James

KT-556-840

2 4 NOV 2023

DISCARDED

TELFORD & WREKIN LIBRARIES

SR

Please return/renew this item
by the last date shown.
Items may also be renewed by
Telephone and Internet.
Telford & Wrekin Libraries
www.telford.gov.uk/libraries

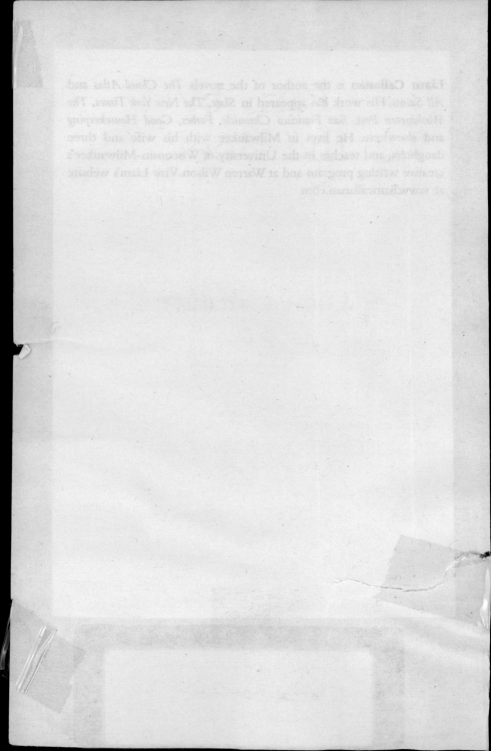

Liam Callanan is the author of the novels *The Cloud Atlas* and *All Saints*. His work has appeared in *Slate*, *The New York Times*, *The Washington Post*, *San Francisco Chronicle*, *Forbes*, *Good Housekeeping* and elsewhere. He lives in Milwaukee with his wife and three daughters, and teaches in the University of Wisconsin–Milwaukee's creative writing program and at Warren Wilson. Visit Liam's website at www.liamcallanan.com.

Paris by the Book

Liam Callanan

ONE PLACE. MANY STORIES

HQ
An imprint of HarperCollinsPublishers Ltd
1 London Bridge Street
London SE1 9GF
This paperback edition 2019

1

First published in Great Britain by
HQ, an imprint of HarperCollinsPublishers Ltd 2018

ISBN: 978-0-00-828198-4

MIX
Paper from
responsible sources
FSC www.fsc.org **FSC C007454**

This book is produced from independently certified FSC™ paper
to ensure responsible forest management.

For more information visit: www.harpercollins.co.uk/green

Printed and bound by CPI Group (UK) Ltd, Croydon CR0 4YY

To the one I found

It is inevitable that when we really need someone we find him. The person you need attracts you like a magnet. I returned to Paris, after these long years spent in the countryside and I needed a young painter, a young painter who would awaken me. Paris was magnificent, but where was the young painter?

— Gertrude Stein
Paris, 1945

PROLOGUE

Once a week, I chase men who are not my husband.

(After everything, I do this still.)

I should not, but there are many things I do that I should not—smoke, own a bookstore, pay for French lessons I always find ways to skip—and this is one. I walk my daughters to school, stare past the parents staring past me, and start my search for that day's man.

I've sometimes begun right there on the sidewalk, trailing a fellow parent, a father, as he frees himself from the clutch outside the massive school door. More frequently, I walk up to the teeming rue Saint-Antoine and sift the passing crowd. Some mornings I find someone to chase right away. Some mornings it takes all morning. Some mornings I follow someone for a while, usually someone just like my husband, or as close as I can manage, or bear—the ink-black hair, the narrow shoulders, the hands that can't stay in pockets, the head that can't stop turning every way but mine—only to lose interest when some errant detail distracts. My husband would never wear blue glasses. My husband would never not yield a taxi to a pregnant woman. My husband would never steal a magazine from a news-stand, an apple from a greengrocer, a book from a *bouquiniste*. My husband would never—and I saw this once on one of my forays, a dad I'd trailed from the school door—kiss a woman not his wife.

Some mornings I find no one. This always surprises me, though I suppose what should surprise me more is all those other mornings when everything is right, when I find a man within a half kilometer of wandering, when I'm able to follow him for a good long while.

Following these men should be more difficult than it is; it's not. Paris is a crowded city, far more so than travel ads and posters portray, and I—well, although I'm fit, have long legs, and helplessly project the "stay away" vibe men adore, I am forty-two, roughly twice the age of any woman who interests men here.

So be it. Invisibility suits me, serves me.

Every so often, too often, the authorities will issue a special warning, a reminder: we must be watchful. And so I am, and so others must be, but I've learned I'm never more invisible than in the wake of such warnings. I do not look like anyone whom anyone thinks to look for.

Even on those days, on any day, it can become awkward if the man I am pursuing leaves the main streets for narrower ones. On busier boulevards, I have trailed someone as close as a meter or two behind, close enough to see the thickness of his hair (my husband's, so thick), smell his cologne (my husband, none, not ever), taste the smoke coming off his clothes if he smoked (my husband, when he smoked, always lied about doing so, and I always uncovered the lie this same way, a scent, a sniff—but still, a reminder that yes, he could lie).

On the quieter streets, I will let the distance stretch a block or more. I'll ponder what I would do if it really were my husband up ahead: embrace him, take up his hand, hold tight as I kick him, cuff him, ask him *why* and *what* and *where*. But it's not him, it's never him, so I'll study the shops, I'll study my phone, I'll read the historical markers and put any man I'm chasing at ease: *c'est juste une autre touriste perdue.*

. . .

Once (and only once), it finally happened. A man I followed confronted me.

This was six months after we'd first arrived. Not so long ago. Long enough; I was different then. So was Paris.

Still, I should have known. I *did* know—I'd known he was going to be trouble from the very start, because he looked too, too much like my husband. Same hair, same glasses, same smile. He gave that smile to a woman at the Apple store beneath the Louvre (almost as popular, as crowded, as the museum above) and that was what caught my eye, that lopsided grin: I didn't even see it was my husband's doppelgänger until I did, and then I couldn't not chase him. He circled the Louvre pyramid's subterranean twin, inverted like an arrow pointing down, as if to say, *this is the place*—which isn't wrong—and then he moved smoothly past all the other temptations for sale in the underground mall there (coffee, toys, luxury toilet paper), before reaching the spot where everyone must decide: down deeper to the Métro, or up to the surface?

And had he descended, I would have let him be, because I wasn't looking for a Métro chase that day. This was an unplanned mission. I'd only meant to buy my daughters—Ellie, sixteen at that point, and Daphne, fourteen—new charging cords; the cheap knockoffs I'd bought them had failed. I wanted to do something right for a change, and be home, cords in hand, when they arrived from school.

But he didn't descend, he climbed, and at the top of the stairs, he did something that made no sense. Instead of continuing on to the crowded rue de Rivoli, he doubled back into the vast plaza the wide wings of the Louvre embrace. He must have wanted just one more look.

So did I.

After a minute or two, he checked his watch and then chose a new path back out to the world, the Passage Richelieu, a colonnaded pedestrian tunnel that burrows through the Louvre's French sculpture galleries. Glass walls allow passersby a free peek, no lines.

Would he look? No.

I couldn't not, but pausing almost made me lose him, and I had to skip a step or two to catch him as he exited, crossed the street, and started north along the rue de Valois.

And now I set before him another test. If he turned right toward the Banque de France, I would drop him immediately; if left, into the Palais-Royal, with its gorgeous gardens and stately rows of trees that I might weave among, I would follow.

He turned left. So did I. He walked faster. I tried not to. He exited through a forest of columns in the northeast corner. Now west, then north; we passed the gates of the Bibliothèque nationale Richelieu, where black-clad pods of researchers and staff milled about on the sidewalk, in the courtyard, attending to the better work of talking, smoking, sipping coffee from tiny plastic cups. Onward. The old stock exchange. Banks. Cafés. Coin dealers and *les philatélistes*, and I began to think that he was going to walk all the way to Montmartre and that I would walk all that way, too. Because.

Because even I will admit that Paris is a theater, ornate, gilded (if worn at the edges), and to live here is to spend most of your time waiting outside to get in, or, once in, to wait staring at the stage, wondering when the rich red curtain will rise. And then something happens. The lights dim, people hush, something somewhere stirs, and you know the show is finally about to start.

I'm talking about the drifts of flowers cascading from window boxes high above the hidden side street; or the busy museum corridor where you realize a statue is staring right at you, just at you, and that its still smile is still sly after centuries; or the meal when the simplest ingredients on a plate before you (perhaps you made it yourself, following the ebullient butcher's instructions to the letter) combine to best, in one bite, anything you've ever eaten before. You wait and wait for the curtain to rise, precisely because you don't know when it will, where it will, or what will appear.

A man, say. Your husband.

I texted Ellie. I told her I would be late, to unlock our store, flip the sign to OUVERT-OPEN to attract the rare customer—

And here, the man I was following interrupted.

Oui? he said.

Not a proper hello at all. I'd been too busy with my phone. I'd kept walking but not kept watch. And now, here I was, this man before me, speaking to me, as had never happened before.

He stood too close. His breath smelled sharp. Pedestrians, dogs, deliverymen, *trottinettes* swirled around us, rocks in a river.

Non, I said. *Non*, when I should have said, *I'm sorry*, and in English, so he would know I was stupid. But I've had more practice with *non* than any other word in France, and so he took me for a local. His voice fell a register as he asked, in French, what was I doing, following him?

Here is what I did not say. That I had lost my husband. That I'd spent the first months going through all the stages various pamphlets and websites and too many books said I would go through—shock, denial, bargaining, guilt, anger, despair—except that I cycled through them repeatedly, rapidly, never quite making it to the acceptance stage invariably promised.

Until I did make it to that final stage, or rather, until I came to accept something else, that the temporary situation I'd found for my family—running a Parisian bookstore we live above—could or had become permanent.

And so began some new stages. French stages. Which, like so

much else over here, can feel analogous to things American but turn out to be profoundly different. In America, you see a man who resembles your husband and smile sadly to yourself. In France, you chase him.

In America, you think, *well, of course you're curious—it's like an unfinished book.*

In France, I *knew* it was because of an unfinished book.

In America, you say, *I lost my husband*, and everyone thinks they know what you mean.

In France, they know better. When I say I *lost* him, they don't say, *I'm so sorry.*

They say, *where did he go?*

And so when I answered the man I'd been chasing, I spoke quietly and clearly, and told him what I told the police when I was still talking to the police.

I said, *I'm looking for my husband.*

What I did not say next, because at the time, the time of this story, *my* story, I could not yet have known?

My husband is looking for me.

PARIS,
WISCONSIN

CHAPTER 1

I've long considered the front of our bookstore a trap, one carefully set.

This is as it must be. Although we are in the wearyingly popular Marais district, we are in the lower Marais, closer to the Seine but farther from the falafel stands and *crêperies*, the pedestrian streets, and thus the crowds, and thus, customers. One side of our block is almost entirely taken up with the blank back wall of a monastery, which may or may not be occupied. Despite all the bells, I've never seen a monk on the sidewalk. Opposite the monastery, a succession of shops like ours, peering out from the ground floors of anonymous flat-front buildings in various shades of cream forever staining yellow. High above, zinc roofs slowly bruise black, windows shrug away shutters. Here and there appear flowers, or their remains. So, too, wrought iron railings, or their remains.

And our store, bright red, like an apple, a wound.

The store has always been red, but it was deeper, bluer, more toward the color of Cabernet when I first saw it. It was my choice to update it to cherry, almost fire truck, red. This caused a mild scandal even though I'd cleared it with our landlord, the store's original proprietor, Madame Brouillard; one painter quit on me before he got started and another quit after scraping and priming. Upon the recommendation of my UPS driver (and unofficial street concierge), Laurent, I finally hired a Polish man who spoke almost as little French as I did and thus didn't care what anyone thought. I asked Laurent what *he* thought when the job was done. Laurent looked up and down the street. The painter had not only gotten exactly right the clarion red I wanted, he'd layered what looked to be thirty-six coats of clear lacquer on top. The place shone as if it had been enameled in molten lollipop.

Laurent said I should sell them, lollipops.

I shook my head.

He shook his.

We sell books. Gold letters say this on the window. BOOKSHOP to one side, LIBRAIRIE ANGLOPHONE to the other. In the middle, our name, a debate. It had been named for the street, which is named for Saint Lucy. This confuses people; across town, there is another street named for her. More confusion: Lucy is the patron saint of writers, but Madame Brouillard said the name sometimes brought in religious shoppers, and most times, no one at all. Once upon a time, she insisted to me, the street had been crowded, not just with book buyers but booksellers. One by one, the stores departed, and many left their stock behind with Madame. The English-language volumes, not the French. The dross, not the treasures. And needless to say, the dead, not the living. She had hardly anything by living authors.

I suggested rechristening the store The Late Edition. *Late* as in we would henceforth specialize in authors who, unlike their books, were dead.

She didn't like it, but she let me proceed, as one of her keenest pleasures is bearing a grudge. I sometimes think it's why she let me, who knew little about bookstores (and even less about French), assume control of a bookshop she'd owned for decades. And it's likely why she watched with interest as the dead-authors angle turned out to be just the sort of Paris quirk travel writers craved (who are quick to note that I make living-authors exceptions for children's books and books of any sort by women).

Madame pays Laurent off the books to bring more stock from storage units outside Paris, where she's piled the leavings of her predecessors. Laurent says there aren't enough customers in the world for all the books waiting there.

And Madame had a very small share of the world's customers. When we took over the store, the running joke was that we were down to three. Two Americans and one New Zealander, who also formed the sum total of my friends in Paris: another joke. And whenever my daughters made it, I would smile to hide the hurt. Not only was it a stretch to call the three "customers," but even more so to call them friends. Still, I was grateful they occasionally bought books.

The truth is, in modern France as in modern elsewhere, Amazon sells books (and snow tires); bookstores sell coffee. Or, the profitable ones do. Those with bookstores that only sell books have a tougher time. It is slightly easier in France, although Amazon's smirk is almost as ubiquitous here as it likely still is in Milwaukee, where my girls and I lived until recently. (Unless two years is not recent? Some days it feels like twenty years. Other days, twenty minutes.) Enlightened France, however, regulates discounting books (or attempts to) and, even more cheering, occasionally provides independent bookstores financial support. Such aid favors the selling of new books, but Madame Brouillard had long ago figured out a way to benefit, by running a second, smaller bookstore that sold new titles in French. It just happened to coexist inside a bookstore that sold used books in English. The French store specialized in children's titles and was in the front half of what looks like the building's second floor but is actually a cramped mezzanine.

The back half of the mezzanine, flimsily walled off, became my daughters' bedroom, which, if they left the door open upon leaving, sometimes became an ersatz English-language children's bookstore: Daphne once complained someone was stealing her old Beverly Cleary books. I'd been selling them without asking buyers just where they'd picked them up.

The kitchen, living area, and my bedroom are on the floor above the girls. With higher ceilings and more elaborate architectural detail, this is the *étage noble*. But in our building, the resident noble, Madame Brouillard, commands the top two floors, which have much better light. She lives on one and her own private collection of books lives just above, or so she once told me. For the longest time, I'd never ventured farther into her apartment than the small sitting room just inside the door (which, like the building, like so much of Paris, looks just like authors and artists have long led you to think: late-sun yellow, delicate furniture, lace, an old crystal lamp atop a tiny table).

Paris, in other words, like Madame's promises to show me the top floor, is a challenge, an invitation, a city that doesn't distinguish between the two. It may be why my conversations with Madame often ended abruptly. Or it was because she knew, long before I did, that the trap I'd set was not for customers but for my vanished husband—and that it had ensnared me instead.

It is faintly ironic I find myself running a bookstore, because almost twenty years ago I was caught running from one, a stolen item in hand. And ironic that I've ever chased any man anywhere in Paris, because on that long-ago night, my husband was chasing me.

Please change the set. Unroll a new sidewalk, erect a different storefront, lower a fresh backdrop. Gone is the Eiffel Tower, and arriving in its place is—nothing, really. Blue skies, clouds if you like. A simple city skyline. Steeples here and there, some smokestacks, but otherwise, clip-art buildings. After all, we're no longer in Paris, but Milwaukee.

And there, on my left hand, no ring. We're not married yet, my husband and I. Two moon-pale Midwesterners, we don't even know each other, which makes it awkward that he's just accosted me on the street—a series of *heys!* dopplering ever closer until I had to turn— about something I have clutched in my right hand. A book. I'm not hiding it, mind you. (I'm not hiding it because I couldn't—it was about ten by twelve inches, a children's book, with a bright red balloon on the cover.)

"Hi," he said with half a smile. "I think you forgot to pay?" He now crinkled half his face to go with his half smile, which was good. It gave him some creases, which gave him some years. He was short, fair, slender but athletic. I'd taken him for seventeen. On his high school's cross-country team. Now I added four years. Later he would add four more: twenty-five. Incredible.

"Oh, I pay," I said. "I pay every day." I got ready to rant about men accosting me on the sidewalk, about men everywhere accosting women everywhere on all the sidewalks of the world—but it wasn't true, not for me, not there, not then.

What was true was that I was embarrassed. Embarrassed I'd stolen something—I'd never stolen anything before—and embarrassed that I'd stolen a children's book. And I was embarrassed I was so poor. I was almost twenty-four, and I had exactly that many dollars in my checking account. I would have more on Monday when I received my grad student stipend, but until then, I had twenty-four dollars, two suspended credit cards, and a surplus of anger. The university library had inexplicably closed early, and I'd decided that I needed the book version of Albert Lamorisse's 1956 movie, *The Red Balloon*, at that very moment to finish my master's thesis on the great (and quite curious) man. Never mind that I knew by heart every frame of this classic Paris film and every page of the companion book—indeed, its every cobblestone and cat (one living, black, another on a building's poster, white).

Many people my age briefly shared my obsession as kids, thanks to rainy-day recess copies of the film that saturated American elementary schools in the 1970s and '80s. I noticed that, as years passed, those children moved on. I knew I had not, and would not. That book was my first love. Like a crush, a companion, a boyfriend of the type I wouldn't really have, ever. That book, that film, *understood* me. Or so I felt. I knew that I understood it. And moreover, I understood its Paris. For other girls (and the odd boy), Paris meant flowers and romance and accordions wheezing. *The Red Balloon* has none of this. It's beautiful, but bracing. Some find it sweet, but I didn't like sweet things as a child and I don't much now. I'm surprised more people— like the staff of the Milwaukee bookstore I was stealing from—don't realize the obvious. Red is the color of warning.

I wish I myself had paid more attention to that warning. I was in grad school then for film studies—film criticism—but had started in filmmaking, because I did want to *make* something, and Lamorisse made it look so easy. It wasn't, especially when I discovered my filmmaking program disdained narrative. How much better *The Red Balloon* would have been, they said, had it been *solely* that: *a close-up of a balloon for thirty minutes—or thirty hours! No dialogue. No actors. Just balloon. What do you think, Leah?* I thought I'd transfer to film studies, and did. There they told me I needed to be interested in films other than *The Red Balloon* and cityscapes other than Paris. For a while, I let them think I was. But I couldn't sustain the fiction; in a very short time, I would burn out, give up. Or as I liked to think of it, give *in*, and to a private truth: I was mostly still interested in making my own film. I didn't know how, when, or what it would be. I did know where it would take place: far from Wisconsin.

And far away from this boy accosting me on the street outside a bookstore.

I ran.

Doc Martens do not make for good running shoes, especially when purchased at Goodwill, a size and a half too big. I worried my pursuer might think I'd stolen them, too. I worried that I was worried what he would think.

When he finally caught up to me, the first words out of his mouth were two I myself was about to say.

"I'm sorry?"

He was beautiful. I know there's a delicacy about the word. There was a delicacy about him.

"It's okay," I said, neatly absolving him for something that I had done.

He'd been in line at the cashier when he'd seen me slip the book out of the store. He'd told them to add it to his bill, impulse-bought still another book, and then he'd chased me. "Take it," he said now, though I already had.

"I'm not sure I want it anymore," I said, looking at it, lying.

"Can I—can I buy you a coffee?"

"How about a beer," I said, "unless you're worried I'd steal that, too."

He wasn't, or maybe he was, because he kept a grip on his glass at the bar when we met later that night. He was nervous or thirsty or knew this about himself: his hands, if left unoccupied, would flutter, rise, fall, paint shapes familiar and not. He'd run a hand through his hair and nod, or rub his face and frown, or draw a letter on the table, another in the air. It was how he spoke. It was how he smiled. It was nerves, yes, but of a generalized sort, at least at that point, and my goal soon became to have him be nervous about me. I wanted to see, and feel, what those hands could do.

And he had these eyes. Gray, but the right iris was stained with a tiny burnt-orange splotch I felt compelled to comment on.

He briefly closed his eyes in reply. "It's meaningless," he said, "in humans. But in pigeons? Eyes? A big deal, especially if you race them, which I don't, but it's how you tell them apart, how you know which one's yours."

And at that moment, I did.

"So, Paris?" he said, now tapping *The Red Balloon*, which lay on the table between us. I winced, I think invisibly. Tap, tap: it felt like little thumps to my chest.

Robert explained that his own favorite children's stories were by Ludwig Bemelmans. The *Madeline* series.

In an old house in Paris
That was covered with vines
Lived twelve little girls
In two straight lines. . . .

I shook my head. Once upon a time—first or second grade—those would have been, had been, fighting words. The hats, the bows, the uniforms? The two straight lines?

But on my future husband plowed. He thought I should be, had to be, a Bemelmans fan, given my interest in Lamorisse: "both *artists*, before—and *after*—anything else!" In his hands appeared a copy of the first *Madeline* book. Which he had purchased for me. To go with the book I'd stolen.

He slid *Madeline* alongside *The Red Balloon*, both books flat on the tiny table between us. I looked down at the covers and then around at the bar.

"Everyone is *definitely* jealous of the date I'm on," I said.

Untrue. But I was definitely anxious. I was protective of my passion, my Paris. So much so, I'd long put off going. Poverty had helped me stall, but so had a cynical certainty that the Paris I'd find would disappoint. It wouldn't be the 1950s Paris of *The Red Balloon*. It wouldn't be as rhapsodically bleak. The balloon, if I found one, if one found me, would pop long before I reached the final page.

(There are many ways to describe cowardice. This is one.)

"The way I see it," he said, continuing as if I'd not spoken, "and I didn't see it until just now, actually, looking at the books side by side: it's weird, isn't it?"

He was weird, of course, and that only slew me more. In grad school, the default was that the default did not make sense. Our lives were dispiriting, impoverishing, and largely nocturnal, so we thrilled to what illuminations there were, even if they flickered in strange ways. Especially if they did. I looked at him, carefully. He looked at the books.

"It's two different ways of looking at the world," he went on. "One city—"

"I don't buy that," I said, though I did like a good fight.

"You're either a *Madeline* person or a *Red Balloon* person," he said. (I didn't buy this then either, but genetics bears him out: both our daughters would have his eyes and preference for Bemelmans.) "Paintings, or photographs. Paris in color, or black and white."

"*The Red Balloon* is in color. It's all about color."

"But its palette—its Paris—is all gray," he said.

"You're looking at the book. Those photographs are just stills. The film is different." And thus I outed myself as the budding (fading) film scholar, whose budding (fading) thesis was that *The Red Balloon* wasn't just any film, and its *auteur*, Lamorisse, not just any filmmaker but *the* French filmmaker of mid-century France. In his landmark two-volume *What Is Cinema?* André Bazin goes on for *pages* about Lamorisse. And I quoted the critic who quoted the famed director René Clair, a Parisian native who supposedly said he would have "traded his whole career to have made this one short film."

"Then you get it!" Robert said.

I did not, but nodded cautiously.

"It's the same with Bemelmans," he said, not to me, but the book. "He's so—I mean, I've always loved this about him—do you know about his backstory, too?"

What was there to know? Bemelmans was all there on the page. *That* was the difference between Robert's hero and mine.

"I'm guessing he'd be horrified his book had become a beer coaster," I said.

"He *wrote* it in a bar," he said, looking up. "Pete's Tavern. Manhattan? Still there, I think."

"You're not—a student? A grad student?" I said.

Now, a smile.

"I was," he said. "Creative writing. But I quit. When I sold some things."

"Furniture?"

"A book. Books? Ones I wrote."

Yes, I heard the plural. *Books.* And now his name, *Robert Eady*— it had taken him this long to tell me. I decided to wait to tell him mine was Leah. Make him earn it, or at least ask.

I shook my head. Out of ignorance, not spite, though it was fine if that was unclear.

"You're not my audience," he said. "I mean, currently."

"Technically, I am. Currently."

"Technically," he said, "the books are for kids—adolescents, younger side?" He described a series of books that started in a "middle school in the middle of the country." The first was called *Central Time*, and central to its plot was the absolute absence of any adults— no teachers, no parents.

"Clever," I said. He replied with a new smile, somehow forced or braver. "What's next?" I asked. "Mountain Time?"

"It doesn't matter," he said. "Because I think I'm already done with all that, or going to be. I'm looking to do something—different."

I sat back and studied him, his eyes: strange and beautiful, proud and nervous, excited and worried, all at once. When I later found out that he, like me, had lost both his parents, I thought: *that's where it comes from, that look; I see it in the mirror more mornings than not.*

"Like, okay, Bemelmans?" he said. I was listening. But I was also consuming him, taking a hit off him, getting the slightest bit high. He was just so animated, electric, and weird, and wiry, and what was under that shirt? I wanted a cigarette. I wanted him to light it for me. I had two left. Did he smoke? We could share! But how to get him outside?

He was still talking. "Bemelmans must have done fifteen different things in his life—waiter, author, illustrator. A million things. But comes to realize, what he really wants to do—serious art, oil paintings. It pushes him to the brink, this challenge—and he pushes through. He does it. He made plenty off writing, off *Madeline*, and he respected that work—he respected those readers—he never stopped writing for them, I mean, on his deathbed, even—but he *lived* for those paintings."

"Don't take this the wrong way," I said, hoping he would, "but—was Bemelmans right to?"

"Don't take *this* the wrong way," Robert said, "but were you right to steal that book? Don't even answer, actually, because obviously you were—the book, the movie, Lamorisse, the *art*—it all means that much to you."

"You're making it sound grander than it is," I said.

"I'm not making it sound grand enough! I don't know Lamorisse as well as you do—but he—he didn't stop with this one film, right?"

He didn't, but I shrugged. "He died young. In a helicopter." Robert nodded. "North of Tehran," I added, both because it was true and because I thought it would get us off topic.

"Iran!" Robert shouted. The bar, which had gotten an eyeful, was now getting an earful. Robert nodded even more eagerly, as though Mideast helicopter crashes were what he had been getting at all along. "So, a lot like Bemelmans, right?" he said. "*Restless.*"

I wanted to disagree. "Restless" wasn't my thesis. But it was Robert's—and I could see, dimly, then brighter, that it might just have been Lamorisse's, once upon a time. Lamorisse had made a beautiful film. And a handful more. And he'd made wine and ceramics and patterned fabrics, together with his family, in the hills above Saint-Tropez. He invented the board game *Risk*. And an aerial camera system called Helivision that the makers of the James Bond film *Goldfinger* had used, and so, too, Lamorisse, in the skies above Iran's Karaj Dam, shooting a documentary for the last shah. I had no idea where Lamorisse had planned on going after Iran.

"I'm taking that book back to the store," I said.

"Which one?" he said.

"Both," I said.

"They're paid for," he said.

Robert carefully took Bemelmans's *Madeline* and tucked it in my bag. As I said, I had never been a Bemelmans fan, not even as a child, but seeing that sunny book slip away caused something to slip in me. *The Red Balloon* depicts a Paris that is gorgeous but also bleak: a young boy befriends a magical red balloon as large and round as a beach ball; they explore the city for roughly thirty-two minutes; then bullies fell the balloon with rocks. There are few deaths in cinema as excruciating as the balloon's, whose once-smooth surface puckers hideously as it shrinks and falls to the ground. This all lasts just seconds, or as any child watching will tell you, just longer than forever.

But in the *Madeline* books, Paris always shines, even in rain or snow, even beside a boy in a bar. If I'd let Bemelmans's book speak,

I knew what it would say: *it's okay if you've not finished your graduate degree and have no job prospects—come play in Montmartre!* I loved Bemelmans.

I had not slept in a week. I was behind in my writing. I was, I vaguely felt, behind in my grieving. Two years dead then, my parents, and they still came to me regularly when I slept, and more disturbingly, when I was awake, never confronting me directly but always flashing in the background, like above-the-title actors now working as extras. I worried they saw me now: I'd stolen a book I didn't really need, only to discover I needed it too much. Because I'd recently vowed I would no longer be the type to let someone see me cry, I excused myself, pointed vaguely to the bathroom, and when I reached it, locked myself inside.

Later, too late, I let myself out, went back to where we'd been sitting, and discovered he'd paid, he'd left, he'd left the book, my book, *The Red Balloon*, on the table. My beer, half-drunk, was waiting, too. I asked a waitress to bring something stronger. When that arrived, I opened the book and went through it, page by page, reimagining my whole project. How had I missed how much the camera— Lamorisse—loved the young protagonist, Pascal, played by his own son, Pascal? How much Lamorisse loved Paris? Loved to fly?

I stopped on page 13. There, on a full-page photograph of the apartment building where Pascal lives, someone with a careful hand had inked: *2559 Downer Avenue*. The photo was from Paris, but the address was right around the corner from where I sat.

And farther up the page, above the window that Pascal's mother or grandmother leans out of in order to dispose of the pesky balloon, Robert had written: *5A*.

Finally, in the balloon itself, four words: *Meet me in Paris!*

Paris. I'd grown up there. Or rather, with the help of Lamorisse's film and book, I felt I had. It did not matter that I'd been an only child in a rural Wisconsin town so small it had only one tavern, which we owned and lived above, although the weight of the place—the alcohol, the smoke, the arguments—sometimes made it feel like we lived beneath. When I opened the book version of *The Red Balloon* (which I preferred to the film, because the book was something I could enjoy privately, repeatedly, while the film required the assistance of a librarian, teacher, or parent), the bar and the crossroads and its blinking yellow signal disappeared. I was in *France*.

I loved the world of *The Red Balloon* because it was nothing like mine. Its streets were tight and strange, lumpy with cobblestones, crowded with odd vehicles and, on one memorable page, cockaded police on horseback. Maybe any kid who looks out on a quiet Midwestern intersection day in and day out would find this fascinating. But I also loved the book for reasons all my own. For much of my childhood, I was on my own. So was the book's young protagonist. The balloon was his only friend. This book was my only friend. I don't know if I was ostracized because my parents ran a bar, or if I had ostracized myself, the girl who knew the date of Bastille Day, the girl who advocated the junior high offer French (the only foreign language option was German, K–12). Day after day, I watched Pascal run through Paris, following the balloon, the balloon following him, me trying to follow both of them, frustrated that I couldn't get any closer than 4,127 miles away.

But Robert's apartment was only blocks away, barely enough time for one cigarette. *Meet me in Paris*, he'd written. When I arrived, all I found was a spare studio with no furniture, save a chipboard wooden desk and a mattress on the floor. A previous tenant's bleached strand of Tibetan flags draped out his apartment window like an escape ladder.

Robert looked surprised to see me. I was surprised to see books piled everywhere, teetering, tumbling like stalactites (he corrected me: *stalagmites*) across the well-worn maple floor, which almost groaned with pleasure as I later did.

Half of Paris looks like Pascal's apartment building in *The Red Balloon*, especially along the street where I now live, which I often walk to clear my head. Or, rather, fill it. Maybe it's only bookstore owners who do this, but when I walk, I gather up as many stories as I can carry. I look, and listen, and wonder: where are those sirens going? Who dropped that orange glove on the sidewalk? That couple walking toward me: is she married to him—or, given the way his eyes dart to me, are they having an affair? Why is this window full of dusty movie memorabilia? Is that onion or garlic or shallots I smell? From that window? From every window? Olive oil or butter? (Butter, surely; the city runs on it.) Does *that* dangling course of Tibetan flags lead to a book-mad apartment like the one I once visited in Milwaukee?

I don't know. I don't go up to strange apartments anymore.

But my street! My sooty, pretty street, my bright red store, and, two doors up from us, a bright white store that sells mops. Very fine mops, but still: only mops. I once asked the owner, an Italian, Roman, Madame Grillo, why she limited herself so; she looked at me and said, *but you—sell only books?*

Behind every storefront, then, a story.

This is true even farther down the street, toward the Seine, where more of the storefronts are closed, or empty. Not long after we took over the bookshop, it looked like a new business was moving in to one of the vacant spots; the windows were cleaned, and inside, a painter appeared. And never reappeared. He left behind an old wooden stepladder, battered and covered with decades of paint splatter: rust red, brown gold, a dozen different kinds of blue. And atop it, a single apple. I decided he must have been an art student moonlighting as a painter—a painter, I like to think, moonlighting as a painter—because the apple's placement was so perfect, and so, too, its appearance: small, round, barn red, with a pale, freckled green tonsure around its stem. The resulting tableau was perfect, a still life, and further proof that on every block in Paris, there is at least one store, door, window, sign, or even brick whose exquisiteness gives pause. Not for nothing does the French expression for window-shopping, *lèche-vitrine*, translate literally as "window-licking."

Which is gross. Or would be, anywhere but Paris.

Every trap requires bait. For months, mine had sat just inside the lower left of the store's front window. A copy of a book. Not *Madeline* nor *The Red Balloon* but one of Robert's, that first *Central Time*, a like-new copy I'd found in the store early on, mistakenly wedged amid the U.S. travel guides. Without even pausing to crack the cover or ask Madame how she'd come by it, I moved the book to the front and left it there, trying not to think what I meant by it. A candle lit, a porch light left on, a mailbox flag flipped up, a signal. Every so often, someone would ask to buy it, and I'd refuse.

But eight months after our arrival in Paris, twelve months after Robert disappeared, it was the prospective buyer who refused. She handed it to me and asked if I had another, "clean" copy in back; this one had been scribbled in. I shook my head. I should have been nicer to her. As I said, we had a steady if meager stream of customers, but only three I would call regulars. An American man, older, from the embassy, who stopped in each week for mysteries. A young mom from New Zealand who came for kids' books but mostly for talk. And a retired art teacher from New Orleans, who lived and painted on a houseboat and told me to hand her something new, price no object, each week. I always did, but I'd never handed her, or the others, Robert's book.

So on this occasion, I should have been more polite, but I wasn't. I was distracted by what this customer—a stranger to me—had found on the title page. A scribble, two words.

I'm sorry.

Close enough to be Robert's handwriting, shaky enough to make me wonder.

When I finally found my voice, what I said surprised me even more: "Half off. Do you want it? Because I—"

Because I what? Even I listened to find out. But I couldn't finish the sentence, and when I looked up, the customer was gone.

CHAPTER 2

My daughters don't consider the store a trap, but onlookers could be forgiven for thinking they do, given the way the girls run from the building each morning as though the façade were about to snap shut.

It doesn't, it won't, it's the school door's prompt closing they fear, and so off they run, me tailing, often to the pealing of bells. Each morning, long after 7:00 A.M., seven bells sound in the monastery across the street, and then seven minutes later come *six* bells from a church we've dubbed Saint Someone. It sounds like it's only a few blocks away, but we've never found it; maybe it really is in a different time zone. Suffice to say, if we ever hear either building's bells and are not already out on the sidewalk, we are late. "Sweet girls!" I call, the last endearment the girls permit me, and only in English, so that no one understands.

"Mom!" Daphne shouts. She is my younger daughter, twelve when we first arrived, perpetually in search of a headband. And I might miraculously produce one, only to have her protest, "This isn't the *good* one. It's too loose—"

"Your brain has shrunk!" This is her sister Ellie, two years Daphne's senior. And Ellie is taunting her with the legend of the teacher who supposedly once prowled their school with a ruler, measuring the skulls of students who were doing poorly: *if you do not work, your brain will shrink.* Back in the States, we'd kept track of our girls' heights with numbers penciled on the doorjamb. When I tried to resurrect that tradition in Paris, Daphne insisted I measure the circumference of her head. That's when I learned about this story. For the record, Daphne's teacher—young, gorgeous, kind but not indulgent, *extremely* serious—does not do this. More important, Daphne's brain is fine. If anything, it may be, like her heart, a shade too large.

"*Courez!*" Ellie shouts. This translates to "*run!*" but also a private joke: the girls studied French for years in the States. Or Daphne did. Ellie mostly waited for class to be dismissed each day, which their tired teacher always did with one word, this one, *Courez!*

Out the door and up the street we go. Ellie first, me after, Daphne chugging along behind us both.

Ellie is tall, slender, as though consonants—those leggy double *l*'s—were destiny. Daphne is shorter, denser: no less lovely than her sister, though the world awaits the person who can convince Daphne of this. She is shy, smart, and reads far above her age. Daphne once told me that Edith Wharton was her best friend and cried when I told her Edith had died almost a century ago. Mornings like this, regardless of what her teachers have assigned, Daphne will lumber up the street bearing half her weight in books. Ellie only ever burdens herself with a phone.

Madame Grillo is often cleaning her sidewalk as we pass. She takes great delight in our morning routine: "*courez, les filles, courez!*" She gave Daphne and Ellie their own mops when we moved in. Ellie gave hers to me. Daphne used her mop so often she asked for a new one that Christmas.

"*Bonjour, Madame,*" I call as we hurtle by.

"*Les Américains toujours passionnants!*" she calls back, although I'm not quite sure that's what she means. Neither of us is a native

French speaker; Ellie insists we are not *passionnants* but *pressés*. Regardless, I like Madame. I think she likes us, or at least the daily show we provide.

If we run hard and the lights favor us—although the lights, too, seem to know we are American, and enjoy making life that much more difficult—we will make it to school just before the doors close. This is a fraught moment, whatever your nationality; one does not want to be locked out. And if you are more than twenty minutes late, you are sent to a special room, something like detention, but whose French name is emphatically more grim: *permanence*. But today, *succès*. The girls disappear into the building, never glancing my way, so mortified are they that I've accompanied them: parents don't belong here. Few come. And those who do almost never go in; with few exceptions, parents are expected to stay outside.

So I do, and this leaves me to study the lunch menu, which is prominently posted on the outer wall. *Cassoulet* today. And for dinner? The school does not serve dinner, but the woman who heads our school takes a particular interest in food, and so sometimes posts suggestions about what *les parents* should serve, based on what our children have been fed earlier. Tonight: *poulet*, chicken. *Non frit,* a note clarifies, I assume just for me: *not fried*.

I'm sure there's no conspiracy—Carl, the older man from the embassy who loves mysteries, says there always is—but the *boucherie* I will pass on the way home will already be setting up its sidewalk rotisserie, the chickens beginning to turn, the fat beginning to drip on the potatoes and onions glistening in the foil tray far below. Ellie was briefly a vegetarian; these very potatoes and onions paved her return to meat. I will turn into our street, and depending on the day and the season, a gaggle of lost tourists will block the sidewalk. Ellie tells me (because, I suspect, someone tells her) such tourists in our midst mean we don't live a "real" Parisian life, but I'm not sure she knows what she means. Carl, fiftysomething, single, says the real Paris no longer exists, which is why he lives thirty minutes out, in a charming village I *really* should visit. Shelley, the retired teacher who is quite happy her husband remains in New Orleans and happier still that he sends her a monthly allowance, says Paris only gets real when it rains. Molly, the New Zealand mom, doesn't care if it's real or not, and doesn't care to learn much French, since she's the "trailing spouse" and her husband will be relocated in two years. "Everyone leaves," she says, and jokes about leaving her kids—three under three—behind.

Some mornings, awaking to the washed linen light that arrives after a rain, hearing a motorbike buzz past and then a bird, then two, then many, and then smelling every last human smell from pâtisseries to pee, I wonder, too: am I really, after all these years—am I really in Paris?

Because I've been fooled before.

Two months after the night Robert caught me shoplifting—two months we'd spent doing little else than making love (toppling books every time), splitting beers in bars, and eating when we had money for that, too—I found out that a travel grant I'd put in for, planned for, fully expected was all mine, would not come through. I'd have to go to Paris some other year. I raged, I wept, I waited at the curb at the appointed hour for when Robert said he would be there to take me to Europe.

Because Robert had said it was *ridiculous* that I'd not been to Paris.

And I'd said, *it is.*

And he'd said, *we have to fix this right away.*

And I'd said, *we do.*

There was a pause, and we both just sat there and fed the silence like it was a fire, and when it got hot enough, too hot, he spoke: "I'll pick you up at five tomorrow."

There are many things a young woman thinks about when she is packing for Paris, for her first trip overseas. I thought about how this was something I'd wanted to do since I was eight, since that wet week when the teacher showed *The Red Balloon* during recess four days out of five. I thought about how the film had hypnotized and haunted me in a way that that other piece of Parisian kid fare, *Madeline*, never did, because Madeline was plucky and colorful and small, and—as a kid, anyway—I'd only ever felt like the film's Paris did, gray and sad and saddled with hope. I thought about how lonely I had been growing up, and how it turned out that that loneliness didn't even compare to how I felt now that I was twenty-four and my parents were *gone*—the word might as well mean its opposite, for it had been two years at that point and I thought of them every day, but especially this day: Paris!

Mom, Dad, I met a boy, and he's taking me to Paris. And my parents, sweet and forgiving, parents so kind, so square, it drove me mad, they would have said "wow" because they would have thought, unlike me, that this boy really *was* taking me to Paris. Of course he wasn't.

I told myself this. I told my dead parents this—sometimes they passed by on the sidewalk below my apartment balcony, looking busy, preoccupied, oddly never looking up—I said it out loud. "It's fine that we're not really going to Paris. It's sweet that he promised to take me. It will be an adventure, wherever we go." I kept to myself that I'd gone to the pharmacy earlier that day and gotten my photo taken, and then the post office for a passport application, where they told me what I already knew, that you couldn't get a passport at a post office in an hour. What they didn't know, couldn't know, was that it didn't matter what anyone thought, not the postmaster, not the pharmacy photographer, nor my parents' ghosts pacing. I just *knew*, because only one thing had ever been true in my life and it was this: I was going to Paris. And I'd just met the boy who would take me.

And there he was, 5:00 P.M. on the dot, double-parked beneath my apartment window. He honked and waved and held aloft a bottle of wine. "*Ah, Paree!*" He told me what that meant, but he didn't have to; no one knew intro-textbook French better than I.

But that afternoon we didn't go *à Paris*, we went *to* . . . Belgium. And then: Wales. And then Norway. Berlin. Montreal. Dunkirk, Gibraltar, Stockholm. Moscow. Even, one Friday months later, Cuba.

And we went to every last one of these places without leaving the state of Wisconsin. The village of Belgium lies just south of Sheboygan. Cuba City, south of Platteville. Montreal, an old mining company town, sits up near Lake Superior. Wales, a wilderness of suburban cul-de-sacs, west of Milwaukee. And so on. Different cities, different weekends. His idea, and I let myself be charmed by it, how it obscured the fact that we couldn't afford to leave the state.

And some of the places *were* charming: Stockholm, Wisconsin, all five blocks of it, is almost as pretty as postcards I've seen since of its namesake. William Cullen Bryant insisted that the Wisconsin Stockholm's wide, slow stretch of the Mississippi River "ought to be visited by every poet and painter in the land." So said a plaque. *And so, here I am*, Robert said.

And here I am, I thought there, and elsewhere, including those towns whose great green tides (of corn and soy) William Cullen Bryant had not endorsed, nor the swing sets we sometimes found ourselves lolling on in empty, forgotten playgrounds, nor the quiet main streets we went down, hand in hand. (I loved holding hands with him—he was *good* at it, made it somehow seem the essence of humanity, which I suppose it is.) I was twenty-four, the adventures were cheap, the trips were fun and sometimes funny. Robert was going places. If I stuck by his side, I would, too. I would even, in my way, help. His kids' books had just been a start. A good start. At that point, they paid for gas and sometimes a cut-rate motel or campsite. His books sold okay, I gathered, but I also gathered that they didn't sell for much. Not enough to take us to Paris, anyway.

Paris, France, that is. Paris, Wisconsin, we tried twice, two different Parises in two different corners of the state. The first one, southeast, just off the interstate to Chicago, disappointed. Flat and brown, blanched houses buttoned up against the last days of summer. The librarian told us this Paris was named by its earliest white settler, a man named Seth. He'd named it for Paris, New York, which sits ten miles outside Utica, if you're curious. I wasn't.

It was in Wisconsin's *second* Paris, however, in the state's lonelier, hillier southwest, that we got engaged.

That had not been the plan, but as we wandered this second Wisconsin Paris—we had found it on a map, tiny print, but once there, could find no roadside signs to corroborate—I remember thinking, *I will marry this man,* just five words, which led to eighteen years, two daughters, and, to date, two continents. How to explain, then? Just the magic of the map. That the whole world, once so distant, was suddenly in reach. I knew this wasn't his doing—it was settler Seth's doing, the doings of so many others—but it *felt* like Robert's magic, like ours, like we could do anything, even conjure Paris from the grass.

Which we did under a full moon not far from the western state line. Here was the second Paris, Wisconsin, here was nothing more than a highway wayside with a gravel parking spot, a picnic table, a tree, a fifty-five-gallon barrel rusting with trash, here was where I said, *propose now.*

He said nothing.

I added, *now or never,* because I knew (every fan of *The Red Balloon* knows) magic is transient.

"Marriage?" Robert said.

Was he asking for my hand, or clarification?

I pretended I didn't understand it was the latter.

"Yes!" I said.

He looked away, up at the moon, which it turned out wasn't so full, but almost full, an egg missing or hiding its yolk. And then he did, or said, the strangest thing: "But, Leah—how would that work?"

Work, that was the verb, the noun, the word I should have paid attention to, that I should have featured when we told our engagement story in the years after. But we didn't, we'd focus on other aspects of that night. We would say how it would have been nice if the moon really had been full, because then it might have been bright enough to find his car keys, which we'd somehow lost and wouldn't find until the dull light of dawn. And we'd say we filled those dark hours prior as best we could, tuning the level of innuendo to the level of our listeners. But the truth is, we spent most of the predawn dark working out the details of our life to come, which, for me, were prosaic, or as he (ever the editor, particularly of me) termed them, poetic. My demands: we would have children, two; he was not allowed to die before me; one day he would take me to Paris, the real one. And he should be sure to keep up with his writing. And me.

He thought. I watched him while he did, wondering then if he was thinking about whether or not he agreed with what I'd just said. But *now* I think he was trying to figure out how to phrase what he would say next, which came out this way: that he was a "work in progress"; that he wasn't entirely the bright-eyed eager boy who'd chased me from a store and subsequently toured me through Wisconsin's roll call of world capitals; that he himself was still chasing something; that he didn't know what that was yet; that if we committed to a life together, he would nonetheless need time away, a day, an hour, a weekend, time alone, to do his work, his writing, to chase his challenge. He'd been born alone, he said grandly, and—

I know what you're after, I said, and he looked up with such relief I almost told him what I knew in my bones was true about him—what I, then, there, naively loved about him—which was that he, too, was ever ready to leap, that his work, his *real* work, was a kind of falling, and the challenge was not how to evade the end—because all falls end the same way—but how to fall well, to fall brilliantly, to light up the sky like the moon as you passed.

But I didn't have those words then, and so he kissed me, and I kissed him, and the sun rose and a truck honked and the keys appeared and I thought, *I don't know what he's after* and I thought, *I can't wait to find out* and then my brain stopped thinking and my heart stopped beating and I was all stomach, which only knew what it knew then, that we'd been pulled aloft, that we were suspended, weightless, cresting, not how long the feeling would last.

We married, we honeymooned (in Sevastopol, of course, a waterfront chunk of Wisconsin's Door County), and then Robert took a "honeymoon from our honeymoon," a quick sprint away to get some writing done while I returned home.

This did not bother me. It pleased me, actually. Energized me. It confirmed my prediction, or more plainly spoken, my desire: I'd landed the boy with the smile, the dream, the restlessness that I took to be artistic, necessary. Mine, all mine. If, post-honeymoon, he'd put his feet up in front of the TV (mine) and held the bowl (his) above his head for more popcorn as I puttered about the apartment (his), I think I would have shot him.

I don't know what he got done on that first dash away, nor on any of the trips that he took after. I do know that he disappeared all the time. I called these jaunts "writeaways," a term whose crassness—or aptness—irked him to no end. But I wasn't irked that he left; it was part of the deal. He could have said, "I told you so," but he never did because I never complained. Because all the other parts of the deal had held, too, even kids, which he'd been nervous about, not because he didn't *want* them, he said, but because he wasn't sure "the universe" wanted him to have them. *Let the universe decide*, I said, and it did. We had two daughters, and we proved to be surprisingly good parents.

In my case, I think my parenting success was by accident, but in his case, it was definitely by design. Books came and went from the library. He took classes at the Red Cross and the Y. We became parents who could be counted on to organize the school's silent auction, babysit the class lizard over spring break, organize the nit-picking party when lice descended (but we should not have served alcohol to the parents; the sight of tequila makes me itchy to this day). And when real tragedy descended, we pitched in then, too. When a first grader was struck in a crosswalk, Robert delivered a eulogy people remembered, and stopped me about, hand flat on my forearm, for years after. If we lived in Milwaukee, I bet they would still. And I bet the crosswalk I painted—which embarrassed the city into subsequently painting an official one—still shines nice and bright. My memories of those days do, too. Each birthday celebrated in our household felt like another victory: *we did it!*

I almost wanted someone to give me a medal—it could be small, like the ones they give mothers here in France who have four kids or more—for all my various parenting accomplishments, including not running a tavern in our living room, as my parents essentially had, and not raising my daughters as underage barbacks. Never once did our girls have to empty ashtrays, haul glassware, bang on the ice machine to make it cough up more cubes. And this showed, or I was sure it did, on our girls' faces: they smiled a lot. The world smiled back.

Not that we saw much of the world, though. Despite Robert's vow, we never got to Paris, not even back to a Wisconsin one. That said, the prospect remained, not unpleasantly, on the horizon of our lives, greatly encouraged, of course, by Ludwig Bemelmans and Albert Lamorisse.

The girls' experience with Lamorisse was mine to curate, and the results were strange. Though we had ready access to the film, our daughters, like me, preferred the book and insisted, in their earliest toddler days, on "reading" it to me. Those are Robert's quotation marks, and it's true, the girls did not yet know how to read. But they nevertheless pretended to, and did so intently, not with real words but unintelligible whispers whose soft, husky sibilance reminded me of skates cutting across pond ice. *Hush, hush:* Robert called it Whisper Theater and professed not to know why I loved it so. What needed explaining? The girls' milky breath on my cheek, their bodies knitted with mine on a beanbag or a bed, the three of us sometimes so exhausted by Lamorisse's story that we fell asleep together, especially nights when Robert was away. If he was there, he'd nudge me awake and I'd pretend to be grateful as he squired us all to our individual beds. But nights he wasn't there, nights I'd surface from sleep around 2:00 or 3:00 A.M. with the girls still beside me, I'd lie awake in the most beautiful insomnia I'll ever know, the book flat across us, and on either side of me, little breaths huffing fast or slow as dreams required.

But as they grew, as they learned to read, they fell harder for Bemelmans. It wasn't really a fair fight. Lamorisse's oeuvre is smaller, weirder (1965's *Fifi la plume*, anyone, where a Parisian cat burglar finds a nightgown, a circus, sprouts wings?). Bemelmans, though he could be equally strange—a 1953 *Holiday* magazine Robert bought on eBay featured a cheery Bemelmans illustration of a murderer dismembering a corpse in a Paris attic—provided endless entertainment. *Madeline* backward and forward, of course, versions in Spanish and German and French and a coveted one in Chinese. And long before I thought them ready, Robert read to them from Bemelmans's essays and sketches written for adults, which recount various adventures, loves, and losses, including that of his brother, Oscar, who plummeted to his death in an elevator shaft at the Ritz in New York. Dark stuff. But also funny stuff, obscure stuff, enough to firmly establish Bemelmans as a member of our family, something like the ribald grandfather who occasionally upsets Mom. Lamorisse, meanwhile, served as the uncle whose exploits are legendary but who is rarely seen. Both dead too soon. Both inescapably intertwined with France.

Which is why, when the girls were old enough, when we had time enough, when we had money enough—well, of course: we'd go. I even took French classes (actually, the same introductory class, many times) and enrolled the girls in a magnet school that offered French immersion (they progressed rapidly, or Daphne did). And I stayed employed, my unfinished film studies degree having somehow qualified me for a job writing speeches and PowerPoint presentations and making the occasional (stunningly scripted and shot) video for the university president.

What I mean is, I did my part.

And Robert did his. He organized carpools and dentist appointments and 3:00 A.M. laundry when vomiting or bed-wetting required. He was an excellent cook and involved the girls in the cooking. Juice-box-size trophies he'd won for coaching tiny teams bejeweled our bookshelves.

He navigated all this uncomplainingly, if distantly, as though he was studying these various activities rather than taking part in them.

And I studied him. I learned to predict when he'd feel the need to disappear—it was like a simmering, a swelling, though that's not quite it, because there was never a sense that anything might explode. Instead, he'd just announce that he needed some "time," and off he'd go. He worked in spurts, taking off on a Thursday, say, and coming back Saturday. Or he'd leave predawn Sunday and return at bedtime. In the meantime, he'd have found a hostel or lodge or a convent. A coffee shop or a planetarium. He'd come home dazed, bedraggled, happy-tired, like a runner post-race. Again, I never complained or questioned: a day away, an hour, a weekend, time alone to do his work. It was what we had agreed.

But what we'd also agreed was that he'd always leave a note. We never received communications during his time away, but always a note before he went away. Three words, *be back soon*, was the custom, unfailingly appended with an estimated time of return that was unfailingly accurate. And it worked. For years. We didn't ask other people to understand (especially after I'd made the mistake of offhandedly mentioning Robert's frequent absences on some soccer sideline, leaving other mothers aghast). Children of firefighters and surgeons and sailors get used to their parents' unusual schedules; so did ours. *Dad's off writing*, Daphne would say if she found the note. He loved hiding these in places the kids might find them, a fortune-cookie-size slip taped to the back of a toothbrush, a purple Post-it tumbling out with the Cheerios. *"Be back soon!"* Ellie might chirp.

I'd been forewarned. We'd had that deal. And I didn't want to go back on it, even as his career took one wrong turn after another. That was how art worked. And it was important for me that he live the life of an artist, a writer. I didn't begrudge him time away, but I somehow begrudged him his anxiety, his exhaustion. Failures aside—or included!—he was living the dream. Couldn't he smile more? And maybe cook and freeze a dinner before he left?

.   .   .

What he did leave, for me, were books. Not every time, but many times, since the very beginning. Something to tide me over while he was gone was the idea, I think—but only think, because the few times I pressed him on why he'd left this or that book, he looked at me oddly. *Because I wanted you to read it.* So I did. Katherine Anne Porter's *Pale Horse, Pale Rider* was the first—World War I, TB sanitariums, delirium, lost love—I swooned for it even as I worried he was trying to tell me something: did he, too, have a terminal illness? No, he said again (and again): *I just wanted you to read it.* So I did, and later, William Maxwell's *So Long, See You Tomorrow* and Aidan Higgins's *Helsingør Station* and James Welch's *Fools Crow* and William Kennedy's Albany novels and Grace Paley's Manhattan stories and Octavia Butler and Muriel Spark and so much Alice Munro. I can't remember them all. I don't even have them all—some were just library books he later returned. For a while, I gave him films in return, but that was an inconvenient age when balancing a screen on your stomach would have crushed you; he never seemed to find the time to watch. I didn't mind. I liked the books, I liked talking about them, but I also liked that it was okay not to talk about them; it wasn't a test. It was, instead, a kind of gift, a treat, like breakfast in bed. I felt catered to, and so when the books began to peter out, when he began to leave without leaving them behind, I grew uneasy.

Where once Robert had sauntered the aisles of bookstores and libraries with a proprietary air, now he slunk through them, or avoided them altogether, eager to avoid embarrassments like the one Daphne once put him through during a playdate visit to a bookstore: taking a little friend by the hand, Daphne went over to the *E*'s to brag on her father's behalf. But there, between Alexandre Dumas, Lawrence Durrell, and . . . Umberto Eco, there was no Eady. Of course not, Robert said quickly, and dragged them over to the children's section. But here there were no *E*'s at all. The shelf went straight from Lois Duncan's *I Know What You Did Last Summer* to Walter Farley's *Black Stallion*. Both favorites of Daphne's, but that was beside the point today. "Where are your books, Daddy?" Daphne asked, or so she told me later.

She wasn't the only one asking. Especially because Robert's pursuit of "what's next" had devolved into an increasingly feeble series of experiments, like the trilogy with an unconventional conceit: the first book was pitched at his younger readers, the second for not-quite-adults, the third for readers who thought of themselves (or were thought to be) adults. The idea was to reel in a new adult audience without losing hold of his old younger one. Or, that was the publisher's idea; Robert was less sure.

Thus began a new season. Of being less sure of everything, of stumbling, wandering, of yet more experiments that were rebuffed and abandoned. It wasn't that he bruised easily—more that his earnestness, his artistness (I'm looking for words other than *cluelessness*), left him forever vulnerable.

Over time, it seemed that everything wounded. He'd taken up sailing through the college and loved it—and then they instituted a safety requirement that you had to sail *with* someone. The girls' resurgent complaints about our lack of pets (Robert had allergies) wore at him as never before, as did the neighbors and *their* pets. For the sake of intellectual engagement (his claim), for the sake of human interaction and distraction (my claim, and correct), he'd agreed to teach a class up at the university, but campus inanities bothered him disproportionately—one had to pay for one's own toner, for example, which he said punished the productive.

And I bothered him. I'm not sure why. The therapist didn't know, either. And maybe that was the reason why I troubled him so: I'd convinced Robert to see a therapist. Actually, the compromise was that we would both go see someone, together. Which turned out to be fine. For me. In our sessions, Robert mostly squirmed or sighed; I brought pen and paper, took notes, asked for tools. We wound up with an entire "toolbox," albeit one filled with simple things. Exercise. Meditation. Plus, "alone time," which Robert liked having validated, and "advance notice," which I liked having validated: the latter meant that you were supposed to give your partner a heads-up about things you wanted to discuss. *We will fight about your time away tomorrow* was how I jokingly summarized it. The therapist asked if I felt like I relied on humor too much.

For the longest time, laughter had been the one thing that had worked reliably for us. I'm not the world's best laugher myself—it may be from all those years of hearing fake, beer-fueled laughter in the tavern—and it's made me a connoisseur. No one laughs better than my children. I once told Robert I wanted to bottle it. He said I'd need a lot of bottles, then. But by the time we were in that tiny room with the humorless therapist, any bottles I'd stockpiled would have gone dusty from disuse. I knew from moment one that I'd married a man for whom life was a struggle. It was, again, *why* I married him. To see him struggle through it through art. To help him. Because doing so would help me. What I didn't realize, and maybe no one does as they tenderly slip on smooth wedding bands, is how much it would hurt.

The therapist said we could discuss that next time, but we stopped going. And Robert stopped giving advance notice. Of what he wanted to fight about, about when he wanted to run off and work. I swallowed my complaints. When we married, I thought I was the one tagging along for the wild ride. An author! An explorer! A man whose mysteries only unlocked more. All in a minor key, of course, but I liked that; minor was manageable.

But no, apparently I'd been the one providing the wild ride, and he the passenger. I was the woman who'd run from the store with a book. When actual squalling children arrived, though, we didn't spend evenings talking books in bars. We were busier than ever, and he was more desperate than ever. I saw it in his eyes, in his hands each time he returned from one of his absences: he clutched fewer and fewer pages. It had once been part of the routine, his brandishing pages at reentry, a thick folder, a bulging manila envelope. But now it was sometimes a single rolled page, two, stuck out of a back pants pocket like a flyswatter. I didn't know what to do. Should I steal more books? Should I steal a look at what he was writing?

I should have, but I didn't. I was too afraid. He swore blank pages didn't spook him, but they did me when they were his. Also blank: the notepad in the kitchen where he'd always left those notes. Always. And then, once, twice, he didn't. And then came the next-to-last time.

On that occasion, after he'd been gone from the house for roughly twenty-four hours, I went looking. It was Ellie's idea that I should check his campus office, though she wanted me to go check for *my* sake. She was curious about the lack of a note but not haunted by it. Pages, quantity or quality, didn't matter to the girls; they had a faith in their father's weirdness. Eccentricity reassured them that he was still unique, and uniquely theirs.

When I found him—leaving his office, just where Ellie had said he'd be—he was walking to the elevator. And he said nothing to me, so I said nothing to him. He pushed the down button. The elevator came. He got in. I followed.

I did not like being on campus this late. It reminded me of my grad school days, and reminded me how they had ended, which was slowly, badly, as one professor after another asked what I wanted to *do* after I got my degree. The answers I gave did not satisfy. Them or me. Teach? A teaching assistantship convinced me no. Research? I was going blind reading blurry microfilm in the library basement. I *had* wanted to make my own film, but school had robbed me of the confidence of saying so, even to myself. When I quit and took up speechwriting, I didn't need a therapist to point out that I'd found a job that involved hiding behind someone else. And if a therapist *had* pointed that out, I would have pointed out that speechwriting paid good money.

Being on campus late also reminded me of when things went wrong at work, when I had to stay after hours to fix a speech or presentation because the president's mood or the university's finances had changed. Mindful of my own family's finances, ever more my responsibility, I would stay such nights as long as required, inserting as many Lincoln or Lombardi quotes as required. My boss favored both men, though the two of them had maddeningly little to say about tuition freezes or the depreciation of an aging physical plant, such as the Brutalist office tower where Robert and I now stood. Here was where the campus imprisoned its humanities faculty. The building's one working elevator was so old that triggering an emergency stop after the doors closed involved pulling out a wooden knob, which I did.

"This is the third time now that you've left without a note," I said. "Not a word. Nothing."

"I think that will set off alarms?" he said, staring at his feet, nodding at the button.

"You already have," I said. "We had a *deal*. We've always had a deal, the best fucking deal any husband—any writer—ever had. An hour away, a day away, anytime, anywhere—"

"Unless there's a tournament—"

"—you only have to leave a note. And fuck off about tournaments"—he said I swore too much, and I did—"five bucks says you don't even know what kind of ball they'll use at Ellie's next match."

"That's a trick question?" he said. (Fine: chess.)

"*What are you doing?*" I said. "Go running. Go sailing. Take some time. But enough with this ducking out here and there. Let's get you some *real* time, a week—"

"I've never done a whole—"

"You've never not left *notes*," I said. "The girls notice—they—we all get scared, okay?"

In truth, I hadn't been scared. I'd been angry. But when I said it, I saw it, that he hadn't really gone this time, nor the two times before—he hadn't gone, but was going.

He looked at me, at the elevator doors shut tight, at the compartment's ceiling and the water that disconcertingly pooled in the light panel there. He looked at the worn walls, the scuffed floor; he was wedged in a corner, gripping a side rail with each hand.

"Listen," he said.

I interrupted him. I said the thing you say to kids, the lie you lie to shut them up.

I mean I said, "I know."

He shook his head. I kept lying.

"It's all right," I said. He wouldn't look at me. "It'll be all right."

He closed his eyes, I reached out to him, he whispered, "*I'm so sorry.*"

"*Campus police,*" the intercom blared. "*What's your emergency?*"

"Let's get you home," I said.

I know I need to find a way to say why I loved him still, even how I loved him. I know it's not enough to point to two children's books in a bar—or two daughters in a drafty house and almost twenty years and seventy-four birthday cakes and 150-odd doctors' appointments, eight zoo field trips, ten million sports practices, one chess tournament, one violin and two retainers gone missing, one thousand times our children were told *you have the coolest dad ever* and one strange, delightful evening at Carnegie Hall onstage with Daphne's entire second-grade class, who, under his tutelage, had won a national poetry-writing award, cash money, enough to adopt a blind tortoise from a turtle rescue group the class named Milton, because when Adam and Eve leave Eden in *Paradise Lost*—which Robert somehow read, parts of, anyway, with all those seven-year-olds—they do so "with wandering steps and slow." And because Milton was blind. And because I loved my husband so very much I fell for a metaphor as bright and red and urgent as a STOP button in an elevator.

"Help is on the way," the intercom said.

"Don't worry," I hushed. He shook his head. I stood. I pushed the STOP button in. The elevator lurched downward.

"It's too late," he said.

I brushed the hair from those eyes, and looked for him. There he was. Somewhere. And somewhere inside, something hurt. I fantasized about being able to reach down inside him, to reset some switch, turn some dial, push or pull a button that said *stop*. I wanted to help him that much. I loved him that much. Enough to say what I said then.

"We'll escape!"

But we didn't, of course.

Until he did.

CHAPTER 3

Robert disappeared from our home in Milwaukee, Wisconsin, twelve weeks before my daughters and I arrived in Paris. The exact moment and means were never a mystery: very early, on foot, out the back door. His departure raised no alarm; he was a runner and liked early mornings best. And it wasn't worth much more notice when he didn't return for breakfast; occasionally he ran long.

When he later missed dinner, I reminded myself that he'd sometimes get consumed by a project, so much so that he'd forget to charge his phone (which he made reluctant use of regardless). After still no sign of him that night, I decided that he'd gone off on one of his "writeaways." Ellie and Daphne asked if he'd left a note. He had not.

And then I discovered he had, a very short one. Six letters.

The first person I called when Robert disappeared was Eleanor. It's not quite correct to call her my friend. Nor is it correct to call her Ellie's godmother—we never had her baptized—but both insist Eleanor is. What is true is that back when I was in graduate school, I'd taken some English classes and she was the department chair. I went to her to complain about a grade I'd gotten from another professor, and over the course of an hour, she convinced me both that the grade I'd received was, if anything, too generous and that if I spoke as plainly and fearlessly on paper as I did in person, I'd never have cause to complain about a grade again. She was right, but I still knocked on her office door regularly ever after, even once I'd quit my program: I was sure she could resolve my life's larger complaints as readily as she had my academic ones.

"Leah," Eleanor said after one particularly long afternoon. "I'm not the chair of your *life*." I smiled, and smile now at the memory. It was the only time she ever lied to me.

Not that I believed all the things she told me, such as, *your parents don't hate you*. I told myself that they did, as they'd died before I'd had a chance to apologize to them for being a terrible daughter. Their deaths came within months of each other my third semester in graduate school, my father after a long illness and my mother after a short one. For the record—and as they themselves would surely protest—I wasn't a terrible daughter. I *had* been bothered by them for being so old for so long, for not providing me siblings, for living in rural Wisconsin, for not having more money, and finally, for assuring me it was "just fine" if I didn't go to college (neither of them had). So many grievances, and so minor, and yet, during their illnesses prior to their deaths, I'd fancifully expected to be in some way relieved when they departed.

I was, of course, ruined. I paid for an elaborate funeral few attended and a massive joint headstone that would have embarrassed them. That used up just about all the money they'd left me; they'd mortgaged the bar to pay for my undergrad degree at a private college, a misspent five-year experience (I'd flunked much of freshman year, including French) I thought I could justify by doubling down and attending graduate school.

Other professors resisted the *in loco parentis* part of the job, but for Eleanor, avowedly single, childless, ageless, it *was* the job. She tidied up my grad school exit; found me that campus speechwriting job; told me, when I showed her the picture of my parents' gaudy grave (I don't know why I did this, but I had to, I kept it behind my license in my wallet), that I was a good daughter and, when I wailed in protest, told me she was sorry we weren't graveside right then. I asked why. She said that would allow her to break off part of the outsize stone and hit me over the head with it.

Guilt, the greediest emotion, wants everything, she said. *Grief just wants time.* And time is just what she gave me.

So when I called her after Robert disappeared, I wasn't surprised she told me to sit tight for another day. But when, on the third day, I called her and said I was calling the police, I was very surprised to hear she already had.

The police had told her what they'd told me, but they told me in person, during the middle of the day, all of this invisible to the girls, safely at school: wait.

I then told the girls their father had decided to get an early start on his summer writing period, always an intensive stretch, and that he'd be home soon enough. Ellie and Daphne exchanged sidelong glances—something didn't quite add up—but Dad was Dad. And our family was our family, which is to say, a bubble, the kind I suppose a woman who loses her parents young inflates automatically. I don't mean I bubble-*wrapped* my daughters, just that my default parenting position was to forestall adulthood as long as I could. The tooth fairy still called on us faithfully to collect the odd bicuspid. Daddy would return, too.

And then it was a week without him, and then it was three, and then it was the last day of school. We were crossing the street with the help of a motorcycle cop pressed into service for the great summer exodus. He blew his whistle, stopped traffic, waved us past. Ellie stopped.

"Ellie, *no*," Daphne said, a hiss, a plea.

Ellie looked at me, several steps ahead, and then replied to her sister: "Well, we know *she* won't."

The policeman pointed to the curb. "Hurry along, girls; catch up to your mom."

"Where's our *dad*?" Ellie said.

And then, tears. Daphne's, followed by Ellie's, the latter's quite rare, almost as rare as a policeman abandoning traffic control after two girls go to pieces mid-crosswalk. Everything that followed seemed to take place in three minutes but in real-world time took at least as many weeks: explaining to the cop—and thus, the girls—that yes, their father was missing and yes, the police knew this; and no, the police didn't know where he was, either.

The detective assigned to us did have a theory, however, which he shared with me when we were alone. "In my experience," he said, "the more dead they are, the more clues you find." He nodded, agreeing with himself. "So no sign," he said, "is not the worst sign."

And so we didn't make signs. No flyers, no posters, no posting online. I didn't want to advertise our loss; to do so would somehow make it real. Daddy was simply away. He'd left no clues. I shared the detective's theory, edited, with the girls. Inane, and yet, it steadied them. It steadied me. I sounded like an adult. I spoke to them as little adults. Robert's disappearance had aged them, but my talking this way somehow ratified that leap.

I'm not sure I should have said anything. Everyone has to grow up sometime, yes. But like most parents, I didn't want it to happen in an instant, outside a police station. I protected them to a degree: little grown-ups they might be or were becoming, but I still took care not to say the word *alive*, and I certainly didn't say *dead*.

. . .

Even though he was. Had to be. Like the police, I had no evidence, except one important piece that I couldn't share with them because they'd think I'd lost my mind. Which I had, partly, but enough remained for me to note that I didn't *feel* Robert in my life anymore. I have a theory that couples are bound with some type of invisible rubber band. It expands and contracts, but it's always there, a slight tug that you may not even notice until you notice, as I had, that it was completely gone.

What I also didn't feel—this will sound awful, but wait—was sad. I felt scared, and angry, and alone. I could see sadness, some dark shore up ahead, but I wasn't there yet because the truth wasn't here yet. I *felt* Robert was gone; I didn't *know*. And yet, amid all the advice I read about keeping the faith, keeping hope alive, I found one tough-talk website that said, *your spouse might be dead. Prepare for that, too.* So I did.

The funeral director who buried my parents had been ashamed at his success in overselling me—my theory, anyway, for why he gave me a pile of books, free, on death and dying and surviving, which had survived on my bookshelves ever since. With Robert three weeks gone, I went to the books and started poring over them anew. It didn't quite make sense: Robert had not been declared dead, and as I've said, we resolutely avoided that word, even the concept.

But I had *lost* someone, hadn't I? I had. And at least one of the books reassured me—in a chapter addressing the death of a loved one whose remains are not recovered—*loss* is no euphemism.

It was a start, anyway. A start into a peculiar descent into a peculiar grief. I found that, at this stage, the practical advice these books dispensed was useful: eat, exercise, sleep. I should not rush past my loss, not feel any undue burden to "move on," but I shouldn't linger, either. Keep moving. I did.

And I kept reading, and not surprisingly, reading about death, widowhood, survivorship, colored my thoughts—my hopes—of Robert. As weeks passed without him, these feelings gathered force, mass, became a scar.

It wasn't right. *I* wasn't right. But has there ever been a wife in the world who's not imagined the death of her husband? Idly or urgently, depending on the situation. Mine was both. And mine was complicated still further by the fact that this was not the first time I'd wondered whether he was alive, whether he'd come back from this or that writeaway right away. I didn't wish him ill—no, the absolute opposite. I wished him well because I hoped it would make him well, which would, in turn, make us all well. I had been losing him, Robert, and when the police asked, *were there any signs he'd disappear?* I lied and said no because I didn't know how to say that he himself was the sign, that he and his words and his smile and his question marks were steadily disappearing, day by day.

I did not want Robert to have died. But I also did not know what else would explain the way I felt, which felt so similar to what I'd experienced after losing my parents: achy, antsy, haunted.

Prepare for life without him. Practice. I did. It helped. I determined I would privately pretend Robert was dead, then, until proven otherwise. And knowing I was pretending would stave off the larger, harder questions.

But what about my daughters' questions?

Ellie and Daphne had held it together until the crosswalk and to a degree afterward, comforted that the police were on the case. But as days passed and Dad did not appear, things began happening. They acted out. Slammed doors. Fought. I asked the pediatrician for advice. *This is normal*, he said, which almost made me laugh, because nothing was. Still: I was to watch for "self-harm"—cutting—or eating disorders—or detailed discussions of suicide.

What I saw was none of this; the only self they were trying to harm was Mom. Suicidal thoughts? No. Homicidal, yes. Their eyes tracked me like I was prey. My jury-rigged survival approach—dead Robert as placeholder, receptacle for my grief-in-waiting—I could see that it would not work for them. Indeed, to declare him dead without producing his body—it would be as if I had killed him.

And so death stalked us, made somehow more powerful, more omnipresent, by our not discussing it. For example: one soft summer evening, walking our neighborhood's shopping strip, salving our sorrows with ice cream, Daphne managed to smear chocolate on Ellie's new top (its purchase an earlier salve). An accident, but Ellie screamed a soul-tearing scream. Daphne screamed a lesser scream, but in it rang the simmering anger of days upon days: at her father for disappearing, at her mother for not finding him, and especially at her sister, Ellie, for taking out all of *her* anger and despair and hurt on Daphne in a dozen different ways. And then Ellie smashed her cone in Daphne's shirt.

Daphne plucked Ellie's phone from her back pocket and threw it into the street.

At this point, the film goes silent for a full minute. Or it does when it plays in my mind. I know that, in real life, the next sixty seconds were particularly noisy, but I couldn't hear them then. I couldn't hear my own screaming, which eyewitnesses told me was even louder than my daughters'.

Ellie's phone was her portal, her jet pack, her favorite toy. Something to be chased without hesitation, a ball bouncing into the street. One southbound car screeched and missed her, a northbound pickup ground her phone into the pavement. At this point, my film regained sound, just in time for me to think I was hearing Ellie's bones crunch like kindling.

They didn't; the pickup, after destroying the phone, had stopped just short of Ellie. Hip did meet bumper, but the driver had stopped so miraculously, precisely, shy of her that all his truck really did was tip her to the ground. She never hit her head. Someone ran up with a lawyer's business card, insisted we go to the hospital. The paramedic said it was our choice. The driver was relieved when Ellie chose not to. I was relieved when Ellie, perhaps because she was so shaken by the experience, perhaps because she was certain I would now buy her a new and fancier phone, hugged Daphne and apologized for yelling at her. Daphne mumbled her own apology, incoherent.

We staggered home. We changed and brushed our teeth. We apologized to each other. Ellie told me what kind of new phone she wanted. Daphne said nothing, stayed bent over a diary Eleanor had given her, scribbling entries Eleanor said I shouldn't read but which I of course did. I later woke Daphne when I saw that day's final line: *Whoever you take next, let it be me.*

Whom was Daphne addressing? I didn't know, and so I hovered over her, wondering how to let her know she was loved, she was safe, she must never, ever wish for death—*sweet girl!*—

And studying her in those brief seconds before I saw she saw it was me, when I was still just some strange dark figure looming, I saw her eyes brighten with fear, and relief, that her prayer was being answered.

I heard a quiet, insistent knock at the front door minutes later.

Though it was almost midnight, I didn't even bother with the peephole. Was it—?

Eleanor.

I'd made the discovery earlier that evening. The note. But not Robert's usual kind, and not in the usual place. Before I shared it with the police—much less the girls—I wanted to discuss it with her, especially as it required some of her expertise, very close textual analysis. I'd suggested we meet the next morning, but Eleanor had said this called for a meeting, wine, immediately. Now that she was here, I tried to wave her off; I told her about Ellie, Daphne, the cones, the phone, the street. Now was not the time, I said.

After Eleanor confirmed everyone was physically okay, she said that this was *exactly* the time. More to the point, past time.

"So again," Eleanor said. "This was where?"

We were in the kitchen. She'd brought a paper-bagged bottle but ignored it as soon as I gave her the "note." Not the usual three words, *be back soon*, but, as I said, just six letters: *CWTCCJ*.

"In the granola," I said. I went to get the box, but she flicked an impatient wrist. I returned and continued. "The weird organic shit that he was forever buying but never ate. Certainly no one's touched it in the four weeks since he's been gone."

"Until today," Eleanor said.

"Until today," I said.

"Because you were hungry?" Eleanor said.

I nodded, because that was easier than admitting I didn't have the stomach for almost any food those days, that I'd gone to the granola for the most pathetic of reasons: I'd accidentally washed his clothes. Right after he left, I'd discovered some shirts of his in the laundry pile, and set them aside for the police to inspect. Which they declined to do, because, as they gently asked, *what would that tell us?* I was too dazed to know how to answer, though in the subsequent weeks I did: *it would tell you who he was.* I kept the shirts in a pile on the floor, sometimes buried them beneath a pillow as I slept. I smelled them and remembered, until one sleepy morning I forgot what I was doing and dumped them into the washer with everything else. And out they went with the Tide. I panicked, I pretended I wasn't panicked,

I went through his closet, some drawers, but the scents there were too faint, too clean. And in the kitchen, looking for some noninebriant that would make me hungry again, I found his granola. It smelled stale. And then I saw the slip.

"So my idea," I said. I was still wobbly from Ellie's close call, but Eleanor was here now. She had her reading glasses on. Time to work. "It's a rhyme scheme, right?" I said. "He loved puzzles? Words? A poem? I mean, you're the expert, but . . ."

Eleanor turned it over. Nothing.

"Not a poem," she said.

"Well, it's not from the granola people," I said. "This is a thing of his. You know him. He loves hiding notes for the girls."

"Do you have a laptop?" Eleanor said.

"Google had nothing," I said, which wasn't entirely true. After I'd failed to find anything with those six letters, I'd set Google to another task, which led me to a French firm that offered to make a perfume from a DNA sample, which they could collect from a variety of sources, like, say, an old piece of clothing, the more unwashed the better—

"Maybe you asked Google the wrong thing," Eleanor said, and found a stool. "Get your computer and let's visit some airlines, starting with the ones that fly out of Milwaukee. Failing that, O'Hare."

"Why?" I said.

"Because six dollars says it's a confirmation code, dearest."

Which was how Eleanor reminded me that most of Robert's puzzles were solved easily; recognize the frame or context and then everything flopped into place. CWTCCJ wasn't an anagram or rhyme scheme but an itinerary. And so we tried one airline, and then another, and then there it was, a three-week trip to Paris. Departing the first of August.

"Surprise," Eleanor said.

Robert had been due to go to Paris in late summer, as Eleanor knew. Earlier in the year, for the sake of cash flow, he'd written an article about children's lit and Paris, and a small publisher who'd seen it had asked if Robert thought it could be a book. With maps. And directions and addresses and opening hours and URLs. And there'd be an advance, some money for expenses.

Great, Robert told me, *I've graduated to writing guidebooks.*

Really great! I said. Because I wanted some kind of light on his horizon, someone other than me telling him, *you're good.* And I didn't ask, *is there enough money to take me? the girls?* because I knew there wasn't.

But I had wanted *Robert* to ask, to explain, to renew the promise that someday we'd go to Paris. Honestly, at that point, I would have smiled at an invitation to return to Paris, Wisconsin, either one, so long as doing so would return to me some older, less wise, less weary, less wary Robert, one who said, "sure," "why not," and "we'll figure it out," and once, when I was in the midst of stealing a book, "I think you forgot something. . . ."

Because I hadn't. I forget nothing. Not the number of cats in *The Red Balloon* or the color of the picnic table where he'd proposed, nor that he'd once upon a time promised to take me to France.

Paris in August is terrible, he went on.

Really? I thought. But what I said was *see? You do sound like a guidebook author!* He turned away, I turned it on: *a real artist would say, "a few weeks, on my own, in Paris? I'll buy the ticket tonight."* After a few hours of furious silence, he said he would. And don't tell the girls, he said, it would be a surprise.

The next morning, the surprise came when he told me he hadn't bought the ticket, and wouldn't.

"You had no idea?" Eleanor asked, peering at the screen. I peered at her, curious how the blame that had pooled just moments ago at Robert's feet was somehow seeping toward mine.

"Eleanor," I said.

Not only had he booked himself a ticket—he'd booked tickets for all of us.

Paris. I would finally—

He had finally—

We would all go to—the actual place. The city. Not the one with the cornfield and the water tower, not the wayside with the picnic table and trash barrel, not any Paris on this continent, but the real city, Madeline's city, Lamorisse's city, mine.

Paris.

Eleanor watched me, waited, but I couldn't speak. So she did. "We've learned two things, then," she said. Her seminar voice. She folded away her glasses. "One, he booked flights—including for himself, I see—and two, he had—has?—a credit card you don't know about." (*Had*, it was later determined. The trip was the last thing charged on it; before that, a year or so of little purchases—gas, food— that roughly corresponded with his various prior absences.)

I picked up the little slip of paper. I now almost wished it were a rhyme scheme, an acrostic.

Can't

Write

Think

Can't

Crashed

Jumped

I felt the world rushing up at me—and I mean that, not the floor, not the carpet, but the world, all of it, including Paris, where I'd wanted to go for so long, and now here it was, the code, the key, the passageway—

I did not want to go anywhere, except maybe to bed or outside to scream. I wanted a glass of something, something worse than wine. But I couldn't get any farther than the sink. I watched myself turn on the water. I watched myself bend to the tap. What was I going to do? Drink, apparently, right from the faucet. I drank for a long while and then turned it off and dried my face. Eleanor waited quietly, hands in her lap.

I waited, too, and when I was ready, I spoke. "We haven't learned the most important thing," I said. The rational part of me—which was also the angry part—was slowly returning. "Why?" I said. "Why this way? It's one thing for him to leave a sad little puzzle behind for me to solve. But it's another thing for him to tease the kids, a code tumbling out of a box, his old m.o., and they'd have gotten so excited—"

Eleanor nodded. "That's the part that troubles me," she said.

"That he was a jerk?" I said.

No, Eleanor said. Robert could be clueless but not cruel, and therefore would not have left the code for his family to find if he'd known he wasn't going to be around when they found it. And it was doubtful we ever *would* have found it without his prompting, given that we never went near that box. What troubled her was that this meant something *had* happened.

What troubled her, she went on, was that I'd been abandoned before, my parents dying so suddenly, so soon.

Our eyes met.

This was not that, she said.

"Got it," I said, instantly angry that she would bring it up, angry all over again at my parents for dying, angriest of all, of course, at Robert.

"But do you get *this*?" Eleanor said. There was *no* question, she said. We should go.

"To *France?*" I said.

"That's where he booked tickets to," she said.

"*Now?*" I said. I'd sooner take a journey to the sun.

"Three weeks from now," she said, "or whenever the reservation is for. We'll pay—*I'll* pay—for expedited passports, and—oh, none of that is an issue. Leah, of course go. And my god—don't come back, not right away. If something terrible has happened here—I hold out hope that it hasn't—there will be, for a time, the distraction of distance. So change the tickets. Take a month. Take however much time you need. Take leave. The university will figure it out. So will the airline. So will the girls' schools. Ellie and Daphne may even figure out how to smile again."

"They'll be devastated," I said, "especially when—"

"They awake tomorrow morning, and the next morning, and the next and the next, and he's not here, in this house, in Milwaukee. *This* is what's devastating them, Leah. This is what's hurting."

I thought of the ice-cream fight. I thought of Daphne addressing her diary, the dark: *take me*. I thought of both girls wishing that their dad was not dead and somehow wishing even more that their mom, their own mother, would more visibly join them in this wish and, better yet, make their father reappear.

I thought of how Robert had darkened everything of late, as though a black frame set upon a scene might come to leach its color into what one saw.

"We can't leave," I said, so quietly even I couldn't hear the words. "Robert is away, writing, and is coming back."

Eleanor could be brusque and businesslike, but like Robert—like the Robert I thought I knew—she was never cruel. She looked at me directly. "Do you believe that?" she said.

"Robert's moved far away, and he's changed his identity."

"Do you *want* to believe that?"

I didn't. I feared that he was dead. Because those books had convinced me. Because I had needed them to convince me. Because the world didn't make sense otherwise, starting with six letters in a cereal box.

"Eleanor," I said, more whimper than word.

Joking, sarcasm, anger was a way of pretending that I was fine, that I didn't miss him. And part of me, I confess, did not. But the reader in me, the makeshift muse, word-drunk and bereaved, she suffered. And, yes, the rest of me, my fingers and mouth and hair and stomach, I missed him like air, like water, like a second skin, like a book you love, you need, but is no longer on the shelf when you go to look because it turns out it was never written.

"And the girls? What do they think?" she said.

Ellie and Daphne thought their father was a hero. And I'd agree if allowed to qualify, a classical hero, someone as heroic as he was remote, someone always off on an adventure. I occasionally convinced myself the solution to his (or our) angst lay in taxonomy. If only I could classify what was wrong with him, or me, our family, that house, that life, then I could solve it. He ran off on his write-aways because that was *healthy*, not rude. He was a good father, had to be, because the girls adored him. So, for the longest time, did I. He remembered Picture Day. He knew which summer camp deadlines fell the fall before. When he was home, he did color-correct laundry, sometimes helped with the dishes, and claimed the girls were telepathic because whenever asked to guess the number in his head, they were, somehow, always right.

And they laughed when he told them they were right because he was lying or telling the truth, it didn't matter, not to them, no more than the fact that he would sometimes disappear for a night, a day, a weekend. It had been weeks at this point with no word. Which meant Robert now fit a profile. I didn't see it myself, not right away, but the police did. *Nobody's that clean*, the police technician said, and the detective eventually had to update his theory about corpses leaving more clues. Because not a penny of our bank account had been pinged, not an electron of his e-mail disturbed.

"Do they think he's alive?" Eleanor pressed. "The girls."

You're going to have to stand a little taller was one of the first things Eleanor had told me, back in the freshest, darkest hours after Robert disappeared, and I had taken that to heart. I stood taller, even as I noticed that taller put me just the slightest bit farther from the girls. They looked up at me and I looked down and we saw each other, but from a new distance. The result wasn't vertigo, but it left all of us mildly ill, and no one asked what was for dinner, what number was in any one of our heads, whether Dad was still alive. *Dad is away* was our collective term of art, and so solid-seeming it had been, too, until it began to teeter in that school crosswalk, and then shattered, like Ellie's phone, in that busy street.

"They do," I said.

"You don't," she said.

"I—can't," I said.

"Can you try?" she said.

I didn't answer; I couldn't. It was the same question I'd asked Robert the last night I saw him. He wasn't happy, he'd said. Wasn't sleeping. Wasn't working.

Can you try? I'd asked. The girls were tucked in bed upstairs; otherwise I would have been louder, because I wanted him to *listen to me*, or to the doctor, or the therapist he refused to keep seeing.

Writing is ruining me, he'd said.

I listened to the clock tick. My heart beat. Myself say, *in this whole house, only you?*

. . .

I didn't eat the morning of our flight and not the night before. I'd drunk some wine; that went poorly. Then coffee: worse.

Worse still, the airport, where every father of every age seemed to have gathered. They lifted bags out of taxis, held doors, ferried lattes in cardboard carriers that were—like much of the world, I realized—designed for four. They scooped up little boys who hugged them good-bye and dropped everything to catch daughters, mid-leap, who welcomed them home. They wore suits, sweats, fatigues. Were shaggy-haired, buzz-cut, bald. As short as Robert, as thin, as haunted, or nothing like him at all. The fathers were everywhere except at the airline counter. Eleanor distracted Ellie and Daphne out of earshot while I asked if a *Robert Eady* had already checked in.

"No," said the woman.

Simultaneously relieved and devastated, I said something about how it was unlikely he *would* check in.

The woman shrugged and delivered a bored speech whose punch line was a $150 change fee.

That's all? I thought. I almost paid it. It seemed cheap compared to how much change my life had gone through since April; $150 wasn't much to change it back, to bring a man back from the dead.

I shook my head. She scribbled something on our boarding passes that the TSA agents took as instruction to subject us to a scouring search. I watched as my purse, Daphne's underwear, and a petite container of Clearasil pads I didn't know Ellie had packed were wiped down with what looked like a Clearasil pad. *For explosives*, the agent said, winking at the girls as if this were a game.

For three weeks, I'd told the girls. *Twenty-one days in Paris. This trip, which we were going to take with Dad, we're going to take our-selves.* Daphne had asked if we were going to meet him there, and in the pause it had taken me to mull whether saying *maybe* was right or wrong or kind, Ellie had said *no*.

I said our only real goal for this trip was to get away, see the sights, see some pages from *Madeline* come to life. Dad had needed a longer than usual writing break, apparently. And, apparently, this was his plan for us: Paris. Besides, they loved Bemelmans, right? Ellie especially. She loved sharing alarming anecdotes from the "grown-up" Bemelmans anthologies Robert had found—did I know Bemelmans claimed to have shot someone? That his governess had killed herself when he was six? That Bemelmans had thought of killing *him*self with a velvet rope from the Ritz? No, I did not. (Had her father thought such thoughts? For the longest time I did not let myself think so. Now I couldn't not.)

To fly anywhere these days means navigating, first, a gauntlet of questions.

Did you pack your own bags?

Did anyone ask you to carry something for them?

Has your bag been in your possession the entire time?

But the most difficult one came from Daphne.

"Did you leave Dad a note?"

"Yes," I said, which was untrue.

Ellie, who had been pretending not to follow our discussion as she played with her new phone, tilted slightly closer to us, eyes still focused on her screen.

"I did, too!" Daphne whispered loudly. "I left it on my pillow."

This was too much for Ellie. Earlier, when Daphne had gone to a bathroom near the gate, Ellie had asked: *is Dad coming back? Tell me the truth, now—Daphne can't hear you.*

Ellie had not been satisfied with my *I hope so* and even less so by my *I don't know*. I braced for the follow-up, *is he alive?* My answers would have been no different: *I hope so; I don't know*. But somehow I knew that her just asking the question would make everything different.

But here, now, Ellie was pressing Daphne, not me. "You left the note on your pillow?" Ellie asked.

"Yes?" Daphne said, not quite seeing the blow that was coming.

"You didn't write 'be back soon,' did you?" Ellie said, furious now. "Like he always did? Because that would be so *clever*."

Daphne's eyes filled, but she didn't break her sister's stare. She just let the tears, when they came, pulse down her cheeks one by one in silence.

Ellie stood and stormed away toward a scrum awaiting a Florida flight.

Daphne fell into my shoulder. I pulled her close. What's always amazed me as a mother is that even as your children grow, they still fit. Infant or tween, their chins can find their own individual ways to burrow into your shoulder, your arms, your chest. And then you breathe in and they breathe out, and our molecules are all mixed up again, indivisible once more.

Daphne wriggled in deeper, mole-like, which meant I had to have her repeat what she said to make out the words: "What did *your* note say, Mom?"

I stiffened, just the slightest bit.

My note, before I'd torn up three different drafts and thrown every last one into the trash, had said that we missed him, we loved him, we were worried about him, please call, please write, please tell us what happened, why this happened, how we can keep this from happening again. My note said *I love you* and *but you make it harder and harder to do so* and *we need to talk,* and we did, but as I scratched one underline after another under that word, I remembered that we never would, because he was—had to be? the police seemed to think? the funeral director's books seemed to suggest?—dead.

I thought of the boy in the bar with the books, the boy who'd loved Bemelmans, the boy who'd bought me a book about a balloon, the boy who said we'd go places. And we had. And now he had.

But where?

Daphne looked up at me, and so I told her what I'd written, which I hadn't:

Meet us in Paris.

CHAPTER 4

What I should have felt when we first landed in Paris is obvious: Paris! *Paris!* Paris! Here were the routes I'd traced with a finger on childhood atlases, as though some miniaturized version of the city might bas-relief beneath my fingertips. It never had.

And it didn't now. When Robert left, it turned out he had taken something—a small thing, perhaps, but still, an important thing: the exclamation point that had always followed the city's name, at least for me. From the looks of the girls, he'd taken it from them, too.

Paris. Somewhere around here someone had once made a movie about a red balloon. Someone else had sat sketching schoolgirls marching about in two straight lines.

And back in Milwaukee, some couple had once argued whether Paris was best depicted in color or black and white. Now I saw—

That the city was spectacular. That it couldn't and wouldn't not be, and if I or my girls missed that exclamation point, we were missing the larger point. Paris wasn't a painting, or a movie, or a poster. It wasn't a prize. And now that we'd arrived, it was no longer a dream, either. It was real.

Then why didn't it feel that way?

. . .

Well, in part, because it was so tyrannically hot. Those first August weeks in Paris, the heat staggered us. Even saying the month's name in French—*août*—felt, and sounded, like a little cry for help.

Not that anyone could have heard us above the din—the city was a city, and this fact somehow surprised us, too: how noisy it was, and at all hours. That I'd booked us a hot, cramped apartment between a hospital and train station did not help. During our daytime adventures, we'd sometimes find a narrow, anonymous passage and duck into it, in pursuit of nothing other than silence.

What surprised me most was how kind the city was to us. Nothing prepared me for this (though the girls, fed on *Madeline*, assumed it their due). I've experienced various Parisian unkindnesses since, but I'll never forget those first days here when so many strangers seemed so warm, even courtly, especially toward the girls. Shopkeepers, museum guards, passengers on the Métro. Men gave up their seats; women stopped me to compliment my daughters' beauty; bakers dropped a tiny chocolate (and then, with a wink, two, three) into the bag with our croissants. And the third Nutella *crêpe*? Free for the beautiful lady—who apparently was me. Paris in August is empty but for tourists, but the Parisians who've stayed behind need those tourists, they needed us. And, I was slowly letting myself believe, we needed them.

But with just four days left in Paris, we also needed Daphne's passport.

It was gone. Eleanor's fault: she'd told me that the first step in raising strong, independent women was to give them responsibility, starting with their boarding passes and passports.

Ellie misplaced her boarding pass between TSA and the plane in the United States; Daphne had lost her passport that morning in Paris. No idea how, where, just that it was gone. Also gone, and more devastatingly: the nascent confidence Eleanor's plan had begun to instill in her. The State Department could help us with the passport, but I wasn't sure who would reissue Daphne's pride.

Not me, because I'd lost almost all of my own, having forgotten to bring the passport photocopies Eleanor had insisted I make. Fortunately, she'd insisted on keeping a set as well, and when I called that afternoon, she said she had the copies right at hand.

I waited for "I told you so," autotext she keeps tucked in her cheek.

But instead: "I'm so glad you *called*," Eleanor said. "I have something to tell you—unless—is this costing you thousands, this call?"

It wasn't; Ellie had known to acquire these chips hardly bigger than a beauty mark that, once inserted into our phones, somehow made calling and texting and surfing cost next to nothing, or so she said.

"Not thousands, but . . ." But I needed to hurry Eleanor along; Ellie was bored and Daphne's face was blotchy with tears and shame. Both were eavesdropping avidly. "Eleanor? The passport's number. That's all I need."

We were sitting on a bench in the shadow of the Eiffel Tower, a destination I'd put off, partly to hold it in reserve as a grand finale, partly because I hadn't realized climbing it, especially at peak season, required an advance reservation.

And partly because—this is silly, or maybe not—I'd long ago envisioned climbing to the top and planting a kiss on Robert once there. *Look who's made it to Paris, France, from Paris, Wisconsin! Eighteen years, and here we are!*

And we were. I let my eyes travel up the structure and squinted. It looked even hotter up there, that much closer to the sun.

"Nonsense," Eleanor said. "It's better to have the page itself," Eleanor said. "I'll FedEx it to you."

"*That* will cost thousands," I said.

"Thousands?" Daphne squeaked. Daphne worried about money for reasons that were obscure to me—had Robert and I once argued over finances in her presence? In Milwaukee, she had collected jars and jars of change. And if we were ever in a bookstore and she saw a discount sticker on one of Robert's books, she took it off.

"No—Daphne, it's okay," I said. "It's just that Aunt Eleanor wants to mail us a paper copy of your passport, and—"

Ellie exhaled long and slow. "Wow," she said finally, and stood. Eleanor's cumbersome suggestion proved just how old she was. But this moment proved to me just how old Ellie had become. She was about to turn fifteen then, a teen. Witness the exhale, the "wow," the shimmering disdain, but most of all, the sheer height of her: when your child achieves (or exceeds) your height, you come to feel barely half their size. Ellie and I could now look each other in the eye. We could wear each other's clothes. She dwarfed me. "Just, wow," Ellie elaborated. And with that, she took the phone from me, explained to Eleanor what was needed—scan, upload, send—and then ended the call, brought up a map, and led us to a nearby Internet café.

Such cafés are all but extinct now and this one should have been then. It was un-air-conditioned, unpleasant, filled with young men who should have spent their last euros showering instead of surfing. The room rang with conversations in a dozen languages, but rules were rules—the manager pointed to a sign, in English, NO PHONE TALKING—so I was ordered out to the sidewalk when Eleanor called back.

"You'll have it in a moment, I expect," said Eleanor. "But can I use that moment?" she asked. "Like I said, I may have found something."

I stared into the café; Daphne stared back; Ellie stared at her screen; the manager stared at my girls.

And an ocean away, Eleanor began to explain that the man whom we thought had disappeared without a trace had left behind a substantial one. Not six letters, but one hundred pages.

"It's some sort of—well, manuscript, I guess," Eleanor said. "With a cover letter. Addressed to a prize competition. It arrived earlier via campus mail, from the math department. My assistant's theory is that Robert must have tried to send something to *our* department's central printer ages ago—it's time-stamped March, a month before he vanished—and the document turned left instead of right at some digital intersection, spitting itself out at a random printer across campus."

"March?" I said. "It's August."

"Five months, five hundred yards," Eleanor said. "That's about right for campus mail. Speaking of, has my e-mail arrived?"

I tapped the café window; Ellie looked over—as did half the café—and shook her head. "No?" I said.

"Shoot," she said. I heard clicking. "Resending. In the meantime, let me read just a paragraph or two, because it's so *very* . . ."

And here my waking dream began in earnest—or I'd been dreaming since arriving in Paris, or since Robert left.

"Okay. 'Please find enclosed my submission for the Porlock Prize,'" Eleanor read, and then paused. "Never heard of such a thing. Mind you, I lead a sheltered life. 'It is'—this is him now—'per the guidelines, a manuscript that, in the spirit of Samuel Taylor Coleridge's great "Kubla Khan," lies unfinished due to the author having been interrupted during its production.' Let's be clear," Eleanor said, "Coleridge wasn't 'interrupted,' despite his claim that a 'person from Porlock' had ruined his poem; no, he was—well, speaking of *brains*, actually—"

"Eleanor, Eleanor, I lied," I lied. "This *is* an expensive call. And I've left the girls on their own in—"

"Shush," said Eleanor. "The competition, it turns out, is sponsored by a brain surgeon. In Grand Rapids, Michigan. Do you know what's a telltale sign of a health care system out of control? Neurosurgeons making so much money they endow literary prizes."

"He's a neurosurgeon?" I said.

"So says the Internet. Which also says one of the reasons for his starting the contest was that he'd done research on the brain's ability to handle interruptions."

"Eleanor—"

"Clever! You interrupted. The man has a point. Okay—let's see, skimming, another paragraph of throat-clearing, some vague groveling—it's a little unseemly—it's also very much Robert, I have to say, but—here 'tis. The synopsis."

"Eleanor, do we have to do this now? Over the phone?"

"It's short," she said.

"So is our time here," I said.

"That's my point," Eleanor said. "The story—Leah, it's set in Paris."

Moments before, the humidity had made it seem like there was too much air. Now it felt like there was none.

"I thought so," Eleanor said, marking my silence. "So here goes: 'Young Robert and Callie Eady'—yes, he uses real names, or his, anyway; I don't know what's up with 'Callie'; makes me think of Caligula—'exhausted with their life in Wisconsin'—I'd say that's overstating things, no?—'decide to take a year off with their daughters'—no names given—'and travel the world.' She's a novelist, by the way, and he's a speechwriter—ho, ho! That's my 'ho, ho.' I'll read on. 'Once around and then home, much improved, in no small part because the plan is to *work* their way around the world.' Okay, and now we get some sheep in New Zealand, grape-picking in Chile, etc., etc., teaching and coaching at a school in Zambia—"

"Eleanor!"

"Yes, yes," she said. "Anyway, none of that turns out to be crucial. But this is: 'Their trip stalls'—Robert's words again—'almost as soon as it starts. Crossing the Atlantic to France, they fetch up in Paris'— *really* not sure about that 'fetch up'—'where their plans to staff an English-language bookstore fall through. To bide time, they spend days wandering the city, quickly abandoning traditional guidebooks to follow paths laid out by the children's books and films their two daughters love, chiefly Ludwig Bemelmans's *Madeline* books and'— you knew this was coming, didn't you?—'Albert Lamorisse's *The Red Balloon.*'—Leah, are you listening?"

I was not. Or I was, but not to Eleanor. I was listening to Robert, through words read by Eleanor, trying to make out the words behind the words.

"I admit," Eleanor said, "it doesn't sound like him."

It did and it didn't. It was true that Robert's recent experiments had been increasingly esoteric—a term he found "judgmental"— and he had been exploring the creation of electronic texts, including an e-book app wherein a finger swipe not only turned pages but erased words. Academics loved it. Techies, too. And some students, some of them his old fans. In short, lots of people who didn't spend much money on books. Which was good, because the app was free. A variety of fame resulted. But he no longer seemed much interested in fame, or much else anymore. And I no longer—well, I didn't understand. I told him so. He tried to explain: *So finishing the book will mean—could mean—finishing it off, you know?* I did, and excitement briefly flared in me. A large part of me also thought it was nonsense. But we were deep in a difficult season, and I wanted something to celebrate, and nonsense would do. It would be like the old days, our early days, when the less sense an act, a notion, a thought was, the more sense it made. Chase a shoplifter from a bookstore! Marry a man who loved *Madeline*! Live for art! *Make* something. And we had. And now we were—erasing that art? That life? *Finished*, Robert had said, *like*—

I know, I'd said, and I'd thought I had known, but now—now in Paris, this. This "prize" or contest, which was all about unfinishing? This *didn't* sound like him, not the synopsis, not the contest.

Unless—was the whole thing—was this an experimental work of an entirely new order? He'd not only made up a new novel but a competition? Eleanor had found the contest's website, but maybe Robert, mad puzzler that he was, had generated that, too.

"It's a lot to take in, I suppose," Eleanor said. "I think I hear you breathing. I'll keep going. There's not too much more. Though—steady yourself. 'But as the weeks wear on,' he writes, 'Paris wears them down, and the family dynamic frays.' And it *would*, wouldn't it? 'The girls fight. The parents fight. And then, one morning, *Robert* comes home from a run, and *she's* gone.'"

"Wait—who's gone?" I said.

"You *are* listening," Eleanor said. "So, yes, *this* is the curious part. She's gone, this Callie character—the wife."

"The wife?"

"The wife, and stranger still—okay, let me finish." Eleanor dropped her voice, caught up in the performance. It was almost fun to listen to, to hear someone else get swept away by another's prose and magic, even if it was only a synopsis. It reminded me that Robert had possessed that magic. It reminded me that it had possessed me once upon a time. It made me realize, briefly, that something similar was happening again, here on a crowded sidewalk in a distant city, my girls behind glass, my husband behind words someone was reading to me. "'There's no sign of her,'" Eleanor read. "The wife, he means. 'There'd been no warning. The police, the embassy, are no help. The father prepares to head home; the children resist. The father's compromise: a final trip to the bookstore where they were to have worked.' Whereupon they find a 'clue.'"

"A clue—Eleanor! All this time you've had me on the phone— why didn't you just—what in god's name is the clue?"

"It doesn't say. That's where it ends. By design, I assume. Indeed, that's the contest's conceit. But here's what *I* think of as a clue: the synopsis and manuscript differ. I'm not sure why, and this is only after the speediest of reads, but it appears Robert changed the manuscript before writing the cover letter. Or maybe after. What I mean is, in the manuscript, there's just this one material change: it's no longer Callie, the wife, who leaves. It's . . ."

She paused.

"Well, it's the husband," she said. "I don't know if that's a clue or the opposite of one. But otherwise, for all this talk of clues in the cover letter, there's no explicit discussion of clues in the manuscript itself. Maybe he forgot. More likely, as I said, things changed. We don't even know if he sent it in, after all—perhaps this was just a rough draft."

We didn't know anything, she said, but I knew this: it sounded like Eleanor was gloating. She'd had a hunch that Robert was alive and well somewhere, and this somehow proved that.

But it didn't. We'd found my husband's manuscript. Not my husband. This manuscript wasn't evidence he was alive. Unfinished, it was evidence he was dead.

Wasn't it?

Eleanor could endure my silence no further. "Oh, but of course," Eleanor said, thinking she'd figured out why I'd paused. "I have anticipated your very desire. My able assistant has already scanned in the whole thing, cover letter and all. And she e-mailed it to you along with Daphne's passport page. Maybe that's why it took so long. No matter—Ellie messaged me while we were talking, said she'd gotten it, was printing it."

"Ellie? Eleanor, you should have . . ." I turned to look through the glass again. Ellie's workstation was empty. I looked at the line for the bathroom; no.

And then I saw my two daughters, sitting at a little round table, Daphne bent over Ellie bent over a messy pile of pages—bent, anyway, until Ellie looked up, saw me looking at her, and opened her mouth.

I opened mine, too, but nothing came out. My grief books were no help here; none of them discussed partial manuscripts that churned out of printers in Paris. What could I tell my girls that they would believe now? Their father wasn't gone, he'd come back? Or their father had come back and gone again? Or their father, my husband, was sitting right there on the table, just beneath those words, staring out at us? I wanted to go in and stuff the pages back into the printer. I wanted to gather them up in one giant, messy pile and hug them to me, and not let go: *I'm sorry I thought you were dead! I'm sorry you ran away. I'm sorry I said I would—*

And then I looked around, and the pages became pages again, and my girls became fatherless again, and I thought, *I'm sorry I thought you were back.*

Here is my own synopsis of what happened next, pared to the minimum and thus truer than Robert's: pay, taxi, room, read, argue, cry, call, embassy, cry, call, read, argue, argue, call, call. Stay.

Stay?

Stay in Paris. The girls' idea. Or, Eleanor later argued, their father's.

I had not read anything of Robert's in manuscript form in quite a long time. (I'd once made the mistake of reading a manuscript of his in bed and falling asleep—a perfectly common event in any reader's life, but, as I learned, unacceptable for an author's wife.) His words, once bound into a book, always seemed settled, set.

Reading him in double-spaced, 12-point Times Roman was an entirely different experience, and not just because he fussily preferred throwback typewriter fonts: the words here seemed jittery, loose, like a photograph in a tray of developer that refuses to fix.

The manuscript wasn't bad; I'll get that out of the way immediately. It didn't sound like him, but then, none of his books for adults—and this was one—really did. But I hardly focused on that, so distracted was I by the fact that he'd *written* something. He'd gone away, and come back waving pages!

And on those pages, a message. To us. This was the girls' opinion, and one they held fast to, despite the cover letter to the prize competition. The book was a message and the message was this: go to Paris, stay in Paris. (Come to think, that may be the synopsis for every book ever set in Paris, even the ones—and there are many, even a majority—about leaving.)

In Robert's manuscript, the family does stay. Despite their grand plans to travel the world, when the father disappears, they go no farther than Paris. They don't go home, either. There's a passage where one of the fictional daughters talks about "missing person protocol," about how it's best to "go where the one who's missing liked going": this resonated deeply with Ellie and Daphne. I wanted to point out that this was taken almost word-for-word from a conversation we'd once had at the Milwaukee Humane Society, where the topic had been the neighbor's missing dog and the destination a park. I wanted to say this but then didn't, because, among other things, when they'd found the dog, he was dead.

The mom in the manuscript manages, and the girls do, too. The bookstore that initially rebuffed the family takes pity on them in the wake of Dad's disappearance and offers them jobs; the mom finds an apartment nearby; the girls enroll in schools. Every so often, mother and daughters take to the streets and walk a route lifted from a *Madeline* book. Many Paris landmarks have cameos, and some less familiar spots, too.

There is occasional talk of clues. But as Eleanor said, no specifics.

We revised our trip's remaining itinerary to follow the manuscript's pages. But just as quickly, the girls' interest in the itinerary waned and so did mine. We'd seen most of Paris's top tourist sites; we'd seen a lot of tourists. We'd not seen Robert.

We had eaten a lot of Nutella crêpes, however. Ellie and I now sat on a bench along a swept path in the Tuileries Gardens just west of the Louvre and watched Daphne search for that hour's ration. We'd expected to find dozens of crêpes carts here but instead encountered countless informal exercise classes, running and leaping amongst the trees and tourists. Ellie had ordered Daphne to go ask someone where we could find food. I'd told Ellie Daphne wasn't her servant and Ellie had said, no, she wasn't: she was our translator. And it was true; the past few days had proven Daphne's superior language skills.

The afternoon was especially hot, which I hoped meant we could forgo further conversation. Across the way, Daphne tentatively approached an older couple. They listened to her with grave, attentive faces.

"Mom," Ellie said, "if we go back home—"

"To our apartment?" In addition to its prime spot between the busy hospital and noisy train station, the apartment had a half bath in the hallway shared with the neighbors.

"Blech," Ellie said. "To Milwaukee."

" 'If'?"

"You know what I mean," Ellie said, and I decided I didn't, not yet. "Anyway, we should leave Daphne behind."

Again, it was hot, and we were in dappled shade, which must have looked pretty, but a solid concrete roof would have done more to protect us from the sun. Our brains were baking, Ellie's especially.

"That's sweet, Ellie," I said, and straightened up. Apparently, it was time for a talk after all. "Daphne's your *sister*." Ellie kept staring at Daphne. "Ellie," I said, "I know it's been hard but—"

"But that's not what I mean," Ellie said. "Look at her. She's, like, thriving over here." And Daphne was. She had moved on from the older couple and was now in an animated conversation with two tall teenagers, everyone nodding, laughing, pointing this way and that.

"She's really good at French," I said.

"No," Ellie said. "I mean, yes, but, like, she's really good at the whole French *thing*. Not just the talking, but the doing, the . . ." She sat back. "I don't know."

"Ellie," I said, expecting, hoping, to be interrupted, because I had nothing to say.

"All my friends keep asking if we've found him," Ellie said, softer now. "If he's come back." She looked at Daphne. "If *we're* coming back."

I tackled the least provocative part of that. "We are," I said. "Just three more days, okay? Then we'll be—"

"Actually—if Daphne stays," Ellie said, sitting up straight, "I want to stay with her." Her face was flush, sweaty strands of hair slicked to her forehead.

"Daphne's not—Ellie—no one's—okay," I said at last. "I know this has been—*is* hard."

"I don't want to go back," Ellie said. She was speaking to the air, to Paris, not me. "Not right now, and not three days from now, and maybe not for a while. I don't want to go back because—because

Dad isn't there, and I—I don't want to—I don't want to be that girl, the one with the ghost parent. I don't want to say a thousand times, *um, no, I don't know*." Now she turned to me. "I don't want to have people say they're sorry for *me*."

This was awful. But it was almost a relief to talk about something I knew how to talk about—girl gossip; I was not in the midst of an international parenting crisis, just an old-fashioned domestic one. "Ellie," I said, "it means they care."

"It means they have no fucking clue!" Ellie said, and we both blinked. "Do you know how many friends so far have told me stories of losing a *pet*? Like, six. Three cats, I think, dogs, a ferret."

"Ellie. Sweet girl. They—"

She coughed and cried a bit and shoved away the arm I tried to drape around her shoulders. People turned. When she spoke again, her volume fell again by half, almost to a whisper.

"He didn't—hate us, did he?" she said.

Mothers' hearts break different ways, that's not a surprise. What always surprises me is that there's always a new way for them to be broken. "No," I said. "Sweetie. Love. No."

"He wanted us to come here?" Ellie said.

"I don't—it seems—I don't know," I said.

"The book—those pages, though. It seems like—it's like a clue?" Ellie said.

No, it's not a clue, I could say, and we'd go home. Or, rather, I'd go home alone, because if I said it wasn't a clue, that there was no hope of finding her dad, I'd lose her—both girls—forever. But if I said, *yes, it is a clue*, then—

"What do you *feel*?" I said. It was a favorite question of Robert's, something he got from one of those parenting books, or something he just knew to ask.

"You sound like Dad," Ellie said.

"Well?" I said.

Ellie shifted.

"I feel like it's a clue," she said.

In another three minutes, Daphne would arrive with directions on where to find the very best takeaway crêpes nearby, as well as a plan for our final hours in Paris, one that sounded innocent but wound up changing absolutely everything.

Before all that, though, this: Ellie, pressing, waiting, wondering where her mother stood.

"And you?" Ellie said. And I thought: I can answer this. It's just an unfinished manuscript. They're just pages. Ellie didn't, couldn't, wait. "Do you feel he's alive?" she said.

I quickly said *yes*, the easier answer.

Except it wasn't. In the United States, it had been easy, or at least expeditious, to pretend he was dead. But here in Paris, with each passing page—each passing day—it wasn't. Nothing was easy here. Everything was Robert here.

Ellie smiled. I tried to smile back. I said I would be a moment, and then I found a toilet, where I threw up.

CHAPTER 5

After that customer had presented me Robert's book, the one with the *I'm sorry* scribbled inside, I remembered I'd once asked Robert why he'd set that novel in middle school. Didn't everyone hate middle school?

That was *why* he'd set it in middle school, he'd said. His book offered an escape.

But schools, strangely, would prove our escape during our first days in Paris, although I don't think any of us thought of it that way. Not initially. Not me. Maybe Daphne knew what she was up to all along when she proposed we stop sightseeing and start school-shopping instead. *Let's pretend we're moving here!* Why not, I thought? I'd gotten good at pretending.

That most of the schools, like most of Paris, were shut tight for August did not deter Daphne and Ellie; working from a list a bemused tourist office employee gave us, we marched from one school to another. We peered through windows when we could and made sophisticated determinations as to the school's quality based on the size of the door, the age of the paint job, the presence of graffiti, and what online reviews had to say.

On one occasion, we found a door ajar in an otherwise barricaded archway. Ellie pulled us through, and where I'd expected a foyer or hallway, we found a quiet courtyard with a dry fountain in one wall and a small lemon tree opposite in a giant wooden box on casters. A wide tunnel beyond opened into a broader, startlingly modern space—some sort of athletic field, artificial turf, countless lines gracefully arcing this way and that, delineating the games and sports of what seemed to be another world.

A woman appeared, my age but more stylish, more serious, slim skirt, dark hair with an unembarrassed strand or two of gray, all pulled tightly back. Ellie said *bonjour* and then nervously switched to English to explain that we were moving to Paris and so looking at schools.

I broke in to say that that wasn't exactly true.

The woman turned to me with a face like iron, silent. Even the girls took notice. She turned back to them. *It's not a simple thing,* she said to them. And here, appropriately enough, began our French education: *no* rarely means *no*, but more often *no, this won't be easy.* If you want it, you must work for it. Because nothing is easy. And nothing was more remarkable than watching as the woman took each girl by the hand—even too-old-for-this Ellie—and led them inside.

There we learned that this was a *collège*—roughly equivalent to junior high, for ages eleven to fifteen—and that the school was a public one and thus *free.*

On our way out, I tried to explain to Ellie and Daphne that every other aspect of Paris would not be free—including the school's cafeteria, or *cantine*, whose menu (we were given a copy from last May) always included a cheese and dessert course and such delicacies as "*navarin d'agneau printanier*"—spring lamb stew.

Daphne suggested I get a job in Paris.

Ellie pointed out that I already had one; couldn't I just do it here?

.   .   .

I'm not sure if it was Eleanor who had put that idea in Ellie's head or vice versa; but after I called Eleanor, she immediately put it in the head of my boss, an old friend of hers. *Whereupon*, as Eleanor might say, the hours to our departure ticked away while a brief torrent of e-mails and calls went back and forth beneath the ocean.

In retrospect, my ambivalence may have doomed the proposal, which was that I would telecommute. That, or the fact that I'd never been all that enthusiastic about the job itself during the long years I'd toiled there. I did love the campus benefits—early on, I especially liked the on-site child care staffed by Early Childhood Education majors—and I loved the hours. As I said, I did work late some nights, but otherwise, 5:00 P.M. was a long day, 5:30, the equivalent of midnight. But the work was numbing, and the president had grown less interested in making what I liked making most—those short videos—and more interested in speeches, texts, *words*. That made me anxious. Over my years as a speechwriter, I'd gone from thinking there was a limitless supply of synonyms for, say, the word *synergy*, to believing that such linguistic resources, at least as existed in my own head, were finite—and that one day soon I might come upon the last bullet point possible for *synergy*, and I'd be fired.

Which would be disastrous. I didn't love my job, but I loved having a job. I was proud of having a job. I was proud of supporting our family—and supporting a fellow artist. And I did believe that, that Robert and I were fellow artists. That I wasn't doing my art yet, not really, was fine. Robert said so. I said so. I was patient. The girls were young. Life was busy. And Robert was struggling, and I watched that struggle, and I worried about it when I had time to worry. One struggling artist endowed a family with a certain nobility (I told myself, entering speechwriter mode). Two struggling artists, on the other hand, would only endow a family with debt.

And so would staying on in Paris with no income. We couldn't stay. (And certainly couldn't stay longer than the ninety days our tourist visas allotted us.) Still, it *was* curiously calming to see the girls excited about something, however far-fetched.

So when the final word about telecommuting came from the university—"no"—I wasn't surprised I felt disappointed. I was surprised, however, that some hidden message seemed to lurk between the lines of the e-mail I received. If I didn't hurry back, would my job even be there for me to claim?

I said nothing to the girls. Not yet. As far as they were concerned, their battle was won, the first skirmish anyway, which was convincing Mom that Dad was findable, was perhaps looking for us, was—surely!—nearby. And look! A bookshop. "His"? We went in. Nope.

And another. No.

France has 2,500 bookstores, and that afternoon, Ellie and Daphne were determined to visit as many as possible. It's not the worst way to see Paris. Parisians treat their bookshops a bit like they treat their bakeries: they are both commonplace and important, not something to fetishize—it's just bread, they're just books—but still due extra respect. The electrical grid, the sewer system: these are essential things, but books, baguettes—if they disappeared tomorrow, one might as well disassemble the Eiffel Tower and drain the Seine.

None of the stores we visited looked anything like the one Robert described in his manuscript. That did not dissuade enterprising Ellie from inquiring repeatedly about her father's whereabouts. She was frustrated that her classroom French came off more clumsily than Daphne's; I tried to explain to Ellie that even perfect fluency wouldn't necessarily mean people would understand what she was after.

What we're after, she mumble-corrected me, but eventually, she stopped asking booksellers about her dad. And, to a degree, she stopped looking. While I used my phone to discreetly research the cheapest means of reaching the airport the next day, Ellie and Daphne wandered the aisles, lost in the books.

I have strange children. Or the world wanted me to think that way, at least when we lived in Wisconsin: my girls grew up loving to read. True, they liked milk, understood football, and were as bewitched by screens—TV screens, movie screens, and most definitely phone screens—as everyone else. But they were strange in that they loved reading above all else. I once found Elizabeth George Speare's *Witch of Blackbird Pond* on the shampoo shelf in the shower. I rinsed the soap scum off, fanned the pages, told Ellie I suspected her and she shrugged. The book reappeared in the shower the next week. And maybe the only way to read about the Salem witch trials *is* under a steady stream of water.

But that afternoon in Paris, books were more backdrop than anything. Ellie and Daphne ran their hands along the spines (it's a family trait, I fear; they just like *touching* them, as if to reassure themselves, yes, there they are) but pulled down very few volumes. Instead, they talked. To each other, and when I drifted close enough, to me. Brave words, foolish words: they talked of staying for a month, a year, a school year. They wouldn't miss their friends, because they had FaceTime and Skype. Their friends would be jealous because Paris was cool and French boys were cute. (Over-the-shoulder selfies in pursuit of a boy in the background were taken frequently.)

Back onto the street. Down one block, then the next. Across one bridge, then another. I'll tell them at the next intersection, I thought: *remember, we're going home. I believe*—no, *I think*—*your father is not here.* No. Do it at dinner. The airport. Some distracting place. Some quiet place. A chapel. A closet. Our economy-class seats.

Our pending departure glowed brighter and brighter in my brain until it was a headache, more than a headache, really, more like a hangover, which I suppose it was. Arriving in Paris had delivered the initial buzz, and then the fantastical idea of somehow staying—this touring of schools, neighborhoods—had gotten me drunk.

And now it was the morning of the last day and we were out walking and what was Robert doing across a narrow street from me in a nameless store?

Robert.

I squinted to be sure; he'd lost weight, had new glasses I didn't much like and a new haircut I did. I didn't startle or scream; what happened next happened too fast. He'd been looking down at something on a table, and then he looked up at me, saw me looking at him, and smiled a slow smile, and then returned to browsing. Like I said, this took almost no time, just long enough for me to realize it wasn't Robert.

Now I saw something else, something even stranger than the man I'd mistaken for Robert: behind him were two girls the same age as our daughters. Wait. Those *were* our daughters. I'd forgotten that they'd asked to go across the street into some store.

And it wasn't some store. It was, finally, Robert's store. It was not the color Robert's manuscript had specified, and it was in the Marais, not across the Seine, as he'd described. But otherwise: the narrow edifice, the luminous windows, the carefully lettered LIBRAIRIE, all of this appeared in his manuscript.

A debate Robert and I occasionally took up was the role of coincidence in fiction—especially his fiction. He favored it. His books often relied on it. I said it was barely plausible in his novels for kids and wholly out of place in his adult work. I may have drawn a line from this to his reviews, sales, and so on.

He said real life was ruled by coincidence. If anything, his fiction didn't rely on it *enough.*

I said, *enough*. And then I swore. And then he left.

Whoever swore first lost: his rule. Whoever left first lost: my rule.

Daphne and Ellie set upon me as soon as I entered, each pulling in different directions. Not that there were many directions to go: had we stretched out our arms end to end, the three of us could have almost spanned the store.

But we could not stretch our arms out; the space was filled floor to ceiling with books. A long, broad wooden counter ran along the right side just inside the door, like an old-fashioned grocer's. Atop this counter, more books, piled in varying heights. The floor was unusual—wide, heavy wooden planks answered footsteps with creaks and knocks, like the deck of a very old ship. I felt like I was swaying, anyway. Everything—every last book—seemed both about to fall and yet perfectly placed. If this was disorder, it was a very precise disorder, and it was also very precisely something else, something I'd read, come to life. More than that, it was an earlier chapter of my own life, come to life once more: the books, the disorder, the teetering stalagmites of paper. It even smelled like Robert's old apartment.

But not every detail matched the memory, or the manuscript. I didn't recall the filigreed spiral iron staircase that Daphne was pointing to; she said there was an upstairs, a children's section with books *en français*! Robert's manuscript did not have this. Nor did Robert's store have what Ellie was calling a "secret door," a bookcase in the rear of the room that slid forward on casters. Behind this was a tiny space, the proprietor's office.

And here she was, the proprietor. She'd greeted me earlier with a *bonjour* and then let the girls tug me about. But now she was at my elbow, perhaps because Ellie was showing off the store's inner sanctum.

"Hello," the woman said, her voice round and low. She ducked her head slightly without losing eye contact. "Marjorie Brouillard."

"Ellie!" shouted Daphne from the top of the stairs. "You have *got* to see this."

Ellie ran away.

"Hi," I said to the proprietor. "Leah Eady." I shook my head. "'Hi'? I'm sorry. *Bonjour.* Or—I should probably say—*pardonnez-moi.*"

She shook *her* head, which made me think I'd gotten that wrong, too.

And I saw that I had: I needed to beg pardon not just for myself but the whole unruly three of us. Scrolling through old microfilmed *Cahiers du Cinéma* in the library basement had taught me many things, but not necessarily plural pronouns and imperative verb inversion. "Oh!" I said. "*Pardonnez-nous.*"

Again, from Robert's manuscript: the bookstore is run by a Frenchman, a handsome middle-aged widower. Maybe the manuscript didn't say *handsome*. But I definitely do recall sensing that the French widower and the abandoned wife were on a collision course, that in the pages Robert had yet to write, they'd embrace, a relief for them and readers both.

But my real-life relief was meeting Madame. It had felt odd while reading to think that Robert had been somehow setting me up.

And yet—and this felt far more odd—this *was* the shop from Robert's manuscript.

"They are *très jolies*," Madame said, looking upstairs. "They—is this the word? They 'favor' you," she added. "Yes," she said, before I could.

We stood there for a moment; I struggled to find something to say in French, until I remembered we were speaking English.

"You are kind," I said. "I apologize for not following them into the store sooner—letting them run amok—"

I stopped when her face soured. Did *amok* mean something different in French?

"You," she said, "look much older than you are." She paused. "Why? This is wrong."

We'd not been in France long, but there were specific aspects of Paris that I already knew I would miss. The food, for one, the fact that any food anywhere, even from a cart, a storefront, seemed better than anything I'd be served in a good restaurant back home. But this directness—granted, no one had been *this* direct with me yet, but I'd come to feel that the most of the many kindnesses I'd received had been on behalf of the girls. I'd come to feel that behind these various fleeting conversations and interactions had lurked the very question this woman was now asking: *what is wrong?*

I wouldn't miss such questions back home. It was one thing the Midwest did quite well, which was to keep any kind of intimacy far at bay, well behind closed smiles. Here was the opposite. Intimacy came quickly. Smiles slowly.

While she was waiting for me to answer, she took a pad from the counter and wrote down the address of a store and the name of what turned out to be a particular brand of night cream.

"It is expensive," she said. "But it is necessary to buy."

It was a silly thing to tear up over—a glance at the paper revealed she'd recommended something I could have found in my grandmother's medicine cabinet, a Helena Rubinstein product—but I did, because all this was again (always) about money, and about Paris, and about being alone.

She let out an annoyed puff and went to the front of the shop, where she flipped the sign to FERMÉ, or closed, and locked the door. The thunk was disproportionately loud, like a portcullis had fallen.

I should have felt trapped but instead was filled with the sudden desire to open up. "We had thought—they had *wanted*, my daughters, to spend the rest of the year here," I said to Madame. "Three months. And so I thought—well, for an hour or so yesterday"—why was I telling her this? I don't know, only that French frankness is contagious—"I thought I might have figured it out; I was going to keep the job I had in the States, but I was going to telecommute—I'm not sure how to say that in French—"

"The telephone, yes," she said, impatient. "I this understand."

"Well—no, not quite, but—"

"It is not working?" she said.

"No," I said, "it is not working."

Madame nodded upstairs. "And the father is—gone?" she said. "The older one tells me this." Madame nodded, as if to confirm my unspoken answer: *these things happen. Men disappear.* If eyes can say this much—and Madame's could—I was almost sure that hers added, *good riddance.* Madame resumed speaking: "The younger one tells me they are looking." Now there was no mistaking what she thought: looking for Dad was a bad idea. "I need help," she said. "To work."

I looked around. I looked outside. Locking the door had been unnecessary. It was not busy. Given the age—the smell—of the room, it did not seem like the store had been busy in some time. Madame saw me looking.

"This is why I need help," she said.

We were standing at the counter. She stood perfectly straight, one hand at her side, the other resting lightly on a stack of books. Whatever Madame needed help with, it wasn't poise.

"How much does it pay?" By her startled expression, I saw I'd spoken aloud. Upstairs, meanwhile, I thought I heard something I hadn't in a very long time—the throaty music of my daughters, laughing. I moved closer to the sound and thought, what I should be asking was how much I could pay *her.* For an hour, a day, a year. To make my girls my girls again.

"Enough," she said.

I didn't understand.

"The money," she said. "The job-money is enough."

Enough, my least favorite word in the world.

"I—I can't believe I'm talking about this," I said. I couldn't hear the girls anymore. "You are kind—I think you're offering something, apologies if you're not—and apologies for asking about pay—but, anyway, it doesn't matter. We're about to leave. Our flight's tonight."

I wondered if she'd heard the laughing upstairs, before. She wasn't smiling. "Do not," she said.

"Mrs.—Marjorie," I said. "Thank you, but—"

"*Madame*," she said: I should not have presumed to use her first name.

"*Madame*," I tried. "We can't just—our visas don't—"

This time I stopped again, but for a different reason. A knock on the glass. Was it Robert now? I didn't look.

"You lose the time," she said.

And I was losing time. If Robert was dead, why *should* we go back to Milwaukee? Maybe the manuscript wasn't a clue but an exhortation: *start!* First stop, Paris, then, the world.

Paris. It was real, and I was really here. Back in the States, back when I'd been younger, I remember thinking that if I ever did get to Paris, France, everything would be instant—I would be instantly fluent, instantly at home, instantly, fundamentally translated. But it hadn't been like that, it wouldn't be like that. It was like the hour hand of a clock, like a slow river that seems stopped until you put a finger to the surface of the water. Flowing toward me now, a bookstore. An apartment. Books, and a new life without Robert. And, strangely, with him.

More knocking. I looked to the front of the shop. A tall man, not Robert. Two children, not mine. She started toward them, but then turned back to me. I studied her face, curious because it had changed, somehow . . . gotten younger? Perhaps the cream really did work.

Or, I finally realized, it was because her mouth, just the corners, was it . . . ? It was—the barest start of a smile.

"*Madame Ea-dy*," she said, trying out my name as she put a hand to the door. "*Commençons*." We begin.

Or so Madame said then. But this is my story, not hers, and so it begins months later, with a theft.

It is eight months since Madame has handed over the keys to the store and the empty apartment above, eight months since I have handed in my resignation at the university, seven months since I have made the twin discoveries that I love all books but not all customers, six months since Daphne and Ellie have fallen into a friendless French funk and begged to return stateside, five months since I asked them about flights home only to have them ask if I was crazy, four-plus months since our tourist visas have expired . . .

And just two weeks since the customer retrieved that *Central Time* book of Robert's from the window. The book with the scribbled *I'm sorry*, the message that made it strangely hard to keep pretending that he was dead, that he wasn't in Paris, wasn't watching us, wasn't trying somehow to reach us and for some reason couldn't do so directly. The message that meant everything, in other words.

Unless it meant nothing at all.

After that customer had presented me with Robert's book, after I, in a stunned stupor, offered to sell it to her for half price, after I'd looked up and found the customer gone but the book still there, I'd come to my senses. Up the book went to my bedside table for safe-keeping.

But this proved a terrible choice, because Robert's book woke me up, kept me up, night after night. It wasn't just the *I'm sorry*, though I studied that plenty—were those his *r*'s? Didn't he have a thing about using contractions? Did the *y* look particularly rushed?—it was the story itself. Again, the book was written for kids, but I could still read it and hear him, and more to the point, see him.

Night after night, open or shut, the book buzzed. Robert said the book offered escape and yet I couldn't escape it. So I moved it back down to the store, back to its usual place, in the window—bottom, left, front, bait.

I convinced myself that was progress. I was moving on. For example, when standing at the register, I no longer felt the book looking back at me, a milestone I eventually chose to celebrate by going over to the window to look at it anew.

It was almost a year to the day that he'd disappeared.

The book was gone.

We begin, Madame had said that first night in the store, but the truth is that this is when our life in Paris began, when Robert's book disappeared, and with it, so much else of what I'd believed about what our lives had been, and would be.

PARIS,
FRANCE

CHAPTER 6

Robert said that for many of his students, beginning was the hardest part. But for him, the beginning was the easiest, because he knew he'd always be able to come back later and edit. The only important thing about beginning was beginning; it's when you finish that you realize where you really started. Or something like that.

Robert and I began in a bar in Milwaukee. Or better to say that our family began a few years later in a house nearby. Or that our lives in Paris began on a quiet street lined with quiet stores, in a particular one whose broad window framed a yellowing and dusty tumult of books.

Or maybe it's better to begin not with the books, but the kids.

The two children who'd been pounding at the glass that first day? They soon came to sit at the counter, coloring, reading—because Madame is their grandmother. More than that, she is their primary caregiver, a task that tires her.

So *this* was why she needed help, *this* was why she had encouraged us to take the empty apartment above the store. We thought we were living out a narrative Robert had written us into; it turned out, Madame was writing us into hers, a story where she was slowly and steadily relieved of her burdens—these charming children, this charming store—by the magical woman and two daughters who arrived from America.

Madame does not believe in fairy tales, and nor, for that matter, does Eleanor: *it's not a question of belief,* I've heard Eleanor say more than once. But here is what I believe. Stories provide a frame, a form, a mold. And a good story, one that's retold for generations, demands you pour the messy contents of your own life into it to see what happens as it hardens and sets.

Word arrives from Eleanor about a check, and then a check arrives, too: $3,000 from the Porlock Prize, which Robert has somehow won, which means that with stretching and scrimping and some savings (and some of Eleanor's savings), you will be able to stay in Paris for a whole semester, before you all head home to reality, Milwaukee, for good, come Christmas.

But come Thanksgiving, a second forwarded letter arrives with a check "for the balance": $51,000, signed "Sam Coleridge." You think about framing it, but instead, you cash it, and it clears.

The story begins, then, on the day you'd planned to announce your pre-Christmas departure, when you instead ask Madame about investing some money in the store. With an eye toward one day assuming—control? This does not translate well.

Like buying it? you try.

Because you want to try this: trade Milwaukee for Paris, a bereft life for a busy one, $51,000 or some portion thereof for a down payment, for the stock, the store, the building.

Madame shakes her head, coughs. Not the building.

But the store, she says, and stops, and, for only the second time that fall, smiles.

The story begins when you pay to paint the store red.

. . .

Paris subsumed us. Navigating the schools, the city, the store, sorting out what our lives now were took all our time, and what often felt like all our breath. I never slept so well as I slept those first autumn months in Paris, and I never had less reason to: my mattress was filled with what felt (and smelled) like sand; sirens pulsed past all night; rats fought noisy nocturnal battles behind our building.

I slept because I was exhausted. Running a bookstore, even a failing one, requires enormous effort. Especially when it comes with twins.

The twins: age seven, Madame's grandchildren, Annabelle and Peter. Their care and feeding, after and sometimes before school, were our charge. Their mother, Sylvie, was estranged from Madame, divorced from the twins' father. She lived in Abu Dhabi, remarried to a sheikh.

Their father, George, unmarried, lived in Paris. Daphne and Ellie (and Annabelle and Peter, and mutedly, Madame) adored George. Crisp, British, impeccable manners and dress, Starbucks cup forever in hand. Daphne initially thought he was a barista; in truth, he was trying to make partner with a large consulting firm. Daphne also worried that he might try to become my partner, not in the store but in life, until Ellie bluntly disabused her: *he's gay.* (He was; he'd told me. And when I'd helplessly raised an eyebrow—*so why did you marry Madame's daughter?*—he shrugged and said, "people change.") He compensated us exorbitantly for the twins' care; I caught a glance or two between him and Madame that suggested they knew the store alone couldn't sustain us all and that it was his duty to fill the gap.

And he also considered it his duty to sort out our visas, extending our stay from ninety days to at least a year. This should have required our departure and reentry, followed by much waiting in line at the

Préfecture de Police, examination of our finances, our health, and our language skills. But George, armed with corporate knowledge and money, found us a back door, with the help of a "friend"—and a law that expedited long-stay visas for foreigners who'd bought businesses. The law had expired, but supposedly they were piloting a new version that required a local partner. George got us enrolled. So long as Madame had a say, we could stay.

For good measure, George had invoked an entirely separate visa program covering au pair work. His "friend" later told him this proved unnecessary in our case, but I would argue the opposite. The twins proved essential to our lives in Paris. We didn't have them every day—sometimes George kept them; sometimes they flew to see their mother, who inevitably returned them ahead of schedule—but we had them frequently, sometimes even overnight. I liked having them with us, and not simply because they distracted us. They were quiet, good-natured. They followed directions preternaturally well, a trait I credited to the amount of time they'd spent acquiescing to the crisp, firm kindness of international flight crews. And like the seasoned travelers they were, they didn't engage in indiscreet conversation. They never asked where Daphne and Ellie's father was, perhaps because George himself was often airborne and their mother's new life so distant it was almost fictional. They must have complained to George about missing their mother. But they never said a word to me. And so I accepted that they accepted their lot. That we all did.

I see now that that was a blind spot, a foolish one. Maybe the twins weren't a distraction but a deception; the more I witnessed their own tranquility, the more I found it easy to think that Daphne and Ellie weren't immediately interested in finding their missing parent, either. Entirely untrue. But what *was* true was that as school put more demands on the girls, as they gradually *did* make French friends and their social lives (mostly Ellie's) grew more complex, the girls had less idle time to devote to wondering where their father might be, and when, as that poignant theory held, Robert might join us.

And as the weeks wore into months, as the twins became their siblings in all but the most strictly legal of ways, as the girls became true Parisians in all but the most strictly legal of ways, the poignant theory wore away. It wasn't that the girls forgot Robert—not a day went by that his name, or work, didn't somehow scent the air—but that the muscle the body devotes to longing (I understand it's in, or behind, the heart) stiffened from less strenuous use.

Daphne, for example, had dutifully continued writing in the diary Eleanor had given her so long ago, though the writing became more exterior, professional—notes on Paris and children's books for Dad's article, which she'd present to him as soon as he arrived. As such, she didn't seem to care if we peeked into the diary or not; it sat on the store counter near the *caisse* and I would glance at it week to week, a paper blog, to see what about Paris was catching her eye: the severely trimmed trees, the thick jade green of the Seine, a weeks-long debate about precisely *which* bridge Bemelmans had painted Madeline as falling from, and a running tally of how many Madeline-aged schoolgirls she'd seen in hats, ribbons, or school uniforms of any kind (zero).

But Daphne's entries eventually grew more spare, going from daily to weekly to whenever. The last entry, just a single question, was weeks old now: *are there NO cats in Paris?* There had to be, but it was true I'd not seen a cat in Paris since the last time I'd seen *The Red Balloon*.

I detected a change in Ellie as well. It wasn't that she was moving on, but she was definitely always *in* motion now, and never more so than the Saturday she led us to no. 4, rue de la Colombe, a tiny corner of the Île de la Cité, that sliver of Paris that occupies an island in the Seine. A little wine bar, empty.

"So?" Daphne said.

"Ludwig Bemelmans, the *Madeline* guy, used to *own* this," Ellie said.

"A bar?" Daphne said.

While Daphne wandered closer to inspect a plaque on the wall, Ellie explained she'd read all about it in one of Bemelmans's "books for grown-ups"—and I briefly wondered if the girls really had cooled to their father's memory. I wondered if I wanted this cooling to occur. It meant less angst on their part, but, uncomfortably, more on mine. I'm not sure if I realized until then that I'd outsourced hope to them, partly because I wasn't sure what I was hoping for. Finding Robert's book, that scribbled *I'm sorry*, had been such a shock that the animal part of me had tried to sell the book right away—it was too much to imagine the person I'd imagined was dead was alive. But then, when the book *did* disappear, it was worse. I'd tried telling myself that, absent the book, everything was the same as before. But it wasn't. I was thinking about Robert, what might *really* have happened to him, more than ever.

And Ellie, apparently, was thinking about Bemelmans.

"Did the book say he sold it because of a bad love affair?" Daphne said, squinting at the plaque.

"What?" Ellie said.

We all studied the plaque now. A timeline of significant dates in the building's history ran all the way back to 1297, but the one that had caught Daphne's eye was for 1953, when one Ludwig Bemelmans, "*peintre et écrivain américain*," had taken over the bar only to turn around and sell it to a young couple soon after "*à cause d'un chagrin d'amour.*" This translated to "heartbreak," they agreed, but a debate ensued as to just what, or who, had broken Bemelmans's heart.

They were talking, my two daughters, in English and French, they were falling for a story, stories, just as their dad had, and so when Daphne said, *Dad would love this*, I nodded, because she was right. Because she wasn't using the past tense.

"*I* love it," Ellie said with a snort.

According to the plaque and website and the Bemelmans essay Ellie had read, the great man himself had decorated the walls inside with murals. Reason enough to investigate further, Daphne and I thought, though Ellie wasn't sure.

And inside, the owner wasn't sure either, only that no trace of the supposed murals remained. Ellie spun on her heel and said we should leave immediately. The owner protested. We should take a seat; his *pâté* was particularly good. Then he turned to Ellie and with a look that revealed this was not their first meeting—surprise one—asked where her *petit ami* was.

Surprise two: Ellie had a boyfriend.

Surprise three: she would bring him by the shop some night to introduce us.

Until then, everything was deferred with shrugs. They'd met at school. His name was Asif. His dad was the Canadian naval attaché. They were "just friends" and had been to Bemelmans's old bar "just once," had not had *any* wine or the pâté, just Cokes.

I couldn't tell if I'd just heard five lies or fifty, and wished Robert had been there to hear her, too: not because he'd ferret out the truth (he was terrible at that) but because here was another milestone, the first boyfriend, that would pass without him. Daphne looked on in awe, either at the effortlessness of Ellie's audacity or at the impossibility that even half what her older sister had said was true.

· · ·

But it was. A few days after we visited Bemelmans's bar, Asif arrived at the store at closing time to meet us, receive my belated approval, and take Ellie out on a date.

While Ellie prepared upstairs, I went to the back room, letting Daphne play shopkeeper—a role she loved, and perhaps took more seriously than I did—and listened for the bell above the door. The first time it rang, it was Molly, the young mom from New Zealand, dawdling on the way home to take over from the nanny. As soon as Molly heard what was afoot, she begged to stay and meet The Boyfriend. I sent her away and returned to the office. Sitting down helped. Checking my e-mail did not.

I looked for a book to distract myself instead, which reminded me once again that I was missing a book, Robert's. I missed Robert at that moment, but I was surprised to find that I especially missed his proxy: of all the books to steal in the store, why had someone taken his old *Central Time* volume?

Had *he* taken it back?

Did that mean he was taking his *I'm sorry* back?

Did that mean he was alive, in Paris?

The rising anxiety felt somewhat akin to what I felt on sleepless nights, and so I retrieved my most reliable cure, an 1888 Paris guidebook we inexplicably had six copies of, *Walks in Paris,* by Mr. Augustus John Cuthbert Hare. I had liked Mr. Hare from the moment I read the subhead he'd slapped atop the book's initial pages, which dealt with cabs and hotels and where to eat: *dull-useful information.* His walks were endless (the book runs 532 pages), borrowed abundantly and shamelessly from other authors, lamented all the gorgeous buildings French "folly" had failed to save, and featured at least one murder, suicide, or otherwise fraught historical death per page. From him, I'd learned that the quite undistinguished-looking rue des Lions around the corner was indeed where once the "large and small lions of the king were confined." I particularly liked that "and small."

I thought: *Robert would have loved this.*

The bell rang. I shoved aside the thought—still automatic after thirteen months—that it might be Robert, and went out to meet Asif.

He all but snapped to attention and greeted me formally: "Hello, Madame Eady." English, I would learn, was his way of showing off; he'd spent most of his childhood in Quebec speaking French. (English was probably safer for him in Paris anyway, as the French can find Quebecois accents more humorously awful than Americans'.)

"Hey," Ellie said, suddenly appearing at the top of the spiral staircase. She smiled at Asif, looked carefully at me, and announced, "I'll be right back."

"Okay!" Daphne said.

"And while I'm gone," Ellie said, "nobody talk." She disappeared.

"Ignore her, Asif," I said, and he pretended to relax, at least until I told Daphne to check on the twins. Daphne's departure would leave the two of us alone.

Asif was smoothly handsome, with lashes longer than Ellie's, and he was taller than all of us. Eight or nine feet, I'd guess. I liked that. And that our idle conversation revealed that an abiding passion of Asif's (driven by military or diplomatic life, I assumed) was safety. Ellie was my treasure, or a large part of the dwindling hoard I had left. I didn't want her stolen away by anyone or anything in Paris; Asif seemed up to the task of protecting her.

Still, when Asif swung his security discussion around to the store, I grew uneasy. Was *it* secure? Night *and* day? I thought about telling him about the king's lions. But I thought: even after I explained, Asif wouldn't get that. And I thought: I wish for Ellie someone who *would* get that, someone like her dad.

My wandering mind had missed Asif wandering into a new topic, books. When I began listening again, I heard him asking me a question. I asked him to repeat it and then winced when he winced; he must have thought I was critiquing his English. No, it turned out, just his canon. Trying to impress me, he asked if I'd read Aristotle, Plato, Shakespeare, Kant; trying to be helpful, I asked if he'd ever read anything written by a woman.

That made him nervous enough to start talking about security again: Asif thought a camera or two would help us catch shoplifters. The embassy had quite a system, he said, and then caught himself. "But I really shouldn't answer questions about it," he said, and then paused, I realized, so I could ask one.

"No," I said. "I guess not."

"My dad's really good with the stuff, though," he said.

"I thought he was good at ships," I said.

Asif looked at me blankly.

"Because he's in the *navy*," I said, and he brightened.

"We even have them—cameras—in, around, our apartment," Asif said, and then caught himself again. "I probably shouldn't talk about that, either."

"No," I said, "because it's creepy." I smiled so he would know to as well.

"What's creepy?" Daphne said, returning with the twins.

"Nothing," Asif said, quickly but suavely. It charmed me—I liked that he was at least aspiring to be an adult—but seemed to irritate Daphne, as would most things Asif in the months to come. It took some time for me to determine that the reason was jealousy, mixed with the fact that Asif was male. Save George, Daphne had not had much kindness in her heart for men since arriving in Paris.

The twins, on the other hand, were smitten. They'd climbed onto the tall stools behind the counter and watched the whole scene, rapt. Their lives were full of exotic people coming and going, and they loved it. In some children, the result would have been shyness; it made the twins, on the other hand, want to pull their chairs closer to the show. What's more, Ellie—self-possessed, American, proud— could do no wrong in the twins' eyes, and she had chosen Asif. The matter was settled.

Peter, decidedly the more docile twin, looked, as he often did, contentedly bemused, like the beloved uncle he will one day be.

Annabelle, on the other hand, looked ready to sub in with Asif should Ellie show even a moment's disinterest. Her face fell as Ellie returned.

"Where are you going?" I asked Ellie, a reasonable question that was met with pursed lips.

"Maybe we'll head down to the Seine," Ellie said. "Look for es-capees." The Seine is lined with pop-up bookstalls; Ellie was forever certain that books stolen from our shop were for sale there. Daphne thought so, too.

Asif nodded grimly. This was *exactly* the sort of security lapse he was talking about.

Daphne rolled her eyes, and then Annabelle did, too, a new skill, one of several that George told me Annabelle was mastering under our care.

Asif's eyes, meanwhile, popped wide when I told Ellie to be sure not to *cross* the Seine and visit Bemelmans's old wine bar. Again.

Ellie was undaunted. "Fine," she said, "we'll go up to the Pompi-dou and hang out with all the drunk American students." I actually liked the pedestrian streets around the glass-fronted, inner-workings-on-view Centre Pompidou at night: there were usually people, buskers, music. After dark, our corner of the Marais was so quiet it could be spooky, lions or no.

"They're not all drunk," I said.

Ellie, afraid (like me) of what I would say next, tugged at Asif. With an exchange of *au revoirs*, he bundled her out the door and ducked his head at me, a deferential salute. Annabelle ran to the glass and thumped on it as they passed. I saw Ellie wait—I saw Ellie impress herself with her own magnanimity—while Asif paused, grinned, and pressed his hand against Annabelle's, the glass between them. Then Asif turned, Ellie turned, and they left, marching up the street, away from the Seine, their hands swinging achingly close to each other, knuckles brushing, heads tilted just so.

I don't know which side of the family deeded Ellie her mane, but I've always hoped she (or he) was pleased with the result. Ellie's hair, the brightest black imaginable, is a mammoth, bouncing mass, planetary, rich and wild. I *hoped* Asif would keep her safe, but I knew her hair would. Her bearing would. Anyone who came at my daughter should know they were tangling with royalty.

I went back to Bemelmans's old wine bar once. Just me, by myself, midafternoon. I could have called Molly, but one thing that Paris, city of couples kissing everywhere, does surprisingly well is cater to solitary diners. And drinkers. I ordered the pâté. Some wine? Sure. Maybe that would fortify me enough to press for more about the missing murals. The *chagrin d'amour.*

Wine had fortified me years before. I remembered getting through three-quarters of a bottle one early evening with Robert. This was, needless to say, pre-daughters, pre-wedding, in fact, pre-Wisconsin

World Tour, but rather in the middle of those very early weeks after we'd met outside the bookstore, when we spent most of our time naked, knocking about in the dark amidst his books.

"You're lying," I said.

I was sitting on the floor of his apartment when I said this, and I had been for the better part of an hour—which had followed an hour I'd spent waiting for him at my apartment before that. We'd been supposed to have dinner. He'd said he had to finish something. I'd decided to come over and stare him down until he did, or offered me his apartment's one chair.

"I'm not," he said, staring at his work. "I really am trying to finish—"

But that wasn't what I'd been talking about.

"About your parents," I said.

During our early days, and nights, together, we'd done the whence-me new couples do and bonded over the fact that we were both orphans—that Robert, like me, had lost his parents. His parents' departure was more tragic than mine. Car crash, dead before the paramedics arrived. I'd thought my parents' own relatively gradual departures (dad, years, mom, months) by wasting illnesses (lung cancer, from years of secondhand bar smoke) infinitely cruel, but what Robert described sounded exponentially worse. I'd hugged him. Gripped him, really, as I was gripped by the fact that I'd found someone, finally, whose orphanhood was worse than mine.

And yet, a week or so later, there on the floor of his apartment—

"What do you mean?" he asked.

And yet, "what do you mean" is not what someone who has lost two parents in a fiery wreck says. Moreover, there was something off about him and this loss. I would have expected some sort of comradeship, some sort of connection between us, a shared shock at discovering the world's suddenly revealed wrongness, with the way that, sun or rain, each new day didn't seem to care that our parents were dead. No one cared, not like me. I was slowly learning to navigate this new reality, but I couldn't see any of this process in Robert. True, my parents had been gone only two years then and his, four, but still, the loss was like yesterday, wasn't it?

Had his really died in a car crash four years ago? Or had they died some other way?

Or had they not died at all?

I asked him.

Now he stopped and turned from his work. He didn't answer. There was a long silence that, the longer it ran, seemed to be an invitation to retract my question. I put the cork in the bottle. I wanted more than anything to leave.

"I don't know," he said finally. "Not really." I watched him get angry, and then lose that anger in the face of mine: he'd lied to me, after all. "I'm sorry?" he said. "The thing is—I—I didn't know we were going to be—together?"

Three weeks old then, our relationship.

"You thought, when you caught me, 'awesome, shoplifters are usually good for a one-night pity fuck,'" I said.

"I wasn't thinking that."

"What do you mean, 'I don't know'? Tell me that much," I said, "before I go."

"Leah," he said. "Don't go." So quiet then. I didn't move. "It's a lot to get into on a first date," he said, "what happened. My life. I'm sorry I lied, though. It was easier, but—I'm sorry."

"Easier? Fuck you."

"Easier than saying, 'I don't know what happened to my parents,'" he said. "Please stop saying 'fuck.'"

He left the chair for the floor.

"The crazy thing is," he said, "I thought, 'wow, for once, you know what? I do have a way, a means of'—that night, with the books, the bar, I thought you were beautiful—I think you're beautiful—I think you swear too much but, I thought, 'the Bemelmans book, *Madeline*, is right in front of us. *Use* that!' I mean, that's never happened on a date before."

"Never?" I said. I didn't feel beautiful. "I would have thought that your standard shtick. What kind of woman doesn't fall for the boy who loves books written for little girls?"

"They weren't," Robert said. "And I don't. I mean, I do love *Madeline*. And Bemelmans in general. But I also love—*Johnny Tremaine. Anne of Green Gables. David Copperfield. . . .*"

And—fuck—a dozen other books about orphans.

Robert only had tattered toddler memories of his mom. Nothing of his dad. Or so he thought. His mother *had* died, but not in a crash, or a car crash. Overdose. His birth certificate did not list a father. Sometimes he remembered things, sensations—sunshine, the beach. Sometimes the smell of cigarettes: Marlboros, he'd since determined. But so many memories of so many foster homes since had supplanted everything else. There had been two, three almost-adoptions, but after a while, he'd just gotten too old. He'd been told to "ride it out." He had, and he swore it was only recently he'd learned the expression wasn't *write it out.*

There on the floor, he was everything I was not: sober, serious, not crying. He'd learned to like being alone, he said. He'd learned to like reading. He'd liked *Madeline* because not only were there no parents but everyone seemed to get along in Madeline's tidy, iron-cotted, light-filled dorm. He'd slept in rooms just like that, he said, and it had never been like that.

"But"—I wasn't calling him on his lies anymore, because they weren't lies, I could see that, the way his eyes had gone stone in the telling, but there were other things I couldn't see—"didn't she, didn't

Madeline have parents? Wasn't it just supposed to be a boarding school, where she was?"

Robert nodded, a smile coming to his face, along with some color. "And I liked *that*," he said. "It was like she was *choosing* to grow up without parents. I liked to imagine that I'd chosen, too. In that—in those places, places where I was—all you want is to be able to *choose*. Clothes, lunch, school. Something, anything."

He paused.

"And that's everything?" I finally asked.

He said nothing, just shut his eyes. And then he went back to his little table and his work and he sat and I sat and after a while, he turned off the light and came to me and kissed me, behind one ear, then another, whispering *I'm sorry* and *believe me*.

Daphne asked if we might have some coffee while we waited for Asif and Ellie to return from their date.

Successive parenting failures in Paris: one, to cocoon the girls from the city enough that they went to bed at a normal hour; two, to cocoon them from the city enough that they didn't adopt its ubiquitous vices. In Ellie's case, cigarettes. Ellie protests she only wants to have them on hand for friends who want them, which I half believe because she herself doesn't directly reek of smoke, and because I'm too tired to discipline her effectively. I pick my battles. She bathes, goes to school. *Succès*.

Daphne's vice is more curious. Coffee. Yes, she's too young. But she favors decaf, and only ever just the one cup at a sitting—a petite French-size cup, not a massive American jeroboam of the stuff— served to her at a café or by her own mother on a night like this, the twins safely in bed upstairs, her older sister unsafely at large in the city, her mother's mind unsteadily roaming from one continent to another.

With the distraction of Asif, the scribbled *I'm sorry* in Robert's book, and the twins coming and going, I knew I'd not given Daphne nearly enough time. She seemed pleased to have it now. She took down her special mug from the cabinet, Daphne-size, cryptically labeled: *biz*. I thought it was some dot-com tchotchke Ellie had found at a *marché aux puces*—literally (and epidemically) a market of the fleas—but no, it was from a real shop and had real style, I subsequently found out: *biz* was French texting slang for *bises*, kisses. And I wanted to do just that as she moved quietly about—coffee, cream, sugar, a saucer, a tiny spoon; she loved the ceremony as much as the first sip—I wanted to kiss her, and not the ever-fraught French *bises* on the cheek (one for someone you just met, two for an old friend, or one for a man, three for a woman? I forever did it wrong) but a kiss planted American mom–style, right on the crown of her head.

"Do you miss Dad, Mom?"

And yes, coffee made Daphne seem more grown up, and grown up suited her. She was born an old soul. I'd had serious, adult conversations with her since the day she was born. That look that infants have, that deep, unembarrassed, unhurried gaze they can give you, as though they are patiently waiting for you to say *something* worth responding to? Daphne never lost that look.

"I do, sweetie," I said, and did not look at Daphne. She and Ellie have Robert's eyes. And though Daphne's come complete with her own (smaller, brighter) splotch of color in her right iris, her eyes have none of his furtiveness. He had such wonderful eyes, Robert, and I forever urged him to *do more with them*, like *look at me*.

"Do you?" Daphne said. I checked to see how much of her coffee was gone. There was an ashtray on a high shelf I dearly wanted to use. More than one night I'd rifled through Ellie's purse, looking for cigarettes.

"Daphne," I said. I did not want to answer this question. I did not want to have been asked it. "What's going on?" I said, and watched her decide not to answer this. Yet.

"I miss him more here," Daphne said instead. "More than in Milwaukee."

I nodded to this as though I missed him more here, too, but what I really was thinking was *of course you do*. Because, of course: here was the unanticipated effect, the danger, of relocating to Paris, to relocating inside the pages Robert wrote. It did not grant us distance but collapsed it. He had disappeared, but thanks to his manuscript, thanks to Paris, we'd disappeared inside him.

"I sometimes wonder if Ellie—?" she began, and I knew I had to cut her off. The sisters could compete in other aspects of their lives, but not in how much they missed their father. Or did they regardless? Outside Bemelmans's bar, I remembered how I had first thought Daphne, then Ellie, Robert's true champion. What I'd not realized, what I realized now, was that they, there—everywhere, always—had been measuring me.

"I'm sure she does," I interrupted, but Daphne's eyes grew so wide, I stopped to clarify. "Does Ellie what?"

"Does—does she see him, too?" Daphne gushed. "Does she see Dad?"

She waited for me to speak, and I couldn't.

I had not told the girls about the customer finding their father's book, of me finding the *I'm sorry* inside. I'd not told them and I was proud of not telling them. *Nothing to see here.* Moreover, I'd not told them that I'd wondered if the scribbled apology was an apology to *me*, that the book's sudden appearance, and then disappearance, was *his* doing. That had little basis in reality. I recognized that, and even forgave myself for it. Such slips were to be expected. Why hadn't I expected my daughters would slip, too?

"I don't see him all the time," she mumbled.

"Daphne—what?" I said. "I'm sorry—do you mean—where—?" What I so readily forgave in myself was frightening in Daphne.

"When I'm out walking," Daphne said. "With the twins, and we'll be coming home and we'll be near something—like Notre-Dame—from one of the *Madeline* books, and I'll think, I should look for him, because this is what he was coming to Paris to do, research locations for that book."

We should have stayed in Milwaukee. Or we should have moved to the desert. Jupiter. Some place he'd never find us. Some place we'd never find him.

"What *we* were coming to Paris to do," she amended. "And sometimes, you know—I *see* him. Just out of the corner of my eye. And I'll turn to ask Peter and Annabelle—they can be very *méchants* about holding hands, you know, especially crossing streets; if you let go for *one* second, they wander off, especially Annabelle—and he'll be gone."

"Oh, Daphne," I said, scrambling. "Sometimes—sometimes I think I see him, too." Because I had, after all, that first day outside Madame's bookstore. "Sometimes people can—sometimes imagination—sometimes we can imagine things so well, so very precisely, that we think—"

"Mom!" Daphne said. "Not '*think*.' Not '*imagination*.' It's *really* him, *vraiment*."

"You've talked to—Ellie about this?"

Daphne shook her head. "Mom," she said.

"I know . . ." She waited for me to continue. "I know," I said, "that we both miss someone, very much."

"Daddy's here," Daphne said. "In Paris."

Molly had told me she wasn't learning French because they'd only be here two years. *And,* she added, the Kiwis she knew who'd lived here ten, fifteen, twenty years—they'd lost some of their *English*. I asked myself now whether I'd done something similar to the girls in a fraction of the time. Stranded them between two languages, two countries, two realities. Or rather, between reality and fantasy. I'd not told them what the grief books had told me, and look what had happened: he was walking the streets of Paris in their imaginations.

And now in mine.

I was so startled, I blurted out the first question I could think of, the one that, *were* he alive, hurt most.

"But, sweet girl—then why wouldn't he come—"

"Maybe he hit his head. Like Pascal!"

Daphne had an odd theory about *The Red Balloon* and its oddly happy ending, when Pascal, who's just lost his balloon to the bullies' rocks, is suddenly rescued, lifted up and away into the sky, by dozens of *new* balloons. Daphne believed the flyaway ending wasn't real; Pascal must have gotten conked by a stray rock; the sunny final scenes thus spin out of his concussed unconsciousness. There is absolutely no basis for this theory on-screen. For some of us, however—Daphne and I chief among them—there's also no basis for the film's actual, happy ending. After all, as Pascal flies away smiling, what must he see when he looks down at the ground? His best friend, crushed in the dirt.

Daphne continued: "Dad hit his head, he's looking for us, but maybe—maybe he doesn't know he's looking. Maybe"—her thumb scratched circles on the table—"maybe he doesn't know what he's looking for."

"Sweetheart," I said.

The circles stopped. "You can keep telling people—strangers—he's dead," she said. "I know you do, you say 'lost,' but the way you say it, in French anyway, I know you mean for people to think he's dead, but—but I know he isn't."

"Daphne," I said.

"And I know you know he isn't," she said.

"Look—" I started to say.

"*I am*," she said, stressing each wonderfully awkward, but thus all the more emphatic, English word. *Je suis* is so slippery, even feathery, by comparison. "I *am* looking," she said. "And where do you think Ellie is tonight? *She's* looking."

"She's *what*?"

"No, Mom—listen. *We're* looking."

And they were.

Not just for him, but for me, for that version of her mother who was interested in confronting uncomfortable questions.

"Why," Daphne said, "aren't *you*?"

Because your father is—

Is not—

But I couldn't say it.

Loss, like French, has its own grammar. Unlike French, immersion only makes it harder to master.

CHAPTER 7

One of the scariest books we have in the store goes by an unlikely title: *Swahili Grammar and Vocabulary*. Published by a "Mrs. F. Burt" in 1923 and bound in bloodred buckram, the book initially hid behind a bookshelf, where it must have fallen decades before I found it. I'd almost tossed it in the trash; I had enough trouble selling English-language books. I'd opened it, though, to see if Mrs. F. had convinced them to at least print her full name inside. And there, on the foxed and browning pages, I found the inscription: *To Anderson, on the night of the lion.*

I decided not to throw it away.

For a while, it went back and forth to school in Daphne's bag. She was as fascinated with the inscription as I was—*was* this Mrs. Burt's handwriting? who was Anderson? what lion?—but eventually tired of it. I reclaimed it from Daphne, studied the odd left-leaning penmanship, compared it to what I remembered of Robert's.

But mostly I thought about that *night*, the one of the lion, how so few words can change everything: a boring textbook made into an urgent mystery. The inscription seemed to celebrate an escape, but had everyone escaped?

I hadn't, not from my conversation with Daphne, not from the question she'd asked about looking for Robert. When I tried to answer, when I couldn't answer, she shook her head and wandered wordlessly to her room. She didn't have to tell me not to follow, and I didn't. She wasn't six anymore, nor even twelve. She and Ellie were both teens, that other country. That mother-daughter rupture, it happens everywhere. Or so I've heard. But it yawns particularly wide in Paris, and did then. They'd gone looking without me. They'd believed he was here before I did.

I was falling behind, which meant I couldn't see what they saw coming next.

I went to my room, dislodged the Swahili book from my bedside pile, and took it down to the shop. The street was completely dark. I'd misunderstood, or only half understood, the inscription. It wasn't the lion that was scary, but the night, *this* night, which, as I stared into it, became terrifying. The book, the store, the window I was looking through, but most important, what Daphne had told me she'd seen, all of this was transforming the street outside and the city beyond from a place I thought I knew well into something once again foreign. I had to find a stool to steady myself as the feeling came over me that I no longer knew where, or who, I was. This lasted all of a minute, then everything returned.

I went upstairs to wait and see if Ellie would, too.

"*We're* looking": and indeed, Ellie and Asif had gone looking that night in Ménilmontant. I know that not because Daphne said so, and certainly not because her sister told me—Ellie arrived home at 1:00 A.M. and I did not rise to confront her—but because of Ellie's phone.

Which I'd found *because* I did not confront her. Ellie slept with her phone at her side, flouting a rule I'd found impossible to enforce. Another rule: I was free to examine her phone's entire contents whenever I wanted, without warning. I'd never enforced this rule

(I didn't like the Orwellian feel of it, but the Orwellian parenting website I'd gotten it from said just establishing the rule could suffice), but I'd never revoked it, which meant there was absolutely nothing wrong with sneaking into the girls' room, sliding the phone off Ellie's nightstand, and taking it to the kitchen, where six successive password guesses failed until a final one—her father's birth date—succeeded.

I went straight to the photos. I skipped the texts. I wasn't *that* kind of mom, I told myself. And so I tried not to look as I looked.

But I needn't have worried; speed-skimming revealed a girl in love with Paris as much as or, if I had to judge by photography alone, more than with Asif. There were plenty of shots of him, yes, including one or two making a sinewy bicep. But there were many more of him framed by an archway: he would often be out of focus, but the colorful garden beyond, sharp and true. There were endless shots of him in cafés looking away from the lens, and not seeing what Ellie seemed to see—others looking at him, at them. Ellie, it seemed, saw what I saw, that Parisians enjoy life's little dramas. What I enjoy about Parisians is that they *expect* drama.

And sometimes, although you are not a tenth the romantic your younger sister is, you create a folder on your phone solely devoted to photos of your missing father. Or so I had intuited Ellie had done. There was a folder for friends, for favorites, for Bemelmans (just two off-kilter shots of Notre-Dame and some of the Seine). And there was a folder for "Dad." I hesitated before clicking on it. I'd feared that the girls missed him less now. I'd feared that I'd *wanted* them to miss him less. But the truth was, we all carried him in different ways. Sometimes Daphne set an extra plate at dinner for him, as we'd occasionally done in the States during his absences. But here in Paris, she just as often silently picked that plate back up and returned it to the cabinet before we started eating.

Sometimes, I caught myself crying. So did other people. Once, a girl not much older than Ellie, waiting with me for the light in order to cross the street, looked over and asked if I was all right. In French, in English. I swear I did not know I'd been thinking about Robert, much less crying about him. The light turned green. The girl was on a bike. She waited for me to answer. A bus waited behind her. *Ding, ding*: the warning bells of Parisian buses sound like they've been stolen from a boxing ring but still manage to clang so merrily it's almost music (until the driver, patience spent, finally uses the horn). The girl pushed off. Then, as now, I wiped my face. I decided not to open "Dad."

Instead, I found the folder that contained tonight's images. I saw that Ellie and Asif had stopped at the chocolatier at the top of the street: *Snap*, tongues, an outstretched arm. A shot of Asif eating, smiling. A shot of Ellie kissing him on the cheek. A shot of a bus. A shot of an empty street. Another empty street, one I didn't recognize, and the blue street-name placard on the nearest building unintelligible. A shot of Ellie pointing at a mural painted on the side of a small apartment building—it was hard to make out, but then I saw it, a giant red balloon, wrapping around the building's top left corner.

Then a shot that was a blur; something had jiggled her arm. Another fumbled shot, another, a whole rapid-fire sequence of them, murky or light-blown, all blurry. And then what looked like Asif's hand, stretched toward the lens as if to cover it up.

And then, on her phone, a video she'd taken, time-stamped tonight. Its first frame was pitch black.

But when things became visible, I became so absorbed that I failed to realize that the sound, which I should have muted, might draw someone to see what I was doing.

Ellie.

She came up behind me and didn't say a word until she reached over, stopped the video, and took the phone. "Nice," she said, cool and quiet.

"Ellie," I said.

"I mean, I guess, you did have that rule. I just didn't think—while I was *sleeping*, Mom?" she asked. "How long have you—"

"Ellie, never," I said. "This is the first time. I just wanted to— Daphne said—"

"Daphne?" Ellie said. "Daphne said *what*?"

"Nothing, El, nothing about *you* anyway, she was more talking about—" Ellie circled around the tiny table and sat across from me. "She said you were *looking* for him," I said. "Dad."

"What?" Ellie said.

"*Shh*," I said, nodding toward the sleepers' rooms.

"Yeah, keep it quiet," Ellie said. "Maybe mute the fucking phone next time you're snooping."

"Ellie!"

"Mom!" Ellie said. "When *were* you going to go looking? It's May, nine months since we got here, thirteen since he's been gone. Daphne's like, 'she's going, she's going looking when we're at school, maybe,' and I said, 'okay, then why isn't she telling us about it,' and Daphne's all, 'well, maybe she's not finding him.' And I said, 'well, maybe she should look harder.'" Ellie started flicking through her phone.

Do you talk about me behind my back all the time, I wondered, or just when I'm screwing up? I wanted to ask this, but couldn't, so instead I said, "Is Asif okay?" I'd not seen much of the video, but enough to see Asif take a spill.

Ellie looked up at me. "Yeah."

"Because it looked like he tripped? He fell?"

"It wasn't pretty, but yeah," Ellie said, eyes back to the phone.

"Are you sure he—"

"Asif is *fine*, Mom," Ellie said. "Super embarrassed. Though he shouldn't have been—that rat was as big as a dog. I jumped, too—if I hadn't, I could have caught Asif before he fell."

"Where were you filming? It looks like some sort of park."

"Oh, Mom, c'mon," Ellie said.

She scooted her chair back around the table toward me. All wasn't forgiven, but for the briefest moment, I pretended it was: she was right here, next to me, she was warm and alive and safe, and she'd moved beside me so that if she'd wanted to, she could hug me.

She didn't. Instead, she pressed PLAY.

Ménilmontant. Paris's Alps, an almost vertical stretch of the city, long famous as a film neighborhood: the light's good up there. Jackie Gleason shot a maudlin vanity pic, 1962's *Gigot*, in Ménilmontant and played the title role, a mute clown. Famed director Dmitri Kirsanoff's silent-film masterpiece *Ménilmontant*, supposedly Pauline Kael's favorite film of all time, was shot there in 1924–25; its violence still shocks. And of course, thirty years later, *The Red Balloon*. Lamorisse knew what he was doing when he set his "children's" film in Ménilmontant. He needed the light, sure, but the dark, too.

Ellie's own video was exceptionally dark and fairly short. She narrated it now; she'd long wanted to visit *le quartier du ballon*—the balloon neighborhood, our slang, not Paris's—but she reminded me that I'd long been opposed; it wasn't "safe."

And it wasn't, or so other parents in our timid corner of the Marais assured me: Ménilmontant wasn't wealthy and hadn't been for centuries. Who knew what happened there at night?

I was about to find out.

Ellie is the cameraman, Asif the offscreen, and quite anxious, narrator: *Ellie, Ellie, I think we should go back.* The streets wind and climb, higher and higher, until the ascent grows so steep the sidewalk finally gives up and becomes stairs. Ellie had shot herself an almost perfect noir film, the night blue-black beyond the occasional streetlamp's glow. I was even a little jealous. All those years I'd dreamed of making films, and here Ellie had made one, if unconsciously. Asif plays his own role well: *let's go,* he hisses, suddenly urgent, like he'd just seen something Ellie hadn't. But they continue to climb the stairs. To their left, bricks, a wall, a building, buildings. To their right, perfect darkness. For a minute I thought it was a cliff, but then a distant lamp's glow summoned trees, grass, a terraced park. Ellie climbs, the POV bounces, up, up, she turns to study the neighboring building, and Asif shouts. Squeaks, really. Brave Asif. The camera spins and two of what had looked like trees now animate, split, and become two men with beards. They walk up to Ellie and Asif. They smile, nod, and when Ellie and Asif stutter a reply, the men smile again and say *bonsoir* and disappear.

"See?" Ellie says to Asif on the film, and to me as I watched. "It's not dangerous up there. It's perfectly fine." A moment later, Ellie urges them higher one more time—*we're almost to the top, and that's, like, a famous shot in the film!* This is when the rat (like all good movie monsters, it goes unseen) startles Asif, who stumbles and falls, along with Ellie, along with the phone. The last seconds of the video are shot from the ground, nothing visible but the flare of a lamp and the black sky beyond. The audio's clear, though: Asif and Ellie swear and apologize to each other. There is a discussion of blood. Of glass. Of being out too late. *I'm so sorry,* Asif says, *your mom's going to kill me.*

Ellie has the last words, before a hand crosses the shot to turn the camera off. She's angry with him now. And by *him,* I mean her dad, but Asif is the handy proxy. Or I am: *Don't worry,* Ellie says, *she doesn't care.*

After Ellie and I finished watching, we fell silent. Robert's manuscript took that family to Paris, no farther. There was, as I said, suggestion of a trip to Ménilmontant in its pages, but no actual scene where anyone in the family did just that.

"So there's no reason to be scared," Ellie said.

I shook my head.

"But you still are, aren't you?" she said.

Nine months in Paris, and I had not been to the neighborhood where the subject of my abandoned thesis was filmed. Even though Eleanor recognized that I was relieved to be rid of the thesis—some part of me still burned to *make* a film, but nothing made me want to finish that paper—she would ask about *The Red Balloon*'s "backyard" occasionally on Skype. I had various ways of evading the question. I didn't say that I was worried I might bump into Robert, though I now think that that was some irrational part of it. Another part was that I'd secretly been saving it up, the last chocolate in the box, because what would top it after? The movie of (and, my deluded self insisted, *about*) my childhood, come to life once more.

In the meantime, though, I'd fended off Eleanor with clever speechwriterisms. I wasn't interested in the "real behind the reel" but rather the *art*, the film, the film whole and complete. If I wanted to see Ménilmontant, I could just press PLAY.

But now I had, on Ellie's phone. And now I had to go.

Ménilmontant rises northeast of central Paris, between Montmartre and the Père Lachaise cemetery, but attracts none of their tourists. That's in part because there's little in Ménilmontant for *les touristes*, nor even for scholars and obsessives of *The Red Balloon*. A wide swath of the neighborhood, including the rickety catwalks that helped residents traverse the precipitous heights, was razed in the 1960s in an aggressive slum-clearing effort.

And so Albert Lamorisse's film, shot in just two months at the end of 1955, got there just in time. To review: a large red balloon and a sweet little blond-haired boy (and briefly, a cat) meet atop Ménilmontant at dawn and then pal around Paris; some jealous bullies eventually hunt the balloon down and attack it with slingshots. The balloon sinks lower and lower, until one of the bullies finally puts a foot to it, and then the balloon lies there, crumpled and spent, just another piece of windblown trash in a vacant lot scabbed with dirt. Then comes the odd ending Daphne and I distrust, when the boy floats over Paris with dozens of other balloons that have rushed to his side, while the boy's great love, that red balloon, lies trampled and forgotten. Lamorisse's original script called for the boy to fly all the way to Africa. In the final cut, Pascal hardly makes it out of Paris, but still, the soaring mood is jarringly literal. To me, the film's real, if unintentional, message is unnervingly dark: beauty is fleeting; jealousy kills.

It's strange that Lamorisse's film makes anyone wistful for postwar Paris, because he takes great pains to show how immediately post- the war still was: Pascal and his balloon are pursued over rubble-strewn lots and the rocky ruins of old apartment blocks; tufts of grass dot the earth here and there, but it's no park.

A half century later, it is.

Some parts of Lamorisse's Ménilmontant still exist, however, starting with the bus line Pascal (and the balloon) take in the film and which I took the next morning, after seeing everyone silently off to school. The 96 climbed steeply up and out of the Marais, eventually letting me off at Notre-Dame—another, smaller Notre-Dame, Notre-Dame de la Croix—which boy and mischievous balloon get thrown out of (by an usher in Napoleonic dress) during the film.

Then it was down rue Julien Lacroix and up the staircase that felled Asif. I can see why Ellie was so interested in the location; the stairs here look much like those in Lamorisse's film, but were actually built much later, around the same time as the terraced Parc de Belleville that the staircase threads through. A couple of young men, smoking, looked up at me from a bench as I passed, one of those long, focused stares that I have become somewhat more accustomed to while living here—France is the land of the frank appraisal—but they didn't smile. I kept moving.

At the top of the stairs, I suddenly found myself short of breath but told myself it was from the steep climb. Still, Lamorisse had been *here*. Pascal had walked *there*. The cat, that lonely, long-ago cat, the first living thing the film chooses to put on view, had sat right *there* while Pascal meandered into frame from my left at 00:00:05, endured the boy's friendly scratching at 00:00:16, and stayed put once Pascal, at 00:00:30, headed down (roughly) the same stairs Ellie and Asif had found. (Part of what's always delighted me about the film is how improvisational it is, and how lucky Lamorisse had gotten with his improvisers, be they cats, kids, or balloons.)

They'd all been right here. My daughter, too. Had Robert? I gripped the railing and breathed. *Robert would love this*, I thought, and thought of Ellie. *I love this*. I took in the view Ellie had sought.

In the film, the panorama is wreathed in smoke and fog, but today was startlingly clear. It's a shame tourists flock instead to the views a kilometer or so northwest in the pickpockety heights of Montmartre; it's quieter here, and the Eiffel Tower easier to spot.

But I wasn't thinking of tourists. I was thinking of Ellie.

And Daphne. Not long after we first arrived in Paris, Daphne stopped on the sidewalk of some street—somewhere in the Left Bank, narrow, residential, pretty enough, but nothing notable in view—and said, "I think I've been here before." After some requisite talk about reincarnation, time travel, and wormholes—both Ellie and Daphne love Madeleine L'Engle's *A Wrinkle in Time*—we chalked it up to another Madeline, Bemelmans's, and of course *The Red Balloon*, and all the girls' years of French immersion schooling. For much of their childhood, these girls had lived in Paris in every way but the real way.

So had I. But I'd never felt quite as Daphne did about any spot in Paris until I'd reached this one. *Here* was the view I'd first seen from Wisconsin thirty-two years earlier, when I'd first seen the film, first read the book. I wanted to shout; I felt shaky. I went into a bakery to steady myself, to tell the baker, *bonjour, hello, I'm back!*

Instead, I just stood there, breathless, grinning stupidly.

He said nothing. Neither did the only other person in the store, a customer clutching a very full paper bag.

Seconds passed. Reality spasmed. The customer vanished.

And the baker began to explain that I'd interrupted a holdup.

But I was already out the door, not thinking, just running, because the thief—the other customer, with the full bag—had also stripped me of my purse.

Behind me came the baker. Ahead of me, the thief.

And then, just behind the thief, closing in much faster than I, someone new. Unfortunately, the first thing that came to mind was an idiom I'd just learned for driving fast: *appuyez sur le champignon,* step on the mushroom. (Another reason I don't drive in Paris: I understand that certain older French cars have pedals roughly the size of dimmer switches—or mushrooms.) The idiom wasn't necessarily appropriate here, but I didn't have time to reflect on that, only enough time to dub this new person Monsieur le Champignon—if nothing else, the word sounded like *champion*, and this he proved to be.

Down we plummeted through Ménilmontant. One staircase, two. The baker disappeared.

A landing or so below, the two young men who'd been staring at me earlier roused and tackled the purse snatcher.

And then they seized my ally-of-the-moment, Monsieur le Champignon. I couldn't tell why, although politicians had been battling with each other, and the police, about racial profiling; I hoped I wasn't on the front lines of a skirmish here.

They released the thief first. He ran off, leaving behind the bag of money he'd stolen and my purse. They released Monsieur le Champignon second, who stood his ground and reached for the purse to give to me. They shouted at him; he shouted back. One held him at bay while the other went into bag and purse and extracted fifty euros from each.

They smiled and spoke. French, but with an accent I couldn't source nor entirely understand. What's more, their smiles, menacing, somehow deafened me, and Monsieur le Champignon, whom they were once again restraining—now with the help of a small knife—had to translate.

Monsieur le Champignon I understood easily: his English was perfect, as would befit a valedictorian from Roosevelt High School in Des Moines, Iowa. These details I learned later, along with his name, Declan.

At this point, though, Declan had more important information: *he says this is their* "pourboire"—*their tip? Their finder's fee. Have you called the police? You're getting robbed twice.* He turned to the men. *Leave her alone*, he said.

Then something happened, and suddenly Declan was bleeding, they were running, he was running after them.

And he would have caught them, too, had not two women from an *Accueil et Surveillance* squad, park rangers of a sort, stopped Declan. I caught up and tried to explain who really was at fault, but unfortunately played my role—frightened, confused American—too well, and they started shouting at Declan. He answered them evenly.

They frowned. I frowned. I'd understood what he'd said well enough to know his French was letter-perfect.

I tried some of my own less-perfect French, and they turned, softened: ah, an *Américaine*. Then they shouted at Declan again. He started to respond, and then stopped, coughed, and restarted. This time I understood him better, though (or because) his French had gotten worse, his accent much more American.

The rangers exchanged a glance before addressing Declan again, not shouting now: *vous êtes Américain aussi?*

Yes, he said, in English, *it seems we're both Americans.* The rangers took a deep breath, shook their heads, as though to take it all in. *Americans in Ménilmontant: what will happen next?*

A hospital, I thought, but Declan whispered to me, *say we're fine,* and so I did, and then I sat. Beside Declan, so I could see his wound— just beneath his chin, it was hardly an inch, but gaped open terribly. I decided that it would need stitches but that those stitches would mend well, and the scar would give him character, though he hardly needed more of that.

After moving to Paris and taking over a bookstore, I read fewer and fewer books about Paris. And far fewer, about anything, by men. Shelley, the retired teacher from New Orleans, encouraged me in this. Some weeks, when I would hand over whatever book I'd picked out for her that week—and for her, gender (or genre) didn't matter, so long as it *was* set in Paris—she would hand me a book in return, usually one she'd brought with her from Louisiana. To a degree, she filled Robert's old role, bookgiver in chief. But her inspiration was more mundane than Robert's ever had been. Her houseboat could accommodate only so large a library, she said, before it would sink;

she couldn't take on more books without offloading others. Whatever the cause, Shelley is how I came to develop a crush on Alice Mattison (American, b. 1941), who in one story writes of a high school teacher whose class "found sex everywhere, even the Gettysburg Address. But it was more than that. If spiders made love on a window . . . they'd pick Ms. Feldman's window."

What I mean is, I'm not sure Declan and I would have noticed each other in Winnipeg. Or Milwaukee. But in Paris, in the aftermath of a mugging, I found myself helplessly noting his looks, and that he'd noted mine. And of course, in France, there was another crucial detail that had not been true in Milwaukee (nor Winnipeg, though I did want to visit there thanks to another author Shelley once handed me, Carol Shields).

"A bookstore?" Declan said. "You own a *bookstore* in Paris?"

During our post-police discussion, I'd kept things focused on him, at least until my phone had started chiming with texts and I'd announced that I had to get back to the store.

What store? Bookstore. *Really?*

Really. I told him the name, the address. I told him about our Bemelmans display. I told him about what had drawn me to Ménilmontant (that is, I'd told him about *The Red Balloon*, not about Robert). I felt myself losing my way—and so skipped ahead; I told him to stop by the store sometime. I did caution him that "it's not what you think," but I didn't know what he thought, not really. His tone was a mixture of admiration, envy, surprise—familiar enough, at least coming from Americans, but to this he added a new, fresh, slightly unsettling ingredient: hunger.

"It's *exactly* what I think," he said, and I have often wondered since exactly what he meant, if he knew how those words stole from his mouth and over to me, in and around my ears, down my neck to my spine, and then skittered all the way, all the way down me, like spiders.

Oh, Ms. Feldman, I thought.

But of course the only person to blame for what happened next was me.

More unpleasant, or unsettling, than spiders: Ellie asking how I'd enjoyed Ménilmontant.

This, though I had decided not to mention anything about my adventure; I said I was late because I'd gotten turned around on the Métro, a known weakness of mine. (I use it too infrequently; I love this city and can't see it from underground.)

But Ellie's ability to pin me down—geographically, at least—was not a known strength of hers. How had she known where I was?

"Here," Ellie said, fingers fox-trotting across her phone. A giant pulsing red dot appeared. That was distracting enough that I missed the background picture—which was a satellite map of our street, rue Sainte-Lucie-la-Vierge, with us in the bull's-eye. "See, it's found you."

This took a moment. "You can track me?" I asked.

"Could you be a little less surprised?" Ellie said. "You *asked* for this feature when we signed up for the plan."

"I did?"

"*Oui,*" Ellie said. "You bought the *forfait familial,* right? Then it's automatic with *all* our phones."

Ellie looked away, but the shame was wholly mine. Of course she tracked me. She was already down one parent. She turned back, tried out a smile: "So," she said, "what'd you find?"

CHAPTER 8

People complain it's hard to find things in our store, but others say that's what they like about our store. When I took it over, years of neglect meant that there was almost no organizational system evident whatsoever. I enlisted the girls' help to reshelve things by genre and then alphabetically by author, but Ellie complained it was taking too long and suggested we do something she'd seen in a magazine: shelve everything by color. Daphne said that was stupid, Ellie said she was stupid, Daphne said *Dad* would think it was stupid, and then I intervened and said the first thing that came to me— that we'd organize the store by country. Because what organization we had inherited consisted of a single bookcase featuring books about Paris.

It worked. That is, it shut the girls up. It's a strange way to organize a store and I recommend it to no one. Genres get jumbled and disputes abound: should Shakespeare sit by Thomas Mann? Yes, if it's *The Merchant of Venice* and *Death in Venice*. But *Hamlet* goes next to Kierkegaard. Graham Greene's *Quiet American* sits by Marguerite Duras's *The Lover* and some waterlogged Lonely Planet guides to Vietnam. Greene's *Power and the Glory*, on the other hand, goes next to Octavio Paz in Mexico. In short, suspect judgment rules. Chess books, Russia. Space exploration, United States. Physics, Germany.

Ellie puts books she can't find a place for in Switzerland and, because she's still attached to her original suggestion, books with green covers (and occasionally Graham G. himself) in Greenland. Daphne's catch-all is Antarctica; she's also the author of little signs around the store that invite indignant browsers to reshelve books as they see fit.

I honestly think our system, capricious as it is, sells more books. I guarantee the man who came in looking for *Thirty Seconds over Tokyo* hadn't meant to buy Basho's *Narrow Road* (or a tattered copy of James Clavell's *Shogun*, for that matter), for example, but he did.

That said, with Declan coming, I had a sudden urge to rearrange the entire store in some more professional manner so it would look like I knew what I was doing. He'd been so impressed: *you own a bookstore in Paris?* It would be awkward if he mistook the shop for performance art.

He didn't, but things still quickly grew uncomfortable the day he came by. Daphne had joined me to homework-procrastinate. (And to check if Ellie had moved *Little Women* away from Massachusetts to Paris, which she regularly did to drive Daphne crazy.)

Declan and I exchanged greetings, and I told Daphne I'd met him in Ménilmontant.

"How?" Daphne asked.

I didn't believe in Robert's telepathy, but I do believe in empathy, and when Declan looked at me and Daphne, he understood what to say next: nothing about muggers or bakers, which was good, because I'd told the girls nothing about that aspect of my trip to Ménilmontant. Declan rumbled through something, in English, about how he—or I—or we—had been looking for the Métro. Daphne nodded to me, and said to him she'd never been in that neighborhood but she'd heard that it *was* hard to find the Métro stops up there.

She said this in French, which was a test. A simple one, administered hundreds of times across Paris every day. *Do you speak French?* That question is never asked directly; rather, a shopkeeper or waiter or baker speaks to you in French and you answer in French or you don't.

But beyond shouting the obligatory *bonjour*, we never administered it in our store. Or I didn't. What was Daphne up to? Declan responded in French. I listened. Declan kept talking. What was *he* up to? Daphne responded, French conversation ensued.

"You speak excellent French," Declan finally said to Daphne, in English.

Equally fluent in nonverbal French, Daphne twitched her lower lip (disdain, mild to medium) and turned to me, chin slightly raised. I'm not that fluent, so I wasn't sure what the chin meant, though it seemed to be a mixture of pride, curiosity, and something along the lines of *I think you think he's cute.*

It looked like Daphne was about to soundlessly add, *what's going on here?*—so I quickly said to Declan, aloud, "they both do."

"Both?" he said.

And the pang I felt then was unfamiliar to me—why should I feel embarrassed to admit that I had children? Because I'd be less of a catch? I didn't realize, not quite, that I was looking to be caught.

"My kids," I said. "I have two."

Daphne watched our exchange with extreme care. I could see her slow down the film we were all in so that she could monitor each syllable that came out of our mouths and every crease in our faces. We were on the cusp of finding her father, I think she thought. *She* had already seen him around town. But now something else was happening. What?

I wanted to know, too.

Declan, because he had a sense of decorum, or timing, turned to Daphne and asked her, quite formally, if he might borrow me for a while—he'd helped me find the Métro entrance up in Ménilmontant, he said, but I had helped *him* buy his ticket when he found he was short on change. He now wanted to repay the favor and buy me coffee.

I found myself a tiny bit in awe. He'd invented a perfectly plausible story on the spot, pretended he (and I) needed Daphne's permission to leave, *and* he'd paid Daphne the great respect of continuing to speak to her in immaculate French.

Or what I thought of as immaculate. It was a great embarrassment to the girls how my language skills lagged behind theirs. It was a great inconvenience to me. I had taken lessons offered by the city, by people who'd plastered flyers on poles, by a woman in Beirut who taught via Skype. I usually lasted one or two sessions. I was too advanced to begin where they always wanted to begin, and too much a beginner to do things like Daphne was doing now, correcting Declan's French: the verb he'd used for *repay* wasn't correct, she explained.

"Daphne," I said. I meant to scold her, but what I mostly felt was envy.

But she only had eyes, clear and alert ones, for him, and he for her.

"And," she said, ignoring me, "*nous sommes quatre.*" With that, she bid us adieu and went to return *Little Women* to its place alongside Dickinson, Thoreau, and Carl Yastrzemski.

"Why did she say 'we are four'?" Declan asked as we settled into a sidewalk café nearby.

The fourth member of my family—Robert—flashed before me, but fortunately, so did our waiter, who took our order and returned moments later. Cups, saucers, spoons were quickly and quietly arrayed before us with all the precision of a dinner at Versailles. *You don't have to tip,* insist the American guidebooks I grudgingly stock. *They want Americans to think they're supposed to leave a tip, but you don't have to; they're paid perfectly well.* I tip. I am American. The system relies on someone overpaying. Even when I receive bad service—when I am ignored—I'm comfortable with paying for that, too. No one checked on me for an hour; I was able to finish a book plucked from our Hoosier shelf, George Sand's *Indiana.*

Declan's question hung in the air, but to answer it would have been to break a sidewalk café rule, one almost as strict as not tipping: don't speak, not at first. Acclimate. Survey your surroundings. I did. Paris cafés force you to; the seating unerringly faces the street. Attempting to rearrange things so you face your companion isn't so much forbidden as it is impossible, given how little clearance exists between tables.

In front of us, a sanitation worker in green coveralls banged by with a cart, followed by three impossibly tall, alarmingly young women—models?—all in white. I like to watch people watch people in Paris; it's a hobby, like bird-watching, a study of color and carriage. I like to see what attracts, who distracts. I myself was so distracted by these three—were they triplets?—I failed to see that Declan was staring, not at them but, patiently, at me.

"I'm sorry," I said.

"Not at all," Declan said. I waited for him to begin a new conversational gambit, but no. *We are four.* I'd have to do the math for him, and so I did, explaining how Daphne had added two sisters and two twins to make "four," how four children might as well be forty, but not really, because they were all so well-behaved—*most* of the time, anyway, and—

And maybe because he heard me stumbling, he finally did decide to change the subject, segueing into a riff on all the *badly* behaved kids he encountered in his role as a study-abroad program fixer—his job was to get students to and from the airport, help them jump lines at the Louvre, extricate them from disputes with landlords, bouncers, and occasionally, the police.

I asked what sort of training prepared him for such a job, and he smiled and said none that he'd done. He'd started, and quit, a JD, an MFA in poetry, an MAT with a focus on French. Now he was enrolled in an international MBA program, which he was enjoying more than he'd thought he would.

"Really?" I said.

He laughed, not a happy laugh. "Maybe not," he said, and looked around. "But *I'm enjoying France.*"

"Even when the phone rings at 2:00 A.M.?" I don't know why I was pressing; some of Daphne's latent animosity must have infected me on the way out. "Sounds hellish."

We were at an outdoor café, the coffee was fine, we wouldn't be troubled for the bill for another six hours unless we summoned the waiter ourselves, and when the bill came, it would only be a few euros. Cheaper than Starbucks in Milwaukee. It wasn't raining.

This is all a long way of saying what Declan then said more directly: "I have my problems with Paris, but this is no hell."

I liked him. Not just because he'd rescued me in Ménilmontant, but because he was rescuing me here, again, in the Marais. The stakes were lower now, or higher; there was no immediate crisis, just a lingering one. I had my daughters, I had the twins, I had my three customers-cum-friends, I had the elderly Madame Brouillard, but I was lonely, and I was in Paris.

Paris can feel like a city of pairs. Not just romantic pairs, though it has those in abundance, but friends going arm in arm down the sidewalk, catching a quick word outside the *tabac*, laughing on the way up the Métro stairs, bending toward each other at tiny tables like ours. The cynic says the tables are the diameter of a dinner plate because they want to cram so many in; the romantic, or maybe the realist, believes it's just part of a long-running Paris social experiment: *force them to sit just inches apart, and let's see if they really talk.*

But I was out of practice with small talk. My three "friends" were no good at it. Carl was like radio; you were just supposed to listen. Shelley, perhaps because she lived by herself, was comfortable with quiet, and some weeks, we'd exchange books but barely ten words. I'd liked that. More, anyway, than when Molly came in and demanded more gossip than I ever had.

Beyond the store—I should have made friends, but hadn't. Hanging out with expats would have required discussing life back home, which would have required discussing Robert. Hanging with French friends would have required French.

So I didn't know what to say. I looked around. The city really does look different when you are with someone. And I was. And I should have just enjoyed that. I *was* enjoying that. And so was he, by the looks of things. I asked him about grad school, Des Moines. His work. He told me about being nervous about what came next.

Because I was nervous about the exact same thing, I took that as my cue and told him about the store, Milwaukee, my life. I said I'd lost my husband. I lowered my eyes. Not because I was pious or even pretending to be, though it would be convenient if it looked that way. The truth was—the truth was that I had *lost* Robert, and more disorientingly, lost my means of thinking about him. After my coffee with Daphne, I could no longer pretend, to myself, that Robert was gone forever. I looked up now to see if I could still sell the story to strangers. Declan looked somber. And unlike me, trustworthy. I wanted to ask him, to tell him, *the thing is, I don't know. I used to tell myself he was dead, but only because it was easier. Now it's not.*

"That's gotta be hard," he said. "And with kids . . ."

Kids, yes. The girls. A steady anxiety, but also a handy transition, and so I launched into a single-parenting confessional I hadn't known I'd had in me: something about food, cooking, diet, dieting, everyone ate well in Paris but me. I should do better by my girls. And those twins.

"It's like they speak a different language, kids," Declan said. "I mean, I'm not *that* old. . . ."

He paused. I'm not sure if he wanted me to ask, or protest, or—what I felt most keenly—if he wanted me to blurt out *my* age. I did not.

"You're making an odd face," he said. Odd? I wanted a mirror to see what *odd* meant. How many wrinkles crosshatched the corners of my eyes, my mouth.

Declan's own mouth was slightly agape now; he was waiting for me to say something. Anything.

I opted for the latter.

"Well, speaking of odd," I said, "of different languages? Up in the park, you spoke this *beautiful* French to those policewomen who were hassling you, and then you changed something, not just your accent but how well you spoke. You suddenly sounded like you didn't really know French well. You sounded American. You sounded like—" I was going to say *me*, but his face had turned "odd," too, that open mouth now closed, lips set in a line.

"Whom they preferred me to sound like," he finally said.

"Why would they not want you to speak French well? I'm sure the one thing this city wants from me more than anything else is to speak French perfectly."

Declan leaned back. I thought I saw a smile arrive, but then it left, and he looked somber. "The 'city' wants different things in different places. From different people."

"Okay," I said.

"Not okay," Declan said. "The problem up there in Ménilmontant is that I was speaking French too *well*. I was speaking like I'd been speaking it all my life, like I'd grown up in Africa. And for Africans here—hell, even black people born in Paris—it can sometimes be a rough ride. As you saw. So I put on my American accent."

I picked up my cup to sip at it, to stall, but among the many French skills I've not mastered is how to nurse a drink—coffee, wine, whatever—two, three slugs, and I am done. Part of the reason is the dollhouse crockery used here. Part of it, then, was how thirsty I was.

"I get taken for American all the time," I said, "and that's not always great."

"Your country has done a lot of stupid shit."

"But you're American, too."

"I'm a black American. Paris has been better to, and for, black Americans for years. Jazz, G.I.'s, but even before that. It's not *parfait*—"

"Though your French is," I said.

"It's good. I'm proud of it. Look, I *am* fluent," he said. "But I still make mistakes. So does France. So does Paris." He took up his *café*. "I suppose I shouldn't love it. And sometimes I don't."

"And now?" I said.

"Now," he said, "I do." He looked at me.

I stared at my cup. Empty, no reflection, and none needed. I knew how I felt: embarrassed. And excited.

And suddenly, quite young.

"How old *are* you?" I said.

"Forty?" Daphne said later that night after I'd returned home. In the wake of Declan's visit to the store, Ellie had asked how old he was, and Daphne had ventured a guess after the twins, who had guessed 107.

"Thirty-one!" I said. Daphne was too young to be a good judge of age, but I corrected her too rapidly. Not so much that she noticed, but Ellie definitely did.

"You asked him his *age*?" Daphne said.

"It came up," I said.

"That seems like a very personal thing to ask," Daphne said.

"Did you tell him how old you were?" asked Ellie.

"How old are *you*?" asked Peter.

"We're getting off topic," I said.

"No, you are," Ellie said. "I thought we were looking for *Dad*."

"Our dad is in Beijing!" Annabelle said.

"Ellie," I said, "listen."

Ellie shook her head and, as had become our custom for discussions involving the ever-absent George, took Peter and Annabelle over to an old globe that spun in a corner of the store.

"It wasn't a date," I said to Daphne, though I needed to say it to Ellie, now out of earshot.

Daphne looked confused. "What wasn't?"

"Coffee with that man, the man who helped me. Declan. He was just saying thanks." Or was I? I couldn't remember the cover story.

Daphne nodded, looked over at Ellie, who still had her back to us.

"Did you tell him about Dad?" Daphne asked.

Even a split-second pause would say the wrong thing, so I immediately said yes.

Which turned out to be the wrong thing.

Daphne smiled. "Good," she said, and pulled a much-folded piece of paper from her pocket. A new clue? "Because it sounds like he could help us find him."

It was not a clue, but a map, albeit one Daphne thought might just lead us to more clues. The map appeared on a flyer that had been dropped off at the store earlier, advertising an opportunity to "walk in the feetsteps of *Madeline*." Never mind that in his books, Ludwig Bemelmans sent Madeline and her classmates back and forth across all Paris, gamboling in the Tuileries on one page and then three kilometers away atop Montmartre the next. Never mind that an obsession with Bemelmans ran deeper in Ellie than Daphne. I'd followed my obsession with Lamorisse to Ménilmontant, and I'd not come back with their dad.

Worse, I'd come back with another man entirely.

"Can we take the tour?" Daphne asked, five words, one breath.

"Daphne," I started to say. Ellie and the twins were returning from the globe. In a moment, I'd hear from Ellie that it had been a bad idea for me to go to Ménilmontant, just as it had been a bad idea for Ellie herself to go, just as it had been a bad idea for us to come to Paris, the globe was out of date, it was stupid to organize the store by countries, and: men were *idiots*.

But for now it was still quiet, still just Daphne and me, still enough time for Daphne to whisper and be heard by me alone: "*I think he found the note.*"

"Who—what note, sweet girl?" I said.

"The one on the pillow," Daphne said. The one in Milwaukee, she meant, the one I didn't leave. The one that said what Daphne said now. "'*Meet us in Paris!*'"

I looked at her. I looked to see if I could see the abandoned daughter I had been after my parents had died, my brain simmering in constant low-level frenzy, *where are they where are they now I just need to ask to say I just need to know if*—

Daphne did not look like this. Her eyes glinted, her nose crinkled. She had no reason, she said, to think what she thought; she just had a *feeling*, she said, *you know?*

She—she actually did this—she smiled.

All I could do was nod.

I'm sure it looked like I was agreeing, though all I knew now was how much I didn't know. I didn't know why Ellie was angry. I didn't know what—or whom—Daphne thought she was seeing around Paris. I didn't know why Declan had been in Ménilmontant, nor why seeing him after for coffee felt like a date, which it definitely wasn't.

I told myself the police had still found no clues—no trace—none. I told myself to keep holding out for proof. Proof: not perhaps-sightings or false twinges or notes left on a pillow or scribbled in a book.

I told myself to remember what was real and what was not.

I told myself to ignore the fact that, increasingly, I could not.

Realizing this, I should have proceeded more cautiously. But what was incautious about agreeing to go on a *Madeline* walking tour in three weeks' time? Or to go out with Declan for a "nice" meal a week before the tour? His idea. Strictly business. We'd discuss the upcoming Madeline tour. *Just from the looks of the flyer, it seemed like we could do a better job*, he said. *My local expertise, your book expertise . . .*

Not that expert, I protested, but what I really wanted to protest, to discuss, was another smaller word, *we*. What were *we* up to?

I wondered exactly that as an opaque glass door slid open in the first arrondissement and we stepped into the *Ballon Rouge*, a restaurant that I'd read about—who hadn't?—but never visited. Though the name, in this context, referred to a particular type of wineglass, Declan felt very clever about his invitation: once he'd discovered my interest in Lamorisse, the man and film had become a steady subject. Declan also seemed quite pleased to insist on the meal being his treat.

It was early afternoon and the restaurant was empty. We were seated by the sommelier, a bald man in a tight black T-shirt. He wore a monocle I belatedly realized was a tattoo.

He and Declan were business school classmates, I discovered. I wondered if they'd done a case study on flowers, their cost and effect. In the center of the room, beneath a cylindrical skylight wide enough to accommodate a Titan rocket, bloomed what looked like ten thousand flowers. Purple, purple, every last shade. Lavender hydrangeas foamed out of pots. Indigo delphiniums shot lancelike from impossibly tall and slender glass vases. Orchids. Dahlias. And also fat pink peonies with faces as furrowed—and as big—as the girls' the day they were born. The *prix fixe* here was 250 euros a person; with wine, I'd seen reports it could climb as high as 1,000 euros. As it turned out, today's bill—as Declan knew going in—would be *zéro*; the restaurant was testing its late-spring menu with "friends and family."

"Even the wine's free," Declan said as a bottle arrived. Wine? We were having wine. I thought I should decline—coffee was one thing but wine another, and—and I told myself to calm down. And that the wine would help me do that.

The sommelier showed us the label, which we nodded over dutifully. I smiled up at him, he grimaced down. We were doing something wrong, but I didn't really care; I've always felt, in exchanges like this at Paris restaurants, particularly over wine, that it's my job to do something wrong. To do otherwise is to dash expectations, deny the sommelier some righteous pleasure, the kitchen some titters. The cork came out with a loud *thwop* and Declan pushed his glass toward the sommelier, who smiled and shook his head and nodded to me. Declan smiled. I smiled. We were all smiling. The sommelier emphatically splashed some wine into my glass. As I reached for it, I considered that I'd not seen enough female sommeliers in France, how there needed to be more, how I might myself study to become one. I watched as the wine surged up the sides, caught all the light in the room and—

The sommelier lifted the glass to *his* lips, sipped, chewed, nodded, and finally meted out a tiny smile. Then he decanted the rest of the bottle into a large wide-bottomed carafe that looked like it had been stolen from a laboratory.

I held up my glass. "To business school," I said.

"And Paris," Declan said.

"And wine."

"And *food*," Declan said, as the first plates arrived.

Part of what makes it hard to cook in Paris—apart from the fact that every last soul here does it better than I do—is that Robert was our chef at home.

Fatherhood brought this out in him. Prior to children, I don't remember what we ate, or his taking much of an interest in food. I think we drank most of our calories. But when I became pregnant with Ellie, he became one of those dads who, abetted by too much time in the OB waiting room with too many maternity magazines, nags his wife to eat better. And *I* became one of those wives who bristled at the guilt being served. I said if he wanted us—me and the baby—to eat better, he could shop and cook. He considered this, and apologized for not figuring it out sooner. No better place to start proving himself fit to be a parent than in the kitchen.

And so we ate fresh, we ate healthy, we ate global. As the girls grew, he expanded his efforts. Banh mi for lunch, zipped into their reusable lunch bags. Borscht for dinner, ladled into their unbreakable bowls. Sometimes we'd have Eleanor over, and Robert and the girls would play cooking show: they were the cooks, Eleanor the celebrity guest (I was the audience). She ate it up. They ate it up.

Saturday, they'd set off to farmers' markets, ethnic markets, libraries. Cookbooks came and went, and with them, trends. We ate vegan, we ate paleo, gluten-free, pesca-centric, Afro-centric. We ate equatorial. We ate tropical. Raw. Grilled. One-pot meals. Ten-plate tapas. Slow cookers. Flash-fryers. I had matching aprons made for them and he bought the girls floppy white chef's toques. They wore all this with pride. I was proud of them—and Robert in particular. They were making meals, but also memories. I ignored the voice in my head that said that this was what procrastination tasted like.

Whenever Robert went away, we ate leftovers, or what the girls called, not quite disparagingly, "mom meals." But the girls and I had actually eaten relatively well since coming to France, mostly because it was impossible not to. We'd never eaten as well as Declan and I did at the restaurant, though, and given the price, I knew I never would again. First Declan's friend had brought vegetables—tiny plate after tiny plate. White and green asparagus, then a creamy concoction studded with little green jewels that turned out to be frozen peas. Cucumber in sesame oil. Then on to the fish: tuna with lemon, followed by a butter custard garnished with smoked salt. A ceramic spoon bore us a single bite of sea bass, here swashbucklingly called *loup de mer*, wolf of the sea. Chard and onions. A clear soup, bouillon, boring until the first sip, when it turned out to be—coconut. Basque veal. And now, ginger, two cubes. One a solid raw chunk, the other solid sorbet. Strawberry *mille-feuille*.

I finished not just full, but exhausted. Eating this meal was as physically passionate a thing as I'd done since coming to France. That I sensed that this had not been "strictly business" gave the meal an even greater charge, and when Declan offered to walk me home, I surprised us both by hailing a cab and pulling him into it. We needed to—see some books, *now*.

But because he is always keeping an eye out for me, even, or especially when I wish he would not, Laurent, my UPS man, was lying in wait. He'd been trying to make the day's delivery, and I wasn't in the store, and Madame wouldn't come down.

I apologized, but Laurent didn't quite listen; he was busy watching Declan head into the shop with a box he—Declan—had offered to take inside. I'm fairly certain that was against the rules, but Laurent had never been one to turn down help. He'd accepted Peter's and Annabelle's offers before.

"This is good you hire a man," he said once Declan was inside.

"He's just a friend," I said.

"This is good you hire a friend," Laurent said. He gave a little smile. I was a little drunk. After pouring our first glasses, the sommelier had said, in English, that the wine would be like "licking silk." It had been.

"That's all?" said Declan, already returning.

"Maybe not," Laurent said. He turned to fiddle with the roll door for a while—just to make things awkward—and then finally nodded, once, raised his eyebrows, and drove away.

"He's interesting," Declan said.

"He brought me flowers the first week," I said. "An opening gift. And then flowers the second week, at which point I woke up and saw that he was looking for a date."

"Oh," Declan said, as flummoxed as I suddenly was.

I'd spoken without thinking this through. During conversations with Declan subsequent to my first, I had built a tidy wall around Robert. He went only by "my husband" and I stuck to my first story, the simple story: I lost him. In doing so, I was only telling Declan what I told any other stranger: *I lost my husband very suddenly, very young.* And they would look at the ring I still wore (just the simple wedding band) and say, *such a tragedy,* and the matter would rest. Or they would ask, *how?* And I would say, *I'd rather not talk about it.* And the matter would rest.

Madame Brouillard knew more—slightly more. I hadn't even told her that Robert was an author. I'd simply said that I'd had a husband, he'd disappeared. And when she asked how, I said the police suspected suicide and that I did, too. She herself was the one who urged me to start saying aloud something I'd only said in my head: *he died*.

Otherwise, *le récit vous suit*, Madame said: the story follows you.

She was right, but looking across at Declan, I realized she was also wrong. The story followed regardless. The goal was to make sure it didn't outpace you.

"So—did you—do you—" Declan started.

"No," I interrupted. Because I didn't date—what would the girls think!—but as soon as I said the word, I realized I was saying it to myself: *no, not until you know what's happened to Robert*.

Seconds passed.

"Are you—talking to yourself?" Declan asked.

"DHL," I tried.

"I'm sorry?"

"I was imagining calling and switching from UPS."

"You're funny," he said.

"Just keeping my options open," I said, which made me think, uncomfortably, of a book I had ordered for Ellie—ostensibly for sale in the shop but very much for her—the *Girls' Guide to Dating with Dignity*. It was for high school students. The cover looked punky and fun, and I liked the publicity materials. Madonna had endorsed it!

She's grandmother-old, Mom, Ellie said, and that was the last she interacted with the book. But I read it with great fascination. If only I had had such a guide in high school, college, and beyond. I'd dated with very little dignity. I hadn't made it easy for myself, true. I was smart and proud of it, into subtitled cinema, and, for three weeks, the marching band (I played the euphonium, something else I will never tell Declan, or Ellie). The book's first rule—its overall thesis, really—was *be straight with your guy*. I'd blown past that one, of course. But one of the subrules to this was—and this astounded me—*tell him that you like him*. Just like that. And the book cautioned that he might say that he didn't like you, or not as much, or not in the same way, and that was fine—a whole chapter followed about how to have a good cry and the value of good friends during such a time, but the book made helpfully clear that all this was *normal*, and most of all, *healthy*, and that none of this could happen unless you started with the truth.

The book, significantly, had nothing to say on the subject of husbands who may or may not be dead. "I really like you, Declan," I said, and waited. For someone to walk up to us with a clapper and yell, *cut!* For Daphne to materialize and ask me to say what I'd said in French. For Ellie to disgustedly shake her head. For Robert to come out from the kitchen and say, *but I said I was sorry*.

"I—I like you?" Declan said.

Maybe only I heard the question mark. But I later heard him quite clearly when he asked if he could come over sometime while the girls were at school. I said *why* and *yes* and he arrived with flowers and wine, and I turned the *fermé* sign on the front door—because it was lunchtime, because Madame Brouillard was out that day and couldn't cover—and we went upstairs.

"To Lamorisse's birthday!" Declan said.

I didn't pretend it wasn't a date. I didn't pretend it was. I didn't pretend Robert was dead, and I didn't pretend he was downstairs, either. I *did* pretend that Declan had gotten Lamorisse's birthday right, though he was off by four months.

The wine was amazing. So, too, the lingerie Molly had brought by earlier that week. Lingerie was her husband's go-to gift every birthday, Christmas—every other Tuesday, apparently—and she had more than she could ever want. Need. I, meanwhile, was someone who clearly *did* need, I think she said. And: "have fun." Inside the still-wrapped box had been a half camisole the weight and width of a tissue.

I'd taken the box out that morning, before Declan came over, before I'd gotten dressed. I went to the mirror and stared: I had lost weight since Robert had vanished, and lost more in France. I had thought I looked drawn, but Declan had reliably, if cautiously, complimented my appearance each time we met, and I looked carefully at myself now. Still the same constellations of moles, still the same tummy that had seen two pregnancies, two daughters, the same body that had done all the work asked of it, and which I increasingly thought stared back at me with a weary *now what?*

Now this, apparently: wine finished, we paged through *The Red Balloon*'s companion book of photographs in my kitchen.

What was I doing in my kitchen with this man and this book?

Laughing. Listening. Dying. We reached the last page. We looked up at each other. He couldn't have seen the camisole arranged just so on the bed in the other room, but he was looking like he had. I looked back down. I paged back to the start.

You love this book, Declan said.

Film, I said.

Balloon, he said.

I exhaled.

I like the balloon fine, I said softly, speaking now to the book's opening spread, a photo of Pascal on Ménilmontant's steep stairs, gazing up at his balloon, the cat looking, too, a shot that's not in the film. *I love this Paris,* I said.

Declan stared at the page, leaned in closer—to me, to the book. *Look,* he said, *we're in the picture!* Smoothing the book flat, Declan pointed to two faint shadows in a doorway. There was nothing there; he was just having fun. I suddenly wasn't. *I can't believe we didn't see him!* Declan said, referring to Pascal, to Ménilmontant, but all I could see, in a part of the photograph I swear I'd never seen before and which Declan showed no sign of seeing now, was a murky figure looking out a window.

As I said, this image, this angle, is not in the film, only the book. In the film, the scene on the stairs occurs under overcast skies. The title photo in the book is so sunny you can almost see the ghostly orange balloon Lamorisse inflated inside the lacquered red one to make the color pop brighter. The trick works; you don't focus on anything else.

Which may be why I'd never seen this figure up at the margin, in the window—a nose, a hand, a face, my husband.

Incroyable, Declan said, still joking, not seeing what I was seeing, because no one could; the photograph had been taken years before my husband had been born. Lamorisse could not possibly have taken a photo of my husband. Which was strange, because he had. Incredible?

Incredible, and I said so, in English.

Just the one word of Declan's in French and just the one of mine in English, but English then did what English does in Paris, start a tiny tear in whatever waking dream you've been enjoying, the cute café now just a tourist trap, the sketch artist just another American, the friend you met mid-Ménilmontant-mugging now just a friend. I said I had to do some things. Declan waited until I looked up. I did and apologized. He looked sad and then smiled, and when I saw him out—professionally, no embrace beyond a quick, firm squeeze of his tricep—I kept the *fermé* sign up and locked the door. I looked at the empty spot in the store window Robert's book had once occupied, and then I went through my secret bookcase door to the back room, sat down, and did what the *Girls' Guide* recommended, which was *cry until you're out of tears.* At which point, the guide said, *stop.*

CHAPTER 9

tay together, said the guide as we set out in the "feetsteps" of *Madeline.* So far, so good. Given the flyer's amateurishness, I hadn't expected much, but here we were: a tour guide, tourists, two British twins, an Iowan, and a mother and two daughters from Milwaukee who wanted far more out of this tour than it could ever provide. *Hold on!* the guide shouted, and I almost shouted back, *no kidding.*

Hold the hands, he amended, now looking specifically at Daphne. Daphne was standing next to Declan and looked at him. Declan looked at me. That meant none of us were looking at Ellie, who let go of Peter and Annabelle in order to swoop in and pull Daphne away. Ellie, who'd never held Daphne's hand ever. Ellie, who may or may not be telepathic but still managed to silently shout *don't you dare* to Declan.

But it was too late. I'd already dared. I'd invited Declan along. Because Daphne had said I could, because I felt bad about the awkwardness in my kitchen on Lamorisse's not-birthday, and because—this will sound ridiculous, but it was entirely true—I wanted that awkwardness to continue.

Whatever trick of the mind had placed Robert in that photograph had unnerved me. Declan, despite, or because of, my attraction, had steadied me. (And was he attracted to me? The *Girls' Guide* had a

159

whole section on *Signals!* that I was too shy to consult.) Patting Declan's arm on the way out hadn't been so much a way to be in physical contact with him—well, it was somewhat—as it was to prove to myself, to whomever was watching, that Declan was real, here in the flesh. Robert was not.

The tour guide, a young man, spoke a sturdy, mirthless English. He clearly had no great love for Bemelmans's creation; this was just a way to make money. Peter asked him what his name was. The guide pretended not to understand Peter's French. Annabelle whispered to Peter the name of a French children's book character they hated— somehow the guide understood *that*, and told them to be quiet. Annabelle then asked me, in English, for a stick. Not an unusual request—she was our budding naturalist and would poke anything, alive or dead—but this did not bode well.

As we walked east along the Seine, away from Notre-Dame, my girls could not stop noting all the *erreurs*.

"He keeps calling her *Madeleine,* Mom," Daphne complained. Peter and Annabelle volleyed the name back and forth. Daphne had a point. The book's rhymes don't work if you don't pronounce the name as it is (mis)spelled, *Madeline*, like get-in-line, and instead pronounce it as it "should" be pronounced, *comme en français*, like Mad-*lenn*. Daphne had brought her own book and kept checking it. "And there are *twelve* little girls in two straight lines."

"Twenty-four!" said Peter.

"No," started Daphne, "it's—" and gave up.

Straight lines of any kind were the least interesting aspect of *Madeline*, or Bemelmans, for my girls. They loved the squiggles, the animated looseness of Bemelmans's art, the pages that looked like he'd scratched them out in thirty seconds (though they were often the result of thirty drafts, Robert said), but most of all the fact that, pretty as Paris was, danger lurked around every corner: in the first book of the *Madeline* series, in hardly 350 words, there's a robbery, a wounded soldier, blood-speckled mist roaring from a tiger's mouth, a snowstorm, a rainstorm, an ambulance ride through the legs of the Eiffel Tower, and, of course, a dead-of-night appendectomy. Both Daphne and Ellie had trick-or-treated as Madeline various times in Milwaukee, but they had had little time for the hats and bows I assembled: they preferred to show off the tiny appendix scars Robert drew on their abdomens (with a Sharpie, which even I had to admit nicely echoed Bemelmans's pen-and-ink drawings).

The girls never articulated their love of Bemelmans to me—Robert sometimes tried to—but they didn't have to; I saw them live it. And now on this tour, I was seeing it anew, as our guide spoke one falsehood after another.

"Seriously? Bemelmans was 'American'?" Ellie looked at me. I had once made the grave error of shelving Bemelmans's adult nonfiction with his fellow Manhattanites in U.S.A./New York. Ellie preferred his entire oeuvre to be shelved with the Parisians.

"He did live in America?" I said, adding the question mark only when Ellie's stare demanded one.

"Was he Belgian?" Declan tried. He wasn't trying to ingratiate himself, or he was. He seemed truly curious. "The name—"

"Belgian!" Ellie snorted. "He was Austrian—not *Australian,* Daphne"—Daphne snuck Bemelmans onto our Down Under shelves once to tweak Ellie, and it still rankled—"born and raised. For a time, anyway. Then Germany." We all turned to look at her. "Then. . . . America," Ellie said.

We'd reached the Pont Neuf, the bridge where, in the series's second book, Madeline falls into the Seine, only to be rescued by a dog Madeline's classmates adopt and name Geneviève. Geneviève, the patron saint of Paris. Geneviève, whose name was Fleabag, Ellie now explained, until Bemelmans's editor made him change it. Annabelle perked up. "Fleabag!"

"I don't remember that from the book," said Peter.

"Not *that* book," said Daphne. "Ellie reads the grown-up books."

Our guide took no notice, made no mention of the dog, the saint, fleas, anything of value whatsoever.

Ellie couldn't take it anymore. "*Excusez-moi!*" she shouted. The guide stopped. The group looked at Ellie. She took a deep breath and asked about the plunge, the dog, the debate—it was a debate for her and Daphne—as to precisely *which* bridge Madeline fell from, because when Bemelmans drew the very *first* drawings for *Madeline*, he was on the Quai Voltaire by the Pont du Carrousel—*mais* . . .

The guide shook his head, furious that we might presume to know Paris better than he did. But we did, we knew this Paris, Bemelmans's Paris—Robert's—very well.

The remaining tourists—we'd lost a few each block, it appeared, as the tour grew increasingly desultory—turned to Ellie.

"*This* bridge—" Ellie began.

"This bridge!" the tour guide shouted and began yelling at Ellie, in French, that this bridge was a very important bridge, yes, but not for anything having to do with her stupid book—this bridge was where, in 1968, brave anarchists came close to killing the American ambassador, and wouldn't it have been wonderful if they *had*, because one thing would have led to another and the world would not now be ruled by ignorant, shit-eating Americans. Bemelmans was *German*, he said, and what horrors Americans haven't inflicted on the world, Germans had and would again.

His scarlet candor (and lying, at least about the supposed assassination attempt) suggested that he did not think Ellie—nor Daphne—nor any of us—could speak French fluently. And indeed, no one else on the tour seemed to understand a word he said. But Daphne understood enough to begin crying, and Ellie to begin shouting. This made Peter huff and Annabelle shriek. The guide answered all this with crude slang that was new to me.

It wasn't new to Declan, though, who took to French to tell him to shut up, and furthermore, to be ashamed for taking these people's money and then providing them with a sham of a tour, and for making kids cry . . .

The guide shook his head, and then backed up a step, then another, and then melted away into the crowd.

Peter and Annabelle went to Declan's side—either to console him or because they knew he'd been sticking up for them.

Je suis désolé, Declan said. "I am sorry" is all it means, though it always makes me think, "I am desolate," and so I was, or close to. Daphne shook her head. Peter looked stricken, Annabelle like she *really* wanted that stick now.

But our tour? I turned to our little group and thought about what to say. *Come by the store—we are less than a kilometer away—buy the actual book, or just browse. My apologies on behalf of Paris. I don't know that guide, but I do live here, and—*

"More than one building or school in Paris claims to be the model for Madeline's school, the famous 'old house in Paris that was covered with vines.' The truth is that Bemelmans modeled it on his own school in Austria—a school for boys."

This was Ellie. Everyone was staring at her.

And why wouldn't they? She was speaking with authority. Head held high. Feet planted. Atop the bridge railing, two hands lightly anchoring her to a lamppost as she swung.

"He spoke German. And many other languages."

I looked at Declan. He nodded to two policemen moving toward us from across the bridge, just beginning to break into a slow jog.

The fathers in the crowd, meanwhile, beamed at this wise and spirited child. So did Annabelle. The mothers looked toward me—I was going to stop this, right? Soon?

Yes. But how to do so without being the *cause* of her fall? I stared at her. Ellie stared back. That meant that she didn't quite see Declan moving toward her from another angle.

"Now, Miss Clavel, we all know her?" Ellie called out. "The woman in the book who's like the teacher or leader or something. Also not German. But anyway, *she* was based on his daughter's teacher. Bemelmans's daughter was not named Madeline. Barbara. His *wife*, though, he met *her* after she'd quit living as a nun in a convent kind of like the girls' *school* to work as an artist's model in Manhattan. But this is the important part: Bemelmans's wife was named Mimi, which was a nickname for *Mad*—"

My old boss, the university president, never, ever understood the importance of a dramatic pause. *What, precisely, is the point?* she would say. And I would say, *it's the entire point; a pause tells the audience, "get ready."*

But my boss's point: she didn't want anyone to be ready. A pause would only give someone in the crowd an opportunity to shout, to heckle, and thereby throw her off balance.

Which is precisely what Daphne did.

Three letters, a single syllable: *Dad!*

Ellie spun.

Dad? The word delayed me a crucial half second. But not Declan, who moved like he'd heard nothing, like he really thought he'd catch Ellie before she fell.

He did not. She dropped too fast.

I sprang to the spot she'd just left.

More magic: she'd only fallen three feet. A broad outer lip extends beneath the railing, and that's where Ellie now stood, relieved. Peter and Annabelle clapped. Everyone did. Ellie looked down at the stony surface that had saved her, and so did I. It was about two feet wide, sloped slightly toward the river's surface, and was tinged with a green that must have been mold or algae or moss—something slippery, anyway, because the moment she extended a hand to me (though Declan's was closer), she disappeared from sight.

What next? Someone screaming (not Ellie); Declan restraining Daphne, Peter, and Annabelle; me running. And shouts and horns and whistles and, somewhere in the distance, growing louder, a two-tone siren, and then another, sharp-flat, sharp-flat, the sound that always reminds me I'm not in Milwaukee anymore, and haven't been for some time.

Ellie chose a good spot to fall into the river, just one hundred meters shy of a fireboat station where frogmen were testing new gear. Wiser still would have been to evade the frogmen and let her mother rescue her, but I'd run down the closest stairs, which led to the wrong bank, and so was unable to intercede when, after plucking her from the water, the firemen turned her over to the police.

Declan, Daphne, the twins, and I caught up with Ellie at the local station—an ornate *petit palais* that looked like an outbuilding at Versailles—where, after a brief reunion, Declan went to work. On the way over, he'd reassured us that he'd extricated many a young American from worse. While the rest of us sat on a bench in a two-story arcaded atrium—the lobby, though it feels silly to call it that—Declan moved a few steps away and argued our case.

Ellie refused to speak to me beyond muttering that she hoped this didn't take hours. I secretly wanted it to; I felt I'd need at least that much time to sort out what had happened. What had Daphne shouted? Who had seen what?

Here is what I'd seen: a bigger drop from bridge to water than Bemelmans's drawing makes it out to be, though not so big that college students (reported Declan) and the occasional fifteen-year-old American girl can't navigate the plunge with *élan*. The only real challenge—apart from avoiding boats, which luck had allowed—is getting out. The current runs faster than it looks. But Ellie never panicked; I may even have seen her smile, which I think she did once she realized she had chanced into a stunt I'd never have allowed. Never mind that the river, though not as polluted as it once was, was not safe for swimming: the appeal was that what she was doing was forbidden. That the frogmen from the tidy red-and-white plants-in-pots-on-the-roof *Brigade de sapeurs-pompiers* barge who rescued her later emphasized this point seemed only to please her more. (Though what may have pleased her most was how handsome her young rescuers were; many, many selfies were taken aboard the boat with the crew, who looked, in the pictures, a bit too obliging.)

Here is what I had not seen, not on the bridge, in the water, at the police station after: Robert.

I pretended I'd heard Daphne wrong. She hadn't yelled *Dad*—or if she had, neither Ellie nor the twins had heard her, because that's all they would be talking about now. And I didn't want to bring it up because—because I didn't want to come off as crazy. Not in front of the police, not in front of my daughters.

And not, come to think, in front of Declan, who returned to us with a thin smile—he'd gotten them to waive the fine, he said—

"There's a fine for accidentally falling into a river?" I said.

"No," he said. "But there's one for standing on the rail. Anyway, doesn't matter."

"Thank you," I said, rising to go.

"In exchange, though . . ."

So there *was* a fine. Or there was something about the visas

George had mysteriously acquired for us. If so, that would be worse than a fine.

"Girls," Declan said. "You just have to talk to someone, okay? Your mom will be there for it. Part of it."

"Who?" Daphne said, worry spreading from her eyes to her forehead, her whole face.

"A *psychologue*," Declan said to me. "A psychologist."

"A *what*?" Ellie said.

Declan explained that he'd had more than one of his study-abroad students routed through and out of the police station this way. Just avoid talking about politics, he said: the only time he'd ever had trouble was when a drunken student confessed ardent admiration for Margaret Thatcher. Otherwise, Declan said, thirty minutes, tops.

Daphne said something then that was so quiet Declan had to have her repeat it: "Did you tell them about"—she paused again, and I waited for her to say something about her father, but she didn't. "Did you tell them about the tour?" Daphne asked. "*Madeline*? That we run a bookstore?"

Ellie put on her let's-do-this face, and stood. "That's probably why they think we're crazy," she said.

Declan offered to accompany us, but the women who'd come to usher us in frowned, and the twins needed watching anyway. So off Daphne, Ellie, and I went, to an office that looked like a hospital ward. The therapist that Robert and I had seen in Milwaukee had had a beautiful riverfront loft downtown, clean and uncluttered, simple lines. It always made me think of a day spa, tranquility, balance, burbling peace. Robert said he always thought of Ikea, all those opaque directions.

But this room made me and the girls think of *Madeline*.

Specifically, the 1950s-era hospital where Madeline has her appendix out. A half-dozen cots ran along one wall beneath fourteen-foot ceilings and a row of massive, openable windows. It looked ancient and unused—but also clean and quiet and calm. There was a bud vase with a single rose, yellow, real, on a desk just inside the door.

Even the flaking paint—also yellow, a pale lemon, the color of the tart the girls were later offered as a snack—was beautiful. And Ellie was able to identify yet another parallel to *Madeline*—wherein the young heroine, recovering from that appendectomy, discerns the outline of a rabbit in the ceiling cracks of her hospital room—which made our own ceiling cracks that much more quaint. For me, anyway. For the psychologist, a bespectacled older man who insisted on speaking to us in English (with a disorienting Scottish accent), it only reinforced his belief that our collective mental health needed attending to.

Once again, Daphne cited the tour, the bookstore, *Madeline*, Bemelmans.

Bemel-mans? No, the man said. *He is not known.*

Ellie began to explain about the books, the bridge, how Bemelmans himself had once been suicidal, although there was no evidence he'd ever gone off a bridge or wanted to—

Mademoiselle, he interrupted.

C'est vrai, Daphne chimed in.

The man looked at his clipboard and then at me.

"Girls," I said.

Ellie ignored me and continued. The initial inspiration for the whole series, in fact, had occurred in a hospital, when Bemelmans, recovering from minor surgery in a ward much like this one, struck up a friendship with a little girl who was visited each day by a kindly nun, a nurse, in that swoopy white thing, like a hat? Ellie looked at me. "Wimple?" I said.

Ellie looked at Daphne. *"Comment dire* 'wimple' *en français?"* Daphne shook her head. The psychologist looked at me. Ellie continued.

Bemelmans and the girl passed the hours deriving stories from shapes made by cracks in the ceiling.

Daphne broke in to point out that there were no smartphones back then. Life was more boring. She said this in French.

Do you use the portables? the man asked me in English. *There are many dangers on the portable phones. I know of America this is different, but this is not America.*

Ellie asked if he would like to hear more of the story. I said no. The man said yes.

The hospital that Bemelmans and the girl—a girl close to Daphne's age—had been in was not in Paris, but another part of France. Did he know it? The Île d'Yeu in the Bay of Biscay, just south of the mouth of the Loire.

The psychologist pursed his lips and then fell into muttering French. "We will go now to the separate rooms?" he said. "Different rooms, different questions, the mother, the girls, this sort of thing."

Does your mother hit you? This had been his opening gambit, Daphne reported once we were home and the twins asleep. She and Ellie said they said *non.*

And did he ask anything else?

She and Ellie conferred with their eyes. *Non.*

But during my individual interrogation, the psychologist said differently. He did mention he'd asked them about being struck—he said that, in his experience, Americans professed to not believe in corporal punishment, but many of them practiced it as soon as they left the United States . . .

But he also said he'd asked them about their father, and that the conversation had gone like this.

Where is your father, girls?

Il est parti. He is gone, the girls said. He asked how long; they told him. He asked them where, and they told him—or rather, they told him they weren't sure. He had pressed them on this point and "the younger one" had finally said, *some people say he is dead.*

Madame, the psychologist said down his nose to me, *she say this with no tears. This is not normal.*

Would it suffice, I wondered, if I cried for them? Their lack of tears was not evidence of resilience, which I'd let myself think for months, but delusion. It was indeed *not normal,* not for their father to have disappeared, not for them to be so certain he was coming back—or, to judge from what had just happened, to judge from Daphne's account over coffee weeks before, that Robert had *come* back. For many nights after Robert left, I cursed him for not considering how his disappearance would mess up our kids—but now I worried how *I* was messing them up. After our rocky early days in France, I'd fallen into the fiction that coming to Paris had been good for them. Because what young girl doesn't want to come to Paris? I always had. And now I was here, just like I'd always dreamed, in a police station talking to a mental health professional.

He continued: *And then the big one say, "but we do not believe he is dead."* He looked at his notes. *And then I ask them, "why do you not believe he is dead?" I ask because this is important to understand. Death is not small, we must be very clear when we speak on it. And so the small girl looks at the big girl and the big girl looks at the small girl and the big girl speaks.*

"'He's looking for us,'" he said Ellie said.

"'I do not understand,'" the psychologist said he told her.

"'You wouldn't,'" he said Ellie said.

I do not, the psychologist said to me.

Neither did I, not entirely, and so that night, tucking Ellie in—taking advantage, as Ellie had, of an extraordinary event enabling something never to be permitted again—I told her we needed to talk. I'd meant to say the same to Daphne, but hadn't found a gentle enough way to do so before she fell sound asleep, exhausted by the excitement of the day.

"I'm listening," Ellie said, lying on her stomach, face away from me, eyes closed. And as her breathing slowed and deepened, as I stroked her hair, as the building creaked its evening creaks and the street outside grew almost completely quiet, but not quite, I listened, too.

I might have sat there all night, in upright sleep, had I not heard the watery tones announcing an incoming Skype call downstairs. I let myself imagine that it wasn't the office computer but some distant church tower, but the bells came again, and I thought, must be—

Eleanor. Ellie had posted her frogmen photos, and Eleanor, for whom Ellie served as her sole access point to the vast, roiling world of social media, had seen them and wanted to know what, exactly, had happened.

So I told her. Everything. Which, in my version, amounted to nothing. I told her about the tour, the rude guide, Ellie's declamations, her plunge and rescue. I didn't mention that a man named Declan had helped us navigate the police station. I didn't mention that I thought I'd heard Daphne shout something.

I didn't mention this, but knew I would have to, and soon. Eleanor was her own kind of gravity when it came to the truth, endlessly pulling it toward her.

"You look pleased," I said, almost angry.

Eleanor sniffed. "I haven't been 'pleased' since Eugene McCarthy won New Hampshire. I am *relieved*, even delighted, to discover, however, that my goddaughter has learned to so ably navigate the waters of life, metaphorical and otherwise."

"Eleanor, I can't—" I said. "Don't be clever. Not now."

"Then I'll be direct," Eleanor said. "Why did Ellie fall?"

"Speaking of water," I said. "How are our renters? How is our old Milwaukee house? You've been kind to play landlord. With summer coming, they're going to get water in the basement—"

"Dry as a bone. Unlike Ellie. Leah, what happened?"

"She lost her footing," I said. Eleanor waited. "Something distracted her." Eleanor looked at me like she already knew what I was going to say. I don't think she actually did, but it's the only excuse I have for crumbling. "Okay," I said. "Daphne shouted 'Dad!' Or what sounded to *me* like 'Dad.' Like she'd seen him. She didn't say a word about it after, neither of them did, and I was going to talk to them about it tonight, but I lost my fucking courage. Maybe it's good I did. Maybe I heard her wrong, maybe she'd just shouted something like *aaaaahhh*—" I stopped. "Eleanor," I said, "what's going on?"

She shook her head. "Leah," she said. "They miss their father." She paused carefully. "Of course they do."

"*I* miss their father," I said, which was so starkly not something I was planning to say, something I had not said, for so long, that I said not a word more, and nor did Eleanor. I could feel her looking at me, and I could feel myself looking away.

I did miss Robert. Single-parenting was like a single-take scene, so much pressure on that cameraman to not trip over the cables, not knock into the boom mic, not mistake which fever was worthy of a 4:00 A.M. call to the pediatrician and which wasn't. I thought I'd mastered it back in Milwaukee—we'd readily survived all those writeaways, after all. But I'll admit, cooking and cleaning and sched-uling and scolding and encouraging: it was hard not having help. And here in Paris, it was hard making the dozens of judgment calls that arose each week. Should the girls have allowances, and if so, how much? And paid out of what imaginary bank account? Should we switch to an international school? Should we get a cat?

Should we go home?

You can sit in a four-legged chair that's missing a leg: it just takes more work, more concentration. And Paris, like a pile of books pressed into service, had served as a replacement leg, at least for a while. Not as sturdy, not as sound, not a permanent solution, but we were holding up. Enough time had passed now that it was possible to forget, for a stray millisecond or two, that he was gone. Thinking him dead had, for the longest time, helped with that. But then some-one would come along and rip a book out from the pile, maybe one with *I'm sorry* scribbled inside, the chair would teeter. And then one of us—Daphne, for example—would shout *Dad,* and someone would fall. This time it was Ellie. Who would be next?

"I'm going to ask you something," said Eleanor.

Now I played Eleanor's game: I said nothing.

"I was expecting to be interrupted," she said.

I still said nothing.

"Well, this is one benefit of Skype," Eleanor said. "Anger or agree-ment, it's all free. On the phone, silence feels so expensive."

I shook my head.

"May I quote an expert to you?" Eleanor asked. "I'm afraid I must, as it's about a topic I know nothing about, which is children. This expert told me the seriousness of a young child's injury is proportional to the time that elapses between incident and scream. Minor things, the cry comes right away. Major things, the scream is a long time coming because so much else is at work: there is the child's gradual recognition of what's happened, there is the drawing in of extra air to deliver a scream at extra volume—"

"I told you this," I said.

"I know you did," Eleanor said.

"Did I address the worst-case scenario, where no sound at all comes, ever?"

She didn't flinch. "You did not. Because who would speak of death, even hypothetically, in regard to her own family?"

I did flinch. I did have to pause before I spoke. And when I did, I found my own breath mostly gone, and with it, the force of my anger. That is, I was still furious—with Eleanor, with Robert, with my daughters even, for resurrecting him, however hallucinatorily—but I was tired, too. That's why I saw him in the pages of that book. That's why I felt his eyes on me, all the time. It wasn't because he was alive and in Paris. It was because I was exhausted and alone.

"He's not a child," I said. "He didn't fall. We're not waiting for Robert to scream."

"No, we're not," Eleanor answered. "We have Daphne, who thinks she saw him—sees him. We have you, who saw a note scribbled in one of his books. We have one hundred pages of a manuscript that *I* found, describing a family who sound a *hell* of a lot like one I know," she said.

We've reached a turning point: I waited for Eleanor to say it. But she said something else, something that made me realize Eleanor and the girls had reached that point long ago, and it was time for me to.

"We're not waiting for him to make some noise," Eleanor said, "because he already has."

CHAPTER 10

Robert was a quiet person; it came with the job, he said. I can remember him shouting three times, I think, in our married life. Once when Daphne, six, broke free and scored the winning goal for her coed soccer team; another time when Ellie, ten, won the spelling bee (on *scrumptious*); the third, and most unusual time, was at the end of an evening we'd spent with some of our fellow soccer parents. As such evenings in Milwaukee occasionally go, one drink led to a dozen, and around 11:00 P.M., calls were made to sitters to buy a little more time, because someone had had the brilliant idea that we'd go dancing.

I loved dancing, perhaps because I'd come to it late; I'd only started going out in grad school and so was in my dancing adolescence. That's not a term, but it's how I behaved. Pre-kids, I'd dragged Robert out once or twice, and he'd been game but not great. After that, I mostly went out with my old grad school girlfriends, and as they grew older or left town, I didn't go out at all. And now here we were, judgment impaired, dancing: nothing special, just the back of a bar, but the DJ was bribable and the music was great. Robert and I danced like clothes on a line in a storm. We put on a show for the twentysomethings, the regulars, who tolerated us because we were entertaining and because they knew we were never coming back. But maybe it was one of them who called the police, who arrived around midnight saying they'd gotten complaints about noise. The lights went on, the music off. Robert stood in the center of the room and shouted: *Noooooo!* There was a deep and sudden silence after that, cued by the cops, who didn't know Robert was harmless, a writer, a dad. They watched him intently. So did the room; so did I. I was grinning because I was drunk and it was funny to see Robert so alive, but then I wasn't grinning because as the *o*'s trailed on, I heard everything else pent-up in him; *no* was not only a complaint about the music stopping, but also the magic he'd once lived under. Maybe I'm reading too much into the moment, but it's what a writer's wife does. That, and go to her husband, take up his hands, kiss him, and then theatrically turn to the cops, the crowd, pretending it was all a show, and bow. *Good night, folks!*

Layered meanings aside, we retold our dancing escapade on soccer sidelines for months. *Remember when the cops came . . . ?* It was one of many Milwaukee stories that didn't translate in Paris. I tried it with Molly and she frowned; to her New Zealand ears, all stories about America seemed to involve police or guns or both. But she said her church's Zumba class was talking about doing a girls' night out; did I want to come? I shook my head.

It's so hard to get out at night, I told her. *The girls need minding, the store needs minding. . . .*

For months I'd been asking the girls to brainstorm some way to increase foot traffic in the store. I'd come to realize that specializing in dead authors, mildly quirky as it was, was also dumb: dead authors didn't give readings; we never had events; other than Molly, most of our customers were over sixty years old. I suggested Ellie and her friends stage readings of late greats. "Sure," she said (a word that, like many in her dwindling English vocabulary, only ever meant its opposite), and set about working with Asif to plan an evening focused on developing apps by and for teens. We stocked precisely no books on this subject.

No matter. On the appointed evening, the store was more full than it had ever been. Even Madame came down to take a look (once she heard the topic, she grimaced and withdrew). I wondered how Ellie had come to know so many people so much older than she was—and then realized that they weren't any older; the twenty or thirty attendees she and Asif had mustered were classmates, teens, but teens who wore heels, blazers, scarfs, beards, soccer shirts, abayas, jeans, eye-catching eyeglasses, and everywhere, smiles. Also smiling, if a bit more warily, were Daphne and the twins, who perched at the one corner of the counter that wasn't covered with food. I'd been worried Ellie would ask to serve wine, but she hadn't and, in any case, gripped a mug of tea as she worked the crowd; she (and Daphne, too, it seemed) had the start of a cold. And then the bell over the door rang as the "special surprise guest"—the event's speaker—arrived.

Declan.

What was not a surprise was that they loved him. He knew this demographic. As it turned out, he did not know that much about coding—but this was admitted with laughter and received with even more. Business school *was* teaching him a few things about marketing, however, that he was happy to share and everyone was happy to hear. When things later broke up, pictures were taken, addresses exchanged. Not a book was bought—or for that matter, mentioned—but Ellie thought it such a grand success I could only agree.

Declan stayed to help clean up. Daphne took the twins upstairs. Ellie walked Asif to the Métro. Declan explained that he'd not told me he was coming because Ellie had asked him to keep it a surprise. He said he'd hoped that was okay. He hoped I was okay. He hoped

Ellie was okay. That *everything* was okay, because it had gotten weird a while back.

I said it wasn't weird, nothing was, though everything was. There was still no verifiable sign of Robert in Wisconsin—no ATM withdrawal, no CCTV appearance, no word that our Milwaukee renters had reported him outside on the porch. But there was every other sign of him in Paris. And that reminded me that I was still married, to a missing person. I felt like I was getting second-guessed all the time, because I could hear Robert's voice all the time: *you're letting Ellie wear* that*? You're letting Daphne read* that*? You're serving frozen food for dinner again?*

Yes, yes, and definitely yes (French frozen food may be this country's greatest gift to civilization since Balzac).

And now I heard my voice ask an entirely different sort of question. *Declan, do you want to go dancing?* Some expat friends of mine were meeting up, I said, and his French could be handy. In fact, I said, it would be handy if he could recommend a place, because—

And then I heard Robert say *nooo!* But faintly, because it was hard to hear him over Declan, who'd just said *yes!* And that he would run home, change, text me with some ideas, couldn't wait, see you soon. Then he was gone.

The truth was, I had no expat friends going dancing, but I'd had a fun night in the store, I'd enjoyed seeing him, I wanted to blow off steam—more accurately, I felt like I might explode. I quickly texted Molly to see if I could make my lie true: *dancing? Now?*

I sometimes thought in Paris about texting Robert's phone, though I knew it was sitting in an evidence locker somewhere, its battery long dead.

Molly texted back: *Leah, it's almost midnight!*

Behind me, at the rear of the store, a cough.

Ellie. How long had she been standing there?

Ellie coughed again. "Don't say it," she said.

I knew other dads who'd prayed that they would have sons, shook their heads at the thought of girls. Robert loved his girls. Told gatherings that his should be the last generation with men. Told me that he was proud to have "overcome" his orphan DNA. He made Ellie and Daphne "miXXtapes" (CDs, actually) that featured only female artists. He wanted his girls to take on the world. I wished that he could see they were ready to.

And I wanted him to see that they seemed to regard me as a test run, Ellie especially.

I needed his help. I needed his appreciation for what I'd done in his absence.

I needed to go dancing. "Don't say what?" I said.

"It's not from kissing Asif," she said.

"Okay . . . ?"

"The cough. We were getting teased by our friends. He had a cold. Now I have a cold. So people think—but I don't want you to think—not that I care—"

"Asif's a lovely young man," I said.

"Don't say that," Ellie said.

"Your cough's from the river," I said. She shrugged. A small provocation, but enough to spur me on. "What made you fall from the railing?" I asked.

Another cough. This one fake.

"It wasn't on purpose," she said.

"I know," I said.

"It was Daphne," she said.

I nodded. "She shouted . . . ," I said, trying to lead Ellie to fill in the blank.

"She shouted what she always shouts," Ellie said.

"She never shouts." Like father, like daughter.

"When you cross the street without her or run up the sidewalk ahead of her or the twins color on one of her favorite books," Ellie said, "she'll yell *aaaah* or 'stop' or 'look at me!'"

"She didn't shout, 'look at me!'"

"She wanted to, though," Ellie said. "She was jealous of me up on the railing, getting all the attention."

"She's not the jealous type," I said.

"Yeah, well," Ellie said.

"Well, what?"

Ellie waited a beat. "She's not Declan's biggest fan," she said.

"This is changing the subject," I said.

"Not really," Ellie said. "Not if we're talking about jealousy."

"We're not," I said.

"She said as long as Declan's around, Dad's not coming back," Ellie said.

"*What?*" I said.

"He's *not* coming back, is he?" Ellie said, instantly hushed, earnest. "Dad?"

All that effort to pretend Robert dead, and I'd told myself this was how it needed to be. But looking at Ellie, I saw that I had needed them to pretend, too, to believe, that he was alive.

Her right ear—the ear closest to me, the one my insufficient words were reaching first—the tiniest strand of hair had fallen across it, and all I wanted to do now was go to her, tuck it behind her ear. As a baby, it had taken her so long to get her hair, and then it came in—and came and came and came, and I'd never been able to keep up since. She'd grown *up* in Paris, and I'd been proud of that, her style, her strut, her poise. I'd had none of that at her age. I'd had a bar towel and a roomful of rheumy men who called me *kid* and, later, other things. Nothing I couldn't handle, but I'd grown up too fast.

Maybe Ellie and I had more in common than I thought.

And so: fuck. I'd wanted my girls to be girls for as long as they wanted to be girls. That Ellie no longer was, was my fault. Paris's. Robert's.

"Oh, Ellie, I don't know if Dad's coming back," I said, and it was almost a relief, to finally say something about Robert that was completely true.

It bought me nothing. "You haven't heard from him?" she asked.

"Ellie," I said, "I would tell you."

"Would you?"

"Ellie."

"You know something," Ellie said.

I know you fell, I thought. I know that river is called the Seine. I know the Eiffel Tower is five kilometers away and Milwaukee, six-and-a-half thousand. I know that your eyes, like Daphne's, like his, are gray. I know I see him in you. I know I see him every day. Every day I see you. I see you and I think, how could it be possible that he's dead?

"I don't," I said, because—did I? I didn't. Not for certain. Nothing that I could let her hang her hopes on. Or mine. Not yet.

She looked at me forever. "You never do," she said, and began to climb the stairs.

How to explain what happened next? I then went dancing with Declan despite my daughter being sick and angry with me.

Or, more truth: I went because she was.

Declan and I texted back and forth for hours—what had seemed like a fun, spur-of-the-moment idea required much more planning, and waiting, than I would have thought. Declan said of course it did; no place worth going to was worth going to before midnight. So I napped, and then paced, and then made coffee, and then listened to the girls sleeping—no coughing—and paced some more. I shouldn't go. I shouldn't have gotten into it with Ellie. I should have had a proper talk with Daphne. And so I told myself I would, tomorrow; I'd talk with Daphne first thing, and Ellie, too. And it would be a better conversation than any tonight because it would come the morning after I'd danced off some stress. Robert took writeaways? I would pioneer danceaways.

Declan finally sent word that a three-wheeled minicab—a very unofficial, and app-based, taxi service he'd learned about from a kid earlier that night at the store—would meet me in about twenty minutes.

I wandered the shop floor. I liked having the store and its stock to myself. As a kid, I'd put myself to bed most nights after a peck on the cheek, after which my mom went back to helping Dad in the bar. I buried myself in books. Not just my beloved *Red Balloon* companion book but whatever the library had, whatever I could buy for a quarter at rummage sales. Nancy Drew and the Hardy Boys and *The Phantom Tollbooth* and almanacs of the Olympics and a solitary 1960s-era encyclopedia, the *C* volume, which I managed to write just about all my elementary school reports out of: "Cheese," "Chess," "China," "Coal," "California," "Cardiology," "Civil War," "Cinema."

That "Cinema" later caught my fancy in grad school was a natural progression, a smug professor once informed me: I'd led such an impoverished childhood. But I hadn't. I'd seen the world, "lived" in France. I liked films (but only on big screens; televisions only ever remind me of the bar) but will always love books.

I briefly worried Robert's disappearance would sour this love—I watched books, or the business of books, slowly ruin him. So it was a great surprise that the business of books, weak as our bookstore's was, went so far to sustain me. But it did.

A grad school friend had once made me jealous on Facebook with a photo of her grinning next to a barn. She'd left school for Hollywood and television: *I wrote this last week, they built it this week!*

I'm no longer on Facebook (it asked one too many times, "Are you in a relationship?") but if I was, I would post a photo of the store, because it was better than what my former friend had posted. Not just because a bookstore was better than a barn, but because the bookstore, like Paris, and like, bizarrely, Robert's unfinished manuscript, was real.

I should not have liked being reminded daily of the manuscript, of Robert, of the fact that there are not only better ways to make money in Paris but also better ways to lose money. But it's such a lovely store. It's such an intimate profession. I like Carl, Shelley, Molly, and my other customers fine. But I love a dim yellow light in the corner, a chair beneath, and in it, just me and the book, at home in the world.

I've never told the girls this, but one reason I like our geo-organizing of the store is that it reminds me of Robert's and my adventures across Wisconsin, the ability to travel such distances—from Moscow to Cuba—in hardly any time at all. But what I also liked of those cities, of every last one of our books, is the hope buried deep within them. Paris, France—or Paris, New York—didn't work out? That's fine. Try Paris, Wisconsin. Such hope is resilient; every town, every book, is a way to say, look, there's a new way, a different way. Every book in a bookstore is a fresh beginning. Every book is the next iteration of a very old story. Every bookstore, therefore, is like a safe-deposit box for civilization.

Like that cave in Norway—Norway, Norway, not Norway, Wisconsin—where they bank the seeds that will save the planet:

deep in my bookstore, we stock those same seeds. It doesn't have to be a large store, just a good one. Our store has a few thousand volumes. They range from 10 words to 200,000. Let's call the average 50,000. I have millions, maybe a billion words in stock. When apocalypse comes—and it does all the time now—come call. Out of my billion, we've got a word or two that will get things going again. Start anywhere. Start with "*bonsoir.*"

As Madame now did. She shimmered into view like a thought taking shape. She'd been in the store's rear corner and was now emerging to meet me.

"Oh, you gave me a fright," I said.

Madame raised her chin. "*Bonsoir,*" she said again.

"*Bonsoir, Madame,*" I said. "*Je suis désolée,*" I said. And then: "*excusez-moi de vous déranger.*" Carl called this second sentence a five-word disarmament treaty; always apologize for disturbing them, even when it is you who have been disturbed.

It worked. "No," she said, "*I* am sorry. I have need to illuminate the light. But I do not like. I do not wish the street me to see, and . . ." She went behind the counter as though preparing to ring me up. The light was just enough for us to see each other's faces, an outtake from an old film. "I used to come down when I cannot to sleep," she said. "*Et vous . . . ?*"

"And me," I said, pretending insomnia had drawn me here, too. I wasn't going to tell her I was going out with anyone, least of all the man who'd drawn a crowd to her store earlier that evening to talk about "apps."

I told myself that if the minicab pulled up now, I'd ignore it, pretend it wasn't for me. I'd go upstairs, text Declan, tell him plans had changed.

I started again. "And . . ."

But I wasn't sure what I was going to say. Over the winter months,

Madame had retreated steadily from us and, to a degree, from Annabelle and Peter, though she occasionally visited them at George's
place. But we saw her less and less on the shop floor, on the building
stairs. At first, I'd chalked up Madame's absences to her exploring her
newfound freedom—and she did visit friends outside Paris, and once
took the Chunnel to London—but I'd lately begun to wonder if she'd
come to regret taking us in, letting me take the reins. (She did not
seem to regret taking our money, enabling her travels as it did.)

"*Oui?*" she said, waiting.

"'Thanks' is what I wanted to say," I said. "*Mille mercis.*"

She leaned on the counter to look more closely at me. I have no
idea how old she was, seventy or eighty or a twenty-year-old yoga
instructor who'd gone prematurely gray. "'Thank you,' yes, but for
what? Why is this?" she said.

"For—for this," I said. "For the apartment, for letting me buy into
the store. For the books."

She smiled. With her eyes, anyway. And she pointed to her eyes
now, a cue, which it took me a moment to recognize.

"And the cream! Yes."

"It is working," she said.

It wasn't, I wasn't using it, but I nodded. Paris was what was
working. *I* was working. I had not made a film yet, but I had found
us a place to live, myself a place to work, the girls a school. My French
was meager, but I'd mastered enough to sell a book or buy a ba-
guette, or a scarf, or running shoes. I used those shoes four days out
of seven to run along the Seine, which meant the weight I'd lost was
not entirely due to stress and anxiety. I was living in Paris, France. To
be able to say so is its own Olympian accomplishment. Maybe two or
three other cities worldwide inspire similar envy. Paris, Wisconsin, is
not one of them.

I don't know how or if Madame knew I was lying, but her eyes stopped smiling. She studied me, she looked outside, she drew a deep breath. "I am silly," she said.

"Madame—"

"No," she said, and began making her way out from behind the counter, preparing to make her exit. Through the secret bookcase door, through the tiny office, up the narrow back stairs. But first, a declaration. "I didn't realize until now," she said, "that you are departing."

In a moment, I would realize I'd misunderstood her—she was referring to the funny little three-wheeled car, Declan's taxi, that had just pulled up—but until then, I thought she'd taken some X-ray of my soul, and that she knew better than I when we would leave Paris.

"Madame!"

"Do the girls know?"

Was this true, that we were leaving? Was she a clairvoyant? How could she know such a thing? She couldn't.

"*Bonsoir*, Madame," she said.

"I think my husband's alive," I said, quiet enough that I wasn't sure she heard.

But she did. "Does he drive a taxi?" she said, and nodded to the window. And so I finally turned and saw the vehicle idling, finally realized that *this* was the "departing" she'd been referring to, that this was what she wondered if the girls knew about.

Or not. "*Bon courage*," she said, and left. It means something like "good luck," but not quite; it translates literally as "good courage," which should have been a helpful reminder. *There are different kinds of courage, Leah, suitable for different situations. Tonight—for a change?—take the good kind.*

The minicab couldn't get near the address Declan had given me; the street was full of people. But once I'd made my way there, Declan found me outside. Kiss, kiss, one cheek, the other, where were my friends? Couldn't come, I said, and he grinned and introduced me to two young women nearby. Old friends? New? Stray students? I tried to see if I recognized them from the store, but I didn't, and of course not; of course Declan had a life outside mine. Of course he had other friends. And some of those friends would be women. Younger than me. Younger than *him*.

Robert had always looked younger than me and I'd always liked that; I thought it made me look sexier and more daring than I was. But now people were looking at me, and I looked at me through their eyes and saw that I was older. I reflexively clenched my right hand—not from anger, but anxiety. That was the hand Robert always held.

Then again, Robert held my right hand because it went with his left; *his* right hand was often sore—from writing, he claimed; he handwrote early drafts. This charmed me early on, and later, chafed. Surely *some* aspect of writing doesn't involve suffering, I'd say, and then, often as not, we wouldn't be holding hands anymore.

A waiter from inside yelled at us. Declan threw his shot back, the girls threw back theirs, I sipped at mine—no idea what it was—and Declan led us in. *Dansons!* he shouted, and I was game, but it was even more crowded inside than out.

So it was going to be that kind of evening: on my feet, no place to perch. Declan drew us into the bar, deeper and deeper, which made no sense, as it was only becoming more crowded, with no space to dance. But then, we were at a doorway in the rear of the room, manned by two very large men. Promising. They let Declan through with hardly a glance, but when I followed, they put a hand out to stop me. "But that is my friend," I said in English. My friend, meanwhile, had already disappeared into the crowd and music beyond.

"*Mon ami,*" I corrected.

"*Non,*" one of the bouncers told me. "*Toi, c'est non.*" Not for you (and not even the formal "you," or *vous*). And there it was. The bouncer was saving me from *myself*. How wonderful for the helpless women of the world that there are so many men so ready to look out for us in all manner of dangerous situations—entering a nightclub, say, to dance.

But now, Declan's other "friends," the young women from earlier, slipped past me with nods and giggles hardly half-hidden. The bouncers smiled as they passed in.

Arguing in French has always been a burden for me, so I decided to accelerate the process. It was a tricky business, the *bakchich*, the little gift to ease the way, and I was never sure how much to pay off whom. (In Milwaukee, it had been simpler: if a blizzard was pending and you needed your snowblower fixed, a fifth of Jack Daniel's got you to the head of the line. Or so I'd heard; such had been all Robert's doing.)

Awkwardly—I liked to think enterprisingly—I had tucked fifty euros in my bra before I left the store. I'd not wanted to carry a purse, and, frankly, I'd not expected to spend any money: that was what Declan was for (along with carrying my phone, which I'd passed to him outside). But here I was, digging around in my top for my emergency cash, something I'd not done since I was nineteen.

Unfortunately, this only alarmed the bouncers, and my subsequently looking for a small-enough bill—this wasn't *that* much of an emergency—upset them even further, and one bouncer started hassling the other. They spoke very fast, in a very broad accent, but I was able to make out what they were saying: they were *embarrassed* that I was attempting to give them money. Well. They weren't alone in that. In any case, their next words I understood perfectly: *vite, vite,* one said, sweeping me in quickly, refusing my money. I didn't press the point. I hid my cash, blinked once, and went through the door, into another world.

. . .

Blue, then purple, then a white flash, then black. Stairs—crowded into a vertiginous spiral staircase, no railing—at one end. A tiny, tight stage. A chandelier, a real one, dripping light. Video projections sliding off the walls onto the ceiling, the floor, the patrons, the bar. I find Declan at the bar. I yell at him for abandoning me at the doorway. He can't hear me; I can't hear myself. The music throbs, surrounds, more pulse than sound, and I feel it there, right there, in my chest, then lower. Declan turns away from me, still smiling, and then, a moment later, turns back, a drink in his hand, something clear, vodka. I shake my head. One of the slinky girls comes up to Declan and he nods, laughs, and hands her his drink. She disappears onto the dance floor. But—I am on the dance floor, which is a sticky matte black. Everyone is on the dance floor. This room—is all music, all dancing.

Declan is a voice in my ear. My left, my right. He says this, that. Look there, here. I do not know if this is what he does when he is drunk or if this is what he does all day long. *Regardez* this church, that corner, that window. Tonight he asks if I see the man in the tux over there; how cool, how funny, how Paris is that? I don't look, because if he's in a tux, it's not Robert. I look. It's not Robert. I nod, I smile, I dance. Platforms suspended from chains sway in two corners of the room, or I'm swaying. Declan leans back to my ear: the DJ is a friend of a friend of a friend. Leans away, dances, spins, is at my ear again: *I was prom king*. I smile, nod. I can't stop dancing. He can't stop talking. I want to be annoyed, but can't, because each line comes with a laugh, with his breath at my ear, with his hands at my arms to steady himself or keep me from floating away. *I know a café nearby,* he finally says and I finally say to him, one word at one ear, *stop*, one word at the other, *talking.*

The parted-lip look on his face, equal parts delight and desire: I did that, I think. I dance. I can do anything, I think. I dance. Anything. I ride the music, slick with sweat, and watch and wait for Declan to lean in again, which he finally does. *Let's go.*

We didn't go far enough. We got distracted by a little café two streets down. Or I did. A short man, wide white mustache, rumpled apron, insisted we stop. He waved menus at us. Declan waved him away. But I stopped. The rest of the city's cafés—that is, cafés that need such assistance—now employ young women, Eastern Europeans mostly, beautiful universally, as their touts. But not here. Here, this man. From another era, from another world, and he bowed, he took my left hand, he kissed it deeply. One more millisecond and it would have been too long, but he knew this. He had kissed, and held, hands for decades. He lifted his face, he swept us into two seats, he lit a tiny cupped candle between us.

Declan ordered a coffee, but I suddenly wanted a beer, and so he switched his order, too. And then we spent a good deal of time laughing. In my Paris scrapbook—and I have one, which I shoplifted from my own store, beautiful creamy pages and a little pouch of old-fashioned photo corners to affix photos, which I someday intend to do, so long as I am permitted to travel back in time and take all the photos I failed to snap the first time around—I will have one page devoted to those two beers, that little table, that night. We talked and we laughed. Really laughed. Somehow, everything became funny. Declan was so beautiful, and so smart, and so good with kids—especially my kids. And, of course, he was good with taxis. Finding clubs. Finding ears.

"You'd think a ring would keep a man away!" I said, raising a glass toward the mustachioed tout, who was back at work on the sidewalk, reaching toward other hands to kiss. Our beers had been delicately decanted into pear-shaped glasses, but I took a swig right from the bottle now, eyeing my little ring as I did. It winked at me. I winked back. Just having fun.

But Declan wasn't. He sipped his beer, too, and turned away.

"What?" I said.

He looked at me carefully, waiting.

"*Excusez-moi de vous déranger,*" I said and smiled. He did not. "Carl said that was a disarmament treaty," I mumbled.

"What—? Wait, who's *Carl?*" Declan asked.

"Oh, Carl is one of my three— " Declan's face, an alarming mixture of disgust and pain, stopped me. "Oh, you're *jealous,*" I said. "Please, I—"

"*Please,*" Declan said.

"Carl is a *customer,*" I said. "Of the bookstore. One of three, the girls joke. He likes mysteries, and he could pass for my grandfather."

"And me?" Declan said.

I shook my head. "No," I said. "No, I don't think you could."

"Leah, don't joke," he said. It's the one thing men (especially psychologists) have been telling me all my life. Men, save Robert. He never said this. Maybe because he never knew I was joking, but still, it was something I liked in him. Robert never told me no. That soccer-night DJ, that crowd, those noise abatement cops, and finally, the world: yes, Robert had told them *nooo.*

But Robert never said no to me, not until the night I'd said, *let's get you help, real help.* Not toolbox help, the kind the therapist had offered us, but the inpatient kind. *No,* he'd said.

"I should go," I said to Declan. "No joke."

"Please don't," he said.

"Declan," I said.

"Leah," he said. "We—we've been spending a lot of time together.

I've liked that. I like—you. I'd like to—not tonight, maybe it's too late, or too fast, except it's not—damn, why is this awkward? It's like being in junior high again."

"I didn't have two daughters when I was in junior high," I said, very intently, to my beer bottle.

"Is that what this is about?" he said. "Because—I mean, of course. But maybe some night, or day—unless daytime is weird—was weird—"

"No, this is weird," I said.

It's possible that men always told me not to joke because I wasn't good at it. Because all they wanted, all Declan wanted—and Robert before him—was a straight answer. *Leah, are we good?*

Declan picked up my hand—my—left hand. His was dry and smooth and hard.

This was what Declan's hand felt like. This was what it was like to be held again.

"*This* is weird," he said, and gently tapped my ring with his thumb, once, twice. Then he let go. I felt like I was on one of those chained platforms from the club and it had just given way. "I mean, I get it," he said, "or I got it, but something happened."

"I told you what happened."

I'd have thought I'd have gotten better at lying, given how much of it I was doing lately.

"No, something happened recently. Not tonight. Something before that. Something changed. We were hanging out, it was fun—"

"It was fun tonight."

"You told me you 'liked' me."

I took a short breath. "True."

"And something happened. I want to say, something happened on that stupid *Madeline* tour."

A longer breath. "Obviously."

He waited, shook his head. "See?" he said. "Like right now, that look: you're not—you're not *here*."

"I couldn't be more *here*. I'm right here."

"You're distracted," he said. A retreat, or so his eyes told me, but I ignored that. "I don't—I don't get it," he said, softening further. It was awful to watch. It must have been worse to watch me. "Unless . . . is there someone else?" he asked. He looked at the ring again. "I don't mean . . ."

What was so wonderful, and terrible, was that he didn't mean Robert. And that I did. There was someone else. There were two words in a book, *I'm sorry*. There were one hundred pages of a manuscript, two daughters on a bridge, one husband who might have been there, too. It was easy enough to imagine, anyway. Easier, if somehow more painful.

I heard my phone ping in Declan's pocket: and there it was, life, the kind of real life I led, as opposed to the fictional, carefree Paris life I assumed Declan led, returning. My phone pinged again, and again, a little anvil across which unease could be bent into anger.

What if it was Ellie? Or Daphne? Or Eleanor, with news.

Or, right on schedule, Robert himself?

Declan pulled out my phone from his pocket and looked at the screen. "Shit," he said. Even from across the table, I could see that it was crowded with messages and alerts. "I'm so sorry," he said, "I must not have heard—or felt—"

He leaned toward me over the table and laid the phone gently between us. "I think you missed some calls," he said.

The screen was more explicit than that: ten missed calls, six voice mails, and twelve texts, the most recent of which, from Ellie, was automatically displayed.

The doctors say they need 2 talk 2 the mother. . . .

CHAPTER 11

Declan offered to summon a "real" taxi, but I refused and got in an illegal cab that sidled up as we stood arguing.

Utter mistake. He wasn't a criminal, my driver, but he didn't speak French, or English, and he didn't know Paris. I wasn't much better beyond the Marais, and so wasn't even aware how off course we were until Ellie—with whom I'd been texting frantically—told me to ask the driver what the hell was going on, because she'd tracked me (or rather, my phone) to Père Lachaise.

I looked out the window. *C'est vrai*, the cemetery. I got the driver to stop, and with the help of the map display on my cell phone and some shouting, I learned that he was taking me to the airport. Of course: it was the only thing he knew to do with hysterical Americans. I told him my daughter was *ill, very ill,* and got out and walked away. He didn't even curse at me. Or if he did, I didn't hear him. Two policemen, though, cruised up. Either they'd overheard me or there was a bulletin out for a madwoman, a cheat, the world's worst mother, at large in Paris.

Although it took some doing for them to convince me that I wasn't under arrest, I finally accepted their offer to speed me to the hospital—the Hôpital Necker-Enfants Malades. The hospital for children sick.

Ellie met me at the end of the block, to walk me into the compound.

"Where have you *been*?" Ellie said.

"How is she?" I said.

"Like, the phone showed me where you were, but—"

"Ellie, Ellie, Ellie," I said as the world flew by. It's not that we were walking that fast—I'm not sure if we were walking at all; I felt like I was hovering, drifting, bodiless, and my vision reduced everything but Ellie to a blur. Where was Daphne? Where was my purse?

Ellie was speaking. French, English. She was speaking to me.

"The doctors have to do this thing called a spinal—a 'spinal tap'?" Ellie said.

"Is that your translation or theirs?" Would the hospital have a translator? Daphne was our best translator.

"It's not a translation," Ellie said. "It's what they said, those exact two words, in English. In French they said something about the lower back, and poking. *'Ponction'*?"

"How did you know to come here? Did Madame send you here? It's miles from the store."

"I knocked on her door, she didn't answer. I didn't try long. Daphne woke me up. She'd gone looking for you in your room—she was—you could tell right away it wasn't good. She wasn't making sense, she fell and wouldn't get up. I called *les pompiers*, and when they came, they said this place was best for someone like Daphne," Ellie said. "Or I think they did. They asked me about you, I said I didn't know, then I said you were on your way, and by then we were here. At a children's hospital. It's like, only for kids."

"It's for kids?" I said. Because my fifteen-year-old couldn't have figured this out. Because I was ignoring what Ellie *had* figured out: how to get emergency services to come to a bedroom above a bookstore, how to get the paramedics to ignore the fact that the mother was not present, how to ensure that she (unlike me) stayed at her sister's side—at least until she had to fetch her mother from a police car at the curb.

"I think so," Ellie said, her voice going higher, starting to wobble. "They gave me an English brochure. It said they invented the stethoscope."

The first entrance we passed gave every evidence that this might be true—a spiky gate, wrought iron, towering, furred with rust. What had this hospital invested in since that first stethoscope?

"Okay, okay," I said. "Ellie: where's Daphne?"

She led me through one lumpily cobbled court and then another, past the smokers, the cryers, lonely faces lit gray by the screens of their phones. We finally reached a modern wing with glass walls, aggressively stylish furniture. A towering cartoon dog with a loud thatch of orange hair stood nearby. He had to have terrorized more than one child.

"*Daphne, nom de famille, Ea*—" I said to the woman at the desk, before Ellie pulled me away.

"We've already done *that*," Ellie said, walking ahead. "But you need to come back later with our *carte Vitale*."

"You can't just march right in," I said, as we did.

"You can't just leave your *kids* to go out—what were you doing?" Ellie said.

"Ellie."

"I'm fine being in charge, all right? When things are normal. But what—what was I supposed to do?" said Ellie. "I wasn't even sure which number to dial—Asif said 112."

It *was* confusing: 911 came in different flavors here, people had preferences.

But none of this mattered. Where was Daphne? Did they really want to do a spinal *tap*? I didn't know where we were going, but I had started half jogging, which now put me ahead of Ellie, which allowed her to see—

"What are you wearing?" she said.

I pulled the skirt down and waved her on. We rushed down one long turquoise hallway and then a yellow one. The color, the design, everything was turned up way too loud, and felt even more so, given that the hospital was way too quiet otherwise. A scream, or two? A cry? It seemed a bitter thing to wish for, but I did. Because where was everyone? Where was Daphne? We walked faster and faster. Daphne! For a minute, we followed a thick red line painted on the floor, and for another minute, orange paw prints. Ellie had mentioned needing our family's health card, but I knew that wouldn't cover the full cost being tallied here. The nonmonetary cost. *What do you want, Paris?* I thought. *Give me Daphne back and I will give you my life.* I heard Paris snort. *I'll give up the store.* Paris waited. *I'll give up Paris.* A massive pair of doors parted and we entered a vast space, teeming with people and lights and sounds. It was like we'd stumbled onto the bridge of a starship. Little podlike spaces sealed behind glass ran around the circumference of the room.

Ellie led me to Daphne's.

I reached for the handle to her sliding glass door and yanked. Ellie yelled and grabbed me—I shook her off and went for the door again. Ellie yelled again; a nurse arrived. She put a hand on Ellie's arm and a hand on mine. She looked us each in the eye in turn. Then she closed her eyes, and took a deep breath. *Do this,* she said, without saying a word. *Breathe.* Ellie did, I did, and the nurse, whom I would now do anything for, pointed to a sticker on the door. INTERDIT, it said in French. "*Forbidden,*" this means.

"But I'm her *mother,*" I said to the nurse, who was now pointing back the way we'd come. And here I'd loved her. I opened my mouth to yell. Ellie stepped between us and, tears in her eyes, apologized a dozen times, a dozen ways, to the nurse. *Excusez-nous de vous déranger.* The nurse replied to Ellie at length in French, then turned to me, said one word in English, *wait*, and left.

Ellie turned to me. "We can go in—they don't want *me* to go in, at all, but they will let me go in if you're 'okay' with it, which you better be. My cough is gone." She coughed.

"Fine," I said. "Ellie, of course, fine. So let's go in."

But I couldn't. Because it took a moment to put the prior hours away. And because if Ellie wanted to go in and see Daphne, or if I did, we learned that we would have to put on hospital masks. And latex gloves. And bouffant caps over our hair. And lightweight fluid- and tear-resistant multi-ply isolation gowns that did not tie in the front like a bathrobe, but in back, where you had to have someone, like your oldest child, tie it for you—which gave her the chance to study once more the clothing I'd originally selected for the night.

"Is this *my* skirt?" Ellie asked.

I didn't answer. I was inside. I was looking at Daphne, who looked nothing like my child. This body had my daughter's features—her dark, swooping eyebrows, her upturned nose, her widow's peak, her very first pimple appearing on her soft, still chin—but she couldn't be my Daphne. Her face was waxen, completely false, unrecognizable. Nausea rose in me like a fist. What a fool I'd been to pretend I could pretend for a minute that Robert was dead. Death had nothing to do with pretending. Life, on the other hand, had everything to do with believing. This body was Daphne's. She was alive and she would only stay alive so long as I stood there and willed it. It wasn't a bargain, or it was, and the cost was everything.

I felt hours pass, but only minutes did. Blood was drawn. Urine through a catheter. And now a man in a white coat arrived and spoke to us. I just heard sounds. When Ellie was born, I'd had an old-school nurse during the overnight stretch, one who muttered of vast health care conspiracies, but who wanted me to remember especially this: the shorter the coat, the newer the doctor. I've had doctors since tell me it's not true, and I have never believed them.

This man's coat hit him at his waist, like a waiter. That couldn't be good, unless things were different in France. But everything was different in France. I looked helplessly at Ellie, who translated for me.

"He wants to know if she's had a vaccine for—"

She broke off and said something to the man in French, pantomiming a pen. He wrote something down. I find French handwriting no more legible than Cyrillic; 1's look like 7's, and 7's, emoticons for anger. I've never been able to read it. I gave the pad to Ellie.

"I don't know what this is," she said, and looked up at the man.

"She's had her MMR," I said. Ellie tried translating. "Measles-mumps-rubella," I said. Ellie shared this, too. He shook his head, pointed to the pad, looked at me.

Ellie looked at the pad again. "Pneumonia?" she said, to him and to me.

"She's never had it," I said.

The man spoke, a long word that, with some patience and the help of the pad, I translated as *pneumococcal meningitis*. I could go back to the file folder at home, the file where I kept their birth certificates and passports and immunization records, but I didn't need to, because I knew. Way back when in Wisconsin, the other moms had said there was something funny with that vaccine—or not that one, but all of them, or getting so many vaccines at once. And so I'd said no, and so Daphne hadn't gotten it, the pneumococcal meningitis vaccine.

And then I felt like a fool, and so she got it. Just not on schedule. Did that matter? *No*, Daphne's pediatrician in Milwaukee had told me.

Isn't that what the pediatrician had told me?

I tried to explain all this to Ellie.

"Holy crap, Mom," Ellie said.

"You got yours on time!" I said.

The man spoke to me in rapid French. My language skills were returning, but slowly, not fast enough.

He may have said something about different types of meningitis, how the vaccine worked most of the time, not all the time, not against everything, and who knows how they did things in America, anyway?

And then I heard *lumbar* and *puncture* and *risk* and—this word I definitely heard—*behave*. I took an extra-deep breath and looked at Ellie.

"Um, he's telling you to *behave*, Mom," she said.

"Yes," I said.

"You got the part about giving permission to 'puncture' her *back*?" Ellie said.

"Yes," I said.

"*Mom?*" Ellie said.

"If it's a *lumbar puncture*," I said—he nodded—"then yes. But tell him I want a real doctor in here, and now."

"*Mom*," Ellie said.

"His coat is too fucking short," I said.

"What are you *talking* about?"

But he understood me. Because, it turned out, he understood English.

"The true doctor come now he watch," he said. "But I make the true *poke*."

"I want true doctor poke," I said, in the fractured English I speak when my fractured French fails.

"I am the *doctor*," he said. "I am finishing the training." He was an intern, then? A resident? I couldn't ask because he then turned to Ellie and continued in French: *your mother is crazy if she wants to*

*take this sick girl clear across Paris to the American Hospital in Neuilly
for a "real" doctor, who, at this time of night, will be a vacationing or-
thodontist from Texas*—I think he meant *orthopedist*, or maybe he
didn't—*covering for the doctors they pretend to have there. I am trained
to do this. We do this here.* He left the room.

The American Hospital, which I'd not mentioned, is excellent.
And 30 minutes away.

"Mom," Ellie said.

"Honey, I'm sorry—I'm so sorry—and I'm so sorry you had to
hear that *imbécile* lecture us," I said.

"Where *were* you?" Ellie said.

I looked at Daphne. Ellie looked at me.

"I wasn't there," I said. Enough with tallying costs. I'd done it constantly in Paris. And I'd added it up different ways, different times,
what Robert had paid for airfare, what we'd paid for the store, how
much food cost and school supplies and secret cigarettes and cafés and
tickets for the Métro. Thousands, tens of thousands, of dollars, euros.
It had cost all that, and now it had cost this. Daphne would not have
fallen ill had we stayed in Milwaukee. And we would have never left
Milwaukee had Robert stayed. If he really *were* around now, if Daphne
or Ellie really had seen him—now, right now, would be an excellent
time for him to appear. I thought this thought until my head hurt. I
wondered if Daphne had, too, if this wasn't meningitis but some kind
of stroke, an aneurysm caused by a longing that had tugged too long.

"I *know* you weren't there," Ellie said. "Remember? Because I *was*."

We parents worry so much about our children doing, or saying,
the wrong things. What we should fear more are those times when
they're right, when we're found wanting, when all we want to do is
apologize—and they're not yet old enough to know that's what they
want from us, and deserve.

"I'm sorry," I said. I was conscious of people outside the glass. I was conscious of them waiting, like Ellie, for me to do the right thing. "I'm sorry I wasn't there. I'm sorry I sometimes haven't even been there when I've been there. I'm sorry I took us to Paris—"

She flicked a hand at me.

"I'm sorry I've put so much on *you*—" I said.

"And Daphne!" Ellie said. "Why do you think she's sick?"

"That's not why!" I said, which I didn't know, but I saw something flicker back into Ellie's eyes—a sense that here might be an adult after all, someone who could say something and make it so. So I said something else I didn't know. "And she's going to be all right."

Ellie looked at me, at Daphne, around the room, and then fell into me, crying. I put my arms around her. "I'm sorry, El," I said, and got ready to repeat it a hundred times more, but the second syllable was hardly out before she pulled away.

"And listen," she said. She blotted her eyes as best she could with the gown. "Stop getting angry with the doctors, okay? We need friends here." We weren't even close enough to hug now, but I felt her physically shrugging me off again all the same. She went to Daphne's left side. I went to her right.

I touched Daphne's hand, her face. They had said not to. Through the gloves, she felt hot, but not too hot. Her color was that same otherworldly absence of color, and her breathing was rapid. She had an IV in, and a display attached to the pole provided a maze of numbers. I had no idea what was good or bad. Only that Daphne was motionless. I wanted to shake her awake. I wanted to scream. I wanted to throw up. I wanted to do all these things, but knew if I did any one of them, I'd be thrown out and Ellie would be left alone, in charge, again.

Why wasn't the doctor here *right* now? Why wasn't a nurse with her at all times? I turned around to look at someone to be angry at, and when I turned back, Ellie was easing her way onto the bed beside Daphne.

"*Ellie*," I hissed. "You can't do that."

"I got the shot," she said. "You said." She was lying beside her sister now, on her side, her eyes wide open and staring at Daphne, just inches away.

"Ellie—it's not—it doesn't work like—you're going to get us in such—what if Daphne—"

Ellie said nothing. I looked around, scanning for a doctor or nurse or, one last time, for Robert. Ellie would listen to him.

And he—he did this so well—would listen to her.

And he would lie down.

I found a way to drop the railing, I got a hip on the mattress, a leg, I scooted in, one centimeter, two, right next to her. I was apt to fall out at any moment and upset the whole business—IV pole, display, tubes, curtain—but I didn't fall. I was finally next to Daphne, who, for her thirteenth birthday, just two months ago, had asked for "one book of my choosing" as well as "something special," which for her was two croissants. One was standard in our family. Two was unheard of. I'd bought her six and she'd said, "too many," but she'd smiled. I'd hoarded that smile.

"Daphne," I whispered. Around us, the quietest hospital in the world clacked and clicked and murmured on.

"Ellie," I said. All that hair of hers barely fit in the scrub cap; it billowed just beyond the horizon of Daphne's profile, a great crinkly blue cloud.

"It's okay," Ellie said, so softly I wasn't sure if I'd imagined the words.

"Thank you," I said.

"For what?" she said, her voice distant, drifting. This was no place to sleep, but it was so late, she'd been through so much.

I didn't answer. I remembered our earliest days in bed together, Whisper Theater, how I had never, in all my imagining, imagined us lying like this, here, now. I listened to Daphne breathe her tiny, rapid breaths and her sister try not to breathe at all. So be it. I couldn't breathe either.

Moments later, the door slid open and the silence fell away as the staff banished Ellie and me beyond the glass, where we watched our very young doctor—now in a coat of decent length—prepare for the procedure while an older doctor, a long white coat barely around his shoulders, a paper mask emblazoned with somersaulting orange welcome dogs, looked on, sleepy and bored. Then the curtain was pulled.

By the time Daphne's diagnosis was confirmed, the necessary antibiotics had already been added to her IV drip. Her breathing evened and her color returned. And that was so glorious that my phone had to work hard to distract me from the scene, quivering as text after text arrived, so many that I finally turned it off. Ellie and I exchanged a look.

The young doctor briefed us, predicted a full and speedy recovery, and then left, grinning like he'd just invented the stethoscope.

When morning arrived, Ellie didn't want to leave, but we agreed she'd go home for a spell, change her clothes, charge her phone. Update Madame Brouillard. Find clothes for me. *I've got some cute new jeans you could try,* Ellie jabbed, which is when I knew she'd be okay. She even let me walk her out while Daphne slept. The greater gift: a deep, unembarrassed hug at the exit by the dog.

After Ellie disappeared, I thought I would make the most of being outside and check my phone. I turned it back on and scrolled through everything I missed, starting with some proximity marketing—a feature I'd tried to get Ellie to disable—from a nearby clothing store. *"Good news!"* was as far as they got with me before I deleted it. It's not only that I disliked how the store, like too many

French shopkeepers, assumed we would communicate in English, but that "news": a tic of Eleanor's that I'd adopted was to treat and use that word in e-mails only as a pejorative. (Woe to those who thought e-mails from her subject-lined "department news" sounded innocent.)

What else had the phone handled for me? A call from Declan, a voice mail from same, and then a text from him asking if everything was okay.

A call from George, no voice mail.

An alert from United Airlines, which I was about to dismiss as more marketing, until I saw it was announcing that someone named ELEANOR was sharing an itinerary with me: *arrive Paris (CDG) on . . .*

Then George called again, and I decided to answer. I knew he was taking the twins on a spring break. It would be handy, of course, to be free of them now—but I wouldn't mind the brief, banal distraction of discussing their logistics. Perhaps George had gotten all the way out to De Gaulle and realized he'd forgotten their passports—the twins had been showing off their various visas and stamps to Daphne just the other night. Or he'd forgotten their bedtime books. Or some item of clothing.

Or he'd forgotten to tell me something: I was a terrible mom. Which I was. What Madame couldn't tell him, I could.

I knew I owed him an apology, and so I issued one immediately, even before I said hello. He paused, and said, *Leah?* And I listened—there was background noise, but it sounded familiar—it wasn't an airport, it wasn't a beach. Was he outside the bookstore? I asked him, apologized again if he'd been counting on me to be there, because—

He snorted and said he was in the hallway—or *a* hallway, of *the* hospital. Where was I?

Maroon scarf, deep violet shirt, somehow paired with a pinstripe suit and socks that both did and didn't match: apart from the welcome dog, George was as colorful a presence as the hospital had seen in some time. He was carrying two Starbucks cups, which made his attempt to hug and exchange kisses with me awkward, but—I realized—awkward only for me. One of the cups arrived smoothly in my hand as we sat on a bench just outside Daphne's room. Ellie had talked to Madame, Madame had called him, he'd canceled the trip. The twins had insisted. And if they hadn't, he would have. Daphne! They loved her. How was she?

I explained that we could be on our way home in as little as forty-eight hours if all went well, but until then, isolation rules prevailed.

"What is this?" I said, looking at the cup he'd given me. I'd talked so much I'd not put it to my lips.

He turned my cup so that he could see what was scribbled on the side. "Scotch," he said. And then: "How are *you*?"

I took a sip and sputtered.

"Jesus," I said.

"Mmm," George said. "I find whiskey the better balm. Apologies for adulterating it with coffee, but I figured you needed the caffeine, too."

I put the cup down and marveled at it, and George, for a moment. "You didn't have to cancel your trip," I finally said. "She's going to be okay. The world still grants miracles. Even to mothers like me."

"Meaning pretty ones?" he said.

I sniffed. I had once been a PowerPoint pro for a university president in Milwaukee, and a sideline parent *par excellence* of many American sports. Now I was in Paris, in a hospital, in my older daughter's skirt, outside my younger daughter's room, exhausted from a night out clubbing, drinking scotch with the best-dressed Englishman in Paris.

"I'm a terrible, terrible mother, George," I said. "I'm so sorry—I understand if you want to take the twins elsewhere from now on. I *recommend* you take the twins elsewhere."

"So American," he said. "An incomplete apology, a willful misconstrual, and bad advice, all in one go."

"George," I said.

"Drink your medicine," he said.

I smiled, or tried to. "You're fired up today," I said. I looked at his drink. "Have you been at *your* 'medicine'?"

"Mine's *sans*," he said, waving his cup. "White chocolate mocha with this new vitamin thing added in. It's better in Vietnam, but then, so are the baguettes. They'll get the hang of it here."

"I hope I do," I said after a pause.

"*Please* do not be silly, Leah," George said. "If anything, *I*—"

"Don't say you're the worse parent," I interrupted. "Because—"

He looked horrified.

"Because I'm not," George said. "I'm a fantastic parent. I lead a busy life, I don't always see my children daily, but they are well-fed and cared for, they don't hate me, and they don't hate their mother. I take full credit for all of this. I take credit for teaching Annabelle and Peter taste and manners and English as it ought to be spoken. There are plenty of subpar parents in the world. I know one who is married to a sheikh and another, much older, who owns a building that houses a bookstore. But you and I are not bad parents, not by a long shot. Your youngest child is recovering from an illness that was none of your doing. Your oldest child was able to get her sister the care she needed in the dead of night in a bureaucracy-mad country not of her birth. You've carved out a life in Paris for yourself and your children and made space for mine. Discount none of this. Leah, you've practically made the short list for the World Parenting Awards." He took a slug from my cup now. "It's not a crowded field, god knows. But still."

"But—George, I . . ." I didn't know what I was going to say; I think I thought that saying something, however, would forestall tears. It did not.

He handed me his pocket square, which I took, and even used, despite the fabric feeling like it cost more than the sum total of everything I owned.

"Moving here—I knew Paris would be hard, but not this hard," I said. "I mean, not just this, but . . ." I trailed off.

He waited before he spoke. "Did you know? I lived in the States for a while," he said. "I went to business school there. California. Shocking, yes. Shocked me, too, that I loved it. Life—school—was so *easy*. I lived two blocks from a drugstore—what was it called? C-V-S—that *sold* whiskey—*and* drugs *and* condoms *and* basic groceries, not to mention a full line of batteries. Socks. It stayed open *twenty*-four hours a day, seven days a week. Handy. But in *Paris*, I live, like you, less than a kilometer from the banks of the Seine. Charlemagne used to stroll here. At least, until he moved the capital of the Holy Roman Empire to Aachen, but that was his mistake. Not mine. Not yours." He looked up. "Maybe it's harder here, some days. But it's better, every day."

I let him make me smile. I looked at my cup. He gave it back. "Did Charlemagne drink before noon?" I said.

Now he smiled, but spoke softly. "Only after he left," he said. He raised his cup to toast mine. "To your health," he said.

It was only after George departed that I finally returned to my phone. United Airlines was telling me what? Something about Eleanor.

Eleanor?

Yes, the phone insisted, and now offered a pent-up series of her texts, truncated, that I'd have to swipe to read in full.

Please call when . . .

Delete.

If you get a . . .

Delete.

Where are you . . .

Delete.

And finally: *Leah, I have . . .*

I swiped.

. . . news.

CHAPTER 12

Normally, word of "news" from Eleanor would necessitate an immediate call. But I didn't want to talk to her right then, and certainly not about her "news," so I precluded hers with mine, via text. I explained that Daphne was in the hospital. On the mend, due to be discharged soon if all went well and—

I know, Eleanor said. *I'm on my way.*

Ellie had gotten to Eleanor before I had, with news of Daphne.

Eleanor now explained that the "news" *she* had been so eager to share earlier was that she'd booked a flight to come see us, but as soon as she'd heard about Daphne, she had accelerated her plans *dramatically*.

The adverb, the implied italics, the drama: all hers. Oh, what she had to do to move that flight! But what else *could* she do? Where, after all, was she needed *most*? And so on. Texts and e-mails rattled my phone throughout our hospital stay and continued once we got home. It would have been annoying—it had annoyed the nurses—but for the fact that this brought increasingly bright smiles to Daphne's face.

Daphne was improving. Maybe it was the prospect of Eleanor arriving. Maybe it was that I'd not left Daphne's side. Maybe it was the medicine. Maybe the doctor's coat had been long enough after all.

. . .

Dramatic acceleration means different things to different people; for Eleanor, it meant that she'd arrive in a week's time, late morning.

During the school day, in other words. Ellie asked to stay home, not just to greet Eleanor but to take care of Daphne. But Daphne stubbornly insisted on attending school—the doctors had cautiously said an abbreviated schedule was okay—and I'd stubbornly insisted that Ellie go to school, too, just in case anything happened. Similarly, I was not going to go out to the airport but would stay nearby, at the store, on call.

"Perhaps Declan could meet Eleanor?" Daphne asked, confused.

They had told us to be alert to any changes in her hearing, among other things, but so far Daphne seemed her old self, if a paler version.

"He's busy," I said.

And he was, sending me one solicitous text after another, all of which I'd ignored: *is everything all right? Can I help?*

Everyone in the world knows more about texting than I do, but no one has been able to tell me how to send a text retroactively, a message like the one I'd like to send now that would arrive to Declan back when Eleanor first arrived in Paris. I could—should—have answered the first question, *no.* And the second, *yes.*

Because Eleanor had much more news than she'd first shared.

Her accommodations weren't commensurate with the business-class air ticket I learned she'd purchased—she had not booked the Ritz—but they were comfortable and awfully close. Awfully. Three doors down, to be precise: the Hôtel du Cinéma.

In all our time of living on the street, I had not realized that it *was* a hotel. In my defense, its storefront was as narrow as ours and it looked like a storefront—large glass windows that, yes, said HÔTEL DU CINÉMA, but behind those windows, piles of hats and wigs and old movie cameras. Classic movie posters on the walls. It should have intrigued me, but instead, had long depressed me. No one ever went in or out. I assumed it was yet another Paris boutique whose existence as a money-making concern, past or future, was impossible to envision.

I was peering in the windows, trying to decide if it *was*, in fact, a money-making concern, when Eleanor's car arrived.

"Look who's here!" Eleanor called as she extricated herself.

"*Bienvenue en France!*" I said, spinning. I tried to move into a hug, but she was already busily overtipping the driver, who bowed gratefully, and thoughtfully opened the trunk so that Eleanor could remove her own five suitcases.

As soon as Eleanor was done, he sped off, and we looked at each other.

"You look good," she said, appraising.

"By which you mean I don't," I said.

"You're thin," she said.

"Not so thin," I said. "Which may be the first time I've heard anyone deflect that comment. Or heard two university women un-ironically take up body image issues within seconds of greeting each other."

"Hardly," Eleanor said, and then she grinned and grabbed me, and gave me a long, deep All-American hug.

We eased out of our embrace, but not fully, each of us staring at the other's distress.

"Oh, it's a damnable thing," Eleanor said. "Damn it all to hell."

"What is?" I said.

"Daphne, sick—"

"Daphne's better," I said.

"Robert—"

"Robert?"

"Oh," Eleanor said. "I mean—just being here, seeing you, I—"

"Robert's still gone," I said. We let go.

"But—"

But it was a long flight, I thought—too long, really, if all she did during it was turn the events of the last thirteen months over and over in her head. It was May. It had been just over a year since he'd been gone. Less than a year since we'd been here. Just weeks since I'd found, and lost, Robert's book with the scribbled *sorry*. "Can we—can we not—not just right *now*?" I said. I swept my hand up and down the street, which looked like it did most weekdays, gray and gritty and perfect. "Eleanor," I said, "you're in *Paris*."

She smiled. It looked like her eyes were filling with tears; I tried to remember if she'd been to Paris before.

"I *am*," she said. "And my god, so are you!" She looked around. "Now where are the two most extraordinary young Americans in France?"

"School," I said. "But they'll be along soon. Let's get you moved in to your—hotel?" We took this as a cue to study the strange façade. "At least I *think* it's a hotel."

"Let's give it a shot," she said.

We needed to give it a lot more than that to get everything inside, and once in, everything only looked more bizarre, less like a cinema-themed hotel than the set of a movie about a cinema-themed hotel.

A narrow young man with a mustache so faint it may have been drawn on appeared from behind a door. "*Bonjour*," he said solemnly.

"Bon-*jour*," Eleanor said. "This is a hotel?"

He looked at Eleanor carefully, and at me. "*Oui*," he said.

"Are you sure?" I said to Eleanor quietly.

"It's really *so* unusual," Eleanor said. She was staring at a bust of

Charlie Chaplin with garishly roughed cheeks. "I bet the kids will find it fun."

"*Madame?*" the man at the desk said.

Switching to French, I quickly told him that Eleanor did not have kids, but *did* have a reservation and wanted to check in.

He answered me in English. "Reservation is good."

"Well, let's get on with this, then," Eleanor said.

And they did. More staff appeared, in 1930s-era movie palace livery—tarnished-button tunics, tiny hats—and swept away Eleanor's luggage. She was issued a pair of "celebrity sunglasses," a gift of the hotel. They looked like Audrey Hepburn's, circa 1961. I shook my head. She tried them on. I started to follow her bags up the stairs, but Eleanor took off the glasses, sat heavily in a chair in the lobby, and patted one beside her.

"I'm sure you're exhausted," I said.

"I am," she said.

"Why don't you go up and rest? In fact, we'll just take it easy tonight, and we'll have our grand reunion tomorrow."

"We are having a grand reunion right now," Eleanor said. She patted the chair again. "Do you think they serve popcorn?" she said. I shook my head. "Pity," she said to the air. And then to me: "Leah, sit, or risk being judged more nervous than I am."

"I'm not nervous," I said, though I was. I'd let myself think that all those Skype conversations were just as intense as being interrogated by Eleanor in person. They were not. "Wait," I said, and sat. "Why are *you* nervous?"

She drew a deep breath and then coughed. Dust swirled around us. "Because I *do* want to talk about Robert. And then I want to talk about him with your girls. He's been gone for so long that—it's time to—"

"Eleanor—"

"Leah—"

"*Eleanor*," I said. "What else do we ever talk about—"

"It's different now," she said.

"It *is* different now," I said. "You're also exhausted now. I'm exhausted now. And if you think you're going to say *one* thing to that poor child just *days* out of a hospital bed, *or* her sister—"

Eleanor smiled as much of a smile as her exhaustion would allow her, which wasn't much. "You *sound* like me," she said.

I looked out to the street, where scarf after scarf passed by. No one looked in. I noted this phenomenon when I was in my own storefront, and it always upset me. All these wonders lining Paris sidewalks—corny wonders, as here in the cinema-hotel's overstuffed lobby, or civilized wonders, as in my tumbledown bookshop—and no one but the occasional tourist even turned to *look* in the window? I myself spent my entire Paris existence not looking where I was going, but rather casting my eyes right and left. Here was a take-out pizza joint the width of a pizza box. Here was a storefront of puzzles. Another featuring aluminum canes and walkers and oxygen tanks painted a blue Yves Klein himself would have envied. Madame Grillo's world-class mops up the way. The painter's abandoned stepladder in the storefront down the block.

I thought I'd assimilated so well to Paris life, but this must have been how the city read me for what I was, a visitor, a tourist, someone who looked in windows. A widow.

"Can I make you a deal?" I said.

"Probably not," Eleanor said, "but you are welcome to try."

"Let us not do this *today*," I said. "You are tired, I am tired, and I don't want to just start in on this with the girls now, not like this. I want to talk with you about *what* to talk about . . ."

Eleanor closed her eyes and leaned back into her director's chair. "The thing is," she said, "I loved you both. I loved the idea of you and the actuality of you. That you existed, the two of you, and the daughters you made, and the cooking shows I celebrity-guested on in your very kitchen—you all were a favorite *text* of mine. Forgive me for that. For being so captivated by such a family."

"I thought we weren't going to talk about this yet," I said.

"I'm sorry," she said, "I'm so tired I don't even know *what* I've been talking about."

Ellie saved us. She came down the street, and *she* looked in the window. Not entirely me nor entirely Robert. I spent a second or two admiring this creation beyond the glass.

Eleanor was watching her, too, but absently.

"It's true, what they say," Eleanor said. Either she was more exhausted than I thought or she really didn't recognize Ellie. "Absolutely everyone in Paris is more beautiful than anywhere else on earth. Just look at this girl."

I laughed. "I do," I said, "every day."

Eleanor looked at me and then stood and stared out the window.

"Good god," she said. "This is Ellie? You've been gone months. She's aged years!"

Ellie caught sight of Eleanor and burst into the hotel, acting for the first time in months like the daughter I had once had in America.

"Auntie El!" she said.

"My dear girl," Eleanor said.

They hugged for long enough I almost thought it was a competition—had Eleanor given me the longer hug, or Ellie?—but they didn't let go, they held on and on, and I realized that Ellie had won, and easily.

Then Eleanor opened her eyes and looked at me, and with a tiny, imperceptible shake of her head, told me that I'd won, too. We wouldn't discuss Robert today.

. . .

First things first. Eleanor didn't even bother following her bags up to her room. *You just know what it will look like,* Eleanor said, *small, a poster of Chaplin's* Great Dictator, *but in French.* (As it turned out, she was wrong: there was a poster, but of *Le Magicien d'Oz.*) Instead, she marched out of the hotel, arm in arm with Ellie, and walked two doors up to see the rest of the family. And the bookstore.

Eleanor admired the store from outside first. She craned her neck to see the sign, and then walked across the street, narrowly avoiding a slaloming Vespa that would have killed her. Ellie went across to join her and I looked at the two of them, godmother and goddaughter, as they pointed to various floors: *this is where we sleep, this is where we eat, this is where the landlady lives.* Arm in arm, the two crossed back—looking both ways this time—and went inside.

Ellie had left Daphne in charge of the register, and Daphne wavered there like a ghost, worn-out from school, her stay in the hospital. She should have been resting upstairs in bed, but she'd tried that and didn't like it. She insisted the store, on the other hand, calmed her. And the reliable absence of customers meant it was almost as quiet as her bedroom. Nevertheless, seeing Daphne through Eleanor's eyes, I winced. Daphne was better, but not completely better. It was one reason I'd not been answering Declan, who'd been texting. I wanted to be able to say everything was fine. It wasn't.

"Tante Eleanor! Bienvenue!" Daphne said, and let herself be swept up in a hug.

"My, my," Eleanor said into Daphne's hair, which, to me, still smelled of hospital. I worried my brain would ensure it always would. "A French welcome! So fancy."

"Les jumeaux sont où?" I said. Because I wanted to demon-

strate some competency, too, in some tiny area of my life. French would do.

"Peter and Annabelle are up in the children's section," Daphne said. The twins had rejoined us at Daphne's express request, and since I wasn't in a position to deny anything Daphne wanted, request them I did. I would be lying if I said I didn't like having them around, too. Their love was easy, powerful, general.

"Ah, yes," Eleanor said. "The foundlings. I'm so curious to meet them."

"Daphne," I said, "you left them up there *tous seuls?*"

"*Ma mère,*" Ellie said, "just because we *live* in a nineteenth-century building doesn't mean we can't have us some twenty-first-century technology."

"*Qu'est-ce que c'est?*" I said.

Daphne held up a little tablet, an iPad knockoff that I was using to forestall her acquisition of an actual phone. Previously, Daphne had prized an iPod hand-me-down of Ellie's, but this tablet was actually quite nice; I'd bought a model with a spiffier camera, quietly thinking that while Daphne was at school, I could explore its filmmaking capabilities. Back in my own school days, filmmaking had meant borrowing loaner equipment that was always missing a key piece or due back before you were done. Now everyone had the equipment (because now everything, including one's phone, was equipment). Anyone could use it. Even me. *Especially* me. I'd finally make my film.

Except I'd first learn that someone was making films *of* me. Of us all.

"Asif rigged a camera up there," Ellie said, "for just this reason."

Eleanor looked at me with raised eyebrows. I thought she was alarmed about the camera—that's what was panicking me now—but then I realized it was the mention of *Asif.*

"Asif rigged a what?" I said.

"Asif is her *petit ami*," Daphne said to Eleanor.

"He's not so *petit*," I said to Eleanor. "Taller than me. Handsome."

"He's a good friend," Ellie said. (She even blushed, which alarmed Eleanor and relieved me; I'd been worried that Ellie no longer blushed about anything.)

"But wait—what's he doing with cameras in my house?" I said.

Ellie sighed. "You know we always lose more books from the children's section because we don't have someone up there. So now we don't have to worry. You just click and watch. On anything. Even your phone."

"That's *fascinating*," Eleanor said.

Everyone looked to me. I imagined a camera swinging my way. Wide shot, close-up, silence.

No one said anything then, until Daphne, my linguist, my wise younger child, said, "*un ange passé*," an angel passed, the expression one deploys during awkward pauses in a conversation. It wasn't perfectly deployed here, but I was grateful for it all the same, at least until Annabelle, who'd chosen that exact moment to descend the stairs, shot a startled look at Daphne.

"*Un ange?*" Annabelle asked. "Is it your *papa?*"

Non.

Eleanor could not believe it. All the food before us was cooked from frozen?

Oh, but *oui*.

We were introduced to Chef Picard by Molly, who "cooked" a meal or two for us early on. I thought at the time that she had quite outdone herself: sliced duck breast with marinated mushrooms; pork tenderloin in a mustard sauce; monkfish; delicate green beans in butter; flaky, crisp apple tarts, more savory than sweet. But as we were soon to learn, all she—and every other woman and man in Paris, and not a few restaurants—had done was remove some packaging and turn on an oven.

Chef Picard is our own nickname; the food all comes courtesy of a frozen food chain, Picard, whose stores I avoided until Molly finally revealed the source of her gourmet cooking. My first impression, when I finally entered one, was how antiseptic it looked. The space was filled with glass cases, flooded with bright white light, and the walls, while cheerily painted, were almost completely blank. But the packages themselves are adorned with museum-quality photographs that, unlike in America, accurately reflect what's inside. I sometimes like making Picard meals just to look at them. And when I do, I often think of Robert's creations. Of the "cooking shows" with Eleanor.

Frozen or fresh, the meal completely charmed Eleanor—I had opted for beef carpaccio with olive oil and basil for her, Ellie, Daphne, and myself, and then *pépites de poulet panées*—chicken nuggets—for Peter and Annabelle. (Molly says the secret is to use the Picard as a base and then add your own tweaks, but I like what Picard makes just fine.) Eleanor quizzed the girls on school (very hard, they said, and it made them feel like school stateside had been too easy), life in Paris (they wished the church bells didn't ring so early and often), and, finally, the bookstore.

"When I was a little girl," Eleanor said, "I dreamt of living in a bookstore."

"You did?" said Peter. I could see he found Eleanor more grandmotherly than his actual grandmother, Madame Brouillard. "What kind of bookstore?"

"Oh," said Eleanor, putting down her fork and knife and taking up a napkin. "I think it was a red bookstore in a faraway place."

"Our father is often far away," said Peter.

"This bookstore is red!" said Annabelle.

"And I dreamt that there was a little *apartment* above the red store," Eleanor said quickly.

"There is an apartment above this store!" said Peter.

"And that I could go and see the books anytime I wanted," said Eleanor.

"We can't do that," said Annabelle. "Our *papa* says we would get distracted."

"I can't imagine there are better things to be distracted by than books," said Eleanor.

"*Mais oui*," said Daphne.

"I think you dreamed of this store *ici*!" said Peter. The same way question marks defined Robert, exclamation points defined Peter. Even the shapes fit each of them—besieged, Robert curved over into a hunch? Exuberant, Peter often popped straight up out of his shoes!

"*Ici* means 'here,'" said Daphne.

"Yes, I think I did dream of this very store, here," said Eleanor.

"Sometimes," Ellie said, "it's a nightmare."

Peter made a face. Annabelle liked to torture him by always asking to have *Mon Premier Cauchemar*—a French picture book about nightmares—read to them at bedtime. Ellie poked Annabelle. Daphne stifled a laugh. I looked at all their faces—this *was* a family, a kind of one, the five of us. Even without a father, even with two kids on loan from another father, we were our own kind of intact, "normal" family, the kind who kidded with each other over dinner and ate beautiful food.

And I thought, once again: Robert would have *loved* this. Not a guess. It was there in the pages of his manuscript. The family loves Paris. It loves almost all of them back.

"Let us *not* talk of nightmares so close to bedtime," Eleanor said.

"I only meant that it's not easy running a store," Ellie said. "Sometimes it's hard. Sometimes people steal things."

"Like the gypsies!" Peter said.

"Peter!" Ellie said. Just a month prior, Ellie (and Asif) had been at a rally in support of the stateless Romani at the Hôtel de Ville, arguing that the Romani were habitually accused of crimes that they did not commit. Ellie decreed that we were not allowed to say the word *gypsies*, nor even to read Bemelmans's *Madeline and the Gypsies*. This was hardest on Peter, since the book featured a circus. (He thought all books should, and not enough did.)

"One time *someone* stole one of *my* books," Annabelle said.

"Oh, dear," said Eleanor.

"Well, if you just leave your own books lying around," Ellie said, "what do you expect?"

"People to be honest," Daphne said.

"Don't we all," Eleanor said, and turned to me. "And when *is* bedtime, by the way?"

"There were some kids just today," Daphne said. "While Ellie was down meeting you at the hotel. A bunch came into the store, and I *know* one of them stole something."

"Ellie," I said. "This is why I don't like Daphne being left in charge of the store all by herself."

"I like being in charge," said Daphne.

"I was only two doors down," said Ellie. "So were you."

We had a simple protocol with shoplifters: let them steal. Sometimes, if the suspect was younger than herself, Ellie broke the rule and would confront him or her (more often the latter, which surprised me) outside the store. I would often undo Ellie's police work by making a gift of the book. One time Ellie had intercepted a young, freckled, overweight girl in the act of stealing *Dieu, tu es là ? C'est moi Margaret !* With apologies to Judy Blume, that's a book I almost think a young girl *should* steal (which is why I stock it even though Judy Blume is still alive—and may she live forever). And adults stole Bibles and cheap Shakespeare editions, while the backpackers, maps.

And one very special criminal, a very special scribbled-in copy of Robert Eady's *Central Time.*

"I think I remembered some of the kids from Ellie's app night," Daphne said.

"Nice," Ellie said. "Blame me."

"I wasn't!" Daphne said. "And maybe I was wrong. There were just so many of them, and I thought, *this is odd*—it just felt odd. Maybe it was because this kid, and I'm not even sure if he was a kid—he was wearing sunglasses and a hat—"

"What did he take?" said Annabelle.

"Probably the nightmare book," said Ellie.

"Ellie," I said, but Annabelle shot away to check. Then Peter said to himself, *Tintin*, and he ran away, too.

"Lovely, girls," I said. "Daphne, I'm sorry this happened, and you won't find yourself in that spot again, all alone in the store, but let's also try to remember not to talk about such things in front of the *jumeaux, d'accord?*"

"I feel *fine*," Daphne said.

Now Ellie got up and ran away.

"Well," Eleanor said.

"Never a dull moment at The Late Edition," I said.

"It makes me worried for you," Eleanor said.

"Don't be," I said. "Shoplifters are—irritating. But normal. You may recall that I stole something from a bookstore once."

"I've heard that story," Eleanor said. "But I thought we weren't going to talk about—"

Ellie returned, staring at Daphne's tablet.

"That's *mine*," Daphne said.

"I know," Ellie said, "it's just easier to see on this—wait—"

"No technology at the dinner table, Ellie, you know the rules," I said.

"I just got the tail end," Ellie said, still staring at the screen. "It only saves the last two hours, and then it overwrites, I guess, so we're missing most of this guy's visit, and I can't even see what, or if, he stole anything, but here he is, going out of the store."

For some reason, she showed Eleanor first. She tilted back her head. "Honestly," Eleanor said, "I'm no good without my glasses."

Ellie gave the tablet to me. Daphne came and looked over my shoulder. "Yes, that's him," she said, and we studied him, and Ellie paused and zoomed this way and that, and we all agreed that yes, in the crowd Daphne had seen, there *had* been a boy who *had* stolen a book. (The camera even allowed us to read the title: *The Cloud Atlas*.)

But here was what was more remarkable by far.

I seemed to be the only one of us who saw that someone *else* had broken free of the crowd to move across the opposite corner of the screen at the precise moment of the "heist" (as Ellie had come to call it). He quickly disappeared from the shot when Ellie zoomed in on the thief, and as I said, he was in a corner of the room opposite from where the heist had occurred. Which meant no one noticed him.

But of course, I did.

I'd know my husband anywhere.

This was different from seeing him in the static pages of a book, imagining that I'd seen him in a photograph taken a half century before. This was a *film*, from two hours ago. This was Robert. This was life catching up to my imagination, or the other way around.

The reason I'd been having more and more trouble, ever since coming to Paris, imagining he was dead was because *he* had come to Paris.

He'd come to our store.

We'd found him. *I'd* found him.

And he'd found us.

I looked at the girls, but they'd already set off with the twins for the children's section to see what else might be missing. I looked at Eleanor, but she just shook her head sleepily at me. I felt my vision freeze and scatter, as though my eyes were just another balky piece of technology.

Robert was alive.

CHAPTER 13

Ellie had left the tablet behind and I took it up now, slowly slid my finger back and forth, REWIND, PLAY, left, then right, not unlike Robert's old experiment, the book that erased itself, back and forth, except this was different. The story got clearer with each pass.

It was him.

It was not a good picture of him. The camera never caught his face, only him moving away. He appeared to have lost a good deal of weight, but still, on this tiny, grainy film, there was his shape, his profile, how he moved. How he moved amongst *books,* that was the greatest marker for me. I remember this from almost any bookstore we ever visited anywhere. He moved through them with a strained delicacy or grace, the bull who knows he's in a china shop and is terrified his hooves will slide out from under him. Books drew him, I knew, not just as things to be read but as things. I've never known a writer who didn't like just *holding* a book, feeling its mass. (And I've found a surefire way to close a sale is to put the book in a customer's hands, let them feel it, fan it.) I get it: a physical book of paper and glue, it conveys its worth through its weight. The reason people once lined their shelves with encyclopedias was not that they thought they'd turn to them daily, but rather that they might daily bear witness to those spines: it's a complicated world, and all that mass was a moat.

But as much as Robert loved books, he'd also grown to hate them, especially in stores where he wasn't shelved, but also in those where he was: what was he doing in the bargain bin? He hated when other people published books he had not published. He hated the books of authors he hated, and he even hated the books of people he loved. At the bargain table of our Paris bookshop, he did *exactly* what he used to always do at every other bargain table at every other bookstore: he lifted up a copy and gave a quick glance beneath. If a black mark was flecked across the bottom of the bound pages—something invisible to absolutely everyone else in the world but authors and booksellers— that meant it had been remaindered. That meant it hadn't sold at full price the first time around. That meant another author had, like Robert, come up short. Those marks were a comfort, I knew Robert thought that. And, needless to say, those marks also meant a bargain. He liked that, too. Because as much as he came to hate books, he also couldn't not love them in the end. When he disappeared back in Milwaukee, my first thought was to go to the library. I told the police this, and they went, and they didn't find him, so I went, and although I didn't find him either, I saw him, I could imagine him in every corner, under a toppled bookshelf, a massive dictionary striking the fatal blow, or perhaps even squeezed to death by one of those mechanized accordion shelving systems. That was the end I foresaw for him, though I'm sure he saw otherwise. Such a death would have been too showy, too apt.

Eleanor gamely offered to take over the bedtime routine, which was incentive enough for everyone to race up the spiral stairs. She dispatched me, meanwhile, to the lobby of the hotel: later, she said, we would *talk*.

And we eventually did, but the conversation did not go as I had planned. After waiting an hour for her—they'd all wanted bedtime stories, of course—and after I spent that hour rewinding, replaying, zooming in, zooming out, proving to my eyes what I'd known immediately in my bones—I shared my discovery with Eleanor. She took it poorly. At first, I understood her reaction to be rooted in her general reaction to technology: not to be trusted. And it wasn't. *But here*, I showed her. I slowed it down, I advanced it frame by frame. I said no, you can't see his face, but you can see his shoulders, his hips, how he moved—I told her all about how he'd moved; she'd had to have seen this herself, hadn't she? I would still need to see him in the flesh, somehow, somewhere, but until then—

She shook her head.

"What do you mean?" I said. "Why can't you see this?"

Her eyes were red-rimmed, watery, but intent. "Because I know what happened to Robert," she said, and then started again. "Leah, this is what I've been trying to tell you. I know that's not him because, months ago—actually, days ago . . ."

I waited.

"I'm so sorry, dearest," Eleanor said. "I called them."

Them: back before we left for Paris, I had met with the police for a final "update." I put the word in quotation marks because there was no update. There was no nothing. This may not have been their fault, but it broke me, enraged me. Displaced anger, I suppose. There was some shouting, a chair I helped fall over, a door I slammed whose glass, I argue, was already broken. But I did not argue, and nor did the police, when Eleanor suggested she become the designated intermediary henceforward. We even signed a form.

I had found I liked having a buffer, liked it up until this very moment, in fact, when my buffer told me that Robert, my husband, the author, Daphne's and Ellie's dad, was dead.

Because the police said so. Because a "preponderance of evidence" said so. Eleanor had dutifully checked in with them the day she left the States, and this is what they told her, my duly designated representative, that this looked to be the determination they were going to make. They were still preparing the report, but—

But I had just seen him.

Eleanor was still talking: "There is not—I want this to sound like a comfort, but I know it won't, and I really don't want to use the word—there is not—"

"There's no body," I said quietly.

She looked surprised, and then nodded. "I'm sorry, Leah."

I studied her for a moment.

"Not sorry enough," I said.

"*Leah.*"

But it was true. Eleanor had sent Robert's manuscript to the girls! Before that, Eleanor had sent us to Paris. And before *that*, Eleanor had believed. That Robert was alive. That I should believe so, too. And now, now that I *knew*—

"*I'm* sorry," I said. "I'm sorry you're wrong." Because she had to be, and so, too, the police. There was no body because the body was *here*, in Paris, and I'd just seen it, not dead, but alive, wandering a bookstore thirty meters from where Eleanor and I were sitting.

I picked up the tablet but could only stare at the black screen. I was too tired or confused or angry to turn it on.

"Sometimes," Eleanor said, "we see things that . . ." She set her lips in a line.

"What did they say?" I said. "What did *they* see?"

"There was a boat," she said. "The college's sailing center."

I was ready for her to say that they'd found a pair of shoes and a note by a bridge. Or an abandoned rental car an hour west of Green Bay. Or Montego Bay. Something so cliché I could say, *not him. Can't be him*. He was a lot of things, but he wasn't ever, not even for an hour, ordinary.

But the sailing center. It had been his one escape. He never went out of a love of sailing, but out of a need to get away, alone, and water worked. He'd first gone there to research an early book of his where some too-young heroine sails from Miami to Cuba. (Of course, Robert reversed the usual direction.) He quickly learned, I recalled, that Lake Michigan wasn't the Gulf of Mexico. No sharks, true, but Lake Michigan wasn't warm, either. It was an inland ocean; weather came up fast. There were more shipwrecks bubbling beneath than historians could count. But with training and grit and, most important, good weather, it could be sailed successfully. So long as you were prepared. So long as you had the right boat. So long as you had a partner, but as I've said, he hated sailing with someone. It would be very much like him to evade this rule. Especially if he wasn't planning on coming back.

"The Coast Guard found a boat not long ago on the Michigan side of the lake, which turns out to be not only a Great Lake, but a gigantic one," she said. "Gigantic enough that this boat—that is, *the* boat, could go missing for as long as it did. And we know it's *the* boat because there's a log there, at the sailing center." I waited, wordless. "What I mean is—you're going to get a long letter from the police, and you should answer the phone when they call next. There are legal things, which will be an agony, but they will ultimately make life easier for you." She paused to let me respond. When I didn't, she went on. "The detective said you'll see that Robert signed out a boat in this log. Robert wasn't supposed to go out alone that day—or any day—but especially *that* kind of day, something about how the wind was code yellow or—who knows? We live in an age that relies on kindergarten colors for safety—he signed out the boat. It wasn't stormy, but the seas *were* high, say the weather records. It's a good boat, what he signed out, but not for that kind of weather. Way too small."

But sturdy enough to bob about that massive lake for a year?

"What day was this?"

"The day he disappeared. Just over a year ago." She looked me up and down. "This is a lot," she said. It was. I didn't believe her, and yet—

"The sailing center?" I asked Eleanor. "Are you—are they sure that—"

"No," Eleanor said. "I mean, I'm not sure, but the police are, and well, that does make me more sure. It's hard to believe that the idiots at the sailing center didn't realize it was missing. They'd even told the police all was in order way back when. But now, a year on, the Coast Guard finds a boat, someone does an inventory—it's very haphazard, mind you. I drove by on the way to the airport to see for myself, and—I don't know if you've ever been—"

I had not; it was Robert's thing. His private pride and solace.

"It's a mess, naturally. Student-run. I mean, there are boats—not a handful, dozens—in all states of disrepair, life jackets everywhere—"

Eleanor's digressions, asides, and general anger—at the police, the club, and, I detected, Robert—softened the blow of her news somehow. And I still had my own solace, my self-delusion. I had my own pieces of evidence, although in the midst of this onslaught they seemed to be disintegrating. Forget the Coast Guard, the police, the student sailing center: what made me most anxious was that *Eleanor* now believed Robert was gone.

"But no *sign* of him at all?" I said.

"Dearest," Eleanor said, and her face flushed as she turned away. "I knew this was going to be difficult," she said to herself. She looked at me once more. "As I said, there are some legalities ahead, and you have to prepare. And I will *help* you prepare. But part of that is talking to the girls."

"*Prepare?*"

"In Wisconsin and most other states, the presumption is that after someone has been missing for seven years and there's no sign, they can be declared dead."

"It's hardly been seven minutes!"

"It's June," Eleanor said.

"Early June!" I said.

"What does it matter, Leah? The thing is, you don't have to wait seven years if certain conditions obtain," Eleanor said. "In all this time, there has been no sign of him at the bank, no sign of him on the credit card, no sign of him anywhere in Milwaukee—"

"Because he's fucking *here*," I said, and pointed to the tablet. "I just *saw* him."

Eleanor looked around the room as if for support, but found none. "And who else?" she said, not angry but insistent. "We all saw that video—your own daughters saw it—and no one saw him then."

"Daphne saw him on the bridge!"

"There, too, no one else," Eleanor said.

"I found that 'I'm sorry' he wrote in that book," I said. "I'm certain of *that*."

"I'm sure you are," Eleanor said. "But are you certain *when* he wrote that? Maybe it was years ago in another used bookstore. Can you be certain *he* wrote it?"

I couldn't be. Because I couldn't check. Because he'd stolen it back.

"I'm certain he wrote that manuscript!" I said. "And you can't tell me you aren't. One hundred pages, and he's on every page, as you were the first to insist."

"And I'll insist that you start with the first page where it says 'a novel,' which means, as I sadly have to remind my undergraduates every single September, that each page following is *fiction*."

"It's real! You've been to the store."

"I've been to your store. But I didn't meet—what was the wife's name?—Callie?—and I'm quite certain I didn't meet the husband, either."

The lobby, badly lit, made Eleanor look old. I'm sure I looked even older. The room swallowed sound, too: my throat felt like it had just spent the entire evening yelling, but I'd been barely able to hear myself speak.

"I'm sorry, Leah," Eleanor said. "I'm angry. Not at you. Or, a little at you, because you won't let me help. But I'm angry at me, too, because I can't figure out how to help. And because I can't answer your questions the way that I should: am I certain the police are right? Am I certain Robert's dead? Am I certain he's at the bottom of Lake Michigan? I don't know. I do know what I now believe, which is that he's no longer with us."

I still didn't look up; I could feel her looking at me, waiting for me to meet her gaze, but I couldn't, so I didn't.

"You need to imagine a future without him, Leah."

And there was the problem, the reason that I was so angry, too. I was already living that future. But it was a carefully constructed future that relied on certain elastic ambiguities, the way seams in a sidewalk let the pavement expand and contract with the seasons. I had good days and bad days, but with each passing day, I learned to live without Robert. And part of me liked life without him. I missed the author, but not the angst. I missed the dad, but not the doubter. I missed the boy who chased me, but I didn't miss the man who'd made me chase him for almost twenty years.

I didn't know what I would say if I caught him.

Why'd you go? Why'd it take us so long to get to Paris?

And then what? Glad you're back?

Good-bye?

That's why I didn't want to hear what Eleanor said. That's why I didn't want him to be dead. Not anymore. If he was dead, I couldn't leave him. If he was dead, I might fall in love with him again. I just wanted him to *be* back. For the girls' sake. For Eleanor's. And maybe— *if* I could have that boy and his books and his smile and his eyes and his Paris and his Wisconsin map of the world—for my sake, too.

But more than anything, I wanted this to be something I determined. Not the police. Not Eleanor. Not even Robert. If I wanted to see him in the pages of a book, or the grainy background of a video, then I would.

Because I had.

I had the benefit, or burden, of being the last person who saw him alive, that last night he was under our roof in Milwaukee, when Robert said no, he hadn't bought the tickets to Paris to research that guidebook, he didn't think he could stomach it, the project, there wasn't much he could stomach right then, and . . .

And I told Robert that if he didn't get his act together, off the page, on the page, I was leaving.

As in going, gone, and not coming back until he'd figured out a way to get better, with or without medication, with or without a therapist, with or without a career in writing.

I waited for him to say something, but he didn't. Instead, as Eleanor now did, he rose and climbed the stairs without a word.

As Eleanor disappeared, I decided that Robert's unfinished manuscript didn't suggest a work in progress, but a work interrupted. The problem was not that we'd lived a life out of, or in, Robert's manuscript. It was that we were running out of pages.

The next morning, Paris shook itself awake, swept clean its gardens, sent water coursing down its gutters, peopled its streets, polished its storefronts, and pretended that nothing had happened the night before, that I hadn't just heard that my husband had died, that I hadn't just seen evidence that he was alive. Perhaps any city will do this after hidden tragedies, but Paris did it that morning with a particular glint, and ignored me with particular intensity. It reminded me of those occasions—far too many now—when I encountered soldiers in Paris, always in squads of three or four, always with hands cradling weapons, walking up some random street that I was walking down. Expat American bookstore owners are invisible to them. No small feat, as I saw that they saw everything: that parked car there, those shuttered windows there, that van, those men, that bag, that *moto* buzzing by. Everything but me. On one occasion, I was so incredulous—the street was otherwise empty, and they passed inches from me—that I sputtered "*bonjour.*" They kept moving and scowled, like they'd momentarily wandered through the frame of the wrong film.

Tfk?

Declan and Ellie had for some time been attempting to teach me SMS French. But I had enough trouble with spoken French, and its SMS variant struck me as needlessly complicated, impenetrable to everyone but teens: *tfk*, for example, is *not* something lewd, although when I first saw it flash on Ellie's phone, I was sure that was the case.

It wasn't. It only meant what Declan now meant, *tu fais quoi*, what are you doing, what's up?

I was up, early, the morning after my talk with Eleanor, and I was wandering the store, having just seen everyone off to school.

I stared at my phone. The few abbreviations I had learned were of no use here: *tg*, shut up; *t où*, where are you; *mdr*, lol. Nothing they'd taught me meant *hearing from you, Declan, makes me realize that we need to meet, to talk, and probably take a breather from whatever not-quite-relationship that we're in, because life's just gotten really complicated for me.* I almost thought to text Ellie "how do you say 'it's not you, it's me'?" but it would be no use; Ellie had lately abandoned abbreviations for emojis, particularly ones that denoted eye-rolling.

So I texted him back a single letter, *Y,* which meant *yes, I'm up,* at least to me.

A moment later, the phone rang. I looked at it. It was Declan.

"'Why'?" he said. I didn't realize he was quoting my text.

"What are you talking about?" I said. "Also, good morning, which is something else I can't remember the abbreviation for." My voice sounded odd, like I was impersonating some less troubled version of myself, which I now hoped I was.

"The letter *y,*" Declan said. "You texted me that." Then a pause. "Hey," he said. "What *is* up? Are you okay?"

"Y meant 'yes, I'm up, I'm here,'" I said. "But it also means I feel bad I've been out of touch. There's been a lot—too much—going on, and I'm sorry. And I . . ."

Wait, I thought, I'm going to do this on the *phone?* I needed to meet Declan. Awkward as it might be—well, maybe it wouldn't be awkward. He was a friend, after all, and a gentler one than Eleanor. I wouldn't have to discuss the police department's discovery. Or mine.

"Are you free?" I said. "Just for twenty minutes—an hour? We should meet."

"Not only am I free—until after lunch—I have an amazing bottle of wine this student's parents bought me for helping them jump the line at the Louvre."

I smiled, or tried to, though he couldn't see, or hear, that. Or maybe he could.

"Leah?" he said. "It's . . . been a while."

"It has," I said, and then, again, nothing. Because this meeting was a terrible idea. What I needed was time—a week, a month, more—to reassess, think things through.

"It was a really long line," Declan finally said. "And they were *really* grateful. And really rich."

"Declan," I said. "I can't—I mean, it sounds amazing, but—let's do coffee, okay? Still free—I'll pay."

"That's not really what I was talking about," Declan said.

"I know," I said. "I'm not really talking about what I'm talking about either."

That sounded more nonsensical than even the worst of my SMS missteps, but as we efficiently made plans to meet in the Place des Vosges, I could hear in his voice—sad, heavy, spent—that it was the one exchange all morning he'd understood perfectly.

Bises, one cheek, the other, and the scent, the smile, almost made me stop and kiss him on the lips. But then my phone buzzed, and there was my other life, interrupting.

Good morning my dear I am sorry for last night I will need COFFEE and now: a text from Eleanor, vital, to be sure, and yet I worried she had absolutely no idea how much she was spending using her American cell phone in France. I shook my head, apologized to Declan, and quickly texted Eleanor back: *I'm meeting a friend.* I'd texted her in English, of course, but I wondered how that *friend* would translate.

We need to TALK, Eleanor said. *See you at the store in a horse.*

"Ellie?" Declan said.

Hooray, Eleanor texted.

"I'm sorry," I said. "I have a little less time than I thought."

HOUR, Eleanor texted.

It took Declan and me far less time to skip past pleasantries to anger.

"So this is how it's going to go down?" Declan asked. The waitress brought our cafés. I didn't really want coffee; I wanted a shot, even a beer. I wanted this to be our first drink, I wanted to be headed off to go dancing soon, and I wanted to be paging through *The Red Balloon* again in my kitchen, and this time, instead of studying Robert's face in a photo, I wanted to close the book and study Declan's.

"I'm sorry," I said again.

"It's been over a week since I've heard from you, you know," Declan said. "I mean, I'm sorry I took you out dancing the night your daughter got sick, but that was *your* idea—"

"Declan," I said. "I'm sorry I didn't call. I'm sorry I didn't answer your texts. You were very kind. I was very distracted. I *am* very distracted. There's been a lot going on."

"I'm sure," Declan said. "I mean—I know. The hospital. Daphne. It must have been very scary."

After I'd fiddled with my cup and saucer long enough to let my own anger melt into sadness, I told him about Eleanor, about everything. Everything I should have told him earlier. I told him that I had not been a widow and now might be—but for the fact that I was increasingly convinced my husband was alive. There'd been a note in a book. There'd been Daphne's shout on the bridge. There'd been the back of someone's head in the fuzzy corner of a frame from a DIY surveillance video system installed by my teenage daughter's Canadian boyfriend.

I told him that almost all my favorite memories of Paris involved him, Declan.

"Like the mugging in Ménilmontant?" he said. "Or the time you learned the French term for 'police psychologist'? Or when you invited me out for coffee to—to do whatever it is we're doing now?"

"Like a fifty-course midafternoon meal lit by a million flowers.

Like a daytime whatever in my kitchen with wine instead of coffee. Like when you took me dancing and kept asking afterward if everything was okay—kept asking, even when I didn't answer."

"You're not answering me now," he said.

"What do you mean?"

"I don't know," he said. "I—if I'm hearing you—"

"You are," I said.

"I can't be," he said. "What you're saying is that a woman's arrived from Milwaukee, and she's told you the police think your husband is dead. There's a boat, some kind of report. Your daughters haven't heard about this yet—"

"And won't," I said.

"You keep pretending that I don't know them, your girls?" Declan said. "Not well, but enough to know that—they'll—"

"Fine, yes, I need to tell them, but that's my problem, not—"

"But that's not—I don't think *problem*'s even the right word."

"*Problème* is an excellent word. In English or French."

"The *problem* is you think—you know—he's still alive. And you think—you think you saw him. You think you were getting messages from him before, you thought you saw him before, but now—now you *know*."

"I think I know," I said.

"Okay," Declan said, but he was agreeing with something he was thinking, not what I was thinking, which was *can you wait? Can you be a friend and just a friend, just until I figure out what's going on?* But when I looked up, he was gone. He was still sitting there, but he was gone, gone from me, and I wasn't getting him back. Not his easy conversation or his eyes or his shoulders, legs, his hands. All of it, gone. My purse savior, dance defender, daytime companion, gone.

"Declan," I said.

"I'm really sorry," he said. "And I mean that, I mean that word every way it can mean. I'm sorry *for* you, I'm sorry for me." He twisted to find the waiter.

"Declan," I said. "This is not—I hope this is not good-bye."

"It's not," Declan said. "It's something way stranger."

Laurent thought something strange was going on, too. Or so Madame Brouillard reported when I returned to the store. I'd not been there for the morning delivery, which meant Laurent somehow roused Madame to have her sign for it (and, knowing Laurent, have her carry the boxes into the store). Madame did not like Laurent (he'd once told her he didn't like books; they were too heavy; he preferred delivering mops). Madame did not like being roused. Madame did not like that the store had not been open of late during my usual hours—noon until dinner—and that she was pestered at *all* hours as a result. She'd not expected *much*, having turned things over to Americans, but she had expected better than this. And, worst of all, the store now seemed to be attracting *dangerous* people.

At first I thought she was referring to the crowd Ellie, Asif, and Declan had convened the other night, but no: Laurent said he'd seen someone "prowling" around. I wasn't as confident as Madame seemed to be that *prowling* was the right word, but the gist of what Laurent was saying was clear.

And so was the gist of what Madame was saying: either I figure out how to run the store better, or she'd find a way to run us out. After all, I couldn't be part owner of a business, as our visas required, if it wasn't in business.

Of course I took offense at Madame's threat—I was supposed to—but I wanted us to be doing better, too. In no small part because I wanted to show off for Eleanor. Maybe every other aspect of my life was a mess, but I wanted Eleanor to see that I'd managed to figure out this much, how to survive in Paris.

And we almost were. We'd spent down much of Robert's prize money, but we were doing okay. Madame's threat aside, the visas George had magically acquired for us were still working their magic. George also helped us negotiate for the assistance the government sometimes granted independent bookstores. If I'd had to pay for tuition or health care, the books, indeed, would not have balanced. But I didn't have to pay for those things; George paid us handsomely, and Madame Brouillard, when she wasn't browbeating me about my poor business abilities, made clear her own failings by not following up with me when I was late with my monthly payments (confusingly, when we discussed them in English, we called this the "mortgage," but in French, she would use the word for "rent").

Originally, I'd thought Eleanor and I would spend her first full day walking the city—the best cure for jet lag—but that would mean shuttering the store yet again. If I had had enough cash flow to hire an assistant (and Molly was all but begging me for such a position), things might have been different.

I was lugging the last of Laurent's boxes into the back room when I heard the bell over the door, reminding me that I'd forgotten to lock it until I was officially open. Too late now, but so much the better; an early sale would help us make up lost ground. It might even be the man who had called in looking for a first edition of Sophie Calle's cryptic 1979 photo essay *Suite Vénitienne*, which we did have and could never sell, because it was Madame Brouillard's own copy and she wanted five hundred euros for it. If I sold it at that price this morning, though, I'd more than cover the cost of closing—or hiring Molly—this afternoon.

"*Bonjour*," I called. "*Bienvenue, bienvenue*," I said, dusting my hands and easing the bookcase-door aside.

"Good morning," said Eleanor, in a tone that suggested it was not.

"I—well, here you are. I was going to be in touch as soon as I squared away things here," I said, blinking hard. "Did you not sleep well?" I asked.

"The bed was awful," Eleanor said. "And I want to apologize for last night."

"Me, too," I said. I paused.

I guess I thought Eleanor would go first. But she said nothing. So I said nothing.

"Well, I'm glad that's over with," I said.

"Not quite," Eleanor said, drawing a folder out of her purse. "They should be ashamed, that hotel, what they charge for printing."

"Oh—? We could have printed that out for you for free."

"I wanted to see it first." She looked at me. "It's the police report. I don't know if my calling them accelerated things or if things just came together, but—here it is. There's nothing new in it, it's everything I said."

I stared at the folder. The stack of pages inside seemed insultingly small. Smaller than Robert's manuscript.

"Like I said," I said quietly. "I need time."

"Leah—" She reached toward me, and I reflexively withdrew. She stiffened, stung, and then put the pages away. "Leah, *time* is what I'm trying to give you."

She looked at me expectantly.

"What?" I said.

"Ellie tells me you've had a gentleman caller."

"I've—what? I'm sure she did not," I said.

"She has eyes," Eleanor said.

"If Ellie has *eyes*, then she saw that I've done something you told me to do—make friends. I'm up to four now. Five, if I can still count you."

"Count me first," Eleanor said.

"Well, number five is just a friend. His name is Declan. He *is* very sweet and handsome. But nothing more. That's clear."

"Is it? To all involved?" Eleanor said. "You deserve to get on with your life," Eleanor said. "*That* is what I'm trying to help you with. I don't want the police report to be true any more than you do. But realize, past the pain, what a gift the report *is*."

"The UPS driver said he saw a man lurking about," I said.

"Did he call the police?" Eleanor said.

"I don't think it was like that," I said, trying not to look at the folder.

"Did *you* call the police? In Paris, or Milwaukee?" Eleanor said, more gently now. "When you 'saw' Robert in the video? When Daphne 'saw' him on the bridge? When 'he' apologized to you by scribbling an unsigned 'sorry' in the pages of a book you randomly found?"

Just a PAUSE button. It's all I want from the world's scientists. A STOP button would be too much to ask for. But a pause, just a pause, when you don't want to hear—

"He died, Leah," Eleanor said. "It's time to use the word, the actual word. And I know it's like he *just* died, but it turns out he's been dead for some time. Enough time that it's now time to take some steps."

How did she do it? With her voice, her eyes, the way she set her face? Take something I'd been certain of, just hours, just seconds ago—that I'd *seen* Robert on that video—and knock it askew? Life had no PAUSE button, but apparently, Eleanor had a button that launched you fast-forward, and I felt that now, a physical pull, past sad-eyed policemen, past lawyers, past Milwaukee friends nodding sorrow, past the girls keening. All of this, about to start.

CHAPTER 14

But everything started with me, with convincing me of what was true, what was fiction. The theory that he was dead had all the evidence, save Robert's body. The theory that he was alive had no evidence, save Robert's—what? I didn't know how to categorize his brief cameo, nor what now seemed, in retrospect, like constant haunting.

I felt Eleanor watching me, measuring me. *I just told Leah her husband is dead, and yet she seems unmoved.* But I was moved, or had moved, from one belief to another.

Press PLAY.

"I'll hear you out, Eleanor," I said. "But will you hear me?" I wasn't sure yet what I would say beyond this.

The store's phone started ringing.

"Please answer that," I said. It was the first thing I could think of. "*That* would help."

Eleanor lifted the receiver. "*Allo*," she said, and looked at me for my approval. I nodded. "Late Edition Bookshop," she said.

She listened.

"Can you speak English?" Eleanor asked. She listened a moment more, then continued. "I don't speak French. This is an English-language bookshop."

She listened again, more briefly. "'Lay-cole'? Is that the author?"

L'école. School. School was calling. *"Allo, allo,"* I said, taking the phone. The school intimidated me now even more than the girls. *"Je suis désolée. Mon—assistanté ne parle pas français. Ça va bien, les enfants?"*

Les enfants, the children, mine, though it turned out they were talking about George's.

When I got to their school, I immediately checked their foreheads—please, God, let us not go back to the hospital where they invented the stethoscope—but they were cool. The woman explained, in English, that their class was going to the park today, but the twins could not go along because they did not have their permission slips signed. I offered to sign right then. The woman shook her head slowly: I was not their mother.

But it was okay for me to pick them up at school?

We were already on the sidewalk outside, and she began closing the door. They didn't have staff to watch the children without slips, she said. *Je suis désolée.*

George texted me that he was sorry, too. But Eleanor was not; the twins had charmed her. Why don't we take them to a park ourselves? Would the Luxembourg Gardens suffice? The hotel had told her it had many diversions for kids.

But we didn't have to go anywhere if I was *expecting* someone, she said.

Was I? I didn't like the sound of those italics, but I didn't want to stay cooped up in the store either, so I agreed to her plan. I called Shelley to see if she might mind the counter. She told me to close the store. I didn't call Carl, because every time he'd given me his contact info, I'd deleted it. I finally called Molly; she said she'd be over as soon as spin class was over. When she arrived, Eleanor, impatient, already had her sunglasses on and acknowledged Molly with barely a nod.

"That's that actress, isn't it?" Molly whispered as I showed her a variety of unnecessary things, like how to record a sale.

"I can't say," I whispered back.

Molly grinned. "I love Paris."

My new employee surreptitiously snapped a photo of us as we left.

The walk ahead wasn't short—three kilometers, forty minutes or likely more—but, because of the oddities of the map, the Métro would have taken us almost as much time. (Not that this kept Peter, who considered the Métro the world's longest and most convenient amusement park ride, from begging that we take it.) I called up to Madame Brouillard to tell her about Molly. She didn't answer. I asked Eleanor if we could postpone talking about, you know. She did not answer.

So it was a relief when difficulties and distractions arose. We passed a carousel that had somehow squeezed itself onto a narrow traffic island by a Métro entrance. Dozens of carousels dot the city, an implausible number. From the air, Paris must look like a whirling machine of countless cogs. It's a marvel the sidewalks aren't more choked with children dizzily staggering away from their rides. I could see that Peter, however, was focused: a carousel *and* a Métro entrance? The Luxembourg Gardens and its swing sets (and especially its sailboats) could wait.

But Annabelle needed to use the bathroom. A small crisis became a larger one, as the first two self-sanitizing sidewalk toilets near the carousel were out of service. Now Peter needed to go. We walked on. And on. We were still well shy of the Gardens and their toilets, so I routed us into the first tiny *crêperie* that presented itself. Hardly the width of a pool table, the restaurant was for tourists. A take-out window opened directly onto the street; a darkened refrigerator case featured a haphazard array of Coke products. The counterman was the only employee and looked no more Parisian than I. Still, I would not have assumed, as Eleanor did, that he knew German, but soon they were chatting away.

Before I knew it, we'd been allowed to use an immaculate bathroom behind an unmarked door. We were then ushered through another unmarked door to a tiny courtyard behind the restaurant. Here sat a table, two chairs, and a small playground set.

Toys.

This was his backyard. His children's toys. I turned to comment on this to Eleanor, but she was deep in negotiations with the counterman.

When he left, Eleanor cleared her throat. "*Luxembourg* Gardens another day," she announced. "Today, we dine in the *Garten* Erdem." Peter and Annabelle looked confused. "My new friend, Erdem— who is Turkish and thus gifted in such arts of the kitchen as Americans, and perhaps even French, can only dream of—is going to lay out a lovely spread for us," she said. "Children, look!" And because Peter and Annabelle cannot fail to be charmed by any special gesture from anyone—a tight-smiling stranger holding open the door at Picard makes them blush—they leapt.

"*Des jouets!*" they shouted.

"Eleanor," I said as the twins tackled the toys. "You are a marvel." And she was. She'd not said an additional word about Robert. I wondered how much longer I had.

"Oh, listen to you," Eleanor said. "And that's even before the wine comes."

Wine: so I had that much time. Erdem delivered a bottle of prosecco. We spent our first glass watching the twins drag the equipment this way and that, carefully arranging the smaller toys. Every so often, one would hand a toy to the other; words were exchanged, everything was rearranged.

"They're running a little store, aren't they?" Eleanor finally said. She reached for the bottle and poured herself another inch.

"It's a side affliction of living above, and in, a bookstore," I said. "Whenever they play, they play this. I don't think they've seen their father enough to know how to play international consultant."

"Don't call it an affliction," Eleanor said. "It's a benefit."

By the time we were halfway through a second glass, Erdem had delivered, and the twins consumed, a small pizza. They went back to playing. Erdem soon reemerged with a special off-the-menu meal he and Eleanor had worked out. Nothing fancy, but somehow quite exotic—a tomato cucumber salad where the tomato and cucumber were largely displaced by cubed oranges and olives. Eleanor insisted that she detected coriander. I said paprika. She asked if Declan was Irish. I said no, we hadn't.

"Excuse me?" Eleanor said, which is when I realized I'd answered the question some wicked part of me imagined she was asking, which is whether I'd slept with the man. She watched me work this out, and then she worked it out. "Good *lord*, Leah."

"Please," I said.

"Oh, god, you *did*," she said. "I can hear it in your voice."

"We *didn't*," I said. "What you can hear in my voice is—actually, I don't know what you hear. What I hear is this other woman, this other me, who's been getting introduced to a new—to a different—life?"

"A single life?" Eleanor said.

"An independent life? My-own-two-feet life. I don't know. It's been—interesting."

"Which is code for?"

"Maybe it's for 'fun,' except it hasn't been precisely that; it's been disorienting sometimes and pleasant other times, but mostly, it's been a new pair of glasses when I'm out with him. Do you know how different this city looks when you're walking *with* someone, when you're sitting beside the Seine *with* someone, when you're having a glass of wine *with* someone?"

Eleanor raised her glass. "I had no idea I was prying," she said. I looked at her. "I mean, I did. But I really was just curious if he *was* from Ireland, because—"

"Iowa," I said. "He's in Paris studying for an MBA, but he's from Iowa."

"Oh, for godsakes," Eleanor said, and leaned back. "Why didn't you say that in the first case? I taught there for a year. The world would be a better place if it was given over to Iowans. There'd be no more war, we'd go to bed on time and drive on *very* tidy roads, yielding every so often to proud and capable Amish and their carriages. We'd eat a lot more pork, true, but I found that, prepared well, it's quite tasty." She speared a fleshy square of orange-flecked red. "As is this," she added. She nodded to the bottle, and so I poured her a final sip of wine, and then myself one, too. There was no way we'd make it back in time to welcome the girls home from school. I got out my phone to text Ellie, to tell her we were delayed, that Molly was manning the store, and that homework should be done before anything else.

I felt Eleanor watching me but didn't look up until I'd hit SEND.

"Just Ellie," I explained, waving the phone. I wanted to prove to Eleanor, if not myself, that I was the kind of mother who always kept her kids apprised of her whereabouts.

"Do you talk to her about Robert?" Eleanor said. "She's never been the fragile type, my goddaughter, but nonetheless—"

"She's a cool customer," I said. "Not like Daphne." My memory, merciless, flashed a picture of Daphne in the hospital, hot with fever.

"Cool she may be, but that doesn't mean she doesn't want to talk," Eleanor said.

"They both do," I said. Flatly, because this was something I felt more than knew. Some days, I felt like we'd portioned out the stages of grief from one of those books: Daphne, to judge from her silences and haunted looks, had taken sadness; Ellie, anger; and I, of course, denial.

The look on Eleanor's face told me that she'd read my uncertainty perfectly. "May I show you something?" she asked, wiping her hands.

"Please don't," I said.

She reached for my phone and then handed it back to me. "Make it do the Internet thing."

"What?"

"The—I hate this word—*browser*. Open the *browser*." I did, and she took it back and painstakingly typed something in, waited for it to load, narrating what she was doing all the while. "You know Ellie's class project? Photography." I shook my head. "I wondered as much. She is, of course, very talented." She handed the phone back. Ellie had produced a photo blog—Paris street scenes, close-ups of various addresses. I sighed with relief. So this was just about a blog (another awful word), about a hidden talent of Ellie's that wasn't hidden at all: I'd been through her phone the night before I'd gone to Ménilmontant. I'd known she was skilled, that she had an eye.

"She *is* very talented," I said, flicking through the photos. I liked how Ellie had avoided the usual suspects—no Eiffel Tower or Sacré Cœur here, just random businesses and signs around Paris. A certain weary bleakness pervaded. My kind of girl. Lamorisse's, too, though she'd dispute that. But that wasn't what Eleanor was getting at.

"Leah," Eleanor said gently, and took the phone. She put it flat on the table between us and began swiping through the photos once more. "Do you see?"

I leaned closer. Had Eleanor—had Ellie—caught him on film, too?

It took a moment, but then I saw what Eleanor saw. Not in every photo, not always in the center, but—there it was. I picked up the phone. And there. And there. The shoe store. The restaurant. The upholstery shop. On the door. The awning. The sign. The menu. *Boutique Robert. Restaurant Robert et Louise. Robert Four. Chez Robert. Editions Robert. Robert et fils.*

"Oh my god," I said to the phone, to Ellie, wherever she was. I looked around the sunny garden, at the happy twins, at the laundry on the line of the neighbor behind. I saw everything. But I'd not seen how my own child—my oldest—ached. I'd not seen how much she *saw*. "This is terrible," I said, once I'd found my voice again.

Eleanor shook her head. "It's beautiful is what it is." I put the phone down. I had to stop looking. "But it does mean—she misses him," Eleanor said.

"I know—I knew that—Eleanor, I'm not a monster—"

"I know you know," Eleanor said. "But I also know that they *don't* know, not what happened to their father. And this is the result." She turned the phone facedown before starting again. "Telling them that the police think—know—that he died, this isn't going to be easier, especially at first, but eventually it *will* be better."

"And then, once we tell them he's dead, Ellie will stop taking photos of 'Robert' around Paris?"

"She may very well take them for the rest of her life. You should at least buy her a decent camera; she's got a future."

"Eleanor—"

"You *all* have a future. But if you don't accept that he's dead, then *she* won't accept it, and Daphne won't, and the mystery's going to pull on all of you forever." She picked up the phone and, with some increasingly hard tapping, figured out how to close the blog. "And down the line, pull in ways that may not be as beautiful as this."

So it was time.

"Make your case," I said quietly. "That he died."

Eleanor took a deep breath. I did, too, but it caught, and it was a moment before I could exhale.

"It's not mine," Eleanor said, and took the folder out of her purse. The report inside was poorly written, but otherwise, all was as Eleanor said. A boat had been signed out. The same boat had been found. No body had been found, but since the "subject's" disappearance, "no evidence of life," online or off-, had been found either. It was the department's recommendation that the surviving spouse petition the court to have "the missing person" declared dead, given that he had faced "imminent peril"—a 922-foot-deep Great Lake—and "failed to return."

I pushed the folder back to her. I didn't say that what unsettled me most were his fingerprints. Not prints they'd lifted from any suspicious surface, but prints they'd had on file—I think from his driver's license or passport. I couldn't say, only that the whorl of lines, its interruptions and breaks, its careful contours, seemed so undeniably *him*, despite the fact that I'd never seen these prints before. They reminded me of his eyes, that burst of color in the one. They reminded me of him.

"I don't know what to think, Eleanor," I said.

She bent down and rustled through her purse, returning with a handkerchief, which she handed to me. I had no idea what to do with it. *Ding, ding*: that warning bell buses sound. I heard it now, that folder on Ellie's phone. The one I'd not opened. "Dad."

Eleanor mimed patting her cheeks. I was crying.

"Leah," Eleanor said.

I bent to my purse to look for tissues I knew weren't there. But I kept looking, to hide my face, and I heard Eleanor leave the table, say something to the twins about "Nutella," and then return. I heard the door to the restaurant creak open, slam shut, and then it was quiet. I straightened up.

Eleanor looked at me carefully. "Okay, crying finished, children sated, Paris paused," she said. "Now is your chance. Make *your* case. The police have made theirs. Hold forth."

After a moment, I began.

"I don't know what to say," I said. "I mean, for months, I made myself believe he was dead. And up until the 'clues' or 'signs' or 'hallucinations'—whatever we want to call them—up until those started arriving, I'd almost done it. I'd almost *willed* him dead, in my mind. I never *believed* it, not soul-deep, but I came to—understand it. Intellectually. It made sense."

"'*Sense*,'" Eleanor repeated.

"Until it didn't make sense. Until pretending he was dead no longer made things easier, but stranger. That's where I am now. That's why this report . . ." *Didn't apply*, I wanted to say, as though it was a matter of jurisdiction, as though what happened in Milwaukee had no bearing on Paris.

"Leah, it's just that—I'm worried that if you don't—"

"Eleanor—fine," I said. "If you've come to Paris to get me to sign some form, and by signing that form, you think that Robert will indeed disappear, then I will sign it. We'll delete him. He's no more than a character in a manuscript, at this point, right? A film."

"Leah," Eleanor said.

"Because it's easier to say that than to ask, what kind of man leaves his family like that? I'm not talking about the sheer burden of abandonment—the doubling of parental duties, the stress of not just doing all the laundry but dealing with every single fucking crisis that children can produce—I'm talking about the withdrawal of love. You fall for someone, he falls for you, you marry, and then he gets tired of it all and doesn't have the decency to tell you. Or to die. Instead, he lingers on, he lurks, he haunts you, keeps you from *moving on* despite your very best efforts to do so. He decides to continue to live the life he had before, just this time from the other side of the window, outside looking in? The police say he's dead. Can they also make sure he stops coming around?"

"Leah," Eleanor said again, just interruption enough to make me stop and think—why *was* he coming around? But I could also hear Eleanor say it: *you, dear—the girls. He's coming round because he loves you.*

But she wasn't saying that. She was saying he was gone.

"Eleanor," I said. "I understand. They think he's dead. Now *you* think he's dead. And yes, I can *understand* this. I just can't pretend to believe anymore. Where's the evidence? I know the evidence is that there *is* no evidence, but—"

"But there is . . . this," Eleanor said. She pulled out another folder, hesitated, and then opened it and laid the contents between us. "I'm switching topics," she said. "Or maybe not."

In another minute or so, we would grimace at each other, collect the twins, pay the bill, and march the whole way home hardly exchanging another word. She'd go to her lodgings and I to mine, and I'd see to dinner and bedtime alone, and then I'd descend to the little office behind the store, turn on the desk lamp, and sit there, surrounded by dust and dark, and open the folder once more.

But that was all to come. There, then, in kind Mr. Erdem's backyard, she looked at me looking at what she'd taken out—and then quickly apologized and began to stuff it back inside the folder. "Damn it," she said. "That was awfully stupid."

It was. But it was my stupidity more than hers, and it started, or rather, ended, over a year ago, the day Robert quit writing.

This was March, just weeks before he quit our family. I remember the day, the moment, quite specifically, as it was Daphne's twelfth birthday. We were having an unusually large party. He made his announcement to me privately a few hours before the festivities were to start. *I'm done,* he said. *I'm done with writing. With paper, with pens, keyboards, with—*

Great, I said. A pause followed. He said, *I'm not sure you heard me,* and though I had, I stopped and waited, because I also hadn't. I was devoting a very small percentage of my brain to listening to Robert, in part because that had become my habit of late, in part because I was focused on the contents of our refrigerator: what did we still need to get at the store, what could be thrown out, what would I say if the photographer wanted to take a picture of this, too?

The photographer. About which more in a moment, but for now, know that somewhere along the way, Robert's agent—long gone at this point—had said that one problem plaguing my husband's career was that he wasn't enough of a "brand." Not enough readers knew who he was.

I had dutifully rolled my eyes, said my lines, but he'd shaken his head and said, *Leah?*

That was all, but that was enough. I would become familiar with the tone, which mixed question with complaint, a tone familiar to more than one married couple in the world. But into Robert's variation crept something new, something I hadn't quite identified then but now think of as nostalgia, longing, loneliness. The way he said my name sometimes—the way he said it every time I'd not responded adequately to some existential plea—made me think for a moment that we weren't speaking to each other in the same room but over a telephone line, long distance, back when it used to cost money: the voices muffled and anxious at every second that went expensively slipping by. I'd not gone anywhere, but it felt, even to me, like I'd moved away.

And so I listened carefully when he said my name the morning of Daphne's birthday, because the inflection mattered; *Leah* could mean "what did you think of that *Times* piece I sent you about that (successful/famous/wealthy/laureled) author" or "I didn't sleep last night and can't do the chore you just asked of me" or, as of that morning, "what's going *on*?"

Awkwardly, this. A neighbor who'd had success with a local neighborhood news blog—mostly because it featured photos of absolutely everyone *in* the neighborhood—was raising money to take it into print. She'd chosen my husband, minor celebrity (ever smaller) that he was, to be the debut cover subject and had sent an incredibly young reporter to interview him days before. Today a photographer was coming.

This was bad timing, as it was not only Daphne's birthday but her Golden Birthday, the magical date when your age aligns with the calendar date of your birth (Daphne, born on the twelfth, was turning twelve) and parents in Wisconsin and neighboring territories are obligated to make a massive fuss. Massive. It was to be a day without rival, something like Christmas and the Fourth of July crossed with the rare return of Halley's Comet, except your Golden Birthday would never, ever come again. I knew parents who had booked restaurants and ponies, and had heard stories of twenty-one-year-olds who went to Las Vegas (and never returned). Ellie, when she had turned nine on the ninth, had asked us to fly her first-class to Disneyland. But we couldn't afford that then, and we had even less money now. Daphne wanted a pony ride. Robert was offering, instead, a make-your-own-book party. He'd move our thirty-dollar inkjet printer down to the dining room table and everything!

So it was not a good day for the photographer to come. But it was the only day the editor-neighbor could get the guy—she was bartering for him—and so she bribed me: what if she had an advertiser give us flowers? I hesitated. *Lots* of flowers, she said. I pointed out the house was crowded enough for this "golden birthday"—and then she squealed: an idea! A new nail place had been begging for exposure—how about an on-site "spa day" for Daphne and her little guests? The photographer would shoot Robert, then Daphne and her guests for a future story and—

And so waivers had gone into the envelopes along with the invitations. Moms called with questions, but mostly thought it fun: tallying appearances in the blog was a local pastime. No one opted out.

Except, that morning, Robert.

I closed the fridge. His jobs today: retrieve the cake (on us) and flowers (free, but delivery not free), and sweep the porch. Easy. Much easier, anyway, than building a little pen for a pony in the backyard, which Daphne irrationally held out hope for: the pony could get a pedicure. They'd braid his mane.

"Let's not talk about quitting," I said. "Even as a joke," I added, giving him an out. I waited to see if he'd take it. He did not. I could be, and now was, inordinately proud of controlling my tone. Robert had no sense of timing whatsoever. He might hit on you as you were attempting to shoplift a children's book, he might disappear from your life years later while out for a run, he might tell you he was quitting writing the day a magazine was coming to photograph him for a story about being a writer.

"Not a joke," he whispered.

"Mom!" Ellie's warning voice, singing from the second floor: Daphne was experimenting with clothes. There was a photographer coming, after all. (As Ellie never let us forget, we had wound up at a local pizza place for Ellie's golden birthday, not a photographer in sight.)

"I'm not going to spoil the day," Robert said, continuing to whisper, though no one else was around. "I just wanted you to know as soon as I knew."

I looked at him, incredulous at what I was hearing, incredulous at the almost excited look on his face.

"You do know I'm proud of you," I said, though I wasn't. "No matter what," I said, though this mattered right then, quite a bit.

"Leah," he said—that voice again. "No toolbox." The therapist's toolbox. At that point, I'd almost forgotten it. I was surprised he hadn't. He'd given no "advance notice," for example, that he'd decided to quit writing. I tried to remember if there was a hammer in the toolbox. If so, I might pull it out now. Did I "rely on humor" too much? No, because that wasn't funny. So no hammer, but I did recall that we were to "speak affirmatively."

"Fine," I said.

A final item from the toolbox: holding each other's hands during difficult moments or conversations (not "fights"). He reached out to take mine. I snatched it away.

"This is *not* how couples fight," I said.

"We're not fighting," he said. "And I thought you'd be—I thought you'd be happy for me?"

"Happy?" I wasn't sure if this was more toolbox talk; the therapist had a thing about happiness: a false god or goal, or something like that. I couldn't recall exactly. Contentment, equilibrium, *that* was what you were supposed to be after. "I'm happy when you're working."

A breath.

"I'm not happy when I'm working," he said.

"Maybe that's how you know it's work?" I said.

"You're not making sense," he said.

"*I'm* not? What doesn't make sense here is what you want me to say, or do. Do you want me to say 'hooray, you're abandoning your gift!' or 'no, honey, don't do it, don't'? Tell me, and quickly, because the next scene in this script involves a happy *child*."

He turned away.

He was struggling. That I understand. We understood. But he never seemed to understand how hard it was on us. Lonely Sisyphus he thought himself, pushing that rock up the hill each morning. But he was too tired to notice that when it came rolling back down the hill each night, it threatened to crush the three of us waiting there.

"Mom!" Now it was Daphne shouting. The anthropologist in me had long noted they never shouted for Dad, except when he returned from an absence of any length whatsoever. An hour, a day, a week. His arrival ever worthy of exultation.

"Okay, I don't know where this crisis came from," I said, "but if this is about the stupid article—no one will read the article. A few will look at the pictures. And by 'few' I mean us."

"That's not the point," he said. "I'm tired of—"

Tired: that was a word from another box, the deep, wide one any couple gets on its wedding day, the one you fill with everything, good or bad, that comes into your lives every day after. It's an emotional trousseau, except you keep adding to it. And if you add too much of one thing—too much angst or melancholy or exhaustion—and too little of other things, like stress-free golden birthdays, or successful manuscripts that become successful books, or successful "experiments" that establish new trajectories, it bursts open, spilling its contents all over the floor, making a mess just hours before the guests are supposed to arrive.

"That is the point," I said. "I know what you're tired of. What I don't know is what I'm supposed to do about it."

A beat elapsed where no one in the house said or screamed anything. The refrigerator hummed, and out front, a car door opened and shut. And maybe *this* is when Robert's next book, his final book, began, when he finally began to write, really write, even as he quit, right there in that room, right behind those eyes looking at me, in his right iris that flash of color that had first inflamed me, marked him for me, this man I loved because he had all those question marks, including that one he'd once appended to that extraordinary word: *marriage?*

Yes, I'd said then. Straight into his shoulder, I'd been hugging him so hard. I'd been so happy.

And maybe I should have hugged him now, held his hand as instructed. But then I would have missed what he did next, something that made me endlessly grateful at the time, although it shouldn't have. I should have recognized it for what it was—the start of something irreversible, the steady unpacking of that trousseau until its every corner was bare.

But I didn't see that. I saw this: a smile. His. A tiny smile, a half smile, maybe even a smile from the toolbox, which said willing your facial muscles to grin sometimes cued a sympathetic response in your psyche.

I'd gotten angry, exasperated, I'd asked him *what am I supposed to do?* And now he said "nothing." I smiled (he was smiling). He turned slightly, and the little kaleidoscopes that were his irises turned, too. He turned back. The color returned. "I'm sorry," he said. "Nothing."

And then he got the cake and the flowers and—who knows how, on such short notice—a pony, who carried Daphne and her friends straight from our yard into the page proofs of a magazine Eleanor had brought to Paris and shown to me beside a children's playset in a cramped green plot behind a Turkish *crêperie*. I'd thought they'd spiked the piece; I'd heard the print edition had never gone to press. I'd checked the blog once or twice since coming to Paris and saw that it, too, had gone dormant. And the editor and I had had a falling-out after she'd sent e-mails with invoices after the party: a "misunderstanding." I'd protested, she'd protested, and finally, I began having my inbox automatically route her e-mails to the Junk folder. I'd thought that was that.

But no, sitting in my office, taking out the pages Eleanor had printed off, I saw that this was that. The editor had e-mailed Eleanor: "*I hear you might know now how to reach Leah & Robert?*" The editor explained how she'd once had a magazine, how it had failed, how we'd fallen out—she didn't mention the invoices—and that she felt bad about the whole thing but wanted to send along the unpublished page proofs of "what might have been."

We'd seen an early draft—just the text, and it had been unpromising. But this was the whole package. WRITE AROUND THE CORNER, chirped the headline on the cover. There was no mention inside that Robert had disappeared; that was part of what so unsettled me. It was both a glimpse into our past and a snapshot of an imaginary present: a family in Milwaukee. A house, a mom, a dad.

What unnerved me more, what later kept me awake in Paris, were not the words but the photographs. They were gorgeous. I don't know if they used a special camera or computer, or if the photographer was on leave from *Vogue*, but the colors, our faces, the detail, all of it was like liquid briefly stilled. Robert's solo portrait was handsome, but there were more photos. Of the party. The pony. Of Daphne astride the pony, scared but grinning, a grin that would stay on her face, and mine, for days.

And finally, a photo of our whole family. They'd chosen a shot of us trying to figure out a shot. We are in the living room, and we're deciding if we should sit or stand, tightly together or loosely apart, smiling or serious. Daphne appears to be the only one who's listening to instructions: she's standing up straighter than any of us, but she thinks what we're doing is funny, and it shows. And maybe it's the makeup the spa folks were playing with, but her color looks ten times better than it ever has here in Paris. Ellie, meanwhile, is mortified, but excited; she has one hand on Daphne's shoulder, her other hand is starting to move toward the camera; she's either saying *wait* or *now!*

I'm behind them with what maybe only I would recognize as my game face—what would be clear to anyone is that I'm inordinately pleased. I look like something had been accomplished, and something had. We'd weathered our argument. The pony had shown up. *Robert* had shown up, and not just physically. And the result? The girls look beautiful. Robert looks at ease. He's possibly happy. He's clearly proud of his family. His lips are just parted; he's about to say something.

What?

I don't know. Only that a month later, I'd threaten to leave. And he would.

Eleanor has a toolbox for arguments, too. I'm not sure if she's aware of this, but I am, as I am of the fact that it contains only two tools: a patient, penetrating gaze and, in case of emergency, distraction.

As I said, our walk home from Erdem's was almost wordless, but not quite: after failing to get me to answer even the mildest questions—*are the sidewalks always this busy? Is this weather often this maritime?*—Eleanor finally asked a question she knew I'd have to acknowledge, as it was about a bookstore.

"Would it be too much trouble to—I'm no good at maps, but I looked earlier, and I'd swear it's right around here—might we stop by Shakespeare and Company? Just to see?"

Looking back, it's interesting to think what we might have seen had we stopped by, but I lied and said we were nowhere near it. She raised an eyebrow, but that was the last I heard from her until we walked up to *our* store.

I don't envy Shakespeare and Company their success. It's the only Paris bookstore, English-language or otherwise, most Americans know (if they know any bookstore here), and, to judge from his manuscript, it's the only one Robert knew. Although the description of the store in Robert's manuscript eerily anticipated what became The Late Edition, the truth is, it was more directly a description of Shakespeare and Company. He describes it as being green, for example, as having a small fountain nearby. And he describes it as busy, something no one would have ever described Madame's store as being. And of course, Shakespeare and Company is busy; they have a history—Sylvia Beach, who founded the store's first iteration, published James Joyce's *Ulysses*, championed Hemingway, and thrived until World War II forced her to close. Another store later claimed the name, and an endless stream of backpackers and tourists (and some locals) have prowled their aisles since.

Not me, though. I'd walked by once or twice but never went inside, finding the parallels to Robert's manuscript somehow spookier there.

Five hundred meters away, however, was the lesser-known landmark that Ellie had once marched Daphne and me (and Asif) over to, Bemelmans's old bar in the rue de la Colombe, just northwest of Notre-Dame. I steered us in that direction now, confident that the stop—and the story of Ellie's enterprising research—would make Eleanor forget about Shakespeare and Company.

But as we reached the corner, all I could do was remember. In the months since we'd first visited this corner, I'd done my own enterprising research, curious as to what *"chagrin d'amour"* had forced Bemelmans to sell the bar. I'd found nothing; in his own account, he describes being dispatched to Paris in 1953 by *Holiday* magazine to draw the city's down-and-out, and subsequently falling in love with a bar that catered to them.

He bought it, with an eye toward improving the premises and thus the clientele. It proved to be a disastrous decision financially, but his essay recounting the experience is affectionate and lighthearted.

At one point, he and his contractors realized that they were not going to be able to update the plumbing, due to the discovery of an underground pre-medieval aqueduct built to service Notre-Dame. As a result, for his grand reopening party, Bemelmans commissioned two limousines—one labeled MESDAMES and the other, MESSIEURS—that spirited his guests off to neighboring apartments to do their business.

It was funny when I read it, but walking by with Eleanor and the twins in the day's last light, the corner seemed grim. We walked on.

Crossing the Seine into the Marais, I thought of Sylvia Beach and her beautiful bookstore, shuttered, the story goes, after she refused to sell her last copy of *Finnegans Wake* to a Nazi officer. She did not wear the yellow star Jews wore, but her young friend and assistant, Françoise, did, and wandering the city as a pair, they faced together the same restrictions all Jews faced—no cafés, no movies, no theaters, no transportation but bicycles, and no sitting on benches. One day, picnicking outside, they took special care to sit on the ground rather than the bench nearby. It was an anxious meal.

The officer never got his book. Or the store. Within hours of the officer's angry departure, friends had helped her move and hide its entire contents. They even painted over the sign outside. The Nazis still found Sylvia, however, and packed her off to an internment camp for six months. Hemingway himself later claimed to have "liberated" the store as the Nazis fled, but Sylvia was spent; though she lived another eighteen years, the store never reopened under her ownership.

Ludwig Bemelmans and Sylvia Beach died just four days apart. I sometimes wonder if they ever met. They must have, even if they spent much of their lives on different continents; it's impossible to imagine that, in a city this intimate, two people who should find each other never do.

CHAPTER 15

Eleanor did sleep in the next morning, which was just as well. I had a strange sort of hangover that I tried to hide from the kids as I bundled them off to school. It was partly the wine-soaked afternoon in Erdem's backyard, but it was also the magazine. It had made me sad to see it—leafing through again, I saw I'd pocked the pages with a tear or two—but I felt different this morning.

But Milwaukee . . .

I looked at the pages once more.

Milwaukee paled in so many ways compared to Paris I hadn't realized that I'd let my memories of our stateside lives go pale, too. But there, on those pages, was evidence: Milwaukee had been marvelous. And so was our family. We had had it in us to smile. Even after arguing, even on that crazy, terrible, funny day, the four of us, we'd figured out a way to grin (and nail a cover shoot). And a photographer had figured out a way to show us as we really were—not beset by chess tournaments and manic weather and a writer who'd lost his way, but a family who could, on occasion, goof around, get along.

We'd been okay.

I went back to the couples therapist just once after Robert disappeared. I wanted to make a confession. I left having made two. The first was that I'd caught myself feeling something terrible about Robert's departure—hard as it was, tearing as it was, there were minutes during the day, sometimes as much as an hour, when I felt *relieved*. Life with Robert could be hard; life without him was, too, but you didn't have to double-check the forecast as much to see if, as your husband sometimes thought, the world really was coming to an end that day because a 150-word paragraph wasn't taking shape. I waited for the therapist to uncap her pen and get out the big red book where she kept a list of the world's worst wives. She didn't. Instead, she said, "that's rational," and since I don't like agreeing with anyone, particularly therapists, I said, "well, let me tell you what's *ir*rational, which is that, despite everything, I don't regret marrying him." My second confession, and one I'd not known I'd had in me until I blurted it out.

But as I said it I knew it, and not just because our marriage had produced two females who, I firmly believe, will someday save the planet. I had loved our marriage, I'd loved *us*. I'd loved our creaky house. I'd loved Milwaukee, its bars and its bookstores. I'd loved Robert's cooking shows. I'd loved that the trailer that unloaded the pony had also deposited a goat because, as Robert said, "what's a pony without a goat?" I didn't know, but it turns out having a pony *with* a goat *and* all the ensuing smiles is like winning the world's largest prize, and the one day out of one thousand when things *did* go right for Robert—a great review, or sale, or that the goddamned comma he'd spent the week moving around had finally settled into the right spot on the page—is an even better prize, but the best was being married. It really was.

"And you still *are* married," the therapist said, which is when I decided I wasn't going to see her again.

In the overcrowded U.S.A./New York section of our bookstore is shelved Grace Paley (an author whose books Robert gave me so often I sometimes forgot I hadn't ever met her in person). His favorite story of hers, "Wants," became mine; it charts the rise and fall of an entire marriage over a scant 791 words. Early on, the husband and wife are young and poor, living in an apartment whose walls are so porous it's impossible to avoid smelling the neighbors' breakfast. Years later, they unexpectedly meet again; the husband, now her ex, crows about his plans—which include a sailboat—and says bitterly to her: "You'll always want nothing."

Sailing aside, Robert was never that husband. And I wasn't that wife, but as the story wife later protests, so will I: I did want, *do* want something, many things, including to have one day made a film that wasn't about synergy; to have raised brave, independent daughters; to have read and loved every book on the shelves of my store.

But more than anything, I had, for the longest time, wanted Robert to be healthy, to be happy. To be here.

He wanted to be elsewhere.

I think I was resisting Eleanor's pronouncement, the police's determination, that Robert was dead because acquiescing wouldn't just mean putting Robert to rest but would announce that we'd been profoundly not okay. Whatever he'd needed from us, we'd not provided. And whatever we'd needed from him . . .

But he'd gotten what Daphne wanted, the pony. And the photographer, the picture. And I had other pictures. I had boxes of them. I had memories. The magazine proofs were just one of many, many pieces of evidence that I had of a happy life. Chasing him out of that very first bar after he'd chased me and my stolen book, that had not been a mistake.

And neither had been imagining him dead. Nor, more lately, convincing myself that he was alive. I wasn't crazy; I was cycling. And eventually the cycling would stop, and I'd come to rest. Alone. In the aisles of a bookstore in Paris.

. . .

So I practiced that life: I stood in the store and sold maps of France, London, Europe, and the Baltics to a tanned-gold couple from Napa and told them where to eat. I sold a copy of Hemingway's *Moveable Feast* to a young man whom I surprised in the act of tearing pages from it. I sold ten copies of *The Great Gatsby* to a young woman who said she was a tutor assigned to an American film production company shooting in Paris; I told her to be sure to stop back. She said she'd bring along the young stars and rattled off their names—I knew enough to nod and smile, but otherwise recognized not a syllable of what she'd said.

I was not a bookseller *authentique*, but—I was learning how to impersonate one. I would sometimes practice on Shelley, the most patient of my three customers. I once pressed upon her Tove Jansson's *Fair Play*, the story of two women artists living companionably in the same house, doing their art. Shelley knew Jansson's books for kids, which feature strange trolls—Swedish, hippoish—called *moomins*, but didn't know Jansson had "written for grown-ups."

"Not *all* grown-ups," I said, "just the artists."

Shelley came back the next week and, houseboat equilibrium be damned, bought everything else I had of Jansson's, including a few stray Swedish-language editions.

Today I was short on artists, though not strange children's books. I saw someone had liberated *Le Poids d'un chagrin*—The Weight of a Sorrow—from the French children's book section and left it by the register. The book fascinated Peter and horrified me: the book depicts sorrow as a massive hairball on muddy green pages, a sorrow so *gros qu'il m'a dépassé, submergé, dévoré, un chagrin si lourd à porter que pour m'en sortir, j'ai dû le grignoter à mon tour.* Or, as Peter once earnestly tried to translate for me—*sometimes the sadness is so big it eats me up, um, heavy door I can't get through, I try to leave but I can't, and so I snack? No, nibble away*—and I asked him to stop.

I put it now in the window with a little sticker that said, in English, FREE.

I looked at my watch; time for some tea, maybe the computer. E-mail from the U.S. usually didn't start arriving until late afternoon, Paris time, which I liked—it gave me a chance to clear out my inbox before the next batch arrived. It was mostly spam anyway. I had few Parisian e-mail correspondents; France, like Ellie, seemed to have moved on to texting long ago. But still, I received a few French e-mails every day, usually from *Electre*, this magical online service that helps stores like ours reach millions more readers (or it would if I could figure it out) and advertisers like *Bongo* (which sells gift cards—in Belgium—in boxes; it seems to make a difference).

And today, an e-mail with no subject line.

E-mail could count as "advance notice," that long-ago therapist said. *Here's something I want to talk about.* I said that sounded like an avoidance strategy—it *is* an avoidance strategy—but it's true, just scanning your inbox headers gives the eye, the mind, a moment to think.

Sometimes, especially if the subject line is blank, it's not long enough.

Leah, it's been so long, too long, so long I don't know if I can explain

Or you decide that you don't want to read it at all, that you're so overcome with disbelief you're forced outside of your body, and thus unable to do anything more than stand there and watch yourself click DELETE.

Which is what I did.

A message from Robert had arrived in my inbox and I had deleted it.

The kettle whistled and I got up and turned it off. I rooted about for some tea, and settled on chamomile. It wasn't until the water began puddling on the floor, scorching my feet, that I realized I was completely missing the cup, and then I set down the kettle and looked at the floor, where I noticed the cup in shards. It must have fallen—when, I couldn't say.

Perhaps, too, the person who was sending the e-mail was not Robert but someone impersonating him—his real name was embedded in the e-mail address, but it wasn't any of his old e-mail addresses—in which case I'd been perfectly right to delete it.

But it wasn't an impersonator.

It really was Robert.

And I really knew this because once I found my way back to the computer and looked and found that folder I'd never explored much before—the Trash—I rescued his e-mail from there and opened it. It was brief, so brief that one could make the case that nothing there provided evidence this was indeed *him*. One could make the case, but I wouldn't. Because it was finally too much. And because no one would have more cause to impersonate Robert than Robert himself: he had done so for years.

It was Robert, then, and he was writing me, and he was promising that we would see each other soon.

Robert.

What surprised me now was how much this hurt.

Where was—joy? Or relief, or even some indignant pride? *I* had been right. The girls had been *right*. He was alive!

He was alive, and that hurt, because that meant he'd been alive all this time. It meant that he'd only leave again.

Because that's what he wrote:

Leah, it's been so long, too long, so long I don't know if I can explain it, even to myself. I do know I want to try. And so even though this is short notice, and probably too much to ask, I think we should meet soon, before I go. I really do—

I fixated on those last three words, *I really do,* because those were what convinced me, that painful, awkward earnestness. It was Robert. And fixating on those last three allowed me to not fixate, not just yet, on the three before, *before I go.*

I opened a window to write a reply and then closed it.

How do you write someone who no longer exists? He wasn't *dead*—Eleanor could argue with me, and maybe the police, too, but I *knew*, just as the girls had known these past months in Paris. He was alive. Here was this e-mail. But I also knew that the Robert I'd *known*, the man I'd married, even if he showed his face, even if I touched him, that Robert wouldn't be there. I'm making it sound like a question of physics; it's not. It's just time plus distance, times Paris, minus love . . .

Maybe it is physics. Physics is the most mind-bending of the sciences, and I was having a hard time bending my mind around this fact: Robert, alive.

Not only alive, but apparently feeling emboldened enough to flit back into our lives. And out again.

I opened the reply window once more. The cursor waited.

He was in *Paris*?

Those two words he'd written—*meet soon*—made it sound so.

Although Chicago was only eight hours by air.

Timbuktu, just seven.

He could be anywhere.

He was here.

He was right here, and I was going to meet him.

No. No?

No; or not yet, because what I needed to do *first* was call Eleanor.

. . .

And Eleanor's first thought was to call the embassy: they could send *Marines.* That's who the ambassador called on in an emergency, and if this wasn't one, what was?

But what *was* this? That was the question Eleanor returned to once she'd settled down. When I called her hotel, she'd flown to the store, brusquely kicked out a customer, and studied the e-mail with her reading glasses on and then with them off.

"People impersonate other people online all the time," she said.

"All this time, he *was* alive," I said. "*Is* alive."

"Neither of us are the least bit good with computers," she said, staring at the screen. "It's really not for us to say if this is genuinely him."

"It *is* for me to say. I'm his wife. Eleanor? It took me too long to accept the truth, but I did. *I was right.*"

Eleanor, who'd arrived shaken, turned paler still. "And if I have my chronology right," Eleanor said, "the girls were 'right' before you. Or rather, they were never wrong. Because they never convinced themselves he was dead."

I shook my head; I wasn't sure where this was going, but wanted to stop it before it went where it shouldn't. "Eleanor—"

I didn't have to even finish the thought.

"Of course. Absolutely not," Eleanor said. "They can't see him. Not this meeting. Not until we know it *is* him."

"It is!"

"Do you—do you want *me* to meet him?" Eleanor said, sounding uncharacteristically unsure.

"Do you *want* to meet him?"

She shook her head.

"No, I do not," she said. "I *would* do this for you, because I would do *anything* for you, but I do not want to meet him because I am enraged at him. I have that luxury. I am not his wife. I am not the mother of his children. I can indulge a pure, uncomplicated anger." She flared her nostrils, I think unconsciously. Had Robert actually been there, a brick across the head couldn't have hurt him more than the stare she now summoned. "What I think is also entirely beside the point. How do *you* feel?"

I felt queasy and nervous, furious and afraid, sad, and most unexpectedly, somewhere deep in my feet, a tremor that felt like the first flutterings of—what could *not* be happiness. And yet.

"Very strange," I said.

Eleanor looked at the e-mail one more time, scrolling up and down, deliberating. She asked if I'd gotten other e-mails. I checked; I hadn't. She said to check again. I said the next time I went into my e-mail, it was going to be to write him one.

"Okay," Eleanor said. "Maybe we don't call the Marines, or even the police, just yet. But we must have a *plan*."

And so we worked one out, starting with what to tell the girls: nothing, we agreed. Possibly nothing ever. Nothing, anyway, until we found out more. And to do that, I'd have to meet with him. In some public place, Eleanor insisted, where she herself would lurk nearby, along with—

Well, was I *sure* I didn't want to call the embassy? Perhaps they could just send "a *small* Marine," she said, "in civilian clothes—"

"The Marines have more important things to do," I said.

"Is there *anyone*?" Eleanor asked.

I thought of Laurent. George. My three customers. Declan.

"No," I told Eleanor.

"We'll make do, then," Eleanor said: a park, not too big, not too small, one with people. And benches. I would sit on a particular bench, and Eleanor and/or the cavalry would sit on another bench nearby.

I told Eleanor that a husband and wife should be allowed some time *à deux*.

"But," Eleanor said, "I just want to be there, to see . . ."

I waited.

But she just repeated herself, to herself: "To see," she said softly.

And that broke me. She wanted to be present for me, but she also wanted to be there for Robert. That she would be there, in close physical proximity, to support me in the aftermath of whatever happened would be a boon. But that *she* would see him, too—that was the real reason she wanted to go to the park.

And, I saw now, the real reason she had come to Paris. If she'd really, truly, exhaustively thought he was dead, she'd have sent the forms right away, just as she'd once sent that unfinished manuscript, the pages that once proved to her that he was alive.

"So be it," I said. "But you can't spook him. I'm *certain* that if he sees you—or a passing policeman, or a strapping crew-cutted Marine lounging nearby, bayonet fixed—he's going to keep walking."

"He won't see me," Eleanor said. "I shall be wearing the sunglasses the hotel gave me."

"*Parfait*," I said, and rose, feeling confident. This lasted until I was standing. I felt dizzy.

"Why now?" Eleanor said. "I can almost understand everything but that. Why does he want to come back and talk with you *now*?"

Perhaps he wanted to know why the magazine had taken so long preparing that piece. At the time, they'd told us the issue would be out in mere weeks. Robert, knowing what he knew of publishing, didn't believe this, and given my old neighbor's plaintive e-mail to Eleanor, it seemed like he'd been right not to believe her.

But back then, it was rush, rush, and the reporter, exceptionally eager, exceptionally young, sent Robert—his hero, it turned out—that early draft, *sans* photographs, just days after the visit.

Robert hated it, especially the *tone.*

Well, I didn't like Robert's. It was late at night, I'd been asleep.

It's like the writer thinks he knows me! he said. *On the basis of one afternoon!*

And one pony, I said. I didn't open my eyes. I could feel him sitting on the edge of the bed. The mattress slouched toward him.

How does anyone get a right to say who you are, what you are? he said.

I opened my eyes. *I married you,* I said.

Leah—

For who you are.

Were, he said.

Husband. Father. Are. I closed my eyes again.

You married a writer, he said. *And I don't think I am anymore.*

I married a shoplifter rehabilitationist, I said. *A kid-friendly kitchenista. A children's-stories-set-in-Paris connoisseur.*

(And he *was* all those things. And more. Some days, it was impossible to think about leaving him. Other days, it was all I thought about.)

I mean, he said.

I waited.

At heart, he said.

I waited.

I married you for your heart, I said. *You, your heart, mine. Your dreams, ours. That's what I mean, mean . . .*

I trailed off as *mean* began to mean its other meaning.

I felt, heard him stand.

I miss when—when we—I miss you, he said softly.

I wonder now if he meant "her," that other wife, the one I once was, the one who'd fallen for the flicker in his eyes, the one who hadn't worried what kind of fire such a flicker would start, what it would burn, how long it would take to fully catch fire.

Or the wife he later imagined, from that other life, that other Paris. That other book.

But I'm right here, I said, and rolled over.

That's what makes it so hard, he said.

Eleanor reluctantly went back to her hotel to prepare. She'd wanted to stare over my shoulder as I drafted my reply, but I repeated my earlier refusals and somehow finally struck a tone she found worth heeding.

After two minutes passed before an empty screen, I was even more glad Eleanor wasn't by my side. And here I'd been worried she would second-guess everything I'd say. Instead, I found I had nothing to say whatsoever. I heard the bell over the door jangle; for the first time, I did not answer. Or rather, for the first time, I didn't feel guilty about not answering it. Let the customer feel ignored. Let the customer ransack the store if she wanted to. I'd hire on Molly full-time.

Allo, allo? I heard after a minute passed. Then the floor creaking its pirate-ship creak. Then muttering. Then the bell again as the customer left.

Robert never suffered writer's block, or so he once claimed in a five-year-old interview published in a magazine that actually was printed: *I do not understand what people mean by writer's block unless it's a real, physical thing. If it's in your mind, great—that's where the words are, too. Just peer over the wall.* He got plenty of mocking hate mail after that; one student even gave him a brick that he'd labeled with a Sharpie: *writer's block.* Robert used it as a bookend.

As two minutes sitting before the computer turned into twelve and then twenty, I began to wonder: is *this* what happened? That a block finally came to afflict Robert, and when it did, its effect was total. That he'd peered over the wall one day and found nothing, nothing of value whatsoever. Robert would quibble with that "of value." If there *was* such a thing as writer's block, it was simply perfectionism by a clumsier name. Words were words. Creativity was creativity.

But I was more sympathetic to Robert's antagonists than his admirers on this point. There are days that a mess of words must seem irredeemably that, a mess.

I typed: *Do you remember the contretemps over writer's block?*

I deleted that and typed, *Contretemps—it's hard to remember now what French words I used back home and which I've acquired here. But do you remember the contretemps over—*

And I paused, because I no longer gave a fuck about writer's block. *Over students' use of profanity in their papers, and—*

I didn't care about that either. I was stalling. I was writing and blocking at the same time, all because I wanted to write, *do you remember the whole raging battle about sleep, about SIDS, about "Back to Sleep," and how we were supposed to put baby Ellie down on her back, but then a nurse whispered to us late one night—so early we were still in the hospital—"put her on her side" and you nodded, and the nurse left, and then we tried it, we went over to the layette where the nurse had just laid Ellie on her side, and Ellie was—she was just a peanut then, a slip of a thing, and she wobbled and rolled straight over onto her face. And you snatched her up, and she awoke crying, and it felt like hours later she fell asleep on your chest, facedown of course, burrowed into you, and we looked at each other, and I swear we both had these eyes full of tears, ready to cry, but then one of us—was it you? It would have had to have been you, I was so tired— started laughing. Just the tiniest little laugh, but then both of us were, and try as you might, you couldn't hold it in, and you* laughed and that bucked her awake, sweet girl. And she didn't cry then, she just opened her eyes wide and stretched an arm, the way you do when you've had yourself a solid little nap, and you said something like "that can't be a bad thing, waking up to laughter." And it really wasn't. I don't remember ever waking anyone up that way again or being awoken that way myself, but I remember that moment there in the hospital, every last atom of it. I remember you had been so nervous about whether we should even have kids, and I remember you holding her and saying, "you were right." I remember her and you and the almost-dark and the punch-drunk laughter and thinking, saying, "I give it all up. Whatever wonders were due me in life, whatever peace, I surrender them because I have known this." And you said—god, when did you say it?—"no, Leah, don't give any of it up." I remember the whispering, that you whispered it. So maybe it was there in the hospital. Our baby sleeping and you saying don't give anything up. And I remember thinking that you were right, that no supernatural bargains should be made involving our daughter and I remember thinking you were wrong, that I would sacrifice anything for her, everything, whatever the cost. And years later, when you left—left me, all of us, while we were sleeping—I wondered if the bill had finally come due.

I lie unasleep now, an ocean away from that life, and marvel at that bargain, how readily I struck it, how long it held. And I wonder if I can yet again mortgage whatever good I have coming to me. Because I want to, I want to say it, I want to say once more that I give it all up, just to get you back, to get us back, to get our family back to whole and your life back to what it was with us.

I do so want to meet you. But if we do, know I will ask: what could I have done? Because our children—they still make me laugh. And Ellie is still beautiful when she sleeps and sleeps only on her stomach.

And Paris conjures magic enough to confound whatever, whoever might come collecting.

I paused.

If you thought we couldn't change, we could—we did—we will.

And then I wrote, *have you?*

And then, nothing.

And then: *come back—just say how. Just say when.*

I don't get interviewed about writing, but if I did, I would say that what writers need fear most is not writer's block but writer's knives, some hammered and sharpened against that selfsame block, able to cut through anything.

Was I wrong to cut everything but the last six words of what I'd just written?

Everything. I cut the story of Ellie, of laughter, of wagers, of magic. I cut "Dear Robert" and "Love, Leah."

I cut "come back."

I cut everything until I was left with this, which I sent:

Just say how. Just say when.

CHAPTER 16

After a minute passed with no reply, I distracted myself by texting Eleanor: *sent word, awaiting word*. She immediately called and wanted details, and I told her there were none. I'd not proposed a meeting place; I'd asked him to. Eleanor began to lecture me on negotiations, how women too often fail at them and how they can and should succeed—the thrust seemed to be *take the initiative*, so I did and hung up on her. I felt bad and texted apologies. She texted back: *this is what I mean*, she said. *Never apologize.*

I checked my inbox again—the French term *boîte de réception* is so fussy, and so lovely—nothing. The bell over the door rang. I *clique*'d on my *boîte de réception*. *Rien*. Nothing. I wished that I'd shut the store while I sorted this out.

Now my phone rang. Robert? (How?)

No, just Eleanor.

To have not greeted one customer so far that day was a forgivable lapse, at least for an expatriate American shopkeeper. To have let two enter the shop without my calling out the required *bonjour* was almost grounds for deportation. But if I didn't take Eleanor's call, she'd only call again. And again.

I shouted a *bonjour* to the invisible woman (just a guess; it was quiet; men are noisy). No answer. She must have been in the far front corner or have climbed the stairs to the children's area. "*Je suis désolée,* I just have to take this call," I announced as I maneuvered out of the tiny back office. "*Une minute.*"

I answered the phone. "*Bonjour,*" I said. "I'm sorry; hello. I'm juggling things here."

"How many things?" Eleanor asked.

"Just—a customer, somewhere—"

"I've been thinking about our—about *your* plan," Eleanor said, "about leaving the girls out of the meeting. I think this is wrong. This is not just about you—it is about *all* of you, as a family. *He* needs to realize that." She paused again. "*You* need to realize that."

"Eleanor—" I said.

"No," she interrupted. "I'm certain about this. I think there's a way to stage-manage it so that you—so that you meet him *first*, but then—and we don't have to do this with a lot of *spycraft*—you and he meet on some bench, and the girls and I will be at a playground a short distance away with the twins, unless, and I advise this, we redeposit the tiny two with *their* own feckless father for the day, but in any case, once contact has been made, once you are absolutely *sure* it is him, you just—*walk* him on over to us." Off-loading the twins was a good idea, but otherwise, I hated this plan, and I'd told her so earlier. "Do you understand?" she asked.

"Eleanor—" I said, and broke off, finally having encountered my customer.

"Say you'll meet him after school, *today.* And you know what? It's fine if we have the twins in tow—let him think you've been *busy.* Because you *have.* And don't worry for a *moment* that you are hallucinating when—*if*—you see him, because I shall be there, too."

I had not been breathing then, not for a long while, and now finally drew a very deep breath in order to speak. But I couldn't.

"You forget, my dear, how easily I contend with silence," Eleanor said. "So it's agreed. I'll meet the girls right outside the door of the school and the twins outside theirs, Ellie and I will sort this all out, and then we'll go *straight* to a convenient, *strategic* park or square. I have a map. I have your brilliant girls. Okay, Leah?" I said nothing. "Oh, you're impossible. Here's what you say now: *thank you, Eleanor, sounds good, good-bye.*"

"Good—bye," I said, my voice hoarse and high.

And she may have said something else; I don't know, because I put down the phone, facedown, as though it was an old-fashioned handset, the kind that used to have a cord and a cradle and a reliable, expectant dial tone.

I heard such a tone now, it was all I could hear, and it was so loud it felt like I was vibrating, like the whole store was vibrating, like I might fall if I didn't grab hold of something, so I did—that is, I grabbed hold of my customer, not a woman but a man, one who seemed as stunned as I was.

So I hugged him. I hugged him on and on, until, finally, slowly, fearfully, as though one or both of us might break, Robert hugged me back.

I was hugging a stranger. The spread of his shoulders was wider, his chest thicker. His chin found my shoulder where it should have, but it only rested lightly there, it didn't fit. His hair, thinner, didn't smell like him. He didn't smell like him. When he spoke, though, the voice was his, and so, too, the eyes . . .

It wasn't a hallucination. He was real. He was Robert, and he was no longer my husband.

"Welcome back," I said, almost inaudibly.

He shook his head, almost invisibly.

"Welcome to Paris," he said.

And I laughed, one laugh, which became crying, which became hacking bent-over sobs. I hadn't cried like this since my parents' funerals and I'm not sure I cried as hard then. I cried so hard now it hurt, burned my throat, burned the muscles of my abdomen, my ribs. Seeing Robert for the first time in forever: he hadn't died; I was about to. It was too hard. It was too much.

He didn't know what to do. He said my name softly, he put a tentative hand on my shoulder, he finally went in search of tissues, and then I had my breath again. I couldn't speak, but I could see him, and the tissues, and it was better. I closed and opened my eyes. Still there, Robert. So, too, the roar in my ears, though subsiding. Not quite enough to make out what he was saying, but enough to hear my own heart, *thump, thump, thump*, enough to hear me say, *"Robert?"* And then the roar subsided further, and I could hear him speak.

"I'm sorry," he said.

I nodded.

"Are you—are you all right?" I said.

I looked at him looking at me. It was him, but it was also not him. He looked concerned, but also curious, like, *hey, this is interesting.* As opposed to, *hey, this is Leah.*

"Maybe we could go—for a walk?" Robert said.

I felt faint. I needed something to steady me, us, and then I looked up and saw that we were in a bookstore. *My* bookstore. My books. My life, now.

"Do you want to see the store first?" I said, my voice hollow. He nodded. I'd been sitting on the floor; I got to my feet, pretending not to see the hand he extended.

We stepped along gingerly, like we'd just tumbled out of a lunar module. Or maybe it was that we were scuba divers, a strange feeling of being both totally immersed but totally encapsulated, separate. It's the only explanation I have for why we didn't immediately start talking about the girls, where he'd gone, where he was going. We didn't talk because we couldn't, not yet.

And so the bookstore spoke up. Around us raged thousands upon thousands of pages of argument. Of stories. Of journeys. Of husbands and wives and spiders in classrooms in Connecticut. I told him Alice Mattison was selling well, and he smiled. I pulled down Grace Paley for him and he saddened. He flipped to "Wants" and started to read it, and I did, too, and then we both couldn't. He closed the book. I described our quirky geographic shelving system, and he said it sounded brilliant. I took him to Sweden, showed him Tove Jansson, and before I could explain who she was he said, *Moomin!*—and of course. Robert knew books. He *loved* them, and couldn't resist as the shop pulled him in deeper.

I'm so sorry, Robert said, not because he'd gone but because, I knew, he had come back and was about to go again.

I went to England. He followed me, but then stopped mid-store, as though afraid what I would pull down next. So was I. Before I knew what I was doing, I reached down an armful of cheap Shakespeare paperbacks and threw them at him. And the rest of the row. And another. And some hardbacks. And more paperbacks. And then Canada, for a giant book, *Sculpture of the Eskimo*, which thudded against him. Alice Mattison flew well, as did Grace Paley. The women knew their way. I went to the window display of *Madeline* books. They threw easy and fast, like Frisbees, like fine china, like saw blades. I couldn't find *The Red Balloon,* but here was a book about lollipops. Some books were too heavy to throw; they fell. The others tumbled about him. For a while, he let them pile against him, and then, as the barrage continued, he cowered and I bounced them off his shoulder, his back, his head. *Please stop*, he said, and I did, not because he'd asked but because I was exhausted. The door rang open. A French voice said, "*bonjour?*" I roared back, "*fermé!*" The person left. Robert went to the door, locked it, and turned the sign. I went behind the counter and sat, head in my hands, and let him do whatever it was he was doing. Picking up, it sounded like. And when he was done, there was a silence, like he was waiting for me to look up at him again, but I didn't. I heard the quiet tramp of his shoes up the spiral staircase to the children's section. He was gone five minutes or an hour. When he came down, I finally raised my head. His face was red, from crying, shame, or the books. One lucky volume had given him a good scrape down his cheek and another had caught part of an eye.

"Can we talk?" he said, sounding like the old Robert, with the old question marks.

And me sounding like the old me: "okay."

"Here?" he asked.

"Here," I said, and waited for him to tell me why he'd disappeared.

Instead—and this was a final clue—he told me how.

That early April morning in Milwaukee, he'd gone out for his normal dawn run, no great adventure on his mind. Then he'd passed the harbor, he'd seen the boats.

It was too windy a day. But also too stormy a season, at least for him, at least creatively. Too stormy and too long. Ludwig Bemelmans had found oil painting in the last part of his life. He did so almost with gritted teeth, the work taxed him like nothing before, but at least he had found something that fed him, freed him. There in Milwaukee, Robert was still gritting, still looking.

Looking, specifically, at the harbor that morning. There was the water, the boats, and the solution: before doing anything else, he would clear his head with a morning sail. No one was about, but he had the gate code, knew where they hid the key to the gear shed. He got everything he needed (except the required companion sailor), signed out a boat in the log, nosed his way out of the marina, then the harbor, and this all felt so good, he had a wild thought: I'll sail clear across the lake to Michigan! A sailaway writeaway. It was a small boat—too small—but he wouldn't be the first to do it. With winds the way they were, he'd make it across in a little less than a day. And he almost did. But then an errant wave took hold of the bow and yanked. Into the water he went, though not before the mast knocked him unconscious.

The lake revived him, but Robert couldn't right the boat. He spent the night crouched atop the upturned hull, waves sometimes tumbling him back into the water. It was late spring, but the water felt like winter. With each successive tumble he grew colder, weaker, less certain he'd be able to climb back atop the hull, less certain he still wanted to.

But then it was morning, and with light came land. "I got to the shallows, the beach," he said, "and that's when it started—when the world and I—when things stopped making sense. I stumbled out of the water, soaking wet, walking through this little park, then some trailer neighborhood. It didn't look like Wisconsin—it definitely wasn't Milwaukee—but I thought, I can't have made it to Michigan. And at first, I didn't want to ask. It was eerie. I saw people, but it was like they didn't see me."

I wondered what those people saw. A soaking-wet stranger walking past their windows? I guess I would have decided I hadn't seen him, either. As long as that man keeps walking, they must have thought, maybe he'll keep walking out of our lives. And he did.

"I walked myself dry," he said. "Which made me only more invisible. It gave me an idea. The idea. I mean, I wasn't thinking about sailing when I started running that morning, and I wasn't thinking about Michigan when I started sailing."

But he said he had been thinking, a lot, about how he "clouded our lives," and so once he started going, he let himself keep going. Because he'd had the sudden sense while jogging that morning that if he'd rounded the corner and headed home—or if he'd turned the sailboat around an hour into his trip—if he'd gone back to Milwaukee at that instant, who knew what would happen?

Even he didn't know, just that it would not be good. He'd reached "that place." He didn't say where it was or what he meant, but he didn't have to. It wasn't on our old maps. It was in his head; it had overtaken his head, actually, and now it stole, terribly, into mine. I saw what he saw, what he'd thought through, what would leave his body prone on some floor, or lowered by firemen from a rafter. Or something else. There were so many ways.

But there were so many reasons, three in particular, why *not* to do this, think this.

"You would have *never* . . ." I started to say, but stopped, because, of course, he hadn't. I'd wanted evidence he'd loved the girls. This was. But also wasn't.

He shook his head. "And I didn't want—I didn't want medicine, doctors, a hospital; there would have been a hospital for sure, right?" He pointed to his head. "A mental—?" He couldn't say it. "Someplace like that. Someplace that would have only made it worse. And I wasn't—I wasn't *sick*, I was just . . ."

Selfish, I thought. Or, put another way, yes, sick. Head-sick enough to leave a family who loved him.

But he was well enough, there in Michigan, to find his way to a shelter. And if he'd stayed longer there, the police probably would have found him, but someone came looking for pickers the next morning. Berries. One kind, then another. I waited to hear him talk about desperate attempts to reach us, but instead I heard about six weeks of blast-furnace sun, black nights in cinder-block dorms. He wasn't the only guy there who didn't have papers, didn't want to talk, was willing to work for half the pay, cash, as a result. And then the crop was in. The crew was moving on, moving south. He thought he'd go with them. But first, home: he wasn't going to pick berries forever, but he decided he was going to be on the road for a while. Some kind of permanent writeaway. New material, a new project.

And so, he said, "I had to find you. To tell you. In person."

I tried to imagine how such a preposterous scene would have unfolded. Exactly, I decided, as it was unfolding now.

Another scene, one more haunting, more vivid: his post-Michigan return to Milwaukee, our neighborhood, our home. His discovery that we weren't there.

He said he'd walked the little retail strip near our house, his identity cloaked by sunglasses, long hair, weeks' worth of beard, and no one noticed him. No one noticed him and he noticed no "missing!" or "have you seen?" posters and we were gone. He began to feel soaking wet again.

I found it hard to believe him. I found it harder not to. Still, I tried.

"You came back? All you had to do was walk up the street—ring a doorbell, ask the renters, or the neighbors," I said. "Walk up to campus and ask Eleanor—"

He shook his head. "Eleanor would have eaten me alive."

"And then *helped* you—"

But he didn't need Eleanor, he said. He'd figured it out for himself. (He spoke more quickly, quietly now, as though talking to himself.) We were gone. Gone-gone. And there was only one place we could have gone. Paris. Those tickets. He'd said he wouldn't buy them, but then he had; he'd hidden the code in the cereal box, and we must have found it. He'd wanted to be there for that moment, and he hadn't been. But that didn't mean the girls and I wouldn't still follow through. Did it? We were doing our part. He'd have to do his.

And so he had. I looked at him. He'd gotten money, a passport, a ticket—all of this without triggering a single alert on a single screen. Or maybe the police hadn't put him on a watch list. Maybe, at some crucial juncture, the authorities had thought *me* the liar. The wife, she was the crazy one. Who *wouldn't* run away from this lady?

In Paris, he found his way to, of course, a bookstore. He'd heard Shakespeare and Company had a cot or two for bookish people passing through, so long as you didn't mind a few chores, and he didn't. His first free afternoon, he went looking, preparing himself for the likelihood he'd never find us.

It took him all of an hour.

He found us, but he didn't come in, because he was beyond certain now that he was hallucinating. He'd wandered past our house in Milwaukee, except it wasn't our house anymore. Renters lived there. I *had* once threatened to leave, he said—I didn't nod, didn't blink, just listened—had I? What happened when? What *had* happened? He was no longer sure. Back home, before everything got really bad, he'd started this manuscript about a family in Paris. And so once he was *in* Paris, he'd gone to this street he'd picked off a map while writing— Saint Lucy, the patron saint of writers!—which meant Madame's store didn't surprise him, he'd seen one like it online, that's why he'd set the story here, but—inside—these people—they looked like us.

He had stood across the street from our store, he said, and stared inside, awestruck, terror-struck. His unfinished manuscript come to life: finding us was evidence he'd finally lost his mind. He ran away, but he couldn't stay away. He started a hundred e-mails to me, to Eleanor, but deleted each one. We'd have thought he was crazy, he said. One day, when there was no sign of us, just some old woman at the register, he'd gone in, scribbled an *I'm sorry* in a book of his. At last, he'd found a book of his on the shelf.

"And I put it in the window after that," I said.

"Did you know it was me?" he said.

I said nothing.

"You did," he said.

"I did," I said. "But I also thought it *couldn't* have been you." Or shouldn't have been.

"I—that's how I felt, about all of it. The girls—Ellie, Daphne"— he could barely speak the words—"I wasn't even sure it *was* them. They're so . . ." I wanted to say, *we weren't sure it was you,* but of course the girls had been, long before me. "I thought, it *couldn't* be them behind the glass, it couldn't be *you* behind the glass. But it was you behind the glass."

"And still you didn't reach out."

He shook his head: "You would have—I thought you would—it would—all disappear. Samuel Taylor Coleridge—this is crazy but— there was this prize—it doesn't matter. Coleridge, this famous poem, he had it all in his head, ready to write, got fifty-four lines down, and then—someone walked in—the dream disappeared."

"We didn't."

"I was sure you would. I got as close to the bubble as I could without popping it."

"Until now."

"Leah, I don't know how to say . . ." He drew a little circle on the counter. Just like Daphne. "But you all looked, you *look* very happy here," he said.

"'*Happy*'?" I said, indignant, because I'd become that Parisian. Happiness is an American emotion, if not affliction. It prevents Americans from seeing how difficult this city, its people, its landlords, UPS drivers, and doctors are, how dangerous its bridges, its river, its bookstores. How fragile its every last stone, story, or film.

And yet, as I'd been reminded, Charlemagne used to walk here. And Bemelmans and Lamorisse and Gertrude Stein and Pablo

Picasso and Joan of Arc and Marie Curie and Edith Wharton and Janet Flanner and James Baldwin and James Joyce and Sylvia Beach, and now me. And Robert.

"We are happy," I said slowly. "Not happy all the time, but the girls have figured some things out. It's been an adjustment. We're still adjusting." I could see the words piling up ahead of me, and I stumbled as I tried to avoid saying them: "and, and now, now that you're back, it'll be, we'll be . . ."

And there it was. The pause. The moment when his eyes, after finding every last place in the store but my face, finally found my eyes. Found them, watched, and wondered. *Was this the real Leah?*

Was this the real Robert? Was this really our life? And how much better would it be with him back? He could—we could—*Robert* could get an apartment nearby, maybe. We'd work something out.

That pause, and then Robert spoke.

"That's what I thought," he said.

"No," I said. "No—listen, Robert—the girls . . ." Was this why he'd surprised me midday, to be sure the girls would be away at school?

"They're—they're doing better without me."

"You can tell that from the sidewalk, from stalking us?"

"Leah, I'm sorry—of course—I miss—there's not even a word for what I feel—"

"'Guilty'? 'Ashamed'?" He nodded, but I shook my head. "*Fight*," I said, and I meant with me, against me, but also, of course, for me.

"Leah—all those writeaways," he said. "I thought they were as much for you all as for me."

"Fuck you."

"I did!" he said. "I needed them—yes. Absolutely. More and more. But I needed them because working at home—or seeing you all at home after working—I saw you see my face, and—I—I didn't like what I saw there. When the girls needed help, they never called for me."

"'Dad! Daddy!' echoed through the house the minute you came home!"

"But they—"

"But they leapt into your *arms*."

"And every time, I thought I'd drop them. I thought I'd disappoint them. I *knew* I was disappointing you."

"You did not."

He stared, waited for the lie I suddenly couldn't say.

"You said I was dead," he said.

"What?"

"The lady up the street here, sells mops?" he said. "I asked what time the bookstore opened and she said she didn't know, 'sometimes open, sometimes close, but hard for her, bookstore lady; her husband dead.'"

"For the longest time," I said, "I tried to convince myself you were."

He laughed, or tried to. "For the longest time, I was sure, too. I mean, up until five minutes ago, when you started throwing those books. They hurt—"

"Sorry—"

"No, it was—I deserved it, and worse, and maybe there's an essay in there somewhere about how e-books will never hurt as much, they don't have the heft . . ."

A pause.

"You're writing again," I said.

A pause.

He nodded his head left, then right. Yes and no.

"That's great," I said. "You . . ." But I wasn't sure what I was going to say, because it seemed like I was sliding toward some sort of equation: you left us, and writing, art, life became possible again.

"Robert, is everything all right? Because—"

"Everything is okay," he said. "Just okay, but okay is much better than it's been. Everything was not okay for a while."

"Because they've got doctors here, too. Medicine. Psychologists. Funnily enough, we've met one or two."

"No—I mean, I'm not—I'm not in that place anymore. Not right now. Like I said, when I went running that morning, sailing, it was bad. I wasn't looking to drown, but I wasn't necessarily looking to come back, either. I thought I'd let the universe decide."

"Don't involve the universe."

"Let the lake decide."

"The *lake*?" I said. "I didn't get a say?"

"I knew what you'd say."

"Is that why you didn't call?"

"I did call!" he said. "From the last pay phone on earth. Long before I got back to Milwaukee. Hours after I left the water. On the way to the shelter. Before the berries. I saw the area code. It's when I figured out I was in Michigan. I called collect. No one answered."

"You tried *once*? You're supposed to call back. To have found a fucking library and e-mailed."

He shook his head. "I've got no excuse, or I just gave it to you. I wasn't in my right head. I didn't want to die, but I did want to be alone. I knew if I came back—'*Robert,*' '*Daddy*'"—and now his eyes filled, finally—"you'd just want to save me. And I didn't want—"

"*Enough*," I said.

"It was already too much."

It *was* too much. In our first days together in Milwaukee, I remember looking at Robert in his all-but-bare apartment, huddled at that cheap desk, surrounded by his stalagmites of books, and thinking he looked so lonely, so alone. But that was nothing, could be nothing, compared to what he felt now, out in the world. I didn't want to know the answer to the next question I asked, but I couldn't not ask it.

"Robert, the girls? How can you bear to be apart from them, to not smell them, hear them laugh . . ." As I said this, his lips moved, but I couldn't hear anything. It was like the girls' old Whisper Theater, all hush and hiss, every syllable so important, intent, unintelligible. Until it finally was.

I loved you. I love you. I love them. Ellie, Daphne. You. And you, Leah. You.

I think I heard that. I know I did, but I leaned in close to hear him, and that became a hug, which silenced him. In the hush, I thought of the girls whispering stories, our little bedtime cocoon, wondering what he'd seen when he poked his head in all those nights, what he'd heard.

What could I say now to him that would make him stay? Did I want him to? I didn't know. If I kept him from leaving, it would be the most loving thing I had ever done for him. And the cruelest thing I'd ever do to the girls. Because as soon as we got him back—I could see this, feel this, taste it in my throat—he'd go again. Maybe years. Maybe forever.

Still, I said it. "Stay."

He shook his head. "Leah, I can't—"

"See the girls," I said.

His shoulders hunched forward like I'd hit him.

"They're all grown up," I said.

"They're beautiful."

"It's Paris," I said.

"It's you," he said.

I thought, this is like the end of the film, not a DVD, but a film, thirty-five-millimeter celluloid, twenty-four frames per second flying by until the reel runs out, *tickety, tickety, tickety*—

But it wasn't that at all. It was a book, and it was ending.

"Parents stick around," I said.

He chuffed.

The shift in tone, the disappearance of tears, was so abrupt it took me a moment to follow. Then I did.

"Okay, no, look—yours didn't—*mine* didn't." He stared at me, cornered. Defiant. I had to fight to not look away. "I refuse to admit we were bad parents," I said. "That I was. That *you* were. When you were around, you were great. And you were around a lot."

"Maybe too much."

"*What?*"

"My writing, work, all those years? It only got worse."

I looked at him square. "You cannot, you *will* not, blame us for that."

"I can't and don't and won't. It was my own fault. I wasn't doing the work."

I meant what I said next. "Robert, the work? Okay, I know, but— who cares? Switch to plumbing. Or painting. Or just cooking for kids. The world has plenty of books. Including some great ones of yours. It's okay if it doesn't get more—"

I didn't hear that I'd added *from you* until I saw it in his face. And once I did, I tried to blurt a retraction, but he waved it aside, not angry now, just exhausted. "I know," he said. "I know it's okay with the world."

He took a breath, looked outside.

"I miss the picnic table. The trash barrel. The empty country road." He looked back at me. "I miss Paris. Wisconsin."

"Robert," I said. "That was—"

"Years ago. But I went back once, one of my 'writeaways.' I never told you—I should have—but I shouldn't have gone back. Table's gone. Barrel's gone. Corn's gone." He exhaled. "I wasn't even sure I was in the right place, but the map said I was."

I didn't need the map to tell me. He had been there, was there now. I could see it in his face. And I could remember that night, that moon, those kisses, that heat.

"Ticket's gone." His voice was very quiet now.

"Tickets?" I asked.

"Ticket. I . . ." He stopped. "I'd bought you a ticket to Paris. To Paris, France. Way back when. Before that trip we took to Paris, Wisconsin. You'd never been to Paris, and I was going to give it to you there, that night, in that Paris. Between savings, what space I had on my credit card, I had only had enough for one round-trip, but I thought, that's enough, for now, *she'll* go, she'll finally go, and then I thought—"

"Robert "

"Then, that night, I looked at you and I thought, 'don't be stupid! Paris? She'll never come back.' And I stared at you and you stared at me and then you were talking nonstop about marriage, and I couldn't believe my luck—this amazing, crazy woman—right here, she wants me to ask her to marry her? And I'm going to put her on a plane? Let her fly away? And we made love and we made our deal and you dozed and I tore up the ticket and threw it into the field, promising myself I would make it up to you somehow, someday, write or make something so incredible it would change our lives. That we'd get here."

"Robert," I whispered.

"*I'm sorry*. That's what I've been trying to say. For years."

"Robert," I said. "We're here. We made it."

He shook his head. "You did."

My cell rang. He looked at the door.

"Stay," I said.

He stared at me.

"Just tonight."

"I have to go."

"Listen to me."

"Leah, I can't—"

His voice was rising and so was mine. "I can't believe we're having this conversation," I said. "That you're here. That you're going to try to leave again after giving me—us—all of twenty minutes to work it out."

The phone stopped ringing.

"I've had a long time to think—"

"I haven't!" I said. "How about an hour? A week?"

I looked toward the door now, too. Why couldn't the girls just walk in *now*?

He closed his eyes then, and I don't know what he saw. Me or that picnic table or that field outside Paris, Wisconsin. Or if he saw Ellie or Daphne, or wherever it was he was headed next. I don't know if he saw that he'd been a good father once, and might yet be again. I squinted hard. I wanted to see it.

"Leah," he said. "Maybe we could—"

The phone rang again. Twice in two minutes?

Eleanor. The caller ID display dredged up a recent photo in case I'd forgotten who the unforgettable Eleanor was. I showed Robert. He managed a kind of smile.

"You know, she's in France," I said.

The smile fled.

Then Ellie's number and face appeared on the phone's screen alongside Eleanor's. Robert rocked back.

I'm too technologically illiterate to do what I did next on purpose, but I somehow managed to answer the phone in such a way that I was speaking to both of them.

"*Oui?*" I said, lifting the phone to my ear.

"Peter—" Ellie said.

"Annabelle—" Eleanor said.

"Where are you?" I said. The panic in their voices made the phones disappear; it was as though they were standing right there with me. But they weren't. Only Robert. "What's going on?" I said.

"Mom!" Ellie said.

"They're gone," Eleanor said.

CHAPTER 17

Peter and Annabelle had it, whatever they call it—twintelligence, the special understanding that twin children seem to possess. This granted them special survival skills. Or so I prayed as the story was now recounted in detail. (Too much detail, but Eleanor and Ellie kept correcting and augmenting each other's tales.)

After Eleanor had collected Ellie, Daphne, and the twins, she announced that they would make the most of the afternoon's sunshine—our first in days—by stopping off at a small park. Peter, eyeing an opportunity in my absence, nominated the Square du Temple, a compact *parc* about a kilometer from the store, with a forbidden pond. Annabelle readily agreed.

None of this interested Ellie, who suggested Grenoble and stomped off, leaving Daphne to explain to Eleanor that this wasn't the name of a park but a town in the French Alps, about eight hours away by bus (they'd once taken a class trip there) or three hours by high-speed rail, the TGV (an option I'd not paid for).

Eleanor proposed a compromise. They would go to the park *first*, and then, if there was time, to the train station to *look* at a "high train." Peter didn't budge until Eleanor wondered aloud if they might take the Métro *to* the park? Sold. Even Daphne agreed.

Not Ellie. She looked up the route on her phone and announced that the Métro made no sense: getting there would require three trains and thirty minutes; walking would take hardly half that time.

Eleanor said she would buy Ellie "whatever you want most in the world" if she accompanied them on the Métro. After some reflection, Ellie agreed.

I wonder what Ellie—or Daphne—thought of as they descended into the Métro and wove their way through the crowd to the platform. What they wanted most was not for sale.

Nor was what Peter wanted—"to take the TGV under the sea to New York"—but before Ellie could explain this was *impossible*, Peter and Annabelle disappeared.

Not poof, like magic, but slam, like the subway car's door muscling closed on the late-afternoon crush, splitting the group: the twins inside, on the train; Eleanor, Daphne, and Ellie on the platform, screaming. Impossible.

As the train slid away, the argument began. Daphne said everything would be okay; the plan had only been to go one stop before changing trains. Ellie said Peter wanted to go to *New York*; the *plan* should have been to walk. Daphne pointed out that there was an *avenue New York* across from the Eiffel Tower; Ellie said the TGV didn't go there.

Daphne said there was a system, a family emergency plan, for this specific scenario, which called for whoever wound up on the train to get off at the next stop, whatever that stop was, and wait, for however long that took.

Ellie said Daphne had confused something she'd read in a book for *real life*, which made sense because Daphne *was the most like Dad* and had *lost a lot of her grip on reality at the hospital*.

And then Daphne had done something awful . . .

"What's going on?" Robert whispered.

"The twins . . ." I said. I held the phone to my chest to mute it. "They're—they wanted to get on the TGV—but they got on the Métro—and—"

"Twins?" he said.

"Kids. Little. We watch them. For money. Because—"

"The girls were coming to see—me? Us? Here?"

"For fuck's sake, Robert," I said. "Eleanor was taking them to a neutral space, a park. She thought if we—if we all met there—"

"Meet them, now?" Robert said, nervous in a new way, scanning the store, even backing up a pace.

I shook my head. My great moral conundrum of moments ago had been transformed into logistics. "They got on a train to go to the park, the doors closed too soon, and the twins' train left the station."

"How old are they?" he said.

"You don't even remember," I said.

"The twins," he said, quietly adding, "Ellie turns sixteen in the fall. Daphne turned thirteen this spring."

I heard Ellie's voice shouting at me from the phone. I lifted it back up to speak, but when I did, I heard Eleanor.

"Okay, okay," Eleanor said. Her department meeting fracas voice. "Ellie is *fine*, okay?" Eleanor said. "Moving on."

"Wait, what happened to Ellie?"

"Daphne pushed her; she fell. Near the tracks, so it was dramatic."

"Oh my god—"

"Not *onto* the tracks, just near the edge of the platform, which Daphne should *not* have done, as *many* people then pointed out to us in various tongues. But Daphne was angry and scared, and my god-daughter was in one of her less helpful moods. Anyway, to review: Ellie is *fine*, and it was all to the good because it finally got us the attention of a policeman, which had been *rather* hard to do. They've issued a lost-child alert, or so I am given to understand."

Ellie broke in. "Mom, the gypsies—" Her slip told me that she was as panicked as I.

"Ellie," I said. "Did Peter and Annabelle know where you were going? Would they know to get off?"

"It was so stupid. Three trains to go five hundred meters," Ellie said. "I don't know—he was talking about the TGV, and Grenoble"—*and New York*, called Daphne from the background—"I don't even know if they know our phone numbers."

"I'm coming to meet you," I said.

"The police say to go home," Eleanor said.

"Please tell them off in your best department-chair voice," I said. "Ellie, do *not* call George."

"Leah," Eleanor said. "I know this has been a lot, of late. I *know* you've been through a lot, but this is out of our hands now."

"George is their *father*," Ellie shouted.

"Leah," Eleanor said. "I need to ask—"

I pressed the red FERMÉ button on my phone.

And then, another surprise, quieter, but in its way, no less startling. Before me stood the old Robert, in full. Calm and overly earnest, entirely and unemotionally focused on the task at hand.

"Leah, what shall we do?" Robert asked.

It almost worked. The sudden return of the man I'd married, and fought with, and made love to, and had children with, and wrapped presents with, and held birthday parties with and for, toasted to through one success after another after another after another until there was nothing left to toast with, or to—had this been the man I'd come to Paris with, not in misguided pursuit *of*, this would be the moment we'd embrace and cry and set about finding these children.

It almost worked, but it didn't. Instead of crying, I began running. Out the door, up the sidewalk.

He caught up with me in front of Madame Grillo's. "Okay," he said. "I'm not going to tell you not to run."

"You're not going to tell me anything," I said.

"What did they say?" he said.

"They said—who? The police? The police apparently told them to go home, as if that made sense."

"Do these twins know your address?" he said.

"Yes," I said. "And if they don't know the address, they know the name of the store. They're not idiots. Nor is their father. Or maybe he is, having entrusted their care to the likes of us. Me. Shit." I stopped running.

"Shouldn't we—you stay at home?" he said.

Home. "No," I said. "I'm going to the Métro station, the top of the street. In case they knew to come home, or in case they told someone where they were going."

I looked at him. I closed my eyes.

"We'll go back," he said. "We'll go back to the store, you and I, and we'll wait."

I listened, I heard that *you and I,* and those three words—that one word, *and*—summoned almost twenty years, a whole world. I heard it, I saw it, and then I didn't. I had moved a family to Paris, I had fed and clothed and schooled two daughters and, until today, successfully minded two more children, and I had done it *myself,* with only the occasional help of a handsome young MBA student and a New Zealand expat and an aloof old woman who once loved books. I once loved Robert. I once threatened to leave. But I hadn't, and if he hadn't, we could have worked together on staying together, he and I. I opened my eyes.

"*You* go back to the store," I said. "*I'm* going to the Métro. I'm calling Ellie and Eleanor and Daphne and telling them to go looking."

"Go looking?" he said.

"The girls have gotten really good at it," I said.

And, I suppose because this part of the story had yet to be written, he said nothing in reply.

And because I didn't know what part of the story this was, I didn't say good-bye.

Peter and Annabelle weren't at our home stop, Saint-Paul, so I raced to the park they'd been aiming for, Square du Temple. No sign of them—and luckily, no *pompier*-frogmen dredging the pond. I went back to Saint-Paul and boarded a train eastward, bound for the end of the line. Eleanor said she'd go west but wound up going south—indeed, Ellie later had to go deep into the Left Bank in search of her godmother, who'd gotten lost trying to follow an invisible trail of bread crumbs back to Erdem's backyard.

Prior to that, Ellie had been thrown off a series of interurban trains at the Gare de Lyon, where the TGV launches for Grenoble. She'd run up and down the aisles of one car after another, yelling *Quelqu'un a vu des jumeaux, de faux jumeaux—très jeunes?*

Daphne, like me, went to our Métro line's eastern terminus, Château de Vincennes, where the twins would have been forced to disembark if they'd not already. I was sure they'd be on the platform. They weren't, Daphne was, and so we retreated, one station at a time, toward Saint-Paul and our store on the rue Sainte-Lucie-la-Vierge, searching each platform for a sign of them. We saw a number of policemen out and about, and Daphne asked them if they were looking for the twins. They all answered her kindly, but scorned me, the American mother who had lost two children.

I received a call asking me to report to the Préfecture de Police immediately—they had not found the twins yet, but there was paperwork to be done, and it was best done now. I hung up without letting them finish. The next call came from the American embassy: Carl. I was startled by his powers of inference, that he knew I was in trouble. Did he, like Asif, have secret cameras installed, too? But no, Eleanor had called the embassy. Carl had gotten wind, and was concerned: a woman named Eleanor had said something about my having a *husband*? And that I adopted two British children? I should come into the embassy to speak with a case officer at my *earliest* opportunity. Carl assured me he would sit in on the interview.

"Thank you," I said, "but I really need to find these children."

Carl replied, "We do maintain a list of English-speaking counsel," and I thought, *not another counselor.* But then I realized he was talking about an attorney. I hung up.

Daphne and I exited at our home stop, Saint-Paul. We checked the *boucherie* and the *boulangerie* and the *chocolatier.* We went to the carousel and Chef Picard's. We went back to the Square du Temple, the twins' school, and then the girls' school, and then circled around the block to Eleanor's hotel. We stopped in every store on the street.

All this resulted in nothing other than so delaying our return to the store that we arrived long after the twins themselves had arrived. They had found their own way home, where a kind man had received them, read to them from one book and then another and then *The Red Balloon*, and then left them all alone in a warm, bright store, guarded by books.

I hugged the twins for so long that Daphne asked me what I was doing, and then I hugged her, too. She started crying then, and apologized for pushing Ellie so near to the tracks. I told her I understood—because I did; I even appreciated the camaraderie of someone else whose anger had sloshed out of its container—and told her that the person she really needed to apologize to was her sister.

"*Mais Zeus!*" Annabelle said, overhearing the story. "Zeus" was Daphne's name for the perpetually stricken man paired with a lightning bolt whose image appears alongside all electrified tracks. NE PAS DESCENDRE SUR LA VOIE, DANGER DE MORT, the yellow signs say. Straightforward enough, and yet, for me, very French: the signs are subtle, the sans serif typeface amiable and quiet, there's no *point d'exclamation!* You either pay attention or, like Daphne, you briefly don't.

"*Ecoutez!*" Peter said. "*Qui est le nouvel monsieur à la librairie? Il est très gentil.*"

There had been a new man in the store, very nice. But who was he?

"*Nouvel monsieur?*" I said. "*Qui est-ce?* What are you talking about?"

When Daphne and I had reached the store, it was empty—or it looked empty. The sign had been turned to FERMÉ, and the door was locked. I had unlocked it, and as soon as the bell above the door sounded, Peter and Annabelle had come racing down the spiral stairs.

"Oh, he's gone now," Annabelle said. "He said that you would be home soon. And you were!"

"Did you hire someone new? *Est-il le nouveau Declan?*" Annabelle asked.

Daphne looked at me with her wide, wise, and, I now saw, forever-sad eyes. I wondered if she knew. Who had taken in the twins, asked them for a tour of the store, asked them about their favorite books, produced a pair of *Lion* candy bars that they ate readily. But Daphne said nothing. And so, instead of studying the twins' faces, fresh from recounting this amazing story, I studied Daphne's. If Ellie or Eleanor had been there, it would have all been different.

But Eleanor was still lost and Ellie was off retrieving her, and it was just Daphne and me and the twins. And Daphne said nothing, so I said nothing.

I didn't tell the twins *that was the girls' father!* I didn't ask them why he thought he could leave them in the store—alone!—after they'd just been found. I didn't ask them for details about what the man looked like or what he said or what he'd touched, where he'd sat, where his fingerprints might now linger. The twins said that he'd read some books to them, and then went downstairs while they read to themselves.

"Where's Ellie and *Tante* Eleanor?" Peter asked.

"Is the man coming back?" Annabelle said.

Before I could answer, Daphne jumped in.

"No," she said.

This stopped me—because it was true, because to hear someone other than me say it aloud made it more true—but it merited hardly a shrug from the twins, who asked to go back upstairs to the children's area. I nodded. Daphne and I watched them disappear.

"It wasn't him, Mom," Daphne said. "That man, the one who stayed with the twins."

I wasn't sure if I should say anything, if this was a dialogue she was having with herself—and if so, that it would be better if I didn't interfere. I lowered my eyes.

But when I looked up, she was looking at me, waiting.

"I know," I said.

"If it *was* him," she said, "he wouldn't have left."

I just shook my head.

"Not without leaving a note," she said, but she didn't quite say it like that; she added a question mark, and it hung in the air between us like a tiny bent pin, useless, dangerous. *Had* he left a note? What would it have said *this* time? What would I want such a note to say?

I couldn't say, only that it would have to be many, many pages longer than the little scraps of paper he once left.

What would Daphne want it to say? That I knew specifically. Not six letters, but three words.

Be back soon!

She was still looking at me. I'd been distractedly answering my own questions without answering hers: *would my father leave without leaving a note?*

"No," I said, and caught myself as my voice rose, as another question mark wavered between us. "Absolutely not."

I called the police to let them know all was well. The police called the embassy. Carl called and asked me to confirm all was well. *"That* was a close one," he said, and for a second, I thought he was referring to Robert. *Yes,* I said.

Ellie wanted to go out to "celebrate" and of course she did; she had ventured out on her own and rescued Eleanor, she had managed to not fall onto the train tracks, she had achieved some sort of rapprochement with Daphne, she had set out in search of the two twins, and though she hadn't found them, here they were, safe and sound and smiling.

And, the most difficult achievement of all (though she did not realize this), she'd not set eyes on her father. She listened to the twins' story of the courteous man and immediately determined that it was Carl. Peter and Annabelle disagreed, but without fuss. Ellie was *la grande sœur*, and they'd long ago learned that she was always right, even when she was very wrong.

I had no interest in dining out, and neither did Eleanor. I wanted to burrow. I wanted to lock the door to the store and then the door to our living quarters and drag a box or two of books over to barricade ourselves in. I wanted a frozen *fête de Picard* and I wanted a lot of wine to go with it. As we started our way upstairs, Eleanor hung back and whispered a suggestion: perhaps Ellie could babysit while Eleanor and I ducked out for a *tête à tête*? I was a step above her on the staircase, and so when I turned to tell her no—eventually, yes, but not right now—I kissed Eleanor on the forehead.

"Don't get fresh with me," Eleanor said, and that somehow made me smile.

I lifted the no-eating-anywhere-but-the-kitchen rule, and we wolfed down one of Picard's more American creations—*Penne rigate au jambon et fromage,* the polyglot label cloaking mac and cheese with bacon bits—while we watched Taiwanese director Hou Hsiao-Hsien's 2007 homage to Lamorisse, *Flight of the Red Balloon*, which Eleanor had checked out of her hotel's lending library.

We didn't finish. Deep into the film, dinner discarded and forks sticking to pillows and carpet, Peter and Annabelle falling asleep, Daphne watching intently, Eleanor watching all of *us* intently, Ellie got up and turned it off.

"There's not enough balloon," she said.

Among other things, Hou Hsiao-Hsien's film involves an absent (though not unreachable) father. I don't know if that's the real reason Ellie turned it off. I also don't know the real reason Robert left. I do know what I saw, and that was someone who was very afraid. Maybe then, there, he was only afraid of me, but I think he was afraid of all of us, of how much we loved him. Of how much that love required his presence. And I think—strangest of all—that he was afraid of Paris. He was afraid of the magic here, which had not only made his wife into a bookstore owner and his daughters into *Parisiennes*, but his fiction into reality.

Except it hadn't, not word-for-word. At one point, for example, not long after Robert's manuscript has the little bedraggled family arrive in Paris, they go exploring. Somewhere along the way, while licking shop windows in an unnamed neighborhood, the wife peels off; the children and father march on ahead. This is foreshadowing of a sort; the husband will disappear in another twenty or so pages.

But first there's this: the wife finishes with whatever her distraction was and wanders up the street after her family. It's some time before she finds them, but then, there they are, arrayed behind the glowing window of a gelato store, in grinning conversation with the staff inside. This flavor or that flavor or both?

The wife has been gone for a good long while, so the obligation is to duck into the shop, all smiles and apologies. But she doesn't. She stands outside and watches them. The shop is bright, her family, too. If she entered, the composition would slip; the bubble, in Robert's words, would pop: the text makes clear that she can almost see, feel, the world sloping and the shop with it.

The wife studies the scene for so long that she's still outside when the family exits. Surprise and delight ensue. The children hold up their paper cups, their spoons: *taste, taste, taste!*

The husband says to her, *I'll go back inside, I'll get you your own, what do you want?*

The scene ends there. It's up to us to imagine the wife's answer, the look on her face, the shape her mouth made as she opened it, or if she opened it at all.

Robert said something when he was in the store with the twins. I saw this on the surveillance video. Not *to* the twins: while he's reading to them upstairs, a customer arrives and Robert must hear the bell—there's no sound on Asif's system—and he goes to the top of the spiral staircase. And pauses. What he must have thought then: that the time had come, that I'd come back with the girls. He pauses, he looks at the twins, who've taken over reading the book to themselves, he looks around the room as if checking for another exit. He looks down the stairs. (Below, whoever it was—the camera doesn't catch them, they must not have come in far—has already left, likely because they were never issued a *bonjour*.)

Robert says something and then takes the first step down.

The twins don't look up, so he must not have been speaking to them. Maybe Robert hadn't said anything aloud. But he'd wanted to say *something*, one word, several—I saw his lips move. I couldn't, not for the life of me, read them.

When Robert comes on-screen downstairs, he's moving more quickly. He looks around the store, sees no one, mouths an easily decipherable "fuck!" (*have Leah and the girls just left again?* he must be thinking), and leaps for the door, one bound, two, bangs into the corner of a table, three, he's at the door. He tears it open. Upstairs, the twins don't appear to hear the wild jangling; they're too engrossed in their reading. Downstairs, Robert leans out the door. He looks up the street toward Madame Grillo's and the Métro. He looks down the street toward the Hôtel du Cinéma and the Seine. Back and forth, back and forth. He goes just outside the door now. The sun on the glass makes him hard to see. He checks his watch, looks inside, looks up at the second floor. He looks up the street, down, and then light and lens align, and the camera catches his face full on. His eyes flash. He turns away.

He makes one last scan of the street. And then he chooses, and then he walks.

I rewound and watched this last moment a dozen times. Back and forth.

I let my finger pause on the screen, which cued a feature I didn't know the software had: *delete recording?*

My decision took far less time than Robert's.

What did Robert want? I ask this less and less. Not because I've become more certain of some particular answer, but because searching for it has exhausted me; my thinking has broken down, perhaps because his did. Perhaps because, bleak as it is to say, he had no model for parents—for adults—living past a certain age. (Neither did I, but then, I had Eleanor.) I do know that he wanted a career, and with it, recognition, some measure of it anyway, but by a yardstick he was always changing—young readers, old readers, readers who enjoyed wiping words clean from a screen—thus ensuring he'd always come up short. And his frustration—his fear—finally swelled to the degree that he felt his only option was to edit himself out of his own life.

Strange, then, that the only clue I have supporting this theory is how he edited himself *into* his own manuscript. For the longest time, the fact that his prize application synopsis has the wife disappearing confused me. Because obviously I hadn't, and didn't. And equally obvious, I thought, was that I was the husband, the speechwriter, and he was her, was Callie. The wife is a novelist, after all, or wants to be one. She's restless, edgy, and maybe forty-one percent crazy. True, she's better on her feet (on the page) than he was, more forceful, strong, smart. But those are changes, or improvements, I would have made, too.

Another notion came to haunt me, however, something even more obvious: that the wife was the wife, that she was me. Because I *had* disappeared. He had stayed. Not in any physical sense but in the dream sense, in the sense we'd had one, a dream, or he had, and we'd started moving toward it that first night when I followed him home from the bar. I'd followed him and followed him, through page after page, year after year, and at some point, he must have thought I said no. In myriad ways, I did. No, we can't go for drinks tonight—we're helping coach this or that practice. No, you shouldn't keep experimenting in ways to lose money, because it seems to be costing you your mind as well.

No, you're not a failure. I said that, too. But he came to believe something else.

And I don't know what happened then, or precisely when it happened. If family life simply overtaxed him; or whether he thought, I'm the only true dreamer left in this marriage, I need to grab whatever balloon floats by, even if it bears me away; or whether all of it, art, life, its intersections, came to feel like foolishness.

I do know that, like the fictional Callie, I grew angry, I grew frustrated, I fled.

I fled without going anywhere. I fled fiction for real life, however pale a second prize or destination that is. I wrote speeches, I made videos. I didn't make my film, but I didn't stop reading—I read the books he gave me, I read shelves full of books I found on my own. I still believed in make-believe. But he must have believed otherwise, and must have believed that that left him the sole presider over a fictional land wholly his own, one he could be present in only by not being present. That's why he couldn't leave us via something as prosaic as divorce. It's why he couldn't stay away from us in Paris.

We were his creation. And he, everlastingly, ours.

CHAPTER 18

Eleanor left. A year passed. Spring returned. Robert did not.
And then—
I'm telling things out of order again.
What happened was this.

I lost my husband.

Robert's disappearance was more profound this time. Somehow, when he left, he managed to leave my imagination, too. I no longer thought I saw him out of the corner of my eye, or in photographs from *The Red Balloon*, or in the pages of his own books. No messages, scribbled or otherwise, appeared. It felt like our fault. Like his appearance in Paris had been solely through the force of my will and the girls' longing—that that was all that had ever caused him to be among us, in fact, for eighteen years. That's untrue, of course, but legally . . .

Legally. After much consultation with Eleanor, I shared with the girls what the police had told me. Or rather, I shared one tiny piece of it. I said the police had explained that if there is no sign of someone for seven years, that person can be declared dead. In other words, I left out the sailboat story, the partial one that the police had pieced together, the one Robert himself had partially corroborated. And without the story, there was nothing. Nothing of him in Paris or Milwaukee—or in their faces. I'd expected screaming or tears, hands at my throat. Nothing, just flat incredulity.

"So we have to wait?" Ellie said.

"Well, it can be accelerated," I said. What was I saying? I listened as I stumbled on. "If the police believe—Eleanor says—there's this process."

Daphne looked confused. "The process *makes* him"—I waited for her to say the word, but she didn't—"not alive?"

"Well," I said, "legally, I suppose it does."

"*Legally?*" said Ellie. Her favorite part of Paris was proving to be the constant parade of *manifestations*—demonstrations and strikes, on behalf of workers, the Romani, immigrants, students—the city fostered.

"But if he *did* come back?" Daphne said.

That question mark again, that bent pin.

"I guess there's another . . . process," I said.

"What's a 'process'?" Daphne said. As Molly once warned, we were all losing our English a word or two at a time. Days before, trying to explain the Vélib' bike-share system to some tourists, I'd been unable to summon *kickstand*. They'd thought I was talking about soccer. Which, of course, is *football*.

But there was another word we'd all somehow lost, in French and English: *père,* father, *papa,* dad. I noticed that when Robert came up now, it was only ever as *he,* as in:

"He's not *coming* back." This was Ellie, and this was a phrase that, as I turned it over and over in the days following, seemed to render superfluous any legal petition.

We lost the store.

I can't say Madame's announcement, almost a year to the day that

Robert walked out of The Late Edition, was a surprise. She and I had spoken less and less, and when she spoke to me, she often did so through George. Do this, do that. I didn't. I knew what she wanted me to do was make money—unable to make our originally negotiated payments, I was supposed to pay a percentage of our sales each month as a way of settling our debt—and she couldn't believe how badly the store was doing. Or so George said. I asked him for his own business insights. *Don't own a bookstore*, he said. I pointed out that we had to.

He said that though he'd wangled us a second year on our visas, a day of reckoning might be coming.

And so it did.

Madame found me one quiet morning in the store and asked if I might come upstairs. I'd not visited her apartment since we'd made our first arrangements. And needless to say, I'd never been all the way up to the attic, the "book floor," which Madame, early on, had often suggested I might visit. But she'd never said when, and it lay beyond a locked door I'd not dared approach (Ellie had, of course; that's how I knew it was locked).

Madame unlocked the door, and I followed her up.

Blue toile wallpaper, a repeating pattern of hunters and stags, enclosed the room, puckering at the seams. A single round window the size of a café serving tray caught a piece of a gray sky. An oriental rug worn through to its warp lay in the middle of the space, which was small, hunched under the roof. A wooden table, almost as large as the door we'd just stepped through, stood on the carpet, along with a single chair. Atop the table, a blotter, a pen cup, some pages. Some covered in handwriting. Some not.

There were no books.

That is, there were no shelves and shelves of books as I'd imagined. There was, instead, a single low bookcase, mostly empty, less than a meter wide and not half as tall. Atop it, a yellow Larousse dictionary and a small cameo portrait of a girl. On the shelf beneath, a dozen books, all identical but for numbers on their spines. Madame handed me one. The cover smooth, soft leather dyed green. The pages were gilt-edged, old gold.

Inside, a single word on a single page: *Un*. One.

She looked to me to see if I understood.

I did; I was once a writer's wife. *Un*. One. Chapter 1. She did not have to remove the rest of the carefully stockpiled journals to show me that those pages were blank, too.

"Madame," I said. "I had no idea." She took the book and put it away. "I didn't know you were a writer. *Un écrivain?*"

She sniffed. I wondered if I'd said it wrong. *Masculin ou féminin?*

"*Un écrivain écrit,*" she said. A writer writes.

And she had not. She'd always wanted to, since she was a child, since she was younger than Annabelle. But so many things had gotten in the way. Life, her daughter, Sylvie. (And Sylvie's father had gotten himself well out of the way—had vanished—before Sylvie was even born. No wonder Madame thought she understood me, and my invisible husband, so well.) Needing to support herself, her child, had gotten in the way, and so she'd gotten herself a job in a bookstore on a street named for the patron saint of writers. In time, she came to own the store, the apartments above, the building. She had everything.

She had twelve gilt-edged green-bound volumes of nothing.

She thought the bookstore would inspire her. Instead, it took all of her time.

And then we came along, she said.

She looked at me to be sure I understood. She was speaking French but that wasn't the problem. I stared back blankly. She sighed and continued, annoyed she had to clarify.

We were the problem.

"I thought, selling you the store, this will give me more time. The time, the *liberté*, I did not have for so many years. But you did not give me the time. Falling in rivers, hospitals, police. So busy! So noisy. This last year, more quiet, but—in the store, too quiet. And the books." She paused, as though working out the next sentence in English. "This is the *problème*. The books down there, louder and louder every night. '*What have you done today, Madame?*' they ask. '*Where is the book?*'"

And I thought, *where is the exit?*

I also felt something else: that I finally understood Robert's write-aways in a way I hadn't before. Claustrophobia has many sources. We were just one.

But it was the one Madame focused on now.

"Leah," Madame said. "This is what I am trying to say: you must leave."

"I'm sorry," I said, turning to go. "Of course!"

Madame shook her head. "No," she said. "The apartment, the store. I am sorry, all of it."

"Madame?"

"You bought the business, yes," she said. "But not the building. And so now—you move."

I'd heard of other expats evicted on short notice by their French landladies; such negotiations had been almost a subspecialty of Declan's. But I'd never thought that . . .

We had an understanding, an agreement, a bond—this wasn't about—this was about *books*. Wasn't it? "Find a new place for the store? For us to live? What about our special visas?"

"I do not know," Madame said. "Especially for an American, this is not easy. Perhaps George can help. Perhaps you can go home, to America. I know people who will buy the stock, the books, all of it. This is the time," she said, and sighed. "When you first come, I think, 'this is what she needs to do, this store—'"

"And the twins," I said.

"They are older now," she said. "George has need of you not so much." It was true. "And you need—you need *more*. I need *more*."

"I—I don't understand," I said, though, degree by degree, surveying the empty room, I did.

Madame looked at her tiny bookcase and then back at me. "Many years," Madame said, "and now few. *Je suis à court de temps*," she added. "Do you understand what that means?"

I did. It meant I could take the rest of the day off. I went downstairs, accepted a package from Laurent, and then endured a headshake from him as I prematurely flipped the sign to FERMÉ.

In the past year, I'd finally gone on a date with him, as doing so had seemed inevitable. It went poorly, as was also inevitable. He took me to a chain restaurant that specialized in hamburgers and told me I'd have to learn how to cook before we got married. But he would pay, he would pay, he'd repeated, as though I'd been badgering him. So *I* paid for dinner and left him at the table. I didn't get deliveries for two weeks. When they resumed, he said he forgave me: if I wanted to pay for things, that was absolutely fine. I said if he wanted to be friends, *just* friends, that was absolutely fine.

I said this in French, and he looked at me like I'd mixed up some key piece of syntax, and I suppose I had. I was plumb out of friends.

When Robert left that second time, it was as though everyone had been waiting for his cue. Carl came by to announce somberly that he'd received his new posting—Côte d'Ivoire. He gave me a wallet-size copy of his official portrait—brown-blazered, American flag at his right—and kissed me, on both cheeks. As I delicately pulled away, he held on to my elbows. *Stay strong*, he said. I tried to, but then Shelley, the quiet retiree from New Orleans, departed, too. No kissing, just an exhale. Her husband had summoned her home. *I suppose it's time*, she said.

When Molly announced that she and her family were leaving, she said it was past time. And it was—for me to fire her. She had been a hapless employee and, it turned out, a bad customer. The week before she left, she returned two boxes of books I'd not known she'd bought. "Just add the refund to my final paycheck," she said.

"But we don't do refunds," I said.

She looked at me, confused. "But I've been giving customers their money back for months?"

I thought about calling Declan, but did not. We'd seen each other for coffee two or three times in the past year, but just coffee. Never wine. Never back to the apartment after. We told each other that it was so busy, we were so busy, Paris was so *busy*. When we parted we said *à bientôt*, which means both "soon" and "good-bye."

And so I strode away from my meeting with Madame Brouillard, up the street, alone. Up the street—not down toward the Seine, toward Notre-Dame, that prettier Paris. I wanted ugly.

Except it wasn't ugly. Wherever I walked, it was terribly beautiful, and I do mean terribly, because sometimes you want the landscape to reflect your soul, you want the skies and streetlights and doorways of every building you pass to frown, turn a shadowed jaw to you, look pale and gaunt. But Paris, even when the sky *is* gray—it was sunny today, so blue above that tourists and locals alike kept stopping to look up—effortlessly, ceaselessly, annoyingly generates magic. I looked down. A faint smell of urine rose from some crevice.

I'll be home in three days, Napoleon famously wrote Josephine; *don't wash.*

Before coming to Paris, I'd always understood that line as nothing more than the plea of a lovesick, sex-mad soldier with the mildest of kinks. After living in the city, I understood it differently, and not just because I'd waited longer than three days. The ideal, the real, they're all mixed up here there's no point in teasing them apart; they'll only come at each other again.

Finally turning, I passed my favorite abandoned storefront, the one with the ladder, the apple, the splatters of paint. It had sat dark for a year, and once, when I could bear to do so, I'd pressed my face to the glass and had seen that the apple, too, had gone. Of course. But tonight, it had its light on, and inside stood a new ladder, a new apple atop it. Green. And with it, a sign above the door, in English: THE APPLE STORE. It would be only a matter of time before Apple got wind and shut it down. But here, now, the apple shone, and I tried the door, found it open, and entered. I called out *bonjour* and received no reply. Everything smelled clean and light. I took the apple. I took a bite. I looked around for the hidden camera as I chewed but saw none, which is, I suppose, the point of hiding. I went home.

Which was where? Milwaukee. We could figure out a way to stay in Paris, I thought, but I also knew that we already had done that once, and doing so had led to this dead end. (Or in French, *impasse*.) Raising kids is about raising yourself as a grown-up, and I was enough of one now to know, unlike Robert, when to leave.

I dragged Daphne on a trip up to the rue de Rivoli to buy one of the *boucherie*'s ready-to-go rotisserie chickens. I wondered if FedEx would be able to deliver it hot to our home in Milwaukee. I don't think I was tearing up over this prospect, but when I placed my order, the butcher looked at me like he knew something was wrong. In Paris, the empathy of butchers and pharmacists cannot be underestimated, and indeed, the *boucher* now offered his prescription: I must buy a *rôti*—a roast, pork, he had one right here, stuffed with apricots and prunes, just put it in the oven.

I must have looked dazed, because he turned his attention to Daphne and explained about the temperature and time, how she would know it was done, how it would be a true tragedy if we cooked it too long. He then explained that we would need to get some shallots and *haricots verts*—green beans—next door and a good burgundy one door farther down. "*Madame*," he said, turning to me and continuing in English, "a little wine for the girl, *aussi*. She is the good help." Daphne smile-frowned and turned away, and though I'd sworn off being surprised by anything anymore, I was startled by what I thought I'd just seen: Daphne flirting? The butcher then gave us, free, six strips of terrifyingly rich bacon—and a little sachet of spices, which he told Daphne to sprinkle on her *mère* as necessary, as the lovely lady was looking a bit grave. Daphne gave a quick, high laugh, said *merci* and good-bye, and then led us from the store. I smiled at the butcher as we left. He raised an eyebrow—he thought *I* was flirting—but I wasn't. I was proud. Of Daphne, and, immoderately, of myself. I'd gotten her this far. Physically, emotionally. Strong enough to navigate Paris. Kind enough to tolerate me tagging along.

"I don't know why everyone doesn't live here," Daphne said as we walked home, packages hanging off us like ornaments.

"It's crowded enough," I said as someone banged into me, but Daphne didn't hear. She was already ahead on the sidewalk, smoothly navigating the crowd. She looked more and more like Ellie; the two of them looked less and less like their parents. I was glad I hadn't successfully brought about a meeting between them and their father. I was devastated that he wasn't here to see the young women they'd become.

As we opened the door to the bookstore, it was dark, which was good, because it hid my face. Daphne said we should have Eleanor visit again—had I seen the sign in her hotel announcing that it had been "refreshed"?

I had, but had wondered at my French, because when I peered inside, the lobby still looked dusty and airless, full of fake movie *bric-à-brac*, its deep maroon walls making you feel like you'd wandered into some darker corner of the human heart.

Then again, I'd noticed one new item on the wall that had once borne a poster of *The Red Balloon*. It was gone, and in its place a poster for another Lamorisse film, *The Lovers' Wind*. Daphne had seen it, too. "I've never heard of it," she said. I said I would tell her about it after dinner. But then she forgot, thank goodness.

Parts of *The Red Balloon* were bleak, but as a whole, it was uplifting, if not inspiring. The end of Lamorisse's life was not.

It is 1968, hardly a dozen years after he had known heady success, and Albert Lamorisse's career has diminished considerably, to the point that he now finds himself producing a film for the shah of Iran.

Lamorisse sleeps poorly and suffers nightmares about dying, about falling, about water.

And this is precisely what happens when, in the midst of filming a tricky shot of the Karaj Dam that Lamorisse wanted to avoid—but the shah insisted; he wanted a documentary that would show how modern and advanced his kingdom is—Lamorisse's helicopter becomes entangled in power cables and crashes, killing Lamorisse, age forty-eight. Navy divers descend in search of the bodies.

The film stock survived, however, and eight years later, Lamorisse's widow and son—Pascal, one-time child star of *The Red Balloon*, now in his twenties—edited the Iranian footage based on Lamorisse's notes. It features all the long, lingering panoramas Lamorisse loved, and almost nothing the shah wanted. The shah fled Iran January 16, 1979. Almost a month to the day later, Lamorisse became an Academy Award nominee once again, posthumously, this time for Best Documentary, for *The Lovers' Wind*.

So all the more piercing, my unfinished thesis argued, is the seven-minute collection of outtakes Lamorisse's remaining Iranian crew assembled as a kind of postscript to the full-length documentary. It contains every last thing the shah wanted, and somehow—the way the images are intercut, sped up and slowed down, brought close or pushed away—manages to indict the shah for Lamorisse's death with every frame.

Knowing the story of Lamorisse's life isn't necessary to appreciate the film, but it helps, especially around the 00:02:30 mark, where the montage abruptly cuts to some B-roll of a laboratory. Right before a test tube begins to fill with what looks like watered-down blood, a man in a white coat reaches to the top of a skinny glass pipe. And there, apropos of nothing, or rather, everything, briefly swells a red balloon.

And so the hotel's poster reminded me, though I should not have needed reminding: clues are always present, should one care to look.

I went downstairs to tidy up while the girls did their homework.

I wouldn't miss this part of owning a bookstore. Picking up after people is never fun. Not if it's your own family, not if it's the stream (or trickle) of customers who march through your store. Granted, our store was organized idiosyncratically, but why customers chose to reshelve books upside down, or spine in, or horizontally instead of vertically, I do not know. It wasn't laziness; some of their efforts clearly *took* effort.

I started with the *Madeline* display, as it had been in particular disarray for some time, with many of its dolls missing. Sold, I hoped, though probably a few Madelines and Pepitos had walked out on their own, too. I admit that our Bemelmans books had, on the whole, gotten less attention from me after Robert left the twins, the store. It wasn't necessarily a conscious thing. Or maybe it was. Or maybe, tonight, it was the glass of wine I'd brought down from the dinner table.

The sidewalks outside were clear, and I was thankful for that. I wasn't interested in putting on a show as I picked up and restaged the windows. The Madeline and Pepito dolls had little Velcro pads on their hands, and I put that feature to use. I pinned Pepito's legs under an omnibus *Madeline* edition that I'd propped on a chair, and had him reaching down to rescue Madeline. Their heads weren't moveable, so that meant while Pepito's face was fixed staring at her, Madeline's stared straight out the window with a grin. I liked that. And then I looked it all over and swapped the dolls' places so that Pepito was the one in distress. I liked that even more. And I put a *Red Balloon* nearby to give him options for his escape.

Enough playing with dolls. I sorted through our Paris bookcase, pruning as I went. Hemingway's *Moveable Feast* I moved to the Illinois shelf. We'd sell less of him there, but that was fine with me. While in the Midwest shelves, I found a mis-shelved James Baldwin and brought him back to France. And M. F. K. Fisher was in Michigan—her birthplace, but it was high time she returned to Paris, too. She loved the city—and, strangely, the station restaurant at the Gare de Lyon, which Ellie had run through shouting during her search for the twins. I knew Fisher would have helped had she been there. Fisher wrote about food, and that led me to Julia Child, whom I expatriated from the Boston shelves—where she sat uncomfortably anyway—to shelve beside Fisher in France. And Monique Truong! I went and fetched her from New York. Not among the deceased, thank god, but I made an exception for her because I loved her book about Gertrude Stein's Vietnamese cook so much—*The Book of Salt* belonged in Paris. I brought these women from their various locales and made room on the Paris shelves by displacing as many men as possible. So long, F. Scott! *Adieu*, Ford Madox! *Au revoir*, Robert Eady!

Robert Eady?

I stopped. Our Milwaukee section—and we did have one—featured none of Robert's work anymore, just books on typewriters (invented there) and Carl Sandburg (once, like me, a speechwriter there).

But this was in Paris. This was not *Central Time*.

I picked up the book. This was new.

A new novel by Robert Eady.

A new novel, *Paris by the Book*. No pseudonym. By Robert Eady.

There was not enough light to read. There was just enough.

I opened the book.

Robert had revised and finished the manuscript.

It still started the way I remembered:

They loved their lives and where they lived, but still they wondered, what happens next?

And then I stopped, and closed the book, and looked at the cover. No Eiffel Tower, brave decision on the publisher's part for a Paris book, just a close-up of—a store like ours. That is, it *was* our store, but someone had had their way with Photoshop, and that was fine. The tangle of vines (cf. *Madeline*) was a nice addition. But the name—the store's name was the same, The Late Edition. I couldn't tell what was in the window—that would have given me a clue as to when the photo was taken—but it was definitely our store.

In France, there is a term, *self-fiction*, that translates into "autobiographical fiction," but not quite. I've always thought the English phrase carried a whiff of condescension or criticism with it, and *self-fiction* doesn't do that at all; it serves more to illuminate something we all do, or should do, and constantly, which is to edit and organize our lives until we find a narrative that suits us, completes us. I've left out until now the detail that Robert, in that moment in our conversation when he took credit for writing *I'm sorry* in that book, his eyes flicked away from mine, and I'd thought, *he's lying.*

Was he? I'm not sure. I'm not even sure it matters, only that mine's the better version, that he'd written *I'm sorry* in that book because he was sorry. Then he'd put his book back on the shelf, a message in a bottle he'd never actually expected to bob our way—and once it did, he'd stolen it back.

But we'd bobbed *his* way, and as he'd told me in the store, he'd watched as much as he could while we did bob, fascinated by what seemed like a hallucination—one that, some days, was more fully realized than others: we seemed to be running the store he'd written, we were living above it, we'd made a *new* family. I wondered if he'd seen the twins—or George—or Declan. Maybe one night Robert had walked by and seen Ellie and Daphne laughing—laughing!—in the front window as Declan regaled them with some story. The scene would have looked so warm and the laughter so genuine, Robert would have stopped to marvel at it, but then would have quickly urged himself on, so as not to be spotted.

Had he seen these things? Had he seen Declan? How many times? On the bridge, for example, where Daphne saw Robert? But Robert insisted he'd been nowhere near that day, and I preferred that version, too. And the manuscript, back in Milwaukee, back in the math department's print queue, the family who buys the store in France? I had let him tell me about it, but hadn't told him Eleanor had found it: I didn't want him to say that he'd not intended us to read it, much less follow it. I didn't want him to say, "I'm sorry," again. Because, strange as it was to have done so, I liked what I'd done with that manuscript, that life, this one. I'd changed jobs, continents. I'd figured out a way to feed my family, with food both frozen and fresh.

The result was two healthy, heroic daughters.

And one beautiful bookstore whose shelves creaked under the weight of several thousand books.

For a little while more, anyway.

I opened Robert's book once again, and this time started from the beginning, the endpapers—a nice map, they paid extra for that—and then a blank page, and then a title page, then an epigraph from Gertrude Stein, and then the dedication.

To the one I lost.

EPILOGUE

And I lost myself in that book.

Back and forth I went in those pages, which meant going back and forth in my memories of Paris, and Milwaukee. I marveled at what he'd done. Not only the writing but also the book's appearance in our store. Had he put it there? He must have. I didn't know for sure and couldn't. I'd had Asif pull the cameras out months before. I did not regret the decision. This was *why* I'd had him pull the cameras; I didn't want to be haunted. It's also why I didn't tell the girls about the book. The next time I saw Robert, if there was a next time, I wanted us all to see him, and I wanted us to see him not in the margins of a book, screen, or crowd, but full on, in person, walking through the front door.

Had he?

The book was cheaply bound and marked ADVANCE READING COPY—NOT FOR SALE. A publicity galley, then. Though it seemed equally possible that the packaging, the binding, like the story inside, was Robert's own doing. That he'd written such a book and then crafted this means of "publishing" it was hardly beyond him; in fact, it seemed to be the very essence of him, right down to the "About the Author" page in back, which, beneath those three words, was blank but for two letters: *tk*. Not French texting slang but an old publishing abbreviation. Don't be fooled by the *k*. *Tk*: it means "to come."

Summer came. Crowds came. And then more crowds came, because Robert's book came. The galley he'd left me wasn't a one-off art object but the first of what turned out to be many, many, many copies. For Robert's book *had* been published by a real publisher, and then magically caught a ride on one of those comets that occasionally illuminates the twilit universe of publishing. The story of the family in Paris who takes over a failing bookstore struck a nerve—with bookstore owners, anyway. And with people visiting Paris. This was even before the *Times* ran its article. But then they did, and the *Guardian* ran theirs and even *Le Monde* theirs in the Thursday books roundup, and then the story, like the book, was everywhere.

Most articles cited our store as the book's "inspiration"; one account also mentioned that the store's original proprietor, Marjorie Brouillard, was a writer herself, with a new project on the way "after a silence of many years." When I read this, I offered her my sincere congratulations and told her we would be out of her way soon. I said I'd heard Madame Grillo was thinking of taking the storefront space.

Madame Brouillard did not respond right away. I thought she didn't want to admit that she'd contacted Madame Grillo about the space. I knew she had, though, because Madame Grillo had told me: *a second store, and just for brooms!*

But Madame Brouillard watched me sweeping up each night after the crowds, she reviewed the sales figures, she calculated what percentage she might receive come month's end. "You do not have to leave *immédiatement*," she said, as though she'd never suggested otherwise. She began her way up the stairs, offering her usual taut smile, but—and this was new—her eyes smiled, too. It wasn't the night cream. She had a parting question for me, *en français,* her words almost shy for a change: *and . . . has the publisher, by chance, found a . . . French translator for your husband's book?*

When the first box of Robert's novel arrived, I split it open privately, in the back office, and turned to the back flap to find out what had come of "to come." Only this: no photo, a very short bio. It doesn't even mention his previous titles, only that this is his last, that he disappeared two years ago sailing Lake Michigan and is presumed dead.

When I asked the publisher who had told them this, they said I had.

When I said I hadn't, they forwarded the e-mails "I" had sent them, including the one where "I" had sent them the full manuscript for their consideration. They said they were glad we were back in touch because "my" prior e-mail address had stopped working, and they wanted to confirm a few matters. Was my contact person at the Milwaukee Police Department, where "I" had sent them to corroborate the story of Robert's fate, still correct? Was it okay to send the police the copy they were asking for, free?

Was the information about making royalties payable to me, in Paris, still current?

Did I know how I was going to explain this to our daughters?

That last question was mine, of course. Daphne and Ellie were very upset when they read the flap. They were almost more angry than sad; they were convinced that the police had somehow gotten their way, that the forms and "process" to declare Dad dead had somehow ground forward without my permission. Then they thought I *had* given permission, and that was even worse. But I hadn't. And when they asked, yet again, if their father really was alive, I said, "I don't know," which was also true.

I did lie, or maybe it wasn't quite a lie, when Ellie said, "so it's our choice"—that is, our choice to believe whether or not Robert was alive. I said *yes*, even though I wanted to tell them that it wasn't, it hadn't been, that Robert had chosen and, for his own terrible reasons, not chosen us.

One conversation, of course, with Ellie and Daphne did not settle the matter of their father's disappearance or "death." Neither did fifty. Skype conversations with a Seattle psychologist Eleanor found for the girls *did* help, and still do. To hear the girls describe it, they've reached a truce. Not their word at all, but it captures things for me: a truce with their father, with the truth, with the psychologist. The good doctor will not insist their father is dead; they will not insist on continuing to search Paris for him.

The psychologist says this is healthy, that the time for searching is past. The psychologist doesn't know about the spoofed e-mails to the publisher and nor do the girls; when Ellie and Daphne asked how the book came to be, I said it seemed as though their father had finished and sent the publisher a manuscript before he disappeared, and that now, the publisher couldn't find him, and neither could I. If pressed, I repeat the psychologist's mantra. The time for searching is past.

But they don't press often. Because they know someone else is.

Eleanor searches. She tells me to tell the girls she doesn't, but I don't, and they wouldn't believe me anyway. She has searched online and offline. She has hired two private detectives, fired both, and is constantly interviewing for a third. She is using her university access to audit courses in criminal justice, French, and, "just in case," forensic anthropology. She has come to know an unsettling amount about jawbones. I often see her using her own when we visit via Skype; for "efficiency" she likes to dine while we talk. Her breakfast is my dinner. I tell her she's nevertheless welcome to join me in a glass of wine. She says she's eating healthier. This explains, though not fully, why I have occasionally caught her eating Robert's brand of granola.

Declan and I dine together not infrequently. After the hotel down the way redid one of its cinema rooms as a "Late Edition" room, they began asking if our store did tours related to the book. I'd called Declan, said I had a business proposition, and then he laughed, and then we were doing tours. Ours is purely a professional relationship now, and better for it, we both agree. We toast to it, in fact, each time he takes me out to dinner, which is every time I pay him. We no longer eat for free; rather, he always tries to spend the exact amount on dinner that I've paid him that week. We keep having to find more and more expensive restaurants. Paris obliges. And so does Declan. He's waiting, and so am I, and neither of us knows quite for what, quite yet. In the meantime, we toast and laugh and drink. And sometimes I hear a three-wheeled minicab whine by, and my pulse goes chasing after it, and I take another silky sip because it's easier than looking at Declan at just that moment.

Declan, I should point out, does not appear in the book.

Robert does. Does and doesn't. In Robert's book, the family lives happily ever after. No posthumous bestseller comes to rescue the store; it makes of itself an old-fashioned success. Week after week, more and more people visit and buy more and more things. Enough money is made that, in one late chapter, the family vacations in the south of France. In another, they take the train to London. There is talk of a trip to Stockholm, but I've already told the girls—don't believe everything you read.

When Eleanor first read the book's flap, she insisted we call the publisher and have every copy seized and the jacket bio changed to something like "Robert Eady is a pseudonym and any resemblance to persons living or dead is . . ." Fat chance. Besides, I've read more than one blogger—for this has become a book everyone has to have an opinion on—who says a good chunk of the book's sales are due to that tragic bio. And I do occasionally see a glistening eye come up to the register if I'm in the store. Though because of sales, I spend fewer hours there. Like everyone else, I now hire aloof French twentysomethings.

But when some sad American does find me and says *I'm sorry for your loss*, I simply thank her—I really try to be sincere—and say, *it's okay*. And then, if the conversation needs to go on—some grab ahold of me and will not let go—I say, *and he's not really gone, is he?* Because I'm really not sure he is. But I don't say that. I say: *he's right here in this book*.

What I believe: that Robert meant to somehow redeem himself by publishing the book—to the degree that the book's royalty stream could absolve him of his failures, including to provide for us for so long. But it's a false absolution, isn't it? Early on, we had the prize money, yes, but beyond that, we largely provided for ourselves (with help from George, Eleanor, and, if I'm being charitable, Madame). I don't begrudge Robert the attempt, though, because it's a painful absolution as well: here, at last, has come success beyond measure, and enjoying it lies just beyond his grasp. Eleanor says it wasn't the world's recognition he ever wanted, just ours, just mine, just to the point that he left clue after clue. Or so we decided; we'd scoured those one hundred manuscript pages before realizing that the girls and I were the book's best clues, and the book's second-biggest mystery: what were we doing in Paris?

In the last sentence on the last page of the published book, as the wife and daughters busy themselves about the store one Saturday, the bell over the door rings.

And so it does each time I leave the store to walk the streets in search of him. Not often and not seriously, and not something I tell the girls, but occasionally, after dropping them at school, I walk on and pretend I'm still in active pursuit. Maybe pretending is all I was ever doing. I don't think so. I do know what I saw in his eyes the last time I saw him, which is something the mirror shows me every day in mine—I saw our girls, our lives. I think, too, that in Robert's eyes, I saw love, longing. What's certain is that bodies, celestial or human, have a pull. It's impossible to imagine he doesn't still feel our tug. It's impossible to imagine him fully gone.

But then it's impossible to imagine I'm a filmmaker, though I really am now. Or that's what the instructor—I'm finally taking classes again—tells me to tell myself when I get frustrated. *Film is about time*, he says, *take time*. So I do.

And time takes me. Summer has finally fallen to winter, and it's cold here. Sometimes, when crowds are thin, I pay to go up the Eiffel Tower, and start my (tiny, high-tech) camera rolling. I don't let myself get distracted by the view to the north, where the vast expanse of the Palais de Chaillot always makes it seem more important than it is, or to the west, because America lies there, along with Belgium and Wales and Stockholm and the two Wisconsin Parises, all those little towns that say, and not just to me, *remember?* And I certainly don't look south, where the thick black Montparnasse Tower feels like a cinder in your eye. I look east. Toward the Louvre, and Montmartre, and Europe—and Ménilmontant. In the meager cast credits of *The Red Balloon*, Lamorisse acknowledges his son and daughter and a handful of others, before acknowledging the support *des ballons de la région parisienne*. Depending on what the day, the weather, and my eyes are up to, it doesn't take much squinting to see all of them, in flight or about to rise.

And down the hill from Ménilmontant, down, down, down toward the Seine, I can almost see my store. I don't need my camera now. I know it. Bright red. And inside, a party well under way, not just my women but so many others, all the living and the dead, including Walt Whitman, maybe Walt Whitman's son—Whitman the textbook author, not the poet, though the son enjoyed the confusion—who started a bookshop named Le Mistral and then renamed it in honor of Sylvia Beach, unable to reopen her own Shakespeare and Company after the war. I think of Sylvia Beach and her shop. I think of mine. I think of distant countries, centuries, cities brought together on bookshelves.

I think of Albert Lamorisse, and his young son, now old, Pascal, who lost his father so long ago, and I think of what Pascal thinks when he sees that old film, *The Red Balloon*, if he even watches it, if he can bear it, Pascal in almost every frame, Pascal looking down at the camera while taking flight in that famous final shot, borne above Paris by a bouquet of balloons. Neither father nor son could have known then how it would end, just fourteen years later, in Iran—Lamorisse in a helicopter with the shah's own pilot as it rises, stutters, falls. There are very few accounts of Lamorisse's death and fewer still that mention this: Pascal, no longer the little boy of *The Red Balloon* but a young man, was aboard the ill-fated helicopter, too. Pascal somehow made it to safety just seconds before the crash. His father did not.

I never told Robert this.

Nor this: at the end of every one of Lamorisse's most celebrated films, the protagonist disappears.

Nor, finally, this, but Bemelmans fan that he was, Robert must have already known: Bemelmans died young. Not as young as Lamorisse, but he never met the grandchildren he longed for. At his death, Bemelmans was working on a final Madeline book, *Madeline and the Magician*, which drew on "Madeline's Christmas" features he'd done for women's magazines in the mid-1950s. But this new iteration would focus on the magician, not Christmas. It survives only in fragments—some paintings, drawings, sketches. (Ellie and Daphne found this arcana; as they grow older, Bemelmans's work for younger readers has somehow become more important for them, not less.) The artist knew he was ill, knew he didn't have long, and try as he might to keep the story sunny, he could not. His life leached into it, as life does. The angular, indefatigable Miss Clavel, who led Madeline and her other charges across all Paris, lies ill, bedridden, beyond the reach of medicine. A magician appears—his name, Mustafa— and with a flourish vastly improves "the old house in Paris covered with vines": a lake appears, a papaya tree, even "mountain goats from the Himalayas."

The girls are delighted, but worry and wonder about Miss Clavel, so sick; would it be too much to ask if—

But of course! Mustafa works his magic on Miss Clavel, and she comes back to life. Miss Clavel is *not* pleased, however, by the changes Mustafa has wrought in her absence and asks him to undo them. He does; she casts him out into a snowy night, where he promptly vanishes.

An arresting sketch survives of the girls tearfully following a funeral cortege bearing the magician's hat, a fez: *we would all love our magician back,* Miss Clavel acknowledges, but some things are not possible, not in real life. Instead, she offers the girls a stray. A cat.

The cat, of course, is the magician, who explains:

> *I changed myself so that I could stay around the house*
> *and be with you—I'll be as quiet as a mouse.*
> *And keep it a secret—*
> *A secret is something which nobody knows.*
> *And with this, our story comes to a close. . . .*

Once upon a time, whenever I saw myself in Robert's words, the feeling was tactile, I was thin and delicate, some pressed form of me, a flattened leaf that fluttered and sometimes tore as the pages turned.

But now I find books so vast, too vast. Not just Robert's, but all of them, all the ones about Paris, all the ones about everywhere. Reading, walking, chasing, longing, I've come to feel that Paris's greatest gift is vertigo, the feeling we get when we discover that that which was so familiar or close is actually so far away. Which is not unlike what I feel whenever I set out in idle pursuit of a man and find a city instead. It's a pursuit that, some mornings, I hope will go on forever, like a favorite book, like my life here. It's only with mild surprise I find I don't so much read anymore, but rather teeter, wonder, take flight, like Pascal, like Madeline, like Bemelmans, like Lamorisse, like my daughters. Like Robert. Like anyone who has ever started or finished a book, or a love affair, or confused the two, in sweet anticipation of the fall.

Finis

It is a nice thing to take over a household so living, complete, and warm, and dig up radishes that someone else has planted for you and cut flowers in a garden that someone else has tended.

—Ludwig Bemelmans
"The Isle of God,"
an essay on the origins
of his *Madeline* series

ACKNOWLEDGEMENTS

Fifty million Frenchmen can't be wrong, but one American, despite (or because of) his affection for Paris, can be; I apologize for any errors herein. I did rely on roughly fifty million sources, however, and am grateful to all of them for the information and advice they gave.

Thank you to my earliest readers, Alfredo Botello, Lauren Fox, Dan Kois, and Emily Gray Tedrowe, and to Christi Clancy, Aims McGuinness, Jon Olson, and Annie Rajurkar. A very special thanks to Caroline Leavitt, whose early enthusiasm made all the difference, and to Susan Richards Shreve, who connected us.

Thanks, too, to all those whose expertise I tapped, including Professor Larry Kuiper, Emily Griffin, and Susan Keane for French language advice. Thanks to Professor Tami Williams for help with French cinema, and Professor José Lanters for help with Dutch zines. To Dr. Kevin Wheeler for advice medical.

To my Parisian readers, Nataša Basic, Sophie Rollet, and Ingrid Johnson, for insights on parenting, Paris, French, the French, and combinations thereof. A special *mrc* to my teen-SMS linguist, Hattie Rowney; to Antoine Laurain for his advice on French bookstores and bookselling; and to Michael Bula and James Frasher for alerting me to "imminent peril."

And to those who saved me from constant peril—my agent, Elisabeth Weed, her colleagues Dana Murphy and Hallie Schaeffer, Jenny Meyer, and the mighty Maya Ziv, this book's editor and champion and merciless savior, and her colleague, Madeline Newquist—*mille mercis.*

A special thanks to my gracious new friends in the UK, Charlotte Mursell and her colleagues at HQ, who helped me translate this book from American into English.

And thank you to the incomparable Daniel Goldin, of Boswell Book Company in Milwaukee, for his insights into the art of bookselling and his support of authors everywhere (this one in particular).

—◆—

I encourage those interested in the life and work of Ludwig Bemelmans to consult a beautiful book by Bemelmans's grandson, John Bemelmans Marciano, *Bemelmans: The Life and Art of Madeline's Creator* (Viking, 1999). Much of the Bemelmans lore I share, especially the material relating to his final project, comes from this book. Marciano acknowledges, as I will, the exhaustively detailed *Ludwig Bemelmans: A Bibliography* (Heineman, 1993) compiled by Murray Pomerance. It's an extraordinary guide for those who want to read beyond *Madeline* (or to know where to read all of *Madeline's* many iterations). For an introduction to Bemelmans's "work for grownups," as Leah and the girls describe it, the anthology *Tell Them It Was Wonderful* (Viking, 1985) is a great place to start. Finally, the exhibition catalogue *Madeline at 75: The Art of Ludwig Bemelmans* (Eric Carle Museum of Picture Book Art, 2014) by Jane Bayard Curley is a rich resource, and includes a gorgeous illustrated essay by Maira Kalman.

Though, like Leah, I treasure the book version of *The Red Balloon* (Doubleday, 1956), the best way to get to know Albert Lamorisse is through his films. *White Mane* (1953) and, of course, *The Red Balloon* (1956) are available in beautifully restored form from the Criterion Collection. Lamorisse's son, Pascal, made a haunting short documentary, *Mon père était un ballon rouge* (2008), that's available from Shellac Sud. Piet E. Schreuders's remarkable magazine, *Furore*, devoted almost an entire issue (no. 21) to hunting down locations and other information about *The Red Balloon*; it's deeply researched and engrossing. I'm grateful to another magazine, *Bidoun,* for introducing me to the piercing montage assembled by Lamorisse's Iranian collaborators after he died. The *Red Balloon* critic mentioned on page 17 is Charles Silver; the quote comes from a brief essay of his on the Museum of Modern Art website.

Even when I was not in Paris, I did my best to live there through books. I benefited from *Paris, I Love You But You're Bringing Me Down* (Farrar, Straus and Giroux, 2012) by Rosecrans Baldwin; *Shakespeare and Company* (Harcourt Brace, 1959) by Sylvia Beach; *My Paris Dream* (Spiegel & Grau, 2015) by Kate Betts; *Americans in Paris: A Literary Anthology* (Library of America, 2004) edited by Adam Gopnik, as well as Gopnik's *Paris to the Moon* (Random House, 2000); *The Red Notebook* (Gallic Books, 2015) by Antoine Laurain; *Time Was Soft There* (St. Martin's, 2005) by Jeremy Mercer; *Petite Anglaise* (Spiegel & Grau, 2008) by Catherine Sanderson; *A Family in Paris* (Penguin Lantern, 2011) by Jane Paech; and *The Only Street in Paris* (W. W. Norton, 2015) by Elaine Sciolino.

I found these sources in a variety of archives and libraries, and I'm indebted to them for their assistance, including the Bibliothèque nationale de France and the Cinémathèque française (this research was supported in part by funds provided by the University of Wisconsin–Milwaukee), the Beinecke Rare Book & Manuscript Library of Yale University, the New York Public Library's Rose Main Reading Room and the Milstein Microform Reading Room, the New-York Historical Society's Patricia D. Klingenstein Library, the Joe and Rika Mansueto Library of the University of Chicago, and the University of Wisconsin–Milwaukee's Golda Meir Library, in particular librarian Molly Mathias, for finding information on a man even harder to track down than Robert.

For those wishing to track down the books Leah mentions, titles include: *Swahili Grammar and Vocabulary* (Society for Promoting Christian Knowledge, 1910) by Mrs. F. Burt; *Suite Vénitienne* (Bay Press, 1988) by Sophie Calle; *Walks in Paris* (George Routledge and Sons, 1888) by Augustus J. C. Hare; *Helsingør Station* (Secker and Warburg, 1989) by Aidan Higgins; *Fair Play* (Sort of Books, 2007) by Tove Jansson; "We Two Grown-ups" from *Men Giving Money, Women Yelling* (William Morrow, 1997) by Alice Mattison; *So Long, See You Tomorrow* (Knopf, 1980) by William Maxwell; "Wants" from *Enormous Changes at the Last Minute* (Farrar, Straus and Giroux, 1985) by Grace Paley; *Pale Horse, Pale Rider* (Harcourt, 1939) by

Katherine Anne Porter; *Indiana* (Oxford, 1994) by George Sand; *Sculpture of the Eskimo* (McClelland and Stewart, 1972) by George Swinton; *The Book of Salt* (Houghton Mifflin Harcourt, 2003) by Monique Truong; and *Fools Crow* (Viking Penguin, 1986) by James Welch. From the children's floor: *Dieu tu es là ? C'est moi Margaret !* (L'Ecole des Loisirs, 1986) by Judy Blume (translated by Michèle Poslaniec); *Le Poids d'un Chagrin* (Editions Auzou, 2008) by Sandrine Lhomme and Roxane Marie Galliez; *Mon Premier Cauchemar* (Chocolat! Jeunesse, 2009) by Selma Mandine.

———

Two notes on intentional errors, or, to use a novelist's term, fiction.

At the time of this writing, France does not have a "magic" visa program for bookstore owners like the one Leah and her daughters enjoy. It's not a bad idea, though. In the meantime, don't overstay, and obey all laws, including those about standing on bridge railings above the Seine.

And any resemblance of The Late Edition to the Marais's late, great Red Wheelbarrow Bookshop (on the rue Saint-Paul, not my fictional rue Sainte-Lucie-la-Vierge) is purely coincidental. My thanks, though, and apologies, to its proprietor Penelope (and Paris): we should have bought the store when you offered.

———

My family thinks about that afternoon all the time. And I thought about them all through the long writing of this book. To Mary, Honor, and Jane, who walked miles without complaint (or umbrellas) on our first treks through Paris, thank you for never pushing your sisters, or me, onto the tracks.

And thank you to my wife, Susan, whose love and support would fill much more than fifty million books, and who, during the writing of this book, tolerated many long absences, sometimes even when I was present: I love you. I'm back.

ONE PLACE. MANY STORIES

Bold, innovative and
empowering publishing.

FOLLOW US ON:

@HQStories